COUPAGE

BLOOD NATION NOVELS

1

Coupage: A Blood Nation Novel

Published 2018 by Kiixink

ISBN: 978-1-9995231-0-7

First Kiixink paperback printing November 2018

Text @2018 by Derekica Snake
Cover Art @ 2018 by Archie the Red Cat

Dedicated to "Spook"

Warren Shawn Snake

My brother passed far too soon. He never read Yaoi; but, he proudly told others to purchase my books.

Also, thanks to SL Publishing Group for getting this story almost ready for final printing before closing their doors.

Glossary

Ancient Vampire - As a vampire ages they get stronger and acquire various abilities. The common ability is immunity to the effects of sunlight. This High Council has set the age of 250 years as the threshold but immunity varies with the individual.

House of the Vampire Nation - There are thirteen Red Blood Houses (families) and two Blue Blood Houses of which one is the Royal House of Von Drachenfeld.

Vampire High Council - Originally the High Council were the advisors to the Lord Emperor. After Sigmund the First's assassination the High Council assumed ruling the Vampire Nation.

House of Assassins - This House is the administrative arm of the High Council as well as the secret police of the Vampire Nation. It has been in existence for eight hundred years and the main goal is to keep the status quo. The Head of the House of the Assassins for the past four hundred years is Hades.

Missions for the House are given a color coded ranking system.

White - Information gathering mission.

Yellow - Assassination - secret operation

Red - Assassination - obvious message to be sent

Black - Assassination - scorched earth policy - everyone and everything is killed.

Blood Nation - There are thirteen 'Blood' Nations that exist along side the human world. Vampire, Lycan, Hellcat, Mystics and Elven are just a few that the human world call legend and myth. The Onaclov Nation of fire demons were annihilated in *Cinder: Book Two*

Blood Nations -

Blue Blood - The Blue Blood shows it mark with a blue flame around the pupil and is significantly physically superior to the common Red Blood vampire. Blue Bloods can only pass on vampirism through procreation or if a blue blood carrier happens to bite another blue blood carrier.

(Royal) Blue Line - The Blue Line is the abilities of the Lord Emperor Von Drachenfeld. The obvious marker is feathered wings which can be called upon at will. The royal family is also able to summon the Blue Hand which can be used as a healing energy or an energy weapon. Just like the Blue Bloods, the Blue Lines must procreate. Last Lord Emperor died four hundred years ago.

Silent Speak - An ability that some Blood Nations possess-almost like telepathy.

Phoenix Wing - A side effect of intercourse with the Onaclov demon. Besides the traditional feather wings, the Lord Emperor has wings of fire that have to be burned every five days to be kept under control.

Blood Massage - Usually only used when normal vampiric healing is too slow due to the injury sustained. Blood is massaged into the wound to aid in healing. Sometimes it takes more than one application.

Hellcat Broadcasting Company - Xavier is bonded with Nightshade the Hellcat Queen. Their type of Silent Speak is stronger and more exclusive-meaning no one else can hear them. Their communication is not hampered by distance.

Scent-Marking - The various Bloods have heightened senses and the Vampire Nation has an acute sense of smell. Rubbing oneself, hair or skin against a fledgling or lover leaves a unique scent signature behind that warns others away. Two scents in a Blood is not the norm.

Hellcat - A mysterious and coveted race of Bloods who have the ability to take on any feline form at will from a domestic housecat up to a sabertooth tiger. They are immortal meaning that once their body dies, their soul is continually reincarnated in another kitten. Hellcats are known to enter a person's mind and fix things so that individual can survive. Due to Hellcat culls in the past this blood has moved even more underground to avoid contact.

The Regency - This is humanity's guard against the Blood Nations. This secret army have been on guard against encroachment from both sides, human and Blood for centuries as peacekeepers however if it comes down to brass tacks the Regency is a successful tactical unit. A unit consists of a Regency Hunter and a Battle Mage. Xavier's parents are the leaders of the North American Regency.

The Seers – a mystic and mysterious race of Bloods who are even more elusive than the Hellcat. They are known as creatures who can see into the past, present and future and to ignore their advice is to court misfortunate. Numerous pleas for Seer assistance by various Bloods has been ignored however when *the Hashmalliam* commands, Lanseng, a beautiful seer is sent to serve.

Phrases in Other Languages and Archaic English

Butled – the act of butlering or performing the duties of being a butler

Elek – (Lycan) Protector

moya mily. Vsyo idyot kak nado – Everything is going to be all right

Mne ni-kog-da v zshiz-ni ne-bee-lo tak ha-ra-sho. - Never in my life, have I felt so good.

Moya Lubov - my love

Tee vsyo, chto mne nuzsh-no. - *You are all that I need.*

Ya bu-du zhit' diya te-bya, lubov moya. - *I will live just for you, my love.*

Zsigmond - (Lycan) defender

Contents

Coupage: *Meaning literally "cutting", a term for blending wines, usually applied to lower quality wines, while the term assemblage is reserved for the blending of finer wines.*
http://dallasbartenders.com/wine_terminology_fr.htm

Prologue

I was having a dream that I had my own personal harem of studly men who wanted nothing more than to pamper the crap out of me. The skilled hands massaging the soles of my feet were slowly bringing me up to an orgasm. Who knew that that spot, oooh yeah right there, was a direct pipeline right to my cock? Lean fingers caressed my scalp finding all those knots of tension and gently working them out. I was boneless; boneless and floating without a care in the world.

Huh, X?

I frowned at that hesitant interjection. Not in my dream harem. I nestled down into my warm furry pillow.

X.

Pillows don't talk.

Wham! I got punched to the gut. Thrashing around I woke up to find my dream men still pinning my feet and brushing my hair.

"What the hell?"

There was a whimper behind me, well underneath me. What the hell? I was sprawled on a dog. Wait…wait a minute. My eyes focused on the twitchy reddish tail that had so rudely awakened me. "What is your problem?"

We are home. Shade turned her head to the window and sure enough the limo was parked outside of the condo.

"I was having such a good dream."

"I could tell, Little One." Armor sent me a seductive grin that was accompanied by fingers lightly caressing my ankle. The foot fetish of his…was something I could really get used to.

Claudius caught me around the shoulders and eased my tensed body against him. "What was your dream, Xavier?"

"Uh, my nightmare was that my future intended wife had figured out that I still had a human family and was waiting at the farm for us while Azrael and Marcus got married. Add to that Azrael's suddenly got a

11

hard on for my sister's battle skills. Oh, and let's not forget I killed five Alpha Lycans who were handpicked by the bitch of the Northern Pack who now believes that I am going to be Lord Vader."

Don't forget you saved this little pup. Shade added.

Thanks for reminding me.

"And I ate another Hellcat."

Claudius shoved me forward and slipped out from behind me. "Vader? I thought the Lycan prophesy said that you were going to be Hashmallim?"

"Do you know who Vader is? Ewoks? Wookies?"

Claudius's refined tone tickled my funny bone. "Wook key?"

I broke out into a tired and somewhat hysterical laugh. This was supposed to have been a quiet day out in the country air celebrating the nuptials. How did so much go so wrong so quickly?

"Little One." I found myself hauled over the sleeping form of the Lycan pup into Armor's warm embrace. "Do not forget that you saved this one's life."

Claudius opened the car door to the street. Shade gave me a gentle tail rub under the chin then she jumped out of the opening. I still found it fascinating that she could jump as a mature two-hundred-pound scarlet toned mountain lion and land in the street as a demure red housecat. Claudius picked up the unconscious pup as easily as you would a stuffed animal and cradled him in his arms as he headed for the front door. Shade sauntered through ahead of him as was her queenly right.

"I couldn't save his littermate." My throat was tight with emotion. Hadn't I suffered enough for one night?

"Lord Emperor?" Havoc, one of my Loyal converts, leaned down and looked into the back of the limo.

Armor kissed my temple as he squeezed my shoulder. "You did your best. That is all anyone should expect from you. I would rather have you try and fail and be here to hold you as you fall apart than to watch you stand by and do nothing." His fist knocked my sternum with enough force that it made me gasp. "This human heart of yours is what is going to make you a great leader for our Nation."

Nation…nation…what the hell was I forgetting? "Claudia! Did I really tell her to find her own way home?"

"Milord, Riot and the second limo has taken the Baroness back to her compound." The woman in black explained as she shifted to pull the door open wider as Armor propelled me forward.

"She's going to be pissed, isn't she?" I bit my lower lip as I stood barefoot out of the sideway.

Armor lumbered out of the back and rose to his full height, towering half a head over her, scanning the area this his molten chocolate eyes. "She is Father's daughter."

"Well…shit."

"Language, Little One." His hands caught my elbow and gently lead me towards the front door. "I think it would benefit both Claudius and I if you explain why the term Hashmallim is akin to this Vader. Marcus would know popular culture more than either of us but he cannot offer up any explanation."

Nightshade's voice sounded in my head. *Are you coming anytime soon? Claudius said the pup isn't as light as he looks.*

I stepped out of this building earlier dressed to casual nines and here I am coming back looking like I've been dredged in ash now wearing a tent of a shirt that almost covered up a bloody micro mini skirt. The polished sheen of the elevator's back reflected the Armor's expression of enamor as he looked at me as if I was the next best thing since bagged blood. I had to laugh because I viewed this ragtag bunch of vampires, Hellcats and now Lycan were mine.

Haley whimpered in his sleep. Stroking his tawny head, I couldn't help my sad smile. "Welcome home."

Chapter One: Yip

My pillow gave a hefty sigh then shifted slightly under me. "What are you thinking, X?"

"Hmm?"

A thumb ran along my brow. "Your forehead wrinkles when you think."

"You would think I would be one big wrinkle then." I settled back on Armor's chest and just stared up at the bright blue sky. We were in the alcove basking in the filtered vampire friendly sunlight.

Rutting, Haley, the new Lycan pup, called it, was more than just sex. It was a contract of protection and a sign of acceptance into the pack. The flame up in my Mom's woods should have been a big enough sign as I had my doubts about becoming a pack leader but at least it seemed to put the pup's fears at ease when he sleepily trundled back to his own room.

I flicked Armor's thumb off my wrinkle.

His hands crept around my sides and interlaced over my stomach. There was nothing sexual in that gentle movement but it still make me feel a little mushy inside. Not that I wouldn't turn down a hot passionate round of sexual healing with the vampire of my dreams but for some reason this quiet time seemed to be important – a peaceful calm before the eventual storm. There is always an eventual storm.

Running my hands down his forearms, my fingers stroked the plain simple band of gold on his left ring finger. I couldn't believe how much that ring gave me such a sense of belonging. It wasn't that I didn't fit in as a human...well yeah, actually, it was that I didn't fit in as a human. Growing up I was a moody bastard who was angry at everyone and everything because it wasn't fair that I was going blind. Look at me now. I have humans and a scary vampire teen-angster lining up to tap my ass.

"My Lord Emperor." How Armor could utter such simple words and make it feel all hearts and candy was a special gift? I was digging this cuddle vibe.

. I interlaced our hands. "Sorry I freaked out on you yesterday at the farm. Sis always knows what buttons to press, even though, I don't think she meant for me to hyperventilate myself unconscious."

Armor leaned forward and nuzzled my hair. "If you fall, I will catch you. When you are down, I will guard you until you can stand on your own strength again."

"I know that, Pretty. You watched over me for twenty-seven days when I was in that coma." I urged his hand up to my lips and kissed the knuckle of his ring finger. "Thank you. That means more to me than you will ever know. But, I can't let that happen again."

"My watching over you?" Armor had the beginning of a hurt look on his face. An expression I wanted to erase right away, so I started explaining quickly.

"My needing to be watched over. I keep telling Sex to think, not just react the way he does most of the time, but I have been guilty of doing the same thing." I shivered as I admitted to myself that I was a little fragile. Too damned fragile in some ways.

"I do not understand, Little One."

"This shit I'm going through with Hades. I can't be protected any more, I shouldn't be. I can do stuff now to protect myself that frankly scares the living daylights out of me." The inner fear that has been trying to consume me rose up again trying to wash away the safety I felt in his arms.

My next words were barely a whisper. "I'm scared. I'm scared and I'm changing. I don't know into what. Am I going to turn out like Emperor Sigmund? Has it crossed your mind that maybe you should get the hell away from me? That it might be safer for you to walk away before I turn into that kind of monster? If I hurt you...I don't know what would happen if I hurt you."

His reply wasn't even hampered by a pause. "Never. I will never stray from your side."

16

I forced my wings out as hard as I could. The feathers chimed wide and stretched out filling the entire hallway. The light was filtered through them, the colors changing like pastel film in front of stage lights. I turned and pushed him flat on his back. "Even through this?"

The expression on his face was pure awe. "Yes."

A blush stained my cheeks. "You say it so easily."

"It is simple because I love you, wings and all." He said it so easily but it was so clear in his expression that he meant it.

I sat back on my heels, balancing myself by pressing my feathers against the corridor walls. "I don't understand you, Armor. I don't. I never did. What the hell is it that you see in me that you can't walk away?" He wrapped me in his arms and pulled me down. I resisted, locking my elbows to keep his embrace loose. "Cause, I can't see it."

"Please, Little One." Armor opened his arms wide. I collapsed on his chest and lay there full of happy contentment. My wings settled across us. I turned my face toward the reflected light now filling the hallway from one of the myriad of mirrored office buildings facing us from across the river. It seemed to be a tenuous boundary between our Vampire Nation and the rest of the world.

"Why do you doubt me, Xavier? I have never lied to you."

"Uh, hello? You had me calling you Marcus for our first year and a half."

He sighed. I rose with his chest as if I was in one of those wave pools on a rising crest. "A rose by any other name would still smell just as sweet. If I walked up to you in that bar and said my name was Armor you would have laughed in my face." He ran his hands down my back and sides hitting and teasing all those sweet spots on my body that made me shiver with desire.

"If I could have seen you I would have been all over you...just like this." I maneuvered myself into a push up over his body, walking myself up on hands and knees sliding my lower, awakening, half up his hot silky skin until I could let my hair trail his chest and pool around his face and neck.

"In the bar?" His hands cupped my hips slowly drumming his fingertips on the curve of my ass. He was tapping out a sexual rumba that made me want more...in a big way, from my big vampire.

My fangs began to tingle. Oh, yeah. I forgot about that little edict this morning and that I was more than a little miffed about it. I kissed his ear and let my tongue flick out. "I don't get fanged. You don't get fanged."

"X!" My fang lightly dragged along the tempting vein pulsed beneath my lips and tongue.

"But that doesn't mean we can't do anything?" I pushed myself off his body as it lounged luxuriously on the leather chaise, folded my wings and sauntered off down the hall, naked as the day I was blooded in this world, in my best catwalk strut. I turned and looked back once I got to the bend in the corridor. He was still laying on the lounge then I saw him tilt back his head until we were staring at each other kind of upside down. "If you want me, come find me."

I flared my wings out then brought my hand sliding up my chest to flick at my push button start. My motor was already primed and ready so one flick was enough to make me shiver with desire. The sound of my wings filled the narrow hall with chimes. "You find me; you can claim me—as hard as you want." I whispered back to him. I didn't have to say it any louder.

He heard me.

Holy Crap!

The plan was to make it to the entertainment room. I could hear him coming up fast behind me. I wasn't going to make it. I needed an advantage so I cheated and lightened my weight, which lengthens my strides and put on speed. Chesterton stepped out into the hall but his butler skills of awareness allowed him to duck back into the doorway as I ripped past him. I glanced back over my wing to see Armor bounce off the wall in an effort to keep from running Chesterton over. Somehow the butler was able to stay upright and unharmed. The goody laden tray wasn't so lucky as bonbons and sweets flew everywhere.

18

I laughed and reached for the door of the entertainment room. A streak of grey came rushing at me from the corner of my eye; I reacted instinctively. Stepping directly into the path of the attacker I swung my left wing around taking the brunt of the hit on it. I staggered a step then pushed back with my shoulder and my wing, knocking my attacker off balance. It was like being hit with a small car, it might be small, but it's still a fucking car. The attacker's nails scrambled on the marble as he brought his feet underneath him. Jumping forward not willing to give the attacker the time to fully regroup I rammed the force of a back flap flinging him down the hall a good ten feet. Crystal vision snapped into place telling me my eyes had taken on the Blue Flame and my fangs had dropped. I dashed forward as the attacker struggled to his feet, smashing into him with my shoulder, driving him back and over in a flurry of legs.

He fought me. My fangs were at full extension as I slammed them down into thick fur. Fur? The pup? Listening to his whine I realized that he wasn't trying to attack he was trying to get away. I used my wings on the walls as braces until I forced him flat beneath me.

STOP MOVING!

Sorry…Master, sorry….I submit to you…Master please…. Sorry… His words were a mixture of sorrow and fear.

I let go of his neck with my fangs but I brought one hand up and around his neck. I could feel his pulse pounding so hard. I could feel my own heart beating a mile a minute. For a moment there, even though it seemed like an eternity ago, I was that young ten year old walking back home in the twilight from a refreshing splash in the farm pond. The attacking dog was nothing more than a blur and yellow fangs that charged out of the woods slamming into me that sent me flying. I remember hitting a tree then saw fireworks as my head exploded into pain. My screams as the dog started ripping me to shreds followed me down into the darkness of unconsciousness. I woke up three days later in my bed, bandaged and bruised, surrounded by my Dad's healing magic and my Mom's prayers. It was more fear than anger that made my fangs descend to full extension but it was that young boy's vulnerability that kept them down. This is why I hate dogs.

19

I snarled at the quaking Lycan. *"I rescue you and bring to you safety. I invite you into my House and this is how you repay me? With treachery!"*

No... Master...I ... thought you were in danger. I was trying to protect you. Master.... please...I'm sorry...I was trying to get around you to stop what I thought was an attacker...so fast... Haley began to mentally sob.

It was a chore to fold my wings across my back. I never took my eyes off the pup. Slowly his head turned and I could see his golden Lycan eyes wide with apprehension and regret. I could smell the fear pouring off him.

"Obey my rules or get out of my House." I could hear the irrational words spilling from my mouth but I couldn't stop it. That streak of grey and the force of the impact had brought back all that terror, pain and helplessness I experienced as a boy. I couldn't handle it then and it was shown to me that I still couldn't. All I could remember was those yellow teeth and the pungent smell and for a moment it layered itself right over Haley.

I sensed Armor's deep concern before he touched my shoulder, before he actually made contact, leaned into it once I truly felt it. He urged me back to my feet and pulled me against him, smushing my wings between us. His massive hand splayed on my upper chest then slid up, brushing against my neck then lightly tapped my left fang. It still wouldn't retract. I crossed my arms over my chest and breathed deep to help regain control, I was trembling badly.

The Lycan pup rolled to his paws and belly crawled to my ankles. His tongue came out and licked at my skin. At the time he was doing that, he kept repeating *I'm sorry.... I'm sorry.*

"I don't want to hear how sorry you are. You need to go to your own damned room and stay there. NOW!" I knew I was being a dink but controlling my wings wasn't enough and they began to tell on me. A slight tinkle of glass chime was ringing in the hall as the adrenaline wore off and my fear trembled through me. As Haley glanced back over his shoulder there was an odd look in those golden eyes but I saw that he was looking past me, to the big man standing there silently watching the whole scene. Then the pup quickly turned and slinked off.

I thought Armor and Chesterton would say something to the pup to try and ease his misery but when I turned to confront them I found they were just staring at me.

I used all my concentration on dissolving my still fluttering wings, not wanting to hear any comments about the physical manifestation of my dog phobia. Armor pulled me tight, erasing the space separating us until I was pressed solidly against him. My whole left side ached. I found out the hard way that ramming into a Lycan, even if he was still a pup, was a painful experience. Once my wings were gone my fangs retracted slowly. Turning on my heel I was taken aback at Armor and Chesterton's expressions as they stood in the hall. It was as if they were staring at a very strange insect under a magnifying glass. Armor's face was cool and unreadable but Chesterton's which normally had the same unflappable look, showed signs of distress. Whatever was disturbing him was beyond his experience and comfort level. Which said a lot in itself.

"What?" I probably had a strange look on my face as well.

"When did you learn Lycan, X?" Armor watched the pup disappear around a corner.

"I can barely speak proper English. I don't know any Blood languages."

Chesterton clutched the silver tray to his stomach. "But sir, you were growling and barking."

I tensed. "I don't know Lycan. I could barely get through introductory Spanish."

Armor took three steps towards me. His eyes belayed how worried he was. "X, what did you tell him?"

"To go to his room and stay there."

"Little One…"

"I shouldn't know Lycan. Armor, what the hell is going on with me? How do I suddenly know Lycan? When does this stop?" My voice broke, I sounded like I was going to start crying. Chesterton bowed and graciously closed the doors behind him as he discretely exited the room.

"I do not know, Little One." Armor's hand came out and caught the side of my face. "But I am with you no matter what is happening."

"You're sweet….and a stupid fuck." Who the hell declares their love by calling their intended a stupid fuck? Me.

"Well, I am your stupid fuck." The fact that Armor accepted that little nick name surprised and touched me even more.

I laughed. I waited for the hysteria or the waterworks but I was struck with a numbness that seemed to have removed my feelings. "Come here, my big stupid fuck." I wrapped my arms around his waist, pressing my face against his silk pajama top. "You caught me…"

Armor set his chin against the top of my head. I closed my eyes and tightened my hold. "Do what you want."

"What do you need, Little One?"

"You." I said as I snuggled into his arms. "Hold me."

Armor pulled me tight to him. I rubbed my cheek against the cool silk. I shivered as his voice slid down my ear canal in deep low rumble of a whisper. "My little rut master. When you were dominating the pup, I don't know how I kept off you. I do not remember you ever looking so commanding or so sexy."

"Hey…what are you doing?"

"It is a distraction."

"The way you usually distract me is more than enough."

Armor snaked a hand down into my jammies and cupped my ass. "Like this?'

"Would you…."

"Little One?"

"Would you put your mouth where the money is?" I oofed as I got a linebacker's shoulder into the midsection. God, I think I liked the bridal pose better than this over the shoulder carry that left me gasping for breath. However, I did get a bird's eye view look at his silk covered ass. I just had to feel it.

Armor took a few quick steps and ducked into the entertainment room throwing me hard enough that I bounced on the leather couch. He moved to cover me, kissing my jaw, working sucking little touches up to my ear. I was surprised that he could be so contained and gentle. Where the hell did my pants go? I saw a pale blue scrap of silk flutter to the ground behind the couch.

"Armor..."

"Unless you are going to say, take me hard and fast, I do not want to hear it." Then he leaned over me and nibbled on the end of my nose.

What the fuck? Armor took my hips in his hands and pulled me up off the couch. I think he did a triple salchow, one of those difficult figure skater's moves, because the room spun around me a couple of times before I landed on my knees on the couch cushion. He smoothed one large hand up my inner thigh then urged me to lift it. He set my knee and calf on the low couch back then kissed my rump. Armor the octopus was back and free ranging. Once he reached his objective everything slowed. I rested my weight on my forearms as he spread my thighs wide, worked his forearms under them, holding them wide and pulled my body tight to him.

"Ah..."

He buried his face in my flesh, his tongue returned home to my ass. I gasped as I clawed at the leather seat cushion. He stood locking his arms around my thighs as he backed away from the couch until I hung upside down against him suspended by his arms and tongue. The front of my thighs were resting on his shoulders as my hands braced on his thighs. I grabbed onto his leg and hung on for dear life. I groaned as Armor slowly teased my back door open. I could feel all the blood rushing to two areas... my groin and my head.

'Please...."

I felt him laugh silently. Oh God, I twitched.

"Do not move. If I drop you, you will split your head open."

"Don't drop me thennn... uuunnn." I felt too vulnerable hanging upside down.

He urged me to press my knees into the side crevasses of the wingback chair as he eased down into it. I ended up resting my weight on my forearms across his thighs. That talented tongue threw coordination out of the window.

"Armmm… uuuhh." I still couldn't make a coherent sentence. I yipped.

Armor stilled. Then he chucked the motion nuzzled his face against my balls and opened asshole. I shivered.

I yipped again. *Fuck me.*

In a move that would have made *Circ du Soleil* performers envious, Armor flipped my weight off his shoulders while cradling my neck, so my back didn't bend in ways it shouldn't, and I ended up with my backside plastered against his wide heaving chest. My legs were splayed wide over his thighs. His hot bar of heat nudged at the underside of my balls. *Oooh, good gawd...*

His hand spread across my stomach until his fingers tangled in my short and curlies then he pushed down as he pumped up slowly, slipping into me in a mind numbing possession. I groaned and growled. It felt good.

"Yeeessss. I have waited for you, Little One."

I screwed my eyes up as he bucked up beneath me. "Huh."

"Beautiful…."

I yipped back at him and bared my fangs. I swung my head and flicked my hair at him. His hand trailed down my neck to my nipple ring.

"I am close, Little One. Come with me." He plucked at my nipple and surged up into me. My whole body rocked. He hit that spot. I threw back my head and howled. He hit it again. I cried out again. I shivered again as fangs dragged over my flesh. *Huh…huh…*

"Now, Little One. Come with me now." He pulled the ring out and away from my body, twisting the metallic ring to the left. I tightened unbearably. He slammed up into my tightened channel and I yowled again as he rubbed past my prostate. My cock spurted. I didn't even stroke it. Armor still held my wrists tight. I groaned and spasmed. Armor bit me with human teeth. I arched my torso back and away from him.

24

"Huh, huh, huh, aaaaahh."

Armor shot his offering into me.

Off in the distance I heard the cry of a wolf in answer to mine. I slumped back against Armor and closed my eyes. My body was coated with a light sheen of sweat.

"Xavier…I do not know what is happening to you." He kissed my shoulder.

"Are you backing out on me now?"

He hunched up in me. I shivered and shuddered. "I am going nowhere. I might have to get a collar and leash on you though."

"You've been trying to do that since I met you."

He chuckled into my ear. The hair of the back of my neck stood up as his breath wafted over my sweaty skin. I let out a big sigh.

"Beautiful?"

"I have to do something, I absolutely loath."

Armor brought his arms around my waist and hugged me as he pulled out of my portal. He caught my wince. He pressed his lips to my temple. "What would that be?"

I grinned back at him and pushed his face away from me. "Shopping. The Pup's got nothing to wear. You still haven't filled out your wardrobe since the fire and the…stalking craziness. Not that I don't love to see you in silk pjs…" I let my voice trail off.

Armor's hands slipped around my hips. "And you have dropped ten pounds so nothing fits properly."

"I was hoping you wouldn't notice."

"There is nothing about you that falls outside my regard."

"I'm damn glad you quit stalking me, because that statement could get creepy really fast."

Armor easily dropped back into the one in charge mode and right at this moment I was more than willing to follow his lead. I think my spine melted there with my orgasm. "We shall shower, collect the Pup and go shopping. I take it we are going to Frederick's?"

"I don't know of anyone else who would close down the store for us."

"Frederick does not do it out of the goodness of his heart."

"So we'll burn some plastic."

Armor kissed my temple and brushed my hair back off my face. "I love you. Do not forget it, do not question it. I will be at your side come what may."

"You….Pretty vampire." I yipped as he swept me off my feet.

"But first, we shower. The pup needs to be scent marked to proclaim that he is not a lone wolf. We however, do not." Armor hand splayed across my ass as he ushered me out of the entertainment room. "X, why did you want to make love here?"

"The plan was to do Sex's male stripper dance for you."

"We will try that again, later." He kissed my nose.

"Okay, what is up with that? Why are you biting or sucking or kissing my nose."

"It is cute and calls out for my attention."

Er, okay.

"Let me take care of you while we are able, Little One. Let me show you the tenderness and gentleness you should have always had in your life. What does that yip mean?"

"Love me." It actually meant 'fuck me now until I howl my release.' My version was a bit more romantic. Armor carried me back to our room straight to the showers. Once we got inside, he slid me down the front of him as if I was a raindrop skimming his body. I smiled at him and pushed him into the shower. We always seemed to do better in falling water.

For the amount of money I was planning on spending, Frederick would keep the store open for us until midnight or whenever while we shopped until we dropped.

Yip.

Chapter Two: Stunned

I didn't even bother getting disgusted waking up in my own drool anymore. What was the point? Just change the towel under my head and get on with it. The hard bristles slapping into my leg brought my attention up to sleepy golden hellcat eye peering from a red panther body who then gestured with her muzzle toward the doorway. Armor was on me. Shade was sprawled against my side like a body pillow and the pup was at the foot of the bed. Everybody had their own room, but they all ended up on my bed. What the hell was that about? I scratched my head and stretched. Did I have fleas?

"Haley, get off." I nudged him gently with my foot. The pup whined and climbed off the bed turned around three times and passed out on the floor. Was that in English or Lycan? Considering it's a new language for me, I'm slipping in and out of it effortlessly.

This is an ungodly hour, I'm not getting up. So don't ask me. Shade groused but the tip of her tail shimmied.

When the hell did a king sized bed get to be so small?

Shade, move your tail.

But it's between two warm pillows.

Oh god, now she's quoting movie lines. *Those aren't pillows.*

Eeeww. Shade's legs kicked in the air as she scrambled to get up and off the bed. The whole mattress shook as she leap off. Her tail was stiff and held straight out from her. She shivered sending her fur out in a frizz around her then I was pinioned by a golden eyed gaze of disgust.

I raised my hands in innocence. *I'm not the one who put it there.*

I repeat, eeewww. She flicked her tail violently with the tip almost vibrating as if she were trying to get rid of cooties. Shade was being a drama queen.

Now that I got two obstacles out of the way I only had one more body to get off me so I could get up. I tried to give him a slight nudge to get him to move but he was firmly entrenched in a deep sleep to feel it.

"Armor, roll over." The slight snoring stopped and the bed rocked as this big hunk of vampire shifted. Instead of freeing me, I was squashed. All the air was squished out of my body.

"The other way!" I pushed on his shoulder to get him turning in the right direction.

Haley gave a low whine somewhere between worry or a warning. *Master, who is that?*

Okay I had enough brain cells firing to know that was Lycan. I blinked my snowstorm of a hairdo out of my eyes to see Claudius standing in the doorway with his hand over his mouth. I don't know if he was shocked or trying to keep from laughing his fool head off. He gestured at me then turned away. I heard his laugh as he walked down the corridor. Considering I thought that Claudius was an unemotional sort of man when I first met him, he sure found a lot to be amused at when he came a calling. I think it was safe to say that little brother was good for him.

Master? Haley whined again in confusion.

"That was Claudius; he's my Father. Do you remember? He saved you in the woods?"

His scent is familiar. Haley's brow furrowed as he sniffed the air.

I climbed out of bed. Shade was stretching when I scratched her head. I jumped as Haley shoved his wet nose were it shouldn't have been. I pushed his face away.

"Jeez, just sniff my hand if you have to check for scent."

He does that. Haley looked puzzled as his paws settled on the edge of the bed. He muzzle gestured to the still snoring lump of vampire who was the only one supposed to be in my bed.

I stilled. "What did you do, watch us?"

Haley glanced down at the floor to avoid my eyes and muttered in a guilty whimper. *You never said I couldn't. That tall, thin human chased me away. After that I just listened. It sounded as if you liked what he was doing. You howled with satisfaction.*

Well I couldn't argue with that. I did like it and I howled with great satisfaction.

Well Armor is the only one I let be that personal with my ass so don't do it again or you'll get thumped by me and Armor, got it? I blinked when I noticed Shade looking at me.

Lycan X? Really? Her voice was more amused than startled.

I didn't even realize that I wasn't speaking, I was growling. I lifted my hand and rubbed my eyes. *Have you got an explanation for this, Shade?* There was complete silence so when I turned and gave her a 'what?' look I noticed her staring at me with an unusual expression of amusement.

Not clue. Her statement was accented with a slow golden eyed blink of barely suppressed laughter.

Okay...thanks, I think.

Are you eating? You're getting a little hard and stringy looking. You need to take better care of yourself X.

What the hell? Everyone seemed to be a critic these days. *Apparently not enough. Don't worry, your Majesty, I'm going to see a doctor. Soon. Take Haley to the kitchens. Please and thank you.*

I watched as Shade sinuously stalked past the smaller beast. Her tail reached out and curled around his head. I didn't know if they talked in Silent Speak or if was just an animal thing, but they headed out of the bedroom together side by side with a much more relaxed Haley, trotting to keep with his much larger companion. Somehow I had managed to get back into my jammies after Armor's and my afternoon delight was over. My stomach growled. I grrrr'd right back at it, tired of the constant remind that for some reason I wasn't keeping any weight on no matter what I ate. I pulled the waist string tighter then went in search of Father.

I stumbled off towards the entertainment room, pushing the rebellious strands of hair back off my face. Yawning I walked into a deceptive human tableaux of Claudius breaking fast. I sniffed the scent of bacon and inhaled deeply. Ambrosia.

"Xavier, I think you would be able to direct armies on the battlefield better than you can direct those in your bed." There was still a remnant of amusement on his lips.

29

Chesterton directed a number of silver services into the entertainment room. Claudius gestured me to sit across from him. Plopping down in the leather wingback chair that had seen so much action yesterday I waited until the staff had vacated the premise before I started peering into domes trays. I had eggs Benedict, OJ, toast, sausage and a plate heaping with bacon along with an extra large bowl of oatmeal and with a coffee mug full of warm blood. My meals were getting bigger. I regularly finished them off, but I wasn't getting any bigger. Thankfully I wasn't getting any smaller...yet. Maybe a little stringy as Claudius had pointed out.

I speared a piece of bacon then waved in the air to make a point. "Not all of them are invited to my bed. Shade just takes over, claiming everything she sees..."

"Typical cat." Claudius added taking a sip from his own blood mug and letting out a little hum of satisfaction.

"And Haley can't sleep alone. He has nightmares. It was easier to let him up on the bed when he came crying to me than to listen to those crying whimpers echoing in the halls. I'm going to have to tell him that the wet nose up the ass is the privilege of..."

T.M.I., X, T.M.I.

Claudius snickered down into his cup of blood. I sat up and just stared at him. "Okay, who are you and where is Father?"

"Sigmund was considered a deviant, but he was not out dominating Lycan pups. He also did not have a Hellcat sleeping willingly in his bed. And not just any old Hellcat but the Queen snuggling on your pillow like a kitten." Father laughed again. Damn that smile looked good on him.

"I don't think you came here to get your joke of the day." I tried to cling to my tattered dignity as I drank my juice. Claudius reclined into a matching chair. He cupped his chin in his hands.

"No, I did not come for that. Hades asked me to remind you about your 7:00 a.m. appointment."

Oh yeah the teenaged boss of me who was perpetually at the expense of his hormones. I picked up a sausage and bit into it. Hmmmmm, tasty. "Asked or ordered?"

"Strongly suggested that it would be in my and your best interest if you showed up on time."

"In other words, commanded." God I hate that prick.

Father arched a critical eyebrow. "You have not left a good impression."

"I plan on going to music appreciation class. Not that it will help much. I have no musical talent and aside from the live stuff that you and Marcus play, I can't stand classical music. Hell, I can't play the tambourine in time. Sex just got up from the coma. He couldn't help falling asleep. He's being unreasonable.

Claudius nodded, "I knew he had done something to embarrass Hades."

"Embarrass Hades? He knocked Sex flat in the lobby then made a spectacle of him."

"He struck Sex?"

Shit, wrong thing to say. Claudius set his mug aside and stood up no longer amused. In the blink of an eye he had turned into an ice cold pillar of purposeful rage.

"Wait!" I scrambled to stand in front of him with my hands splayed across his chest as if I could physically stop him. I knew I presented a less than imposing figure in my pjs compared to the natural casual elegance that embodied my vampiric father. Still, I couldn't have Claudius gunning for Hades. What Hades wanted he couldn't have and it was up to me to tell him that. "This is my problem. I'll handle it."

"Sex is my chosen." The aura of good humor that had surrounded Claudius moments ago had cracked and fallen away like a shattered candy shell. Candy? That wasn't a sentiment that I would have used for Father but it had little brother's feel all over it. Right now, all I could sense with a disturbing stillness. Father's blue eyes were ringed with crimson fire. Good Lord. If he went all postal on Hades, he would end up flat on his back suffering from hemlock poisoning and in Sex's need for vengeance; we'd all end up stapled to a wall again, this time by Hades himself.

31

I swallowed but stood my ground. "This is a House matter." I tried to use my most supercilious tone of voice and was secretly glad it didn't crack much. This was my problem and I was the one to fix it.

Claudius nailed me with a hard cold gaze. His tone of voice had dropped to a monotone. Oh fuck... "A House matter?"

"This is a Von Drachenfeld matter, Father. He is Sex Von Drachenfeld, not Du Bussey. As Head of the House and as his eldest brother, it is my job to protect him; to be the one to avenge his honor and lay down the ground rules. We both know that I have not been doing that. Father you know you can bypass me, but you'd be undermining my authority. I don't need that right now."

"Xavier." Claudius whispered back to me with a voice that cracked slightly with anguish. I'd never heard him speak with such emotional pain. Sex was allowing him to get in touch with his buried feelings but he had to take the good with the bad.

"Let Sex stand on his own, Father. He is far stronger than you think. Azrael and I have his back." I turned to the door. Armor stood there looking like a God that crawled out of bed after a night of debauchery. Which he did and he was. He reached down and yanked human-form Haley from up off the floor on the other side of the wall.

"X, your Lycan needs more lessons in dominance."

Eavesdropping is not tolerated here, pup. I growled at him.

Haley hung his head. Armor dropped his hand from Haley's red leather collar that we picked up at the Joker's Wilde the night before. The diamond studded "X" dog tag sparkled in the artificial light. Haley crouched, sidled up to my side and dropped at my feet. He leaned over and kissed my outer ankle. I glanced up at Armor as he crossed his arms on his chest his face a mask of irritation. He looked down with disapproval at the pup but when the youth was eyes-to-the-floor with obvious dismay at being in trouble again, he flashed me a bright smile then frowned again as the pup glanced back his way. I was grateful Haley had clothes on this time. Someone had said to "start off as you plan on continuing on" and I had a sneaking suspicion that it was it was

Father. I let out a big sigh. It was clear that Armor felt that he had to fight a Lycan pup for rank in my House. Gees.

I forced myself to speak human…English…whatever. "This is the second time that you have disobeyed me, Haley. You will be punished. This is disappointing. I thought last night's show of dominance and ranking would have been enough."

The whole chair shook as he leaned against it. "I am sorry, Master. I just want to be with you."

"Father is my right hand. Armor is my left hand. What they tell you to do, you do. You will obey their words as if they were from my mouth."

"Yes, Master." There was that grating puppy whine again but this was for his own sake. A Lycan trying to learn Vampire hierarchy was just as bad as a human trying to figure it out so we had to turn House Von Drachenfeld into his pack, and he had to learn his place in it. "Sorry Master, I'm really, really sorry."

"You said that before. Now go with Armor. He will show you your rank in my House. You said you understood it yesterday, but it doesn't appear so. Does Father need to dominate you as well?" Claudius looked coldly at the Lycan. Haley quickly shook his head negatively quite reasonably wanting nothing to do with the vampire who radiated such menace right now.

Armor rolled his eyes at the pup's sudden timid air, then gestured for the youth to come to him. If Armor didn't want to do this he would have told me outright and Haley grabbing a handful of t-shirt back told me he wasn't all that adverse. I think. Oh, the hardship of having sex.

Claudius looked back at me. "Dominance issues? Did you rut with him?"

I stopped picking at the breakfast leftovers. "Armor said I needed to do it. It was necessary for the pup's protection."

"You love to complicate your life, Xavier."

I got a sick feeling in my stomach. "Oh, God. Don't tell me I just took another mate."

Claudius was silent regarding me with a wry intensity. I pinched the bridge of my nose almost ready to burst into tears. Could I complicate my life any more than I already had? Apparently so.

Father gave a chuckle. "No, I cannot do it to you even though it is tempting. You look so distressed. No, you do not have another mate. However, you do not have another Lycan and you have promoted him behind Armor. He is now your personal guardian."

"Meaning?"

"If anyone gets past the Loyal, the pup will place himself before you. You are his Alpha. He will die for you." That wasn't something I wanted to hear but Father wasn't done talking. "Armor and I are right behind you in this pack as High Betas. He will obey us but he will live his life only to protect you at any cost. It's a heavy burden for someone so young but he has a core of cold steel. Once he sets his mind to something, he will carry it out regardless of the consequences."

I lost my appetite. I pushed my plate away and closed my eyes. "You should have a manual printed up."

"Pardon?" Claudius paused as he reached for his mug.

"I said, you should have a manual printed up. The dos and don'ts of being a vampire Emperor. Don't rut with Lycans. Just…don't move at all, cause when you do you're fucking something up or over, or on."

"Are you done feeling sorry for yourself, Xavier?"

"No, I got a few more sobs in me but go ahead." I got a slap across the face. Holy crap! It wasn't as hard as Hades but it was enough to ring my bells.

"I will not tolerate disrespect from you, my son. You were not given an owner's manual as a human. You stumble along in that life under the guidance of your parents. Then you are set free from their home when you have learned how to survive."

'You are still a child as a vampire - little more than a fledgling. If I see you need direction or correction, I will distribute it quickly. Your first Vampire Father failed you. Armor did not have the capability to be your Father; he didn't have the experience. Armor probably had a total of one year out in the world in all of Marcus's 240 year lifespan. Marcus has always been the dominant personality. Armor tried to do right by you but it was the blind leading the blind. After a while I could not bear to watch it further- especially when he had Marcus tear your mind open in a jealous rage."

Claudius caught me by the back of my neck and urged me forward until we were forehead to forehead, "You are too powerful to be under the influence of mood swings, Little Blue. You are so young to be in the middle of this, but this is where you are. Master your flame and you will control yourself."

"How can I master something when I don't know what's going on? Do you know what's happening to me? Yesterday I just started growling in Lycan. I can hear that pup just like I can hear you talking and it's not like when I tried to learn Spanish in school. I'm not hearing it as Lycan and then searching for the human equivalent, it's just there. And, it's not like Hellcat and it's not Silent Speak." I ended up pressing the flat on my hands against Claudius's chest.

"Did you try to learn Lycan?"

"I....I didn't even know I was speaking another language until Armor and Chesterton pointed it out."

"The only thing I can think of is that your mind fuck ability has increased and that is not unusual because it should be a trait of the Royal Blue line." Claudius cupped a cool hand around the back of my neck offering up some personal support. Again, I laid this expression of comfort from the former First of assassins at Sex's feet. They were good together. Good for each other. Father controlled those sudden urges Sex felt too often and Sex made Father more...human.

Yip...Yip...Yip.

Having a Lycan in the house was just like having a dog in a small apartment, he really wasn't all that quiet. I sighed. *Well someone was having fun this morning which was more than I could claim.*

I raised a hand to my still burning face. Couldn't really argue with him when he had a slap that felt like a redwood falling on you. A lesser fledgling would still be prostrate on the floor. That was part of Claudius's charm; he always brought everything down to the brass tacks.

You didn't have to sit there and puzzle out the meaning of his words. He smacked you in the face, physically if necessary, with them in a well meaning sort of way.

Claudius kissed my temple. "Sit. Eat. You will have a long day ahead of you. I have arranged for the Medical department within Shadoe Incorporated to take a look at you. You have dropped weight, Xavier. Weight you cannot afford to lose. Your first appointment is at 2:00 p.m. on the 20th floor. Be prepared to have a full examination."

I had a feeling that the embarrassment and uneasiness I had with the 'turn your head and cough' scenario was going to be nothing compared to this doctor's appointment.

Father continued, "I have sent out messengers to contact the Seers. I have not had a reply as of yet."

Arrrrooooooowwwwww! The halls rang with another of the pup's vocalizations.

The hair on the back of my head stood up as the howl of satisfaction echoed through the building. It did echo, right? I couldn't be the only one listening in to this unconventional Vampire-Lycan relation, right? I glanced over to Claudius. "Tell me you heard that."

"I heard." Claudius set his mug down again then leaned closer in to me.

I started when I felt a finger trail down my throat. Blue eyes watched a finger trail along the gold chain at my neck and the locket that nestled the small hollow at the base of my throat.

"You are wearing it." Claudius's fingers curled around it lifting it up off my skin and a slight curl quirked his lips into a smile of satisfaction.

"It's not bothering me. Armor hasn't said anything about it but he knows what this means to you and Sex."

Claudius pulled me towards him by the locket and the kiss I got was definitely meant for Sex. I wouldn't say he raped my mouth, but when Claudius wants a kiss, he's getting a kiss. His lips ran over mine. His tongue snaked out and teased my mouth open, flicking at my teeth and rubbing along my tongue. I had just finished eating and personally I would rather have a toothbrush in my mouth right now but when I tried to pull back but he caught the back of my head and angled my head to the left. If he didn't mind the lingering taste of bacon and eggs, who was I to get in his way. He coaxed my tongue into a slow lingering dance. For once, his hands never strayed below my neck. Who the hell knew that the gentle stroking of knuckles on the nape of my neck could be so sensuous?

"Thank you."

Huh? Thank you for what? My eyes were crossed when he let me go. What the hell? I blinked away the sexual stupor. Papa Fang ready knew how to get his groove on. Claudius settled the locket back on my neck but let his thumb linger over it. "Uh, you're welcome..."

"Sit down, before you fall down." Claudius lightly tapped me on the chest.

I was lucky I was standing in front of my chair because my knees collapsed. I looked at him, "What the hell did Hades do to you yesterday?"

Claudius flipped his long black locks over his shoulder and picked up his blood again. "Hades has decided to try being cute - courteous and cute. He is trying to get back into my pants with manners and the niceties."

"He doesn't get it, does he?" I was going to wait until my heartbeat returned to normal before getting up to start the rest of the day. Damn, if this is just a sample of Claudius unleashed it was no wonder Hades was so stuck on him.

"I am the only thing he wants that he hasn't gotten. Once, I would have given in to him, just to keep him out of the rest of my life, but I was shown the error of my ways."

"Crap, does that mean he's going to be all pissy with me?"

"Probably. You know Hades can act like a moody teenager when he does not get his way."

Out of the corner of my eye I saw a grey blur pass the door. I don't want to know. I picked up my OJ and sipped at it studiously ignoring whatever was happening out in the hall.

Claudius had seen the same blur but deemed to acknowledge the pup. "It is good you collared him. There are rumblings out in the Lycan Nation about the apparent disappearance of this little pup. Lycan, Britta the Elder, has sent out inquiries to the different Bloods searching for him, however there is no mention of the loss of an Alpha pack. The High Council has already questioned me about the incident. I only told them that I would look into it. However, I had to inform Hades that you had this pup under your protection."

A big sigh escaped me. "Why does this sound like it's something I'm not going to like?"

"Before his branding…that little pup was the only remaining grandson of Britta the Elder. There are countless daughters and granddaughters but Haley was the only male. You should remember from your parents that Britta the Elder runs the Lycan packs in this section of the world."

That Lycan pup who likes to stick is wet nose up my ass is royalty? "He was a prince?"

Claudius furrowed his brow. "Not really. The Lycan Clan is matriarchal. Males are not that highly valued except as protectors and breeders. Still, he is of her blood line. Britta branded him in a rage. Now she regrets. I do not know if she truly wants him back or if she wishes to finish what she started."

"Haley could go back home?"

"NO!" I turned and looked at the door. Haley had changed back from the wolf form to a human one. The pup stood there in all his glory, naked and flushed with Armor's recent dominance. "I've been accepted into the von Drachenfeld pack. I'm marked with the pack's symbol and I'm ranked." The golden hue of the Lycan's eye began to glow with an inner fire as he yelled at us. "I am part of this pack and I have sworn an oath to Hashmallim."

That Hasmallim crap. I didn't need to be hyperventilating into a paper bag again.

"Get some clothes on." I growled out an order. Claudius looked at me with a blank expression. Damn, I switched right to Lycan without even thinking about it.

Haley ran into the room and dropped to his knees at the side of my chair. His hands came out and grabbed my foot then pressed his forehead onto my calf. "Do not send me back there. Grandmother knew what she was doing when she set the brands on our shoulders. She sentenced both Derry and me to death. I have no pack. I belong here now."

Haley turned on his knees and presented himself for dominance. Oh god. I raised a hand to my face and closed my eyes. Before I ran afoul of Marcus and Armor, I would have gladly paid for sex. I wanted it so badly with almost every fiber of my being from the time I was fifteen until I hit twenty-nine and I got nothing, nana, zip. Now, I can't get away from it. I can't even eat breakfast without something popping up. Popping up. Ha ha.

"Master?" Evidence of Armor's dominance was running down inside of the pup's leg.

"I submit to you." He dropped his shoulders to the tile.

What did this say about me that I wanted my oatmeal more than a fluffy piece of tail?

The grandfather clock chimed 6:00 a.m. Saved by the bell. "Claudius?"

"Hades was... how did you say it, pissy, when I left yesterday. It would do well not to add to his ire by being late. I will see to the Pup."

"Hashmallim?" Haley had a confused look on his face.

I made an effort to be sure that I was speaking human, "I have responsibilities Haley. I have to get ready to leave. Claudius is my right hand. He is my proxy. Do you understand?"

"But...but...but."

Claudius reached down and took a hold of the red collar. "Lord Xavier has to go. Come little Lycan. Take me to your room."

"You can say no, Haley." I spoke to him in Lycan.

"He is your proxy. I offered my submission." Haley caught Claudius's hand and lead him from the room.

Oh my God, what the hell was I getting into? Into? I thought I was getting thrown into the deep end of the pool, I didn't know I was getting dumped into the middle of the fricking ocean. Now I had to go and deal with Mr. Hemlock Pissypants and music that should have gone the way of the dodo. Not that I'd say that to his face…or think that. I was getting a headache already just thinking about it and it was only 6:00 a.m. in the morning. I shouldn't have said that. When Father or Marcus played that longhair stuff, it just sent shivers to my soul. I think it was the company I was going to have to keep that was making me dread it. If I could have run screaming from the room to hide under the covers to get out of this I would have. As it was, I dutifully finished my orange juice and headed back to shower.

I heard the shower running when I finally got back to my bedchamber. I was so tempted to hop in with Armor, but then one thing would lead to another…and another... and another. Crap. I was turning myself on just thinking about my big monkey. I needed my wits about me today or I'd end up naked on my back on Hades office carpet again.

I busied myself grabbing some clothes. I actually wanted a suit for today to show Hades that I was a professional. Nothing fit, and almost my entire current wardrobe was big enough now that it looked sloppy. The suits I picked out at Frederick's last night wouldn't be tailored until later today, or tomorrow. I pinched the bridge of my nose. My thoughts travelled back to our late night shopping trip. I can't believe we…well, rutted like coven fledglings on the carpeted floor of the big and tall section.

It was the little smile on his face when he finally finished ringing up all our purchases that told me Frederick was about to make another modeling request. "August 4, 2:00 p.m. at the Convention Centre."

I frowned at him. "What does that mean?"

40

"You'll need to be at the Convention Centre for hair and makeup. The show starts at 4."

"What makes you think I'm doing another fashion show? I told you that the last one was it. I've been officially retired."

Frederick laid a CD on the counter. "Funny thing. Those ads you did really helped make the store very popular with the hip and young and trendy. Unfortunately the young and hip, don't always have the money to be trendy and they head for the five finger discount aisle. I had to install a state of the art theft detection system. There isn't a part of the store that isn't covered."

Oh crap, fricking busted!

Armor coughed and walked away to become very busy looking at a t-shirt.

"It's a charity event, Lord Xavier. It is called Heaven & Hell. I wanted to have you as the resident devil with your flaming red hair, but I can make you the Seraphim with your white locks."

"Give it." I held out my hand. He moved the cd out of my reach. "I said give it here."

Frederick paused then reluctantly slid the disk across the counter.

"All you needed to do is just ask. It is for charity."

"But you say no all the time."

I tucked the CD into my shopping bag. "What's the charity for?"

"Supplementing the money needed for programming for the youth of the city. Sports, arenas; keeping them busy so they don't have time to get into trouble. A couple of the public swimming pools were fire bombed and they couldn't be fixed, even though a private benefactor stepped up with the funds. They will be replacing the pools but not until next year."

He had me at firebombed. Damn it! "Ok, ok. I'll do it."

Frederick was so intent on convincing me to be a part of his fashion gala that he didn't realize I had said yes. "You really should think about doing it, Lord Xavier."

"I said I'd do it Frederick. What is your goal?"

"We're shooting for $50,000."

An idea popped into my head. This was a way to help out the city as well as take care of the guilt I had for ruining so many children's summer by exploding their public pool during my Phoenix burns. "I'll match anything you raise. It'll come out of a private confidential foundation. I don't want people pestering me for donations."

Frederick was literally bouncing up and down on his toes he was so excited. "Do you want to be in on the planning committee?"

"I'll see if someone will sit on it."

"Will you do publicity photos?"

"You're pushing it."

"You'll bring in corporate sponsors if you do."

"Fine. Call Chesterton and make an appointment." A sparkle caught my eye. There was a "x" pendant hanging with the rest of the jewelry in the glass display. "I'll take that."

I glanced around and saw that Armor had ushered Haley back out to the limo. "...and do you remember that fetching red number you had for Ar... Marcus a while back?"

Damn, I almost gave Armor's secret identity away.

"That was last season."

"Design me something like that for Marcus again. It doesn't have to be red but it really suits him. Oh and can you have it delivered." It felt strange to be calling Armor, Marcus, but there was a method to this madness. Who wanted their Master of the Territory to be a split personality? Crap, I was the new Master. I doubt vampires would be happy with a multiple personality in charge. Besides, Armor had already said, a rose by another name was still a rose. Armor and Marcus were beautiful blooms on the same stem.

I laid a piece of plastic on the counter. I liked the way that x pendant sparkled in the light. "I'll take the pendant now."

Frederick looked at me. "You have changed from the first time you came into my store, Lord Xavier."

I smirked, "I do believe I was blind when I staggered in here."

"You were four days old."

"There are some days, I feel like I am still four days old."

"Here you go, Lord Emperor." I rolled my eyes as Frederick pushed a number of bags across the counter. Since Armor had his hands full with Haley, the squirmy excitable puppy, I figured I could carry the clothes.

A black suit sleeve reached out beside me and gathered up the Von Drachenfeld's purchases. Another man in black, self appointed, bodyguard gathered up the other bag the first didn't take. Well, there seems to be time when it's good to be an ancient archaic authority figure.

Frederick watched his mouth hanging open as my entourage exited the building. "You are far from four days old."

I broke out into a laugh. "Thank you for your hospitality, Frederick... and accept my apologies for using your store so shamelessly."

Frederick bowed and handed over the pendant in a small black box. "Thank you for agreeing to do this charity fashion show this time, Lord Xavier. I promise you that it will be nothing but taste and decorum."

Turning on my heel I came to stop as my eyes zeroed in on that damned kilt poster that started all this hoopla for the red headed Sexy. He did look hot... and desirable. "The High Council has told me that my face is too recognizable. I think the exact words were, it's time to let that beautiful face fade from the light of day."

Actually, it was the House of Assassins and the blonde menace known as Hemlock Pissypants; but, once again simple vampire folk didn't need to know about the dark underbelly of the Blood Nation. I grinned back at Frederick, "You just thought I was being an ass didn't you?"

His face flushed red which meant he had been calling me a dink behind my back. His eyes widened. "If the High Council doesn't want you to be visible. Should you be doing the charity? I don't want you to get into trouble."

"They are learning that I don't respond well to high handed authority. What I do is my business. Thanks for staying open for us, Frederick."

"You just gave me this month's sales in three hours. Any time you want me open even if it is at 4 a.m. in the morning, I will gladly do so, Lord Emperor."

On the ride home Haley was beside himself with excitement. I don't know if it was the fact that he had three bags of new clothes, or that he could free range in the back of the limo or that he now had a red leather collar around his neck. Watching him zip from window to window tired me out. I didn't think he could get even more hyper but he ramped it up when I showed him his 'x' dog tag. He sprawled across my lap on his back his throat extended in a sign of submission. He quivered with anticipation as I worked that 'x' onto the ring. When I was done Haley was up and trying to squeeze his upper body through the partition that divided the cabin from the front to see himself in the rear view mirror.

I noticed Armor wasn't that enthused with the Lycan's antics until I tapped his ring finger. "What do you think means more to me?"

Almost instantly I found myself sprawled on my back.

"I do." His voice dropped down to a low sexy growl. Suddenly there was an innocent looking face resting on the seat beside my head, eyes wide and interested as if the pup was a keener in a lecture hall. After that, I was pulled upright to a vertical position and set back on the seat, but a warm arm crossed my shoulders and a hot palm rested mere inches from my push button start. Once Haley realized there wasn't going to be a another display of vampire loving 101, he curled up on the seat beside me and passed out.

Shades of the green eyed monster there, Armor.

Now that we were back at the Penthouse and the pup was escorted to his bedroom because honestly, my bed couldn't take anymore occupants, I wandered over to the master bath. All our assorted bags had been dumped at the foot of the bed and Armor had left a trail of clothes from the bed to the bath. That was out of character for him. He was more of there's a place for everything and everything in its place kind of vampire. I can only assume that it was something he had to learn from Claudius. I gathered up the strewn field and dumped it in the hamper before walking up to the running shower and opening the door. Steam billowed out.

"Are you jealous of that pup?"

Armor turned around squinting from the shampoo running down into his eyes. "What?"

"Are you jealous of Haley?" He turned is face up to the showerhead and I drooled as I traced the soap trail with my eyes as it slid down his so perfectly proportioned body. Who was the king of the sea? Charley? No that was tuna royalty. Neptune. My big vampire had the soaking wet body of a sea god.

"Why would I be jealous of a little wolf?" He couldn't look at me as he said that.

Oh my god, he was, he was so fricking jealous! I stepped into the shower fully clothed and buried my head against his neck, wrapping him tightly with my arms. "What were you going to do, brood and turn all Marcus on me? Talk to me, Armor. I shouldn't have to try and read your mind. I don't think either of us would benefit from that."

We stood for what seemed like an eternity in the hot shower until Armor finally started moving. His arms came around me and he squeezed me tightly to him. Avoiding my eyes, he stared down at the water circling the drain as if it was the most interesting thing he had seen in weeks. "When you switch to Lycan, I do not know what you say to him."

Armor's voice sounded like regretful petulance. His face was still turned away and his wet hair kept me from seeing his eyes. I let out a big sigh. "Most of it has been 'get your nose out of there'. Really, a cold Lycan nose up my ass is not the best way to greet the day."

I swallowed a groan of pain as he tightened his embrace...really tightened it. He was going to snap me in half. "You were supposed to be mine. Only mine. I will share you with Claudius but I should not have to with anyone else."

"I'm yours." My voice was strained but he didn't hear it. "Armor!"

He picked me up off my feet with that rib cracking hug, the side of his face pressed just as hard against my cheek. "I love you, Xavier. I love you so much it hurts. When you leave, what I am going to do? Will I even have the will to survive?"

45

I squeaked as his hold tightened even more around me. "Armor! Armor?"

Suddenly the pressure lessened as he dropped me back to my feet and he sank to his knees as if his leg bones melted. The whole of his weight slumped on me knocking me back against the tiled wall.

"PRETTY!" I caught a handful of hair to keep his head from smacking the wall.

Slowly his body stirred and his weight lifted up. The desperate embrace that lingered on me fell away. The face that looked up at me was the same as the one that slept beside me but it was the eyes that gave the change away. Marcus cautiously pushed himself off me, rising up under the pulsing shower to stand in his signature slouched form. How I kept from skittering away from him was nothing short of sheer force of will. "Where's Armor?"

Marcus stepped back to the far corner of the shower. "He...he had to leave. He has never been afraid before."

"Afraid? Of me?" Well aware of how vulnerable I looked sprawled out on the shower floor, I scrambled to my feet and stepped out placing the thick glass shower partition between us.

"Of being alone." Marcus pushed his hair back out of his face. "He has seen the sacrifices that others have made to be with you and for the first time he has found himself lacking."

"Oh for God's sake! I never asked for any sacrifices. Not from him, not from anyone. Send him back." My clothes were soaked and now clung to my body in a cooling clamminess that was making me shiver. It might have been how close Marcus had been but even though that stalking episode was over, I could now admit that he had scared me spit less.

Marcus turned toward the corner of the shower for a moment before he started speaking. "He doesn't want to talk to you right now, Xavier. He knows that leaving you is unfair but this is new to him. I've never allowed him time to experience the world, to gain knowledge, to become whole. He has nothing to compare this emotion to. I can't help him. You can't help him. Let him find his way through this. He will be

46

stronger if he can." Marcus reached out and turned off the shower. The immediate silence was overbearing.

Marcus stood in the shower not making any moves to get out. "You should be getting ready for work. Hades will be waiting for you."

"Fuck Hades. If Armor needs me, I'm staying here." Crap my voice broke.

Marcus was silent for a bit then hung his head. "Armor said he doesn't want to see you right now. He doesn't want you around. Go."

Marcus raised his head and stared at me directly in the eye. "Go, Xavier. I will deal with my brother. Excuse me." Marcus edged his way out of the shower careful not to come anywhere near me.

I whispered. "Did I…did I break him again?"

Marcus reached for a towel and wrapped it around his waist. "Not you alone this time, Lord Emperor. Our world is a cold and cruel place. It is encroaching on our Eden—you and Armor's Eden. He is realizing for the first time, that all his skill, all his strength and size will not win this battle."

"What battle?"

"The Nation wants you, Lord Emperor. The Nation doesn't care for a fractured love sick Vampire. You belong to our world. You cannot belong solely to him."

"I love him."

"Yes you do, Xavier. But when Hashmallim is finally here, he won't care if a splintered psyche loves you." Marcus matched me gaze for gaze. I stood shivering in my wet clothes.

"You know that this Hasmallim is coming, don't you? You've known for a while. I should take brother and leave, but I love Azrael just as desperately as Armor cares for you. So that leaves us little option. Go to work, Lord Emperor. Maybe he will be back to greet you when you return home."

With those quiet words, Marcus carried my love away, leaving me standing wet and alone. What the fuck just happened?

Chapter Three: The Winner

"Lord Xavier?" The tone had stepped up into worry. Haley must have been talking to me for a while…in human, and I hadn't heard a word he was saying. In human. I raised a trembling hand and pinched the bridge of my nose and counted to ten in order to control my rising panic that I had to really think hard about talking in human. I felt arms come around my waist as my little Lycan pressed himself to my back. There was nothing sexual in the act he was trying to give strength and comfort. That was my job. Jeez, I should have been fired and kicked to the curb months ago.

The elevator doors opened to Hades inner sanctum. 7:00 a.m. on a beautiful summer morning and I wanted to die. But I couldn't. *Shake it off. Shake it off.* I had the pup with me because Marcus was roaming the halls. I forgave him, but I didn't trust him and I didn't know how he would react to the new addition especially since Armor had such a bad reaction to the pup.

Early this morning after Armor disappeared; I stripped off and showered mechanically then finished dressing. I stood outside of Haley's room listening like a pervert as Father showed the pup his place in the pecking order. I shivered involuntarily as the yips sped up and a howl echoed in the hallway. I waited for a moment knocked on the door then walked in.

Claudius had the pup speared on his lap. He stroked Haley's hair and scratched behind his ear. Claudius met my eye evenly then gave a nod as if to say the lesson was over and the pup had passed with howling colors.

"Now that you're collared, do you need to be scent marked?" Haley wriggled like a puppy, snuggling back against Claudius and rubbing the back of his head on Father's shoulder. There was a sense of…peace? Or at least, contentment emanating from the Lycan now.

"No, Master."

"Take a shower, get dressed. You are coming with me today."

The pup gave a different yip which was obviously an okay and began to move completely off of Father. Claudius tightened his hold and pinned the pup youth to him.

"Xavier? What is it?" Father immediately picked up on my concern. He seemed to have a nose for trouble.

"Marcus is here. Can you watch him today?"

"Why is Marcus here?' He looked concerned.

"I'm not the only one the Hashmallim prophecy is freaking out. Armor lost it this morning. I'm taking Haley with me for his own safety. If you're not busy today, I'd like you to stay and keep an eye on Marcus."

Claudius let the pup go. "Go get ready."

Naked Claudius stood up and wrapped his arms around my chest and settled his face against mine, "I will redouble my efforts to find a Seer. Why are you not crying?"

"I'm numb. If I give into what I know I should be feeling, I'm going to be a basket case. As it is, I'm going to be late getting to Hades place. I can't show him weakness. He'll walk all over me." I didn't add the word, "again."

"You are stronger than you realize, Xavier. Remember that. Wait. I thought Hades wanted to see Sex."

I gave Father a thin smile. "I think it's about time, Hades realizes he can't always get what he wants. Besides, we have to establish some operating principles. Sex has given in to his every whim. There was no call for any violence, nor was there any need for public humiliation. I don't care if he kicks my ass into next week; he is going to understand that."

"Then I will leave the matter in the House's hands." Father kissed my temple. "I'll have the First Aid kit ready for you when you get home."

I patted his hands. "The sad thing is, I'm probably going to need it."

"You never know with Hades. He just might surprise you. You might want to change out of that bowling shirt. You know how much he likes those."

50

I fingered my shirt. It was the last one left. "Have Haley wait for me at the elevators. I don't think Marcus will cause any problems, but it's better to be safe than sorry."

Father lowered himself into reverent pose. How the hell can he do that, buck naked and still look so elegant doing it? "Thy will, will be done." He caught my hand and kissed my knuckles.

Marcus knew better than to hang around my bedroom so I didn't worry about running into him. I slipped a white tee then a light green dress shirt on over it. Even my fitted tee's were a little loose now. Not that stylish but I really didn't care if Hades got all shreddy. I headed out of my room and caught the elevator down to street level.

We had an old dog named Duke out on the farm. I didn't really have too many memories of that dog but I knew we had one. It wasn't until I got mauled by a stray when I was nine that I really grew a dislike and fear of them. Lycan were isolationists. To simplify things their mantra was, "You stay out of my business and I'll refrain from biting your face off." The few rogues or lone wolves were too worried about building their own pack by any bite necessary to bother humans but there are always a few bad apples in the bunch. Those were the ones that the Regency Hunters took care of. Watching this pup bound side to side in the limo left me at a loss for words. Haley didn't fit in that model. I swear if I put the window down he would have stuck his head out.

Hitting the Shadoe Incorporated elevators from the parking garage at least let us by-pass regular security. When the elevator stopped, I pulled the key from my pocket turned it then placed my palm on the reader that popped out. The elevator began to ascend again. This was done all in silence.

"Master?" Haley's tone was tentative and full of worry.

Huh? Glancing up I noticed that we were at the penthouse level. Instinctively I stuck my arm out to keep the elevator doors from closing completely. Gees, I had to get my head out of lala land before Hades handed it to me on a platter. I turned to the left and headed down to the room where Sex had ended up pinned like a butterfly to the wall. I don't know what I was expecting, a bloody smear left behind as a trophy maybe. Hades would have had it cleaned up before the blood soaked into anything expensive.

There was a cold deadly vibe in the cracking voice. "You bring a Lycan into my personal living quarters, First? A bold move, what are you trying to tell me?"

I tilted my head slightly since Hades had made it clear before that he didn't want me doing the reverence thing to him. "Since I don't have a parking space in the lot downstairs we would have had to park on the street. its 100 degrees in the shade at 7:00 a.m. in the morning, I'm not leaving him in the car with the windows cracked open for air."

"The other option was that you could have left him with security in the lobby."

"Haley hasn't done anything to warrant be locked up in a holding cell for the entire day."

"Then you should have left him at home."

"Let's say that wasn't a viable option at this time. Haley has promised to be on his best behavior."

I could see the wheels turning under those blonde curls. He clicked in a lot quicker than I expected and then surprised me even more by not jumping on it. The little ass had some tact after all…or so I thought.

Hades tossed a leash at me. I caught it instinctively. "And we will make sure that line of action continues."

Haley had moved in front of my body at the first sign of Hades making a move toward me. His low growl said, "Back off."

"Behind me, now."

Haley kept his eyes on the blonde asshat but obeyed…for once.

Hades regarded me like a boy with a magnifying glass on a sunny day, who had just found a colony of ants. Oh crap, I spoke in Lycan again.

"There is a ring by the elevators. Secure the Lycan there. Once that catch closes, it sets up a magical connection. If anyone other than a Vampire opens that leash, your little wolf pup will be dead."

I took a step forward, "Are you threatening me by threatening my pup?"

I felt a light touch on my back, "Its okay, Master."

Glancing over at Haley he stared at Hades but then he turned at gave me a yip. "Are you sure, Haley?"

He shrugged. "Lycans are not generally house pets for a reason. I will behave myself."

There was a ring on the floor just opposite the elevators. I looped the leash through the handle then clipped the end to the red leather collar. "Do you want a chair?"

"A pillow would be nice. Your Father was very dominant." I snapped my head around at the comment but Haley's face was open and sparkly holding no sign of anger or resentment.

I stilled. "Do you need healing?"

Haley shook his head. "It is nothing more than the usual from a fellow Lycan. I did not expect it from a Vampire. It will pass."

I headed back into Hades room and looked for the biggest pillow I could find. I could feel his pale blue eyes regarding my every move. I carried it back to Haley, waited to see if he was comfortable. "Let me know if you need anything. Just give me a yip and I'll come a running."

I offered up my ever present mp3 player then headed back to join Hades. He had, the only way I can describe it is, displayed himself on the couch – legs spread wide, head resting on a crimson cushion, arms crossed languidly across his waist --a reclined figure of sexual nonchalance. Yeah. Right.

"Now, Xavier, why am I graced with your presence instead of my lovely little boy? Not that you are not appreciated."

Welcome, said the spider to the fly. I thought with some amusement but I kept that to myself. I was here on a mission.

"We need to set some ground rules for you - a code of conduct." I sat down on the matching couch opposite from him.

His eyes narrowed. He didn't like that one bit. "Ground rules for my freely offered slave."

"We both know that it wasn't freely offered. You have a light touch on the chess board, Hades. None of us saw that trap. I don't think Father saw that either."

53

"My, you are feisty this morning and bi-lingual. You sounded very erotic growling and yipping to your pup. Speaking of which, there was been an official inquiry regarding the disappearance of a very talented Alpha pack."

"I killed them." Hades blinked. I don't think he was expecting that blunt of an answer from me. "They trespassed on Hunter territory and I had permission from the owners to remove them."

"You and who else?

"Father rescued the pup. I took out of the pack."

"Five fully grown Alpha Lycans?"

"Well I got four. A hellcat got the fifth since it had gotten off the property."

"Where is this Hellcat?"

"I ate him." It sounded better than I sucked his soul into my essence and burnt his carcass to ash.

"You ate him?" Hades sat up, "Are you insane? That is what started your great grandfather down the road to madness. Is this the start of your medical problems?"

Well, Hades was the head of the House of Assassins. I was his First. Claudius, his Second. He would be notified of any and all requests regarding his go-to-guys. "I think its part and parcel of what is happening to me."

"That is why your hair is white?" Hades made it sound like a statement of fact.

"No, my hair is white, because of hemlock poisoning and you. I'm eating three meals a day because of the Hellcat and other things. By the way, Hans is quite enjoying his employment at my House."

Hades had nothing to say about that. There was a slight tightening of the skin around his lips but other than that no outward signs that he was miffed that he had lost his spy to my one upmanship.

"And another thing, this…music appreciation stuff is not necessary. You are encroaching on my personal privacy. Your music is a taste none of us want to acquire."

Hades dismissed my concerns with a wave of his hand. "Edward offered up his terms. Any time I called, he would come. Anything I wanted, he would do."

"However, Sex is not free to act alone. You know that. Besides, you know what I am referring to."

"Enlighten me, Xavier."

"Giving him a concussion in front of the whole of the opera house audience; making him dance like a desperate stripper in your bar. Sex has given into your demands without protest no matter how perverted."

"He came with blood vengeance in his heart." Hades fingers plucked at the cushion's fabric button. Hmmm, was the little pervert nervous about this little heart to heart?

I didn't think he was as composed as that. I pushed him a little more. "Which you already punished him for. I think everyone would agree that the resulting twenty-seven days in a coma is more than enough punishment for something he had no chance of carrying out. Using Claudius as your shield was cowardly."

"So, you are reneging on his offer."

"I am modifying the terms."

"And if I do not agree to these new terms?"

"You really don't have choice in the matter."

"Are you challenging me, yearling?"

"I am stating fact. You cannot make any of us, do anything against our will. Sex has offered up his body to you for protection for his brothers and his Father. I am telling you, I will not have my little brother harmed or demeaned in any way. I also will not lose any more time than necessary to you. We have a schedule. You will have to work your way into it. You will block time if you need Sex on his off days."

"I don't appreciate this tone you are using with me, Xavier."

"Is it the tone of my voice, or the conviction of my words?"

"Touché." Hades leaned forward and his eyes flared red. "And what if I decide to take offense to your tone and conviction."

"Then we end up in a situation like you and Father. Do you really need your First and Second despising you."

"Assassins have vanished for less, Xavier." There was no subtlety in his voice now. I was pissing him off. Good.

"Why have you entered into the world of politics, Hades?" I figured I might keep my head if I went on the offense. "Why have you tipped the scales in favor of the Empire? Why have you backed those in favor of dissolution of the Council?"

"I see Claudius has been talking to you."

"Talking works wonders. It strengthens our father and son bond. We seem to be communicating very well."

"I have always been a Royalist, Xavier. I have never hidden my allegiance to the Emperor. Even after he fell, I stood with the Blues. Unlike many of the remaining Blue houses, I was able to defend myself against attacks – assassination attempts and coups. Eventually I returned as much carnage as I could with those who trespassed against me and mine so those attempts soon stopped."

"So this has nothing to do with the fact that you think you have me in your back pocket."

"It has intrigued me that I might have influence over you, Xavier."

"It isn't as much as you hope."

Hades cocked his head at me, "Where did you suddenly get the backbone from, my little Emperor?"

I narrowed my eyes. "I've always had it. I wouldn't be fractured now if I didn't have it. When I wouldn't bend to Armor's will, he split me. Out comes Sex to deal with the horror. When it came to Marcus, you and all that pain and killing; out comes Azrael. He sends his good wishes on your continued health, by the way."

"Return my sentiments to the Angel of Death. Any other demands you want to lay at my feet, Xavier?"

"Leave Father alone."

"What happens between Claudius and I is not your concern."

"I would like to believe that Sex's sacrifice was motivated by his worry for his brothers, but that would be a huge mistake. We are an afterthought. He offered himself to you to save Claudius. You promised never to touch him again."

"I have not touched Claudius."

"Roses. Brunch. Father stepped back into role as First because you had me down. You tossed him aside after you did all the damage you could do now…now he has begun to live again, you want to step in and take him back."

I pushed the blonde teenager too far. He jumped to his feet and reached across the coffee table for my neck. I brought my forearm up, blocking the grab and twisted my body backwards. Slipping over the back of the couch and landing in a crouch, I popped back up to my feet as quickly as I could. Hades kept coming. I danced back until I hit the back wall. Oh crap, it was the same place Sex got stapled to. A fist flew at my head. I ducked. The whoosh of air past my ear as he missed and connected with the wall. I pivoted around, brought my left arm up in a clothesline and rammed Hades as hard as I could. He was off balance to begin with. He staggered back and went over the couch.

"You've gotten slow, Honey Bee."

That blonde head popped up from the side of the couch. The blue eyes were widened and for a second I thought I saw fear before they narrowed. I saw him coming but this time, I couldn't get out of his way. He flattened my lungs with the force of his punch. I hit the wall hard and hung there for a second before I started my cartoon slide to the Italian marble tiled floor. The back of my head had bounced off the wall and I could hear the rush of the train called unconscious coming for me. The side of my head connected hard with the floor. I just had my ticket punched.

Hades caught the front of my shirt and hauled me off the floor. He shook me like a Schnauzer with a chew toy. "What did you call me?"

"Asshole." I hissed in a garbled whisper. My world narrowed to a pinpoint of light, and then even that was gone.

"Haley, shut the fuck up!" I knew I was growling this time.

The distant whine stopped. I felt a rough tongue lick the side of my face. I groaned.

"Master?" Where the Lycan salvia was still drying, warm lips now pressed. A hand stroked my forehead. "Master…"

I opened my eyes then had to close them again against the bright clinical lights above me. I went to raise my hand then hissed as I pulled on the attached IV. I squinted and found myself on a hospital gurney, somewhat strapped down with all sorts of crap taped to me or stuck in me. Shit. Hades put me in the hospital….again.

I heard Haley move and something tightened on my wrist. A straw was placed against my lips. I blinked to clear my vision and saw Haley's pale topaz eyes looking down at me with such concern as he held a glass of apple juice for me to drink. I lifted my other hand and found his leash clipped to my wrist. "Drink, Master. The doctor's told me to make sure you drink this all. They have taken a lot of blood from you. Everyone is concerned."

I took a big drink. Appley goodness exploded in my mouth….but it wasn't the same potent essence that was my Armor. Crap.

"Where am I? How long have I been out?"

"We are still in the building, Master. It has only been about an hour. The teenager called for medical help right away. There was blood coming from your ear."

Great. Hades cracked my skull open, again. I closed my eyes and ran through math tables. Then I began to list off those who meant the world to me: Armor, Azrael, Sex, Claudius, Claudia, Marcus, Haley, Chesterton. I seemed to be okay.

"Thank you for staying with me, Haley."

"You are my Alpha. I should have been with you when this happened, then maybe it shouldn't have happened. You would never have gotten hurt." There was a tightness to his voice and his nose was runny.

"Are there any blood packs here?"

"No. I can ring for one or you can bite me, Master."

"Armor wouldn't let me bite you before. He didn't say why, I was too busy to ask…"

"You dominate well, Master."

I let out a self depreciating laugh. I think this was the first time someone called me a good fuck. Where the hell was my stupid fuck, when I wanted him? "Ring for some blood packs, Haley. I'll heal myself, eat and we can get the hell out of here."

"I thought that you would have liked to take this with you." That creepy adolescent voice sounded from the far side of the room. Haley began to growl. I turned my head slowly and saw Hades holding up an epi-pen as he lounged against the door frame. "Winfield has decided to play ball. This is the antidote that Princess Sarah Elizabeth needs."

Winfield? Princess Sarah Elizabeth? Who was…oh, ooohhh. It was that man Hades was trying to make dance to his tune. The princess was his daughter, the one who Sex had to poison,

"I was going to give this to Sex after his class. Well, after we got out of bed. He seemed upset over having to harm the child. Will Sex come out and play?"

"You just cracked my skull open. No, Sex is not coming out to play."

"And, still you are belligerent." Haley let out a low soft growl of warning to the Head of the House of Assassins. The kid had guts.

"Keep your Lycan in check, Xavier."

"Haley, please call for those blood packs." I had a headache that was romping through my brain like those giant drums they had in Japan. Boom, boom, boom.

I shook the leash free from my hand. Haley slipped out of the door passed Hades who didn't bother to get out of the way. I thought for a moment that the pup would have run directly into Hades but the fact that he showed such good restraint made me proud. Once the pup was gone I was given his whole attention. "Why did you call me Honey Bee, Xavier?"

"What? I don't remember calling you that."

"Are you in pain?"

59

"Yes."

"Good." Hades came to the end of my bed and picked up the chart at my feet. "I will acquiesce to your scheduling request, Xavier."

"And Father?"

"What happens between Claudius and I is not your concern."

"You do know that he can't stand the sight of you."

"I know that, First. I have to make amends for my actions. I will continue to try. As I told Sex, I will not touch him, but I do want him in my life. If it has to be as an enemy, I am desperate enough to take it."

An orderly came into the room carrying a couple of blood packs. He bowed to Hades then crossed over to me. Haley circled the man and followed him closely, those topaz Lycan eyes watching the man intently. It was easy to tell that Haley's scrutiny was making him visibly nervous. Our conversation stopped until the orderly left.

"Since you were in need of medical attention, I had your physical examination moved up. I have placed you as a priority to the medical department. We should have some answers by this afternoon."

"Can I take this off?" I gestured to the IV. Hades approached slowly. I saw Haley watching him with the eyes of a predator as his upper lip began to curl in a warning snarl. Gesturing with my fingers of my other hand, Haley settled down.

Good Boy.

Hades carefully pulled out of the IV and began unhooking the rest of the monitoring devices. He handed me a warm blood pack. I fanged it and took long lingering drags. I didn't need any monitor to tell me when I had enough reserve to kick the Healing Light into gear.

Haley backed away whimpering as I was engulfed in blue flame. Lingering pain faded and the hairline skull fracture knitted and a whole bunch of other sundry minor wounds healed. Once the Healing Light died out, I grabbed up the other blood pack and drained it. I wanted my power bar recharged so I could get the hell out of here.

I tried not to flinch as Hades reached out and swept my white locks off my face. There was such a lost boy expression on his face and I knew that I wasn't the one with him right at this moment.

60

"Have you ever apologized for raping him?" I took his silence to be a no. "You might want to admit that you wronged Claudius. Just because he gave into you as First, doesn't mean he wanted to."

"Armor…you should hate him. Why do you love him?"

"He did other things besides…" I glanced at the pup. "It was those other things that got to me. He showed me that he cared, really cared for me. You used Claudius like a fuck toy. It's no wonder he only views you as his employer."

I could see that those words cut deep, "Two hundred years and he only sees me as the Head of the House of Assassins." Hades blinked a film of tears away.

"Who's fault is that?" I felt stronger. I sat up and my head didn't hurt. I started a bit when Haley began tonguing my ear then moved back to my hairline. He was cleaning the minuscule blood trail from my ear and neck. I reached up and patted his head. He gave back a little yip of satisfaction.

Hades handed me the epi-pen and a small card with the address on it. "It doesn't matter who delivers it. It should be done today though. She is a small child and I do not think she will last another day."

Hades turned and headed for the door. I slipped off the gurney and stood up, feeling good. I grabbed the pen and the card. I ruffled Haley's hair as he handed me his leash.

"Oh, my Angel of Death. You are the first to knock me off my feet since I joined the House of Assassins. You might want to pass that on to Azrael." Hades said that over his shoulder as he left the room.

"He already knows."

Hades gave me a backwards wave and disappeared out the door. I stared after him. I had won that encounter. Sure, he fractured my skull and put me in the hospital—but I got his acquiesce. I laughed. I took a stand and I won.

"Master? Are we going home now?"

"Not yet, little pup." I held up the epi-pen. "First, we are going to save a life."

"After that?"

"I'm going to kick some sense into my big monkey."

"Can I watch?"

I glanced down at his wide unblinking eyes. "You're going to anyway aren't you."

"Yes."

I ruffled his hair again. "You can watch, but you don't get to join in. I need to dominate my mate. He has forgotten his place."

"You dominate well, Master." Haley pressed up against me, and then moved forward toward the door, pulling against the lead.

"Let's get the hell out of here." I grabbed my Glocks and dagger from the side table and geared up. I followed my Lycan out feeling like a million bucks. I won.

Chapter Four: Angel of Mercy

I watched Haley and kind of longed for simpler days. I swear if I let him, he would have the back window open and would be hanging out in the sunlight. He looked at me once with a little pleading in his eye as he pressed his forehead against the tinted window. I just had to say one word.

"Vampire."

That ended that. Vampire combined with sunlight left a very icky and stinky mess behind.

He stared out at the buildings and people as we sped toward the Winfield residence. "Haley, tell me about yourself."

He sat down and looked at the carpet. "I belong to your House."

"No, I mean before the woods."

"I am not a part of that pack any more. It is forbidden to talk about things that happened there." His fingers fiddled with themselves.

"You can tell me nothing of your life?"

He shrugged. "What I can tell you, you already know, Master."

"Is this because I'm a Vampire that you can't talk about it?"

Haley came close and knelt between my legs. His golden topaz eyes were still sad as he regarded me. "Yes, another Lycan, I could talk to. But I am branded now. No Lycan in good standing with the Northern Pack will acknowledge me and if given the chance, they would kill me. Thank you, Master. Thank you for saving my life and bringing me into the safety of your pack. Thank you for taking care of Derry."

"Your litter mate fell just after you crossed the wardings alerting us to your presence. There was nothing I could have done for him. Can you at least tell me why you were branded?"

Haley lowered his gaze and shook his head. "I am sorry Master. Please don't ask anymore."

I sat and truly looked at him. He was a young man, who I made mistaken for being seventeen but he could pass for nineteen or maybe twenty but not twenty-one. Still too damn young to have such awful memories of his litter mate's death. "Can you tell me how old you are?"

"Forty-five."

I blinked in shock. "Uh? Forty-five years... human years or wolf?"

"Human, but I am still a pup to the Lycan. I wouldn't have been considered anything of consequence until I hit at least sixty-five. Then my Lycan form will begin to fill out. Right now, I'm a little bigger than a German Shepard. Don't worry. I can protect you, Master even if I am still young. I am stronger than most my age and can at least hold my own with older non-Alphas. I will protect you with my life. When I reach the Age of Change, I will be as big as the Alphas who were chasing me and Derry. My father was huge."

I was stuck on forty-five. How the hell old do they get? I cursed myself for not listening to Mom and reading up on the Hunter lore and stuff. At the time I thought why the hell should I pay attention? I was going blind. What the hell could I do to help out besides play bait? All that Hunter knowledge I denied myself was now denied to me forever because of what I was. I looked down at my arm where a slight bruise remained from the IV. Now I'm a Vampire.

A sick vampire. Or was I even a vampire anymore?

Haley whined. Okay, that got old real quick. "What?"

"When you get sad, I hear it in here." Haley winced and rubbed at his temples.

"Jeez, sorry." Crap, now I'm broadcasting. What the hell was I going to do...ahhhh. I mentally pushed my shield wider then constructed a smaller shield inside to keep my thoughts from leaking out. Well that was the plan any way. "Better?"

Haley scrunched up his face for a moment. "It's gone. You're strong -- for a male."

I think I was just insulted. "Uhhh...I don't understand."

"I hear you. It's like the pack cry. Only the Alpha females have it. They can call the pack from anywhere to one location. I've only known the female Lycan to have it...and now you, Master."

Oh god. I brought my knees up to my forehead. What the hell was happening? What the hell was I? A hybrid of demonic species? Vampire, Ocanlov, and now Lycan? *This ain't happening. This ain't happening.*

"Master?"

Haley crawled up on the seat beside me and I felt his arms go around my head. "Don't be worried, Master. You have your vampire pack. They are strong. Your Father will keep your enemies away. Your mate will be your strength and your fangs. Even the tall thin human is part of your pack. He loves you as strongly as your true Father does. You need only to call for them and they will come running."

I felt his nose nestling my ear. "I pity those who would come against you, Master. You look weak when you are alone. You are thin and small." I popped my head up. I was taller than this punk ass kid…who was fifteen years older than me. Haley sniffed my hair reassuringly as he kept the light hug around my hair and face. "But I have seen your capacity for destruction. Your enemies will tremble before you when you unleash your wrath."

"And if they don't?"

"Your pack is stalwart and when your enemy flees we will run them to ground and tear out their throats." Haley's voice was full of pride when he said this.

Carnage, bloodshed and gore. It was like I was sloshing out a swash of chum behind me calling all sorts to predators to me. Creatures who for some reasons wanted to serve me…or serve under me. I pinched the bridge of my nose. I was getting another headache.

"What are you to me, Haley?"

"I am your pet."

I twisted and looked at him. His eyes were closed and he hung onto my hair, rubbing his face back and forth on it. Out of all that he was saying about death and mayhem and packs and ripped throats, I didn't expect – pet.

"I am too small to be your *Elek*, so I must be your *Zsigmond.*"

I stiffened in his hold. "My Sigmund?"

Haley released me and looked down at me his pale brownish gold eyes watching me with interest. "No, I said *Zsigmond*. I cannot be your protector- your *Elek*; I must be your defender – your *Zsigmond*. I am too small to hunt down your enemies. I must stay by your side and keep them from getting to you. Yes, I am your *Zsigmond*."

It still sounded like Sigmund to me. Holy crap, I am never going to get away from that name.

I reached out and lightly stroked him behind his right ear. He reacted like a cat with a hypnotizing tickle spot. He froze with a smile on his face as I touched his skin. A low rumble rose out of his throat. I snatched my hand back. I was turning him on and right now I was too damn weak to have to rut with him. I just had my brains trying to leak out my ears less than an hour ago.

Haley jumped me. We fell over in a tangle of limbs. I was about to start defending myself when he ducked under my arm and pressed his back against my chest snuggling close then he gave a sign of contentment.

"I like to sleep with you. You're warm." I noticed that was in Lycan. Well at least I was kind of picking up the shift of language a bit now.

Haley had been through a lot in a short period of time. He nuzzled up against me, went boneless and drifted off. That was trust. He panted in his sleep like a dog. The little girl's address was way across town. It would take a while to get there. I stretched out, pulled him close and drifted off.

A boy and his *Zsigmond*.

I woke from a dead sleep as a hand thumped into the side window of the limousine. Haley was moving before I really got my wits about me. He slammed into the closed door. He growled snarling at the would-be intruder.

Who ever it was backed off quickly. Haley reached for the handle and swung the door open. Sunlight flooded in. I felt it burning on my skin. I clenched my eyes shut and crawled blindly toward the open door meaning to shut it. There was some shouting then the door was slammed shut. Holy fuck. I grimaced. My flesh felt like I had just rubbed sandpaper all over my arms and face.

"Lord Xavier, are you all right?" Riot, my self proclaimed man in black/chauffeur /bodyguard, called back to me through the intercom.

"No." I hissed back at him. Crap, I was just pan seared for ten seconds.

"We will secure the Lycan and return to base."

"Are we at the Winfields?"

"Yes, Sir. It was the Winfields's personal security that approached the limo, Sir."

I opened my eyes and blinked. Well I wasn't blind. "I've got a mission to complete. Just get me to the front door."

What did Haley say? I could call the pack. I ignored the burning sensation in my skin, dismantled my inner disco ball of protection.

HALEY! Get your ass back to the limo now. Stand by the back door.

I crawled over to the small fridge and whipped out a blood pack. My flesh was on fire and I combined it with an ice cream headache as I sunk my fangs into the cold crystalline fluid. The fridge was set too cold. I sucked on the blood pack until it crumpled in on itself from the force of my suction. Okay, now it felt like a minor sunburn. This I could handle. I pushed myself to my knees then sat back of the seat. Damn that Lycan boy moved fast. Er...man. He was older than me. This is probably what Father felt like when Sex would tear off on some half baked idea.

Hey. Sex protested.

Well, it's true. Now that I see it for myself, you can be awfully annoying. I touched the side of my face fully expecting to feel bubbled skin. The protection of vampire friendly window tint isn't worth squat when the door is hanging wide open.

HEY! Sex protested again.

But, we love you anyway, Sex. You know where we are? I broke my fangs into the second blood bag slushie.

I heard. X, can I do it? I really didn't want to hurt her. Sex sounded dull and calm. Subdued really didn't suit my little brother.

Hades cryptic little message gave me the chills. It might not be pretty. Can you handle it? I don't think we should be exchanging in the present of humans... The little Lycan was now standing beside the back door of the limo and I could hear his whine. He was truly contrite. That sentiment and two pints of blood would get me somewhat back to normal.

...or Lycan. I can't believe you...ahem -- dominated...him X. And, the killer is, that magnificent piece of ass thinks you're a rut master.

In my mind's eye I could see Sex's infectious smile. That time we were all trapped in that coma, when I finally got the meet the other parts of me, well Sex took my breath away -- white on white and mini micro skirt...and those Phoenix wings. In that place, the Darkness as he called it, I had our flaming red hair and our original Emperor's wings in shades of red, oranges, greens and gold. I thought I had protected him, both Sex and Azrael, from that demonic rape but he was the one who still ended up bearing the brunt. And he did it with a smile on his face. How did that song go? He would do anything for love? Little brother was stronger than I ever suspected.

It's quality, not quantity. I think that this is as good as it's going to get for now. I tossed the empty blood pack on the floor.

Watch and learn, elder brother. Let's do it.

I blinked and grimaced as the pain hit me. That is one thing about being in the Dark, you don't feel anything...well except what you carry around with you. I used to carry despair. I liked love a whole lot more. And it wasn't really dark anymore, my Phoenix wings lit up the area around me. Az even came and sat in my light for a while. He would only grunt at me, but that was a hell of a hot better than listening to him curse and call me stupid.

I won't be long, elder brother.

Secure the Lycan. X called back to me.

I reached down and picked up the leash. It gave my finger tips a tingle. I could sense...magic. I shifted my vision, the same as I would when hunting for bloodmarks and saw a small one on the catch of the metal clip. Hades wasn't kidding. This would take the poor Lycan's head off.

"Master?"

I patted my shirt to make sure I still had the epi-pen.

Don't tell the Lycan about the brotherhood, yet. X's voice was getting faint and then he was gone leaving me in charge…in the middle of the morning…with a bitch of a sunburn.

"Lord Xavier?" A Loyal called from outside.

I nodded. Yeah, as if X could see that right now. I squinted through the darkened glass. "I'm good to go…Turmoil."

Riot and Turmoil. Who the hell was picking these names? Oh yeah, Hades the blond wonder kin. What did he do, just open up a thesaurus and pick out something? I never really thought of it. How many assassins were ranked? Maybe he did need to be trite and condescending. Nah, he was just a dink. What did X call him, Hemlock Pissypants? I broke out laughing. It was funny. I wouldn't call him that to his face though. I was just getting used to the taste of latex. I'd take that any day compared to the alternative.

I set my goggles on my face and opened the door again. Turmoil stood close to me under the shade of a huge freaking umbrella. "What did you do, mug a picnic table?"

"The sun is intense this time of year, Lord Xavier."

Well hell, it's summer. Haley stood at the side of the car. He looked down at the pavement. "I'm sorry, Master. I forgot you can't be in the sun. Did I injure you?"

"If that's your version of Zsigmond…I'm up shit creek." I quirked a slight smile on the un-scalded feeling side of my face.

Haley whipped his head around and stared at me. He cocked his head to one side and I could feel his inquiry. I stepped up and caught him by the back of the head and dragged him close. "You can feel me, can't you? You know I'm not elder brother. We'll talk when I get back." I snapped the lead on his collar and he looked away like I had beaten him across the nose with a newspaper.

"You have two options. You can stand in the sun and wait. Turmoil will hold your leash from inside the car. Or, you can stay in the car…again, your leash will be secured." I barely kept from dancing backwards as the pup dropped to his knees and kissed my ankles through my pants. This was just creepy.

"I am sorry Master. I await your punishment."

"That wasn't what I asked you, pup."

"I will stay in the sun."

I pulled away from his hold at my ankles and gestured for Turmoil to lead the way to the front of the Winfield manor. I saw the sidelong glance. Okay, all of that was in Lycan and I'm freaking out the Loyal. I didn't expect to get that lingual offering that had come to X as quickly as to come to me. These gifts were not being distributed among the brotherhood evenly.

Winfield's guard opened the hugely ornate wooden door. Turmoil ushered me inside then headed back for the limo. Haley was still on his knees by the limo watching me with pure curiosity as the huge wooden door shut behind me with an echoing bang. I turned and looked at the foyer of this place. Wow. They had money and combined it with a good sense of taste.

Another guard came up and glared at me. "Hands up, we're going to frisk you."

I put my hands on my head. "I have two Glocks in my holsters. I have a dagger on my forearm. I will take them out and hand them over."

"Do it slowly."

I brought my arm down and twitched my dagger free. I set it on the small side table beside me. I used that same arm to pull one Glock free and lay it on the table. I put my hand back on my head and repeated with the other side.

The man patted me down, taking the epi-pen from my pocket. "Come with me."

I followed him up the winding staircase making sure to stay out of direct sunlight. I didn't need another jolt of intense vitamin D to my system. I shuffled along the carpet. I knew another guard was following along behind. His movements were silent but his…aura, essence, whatever…was screaming for vengeance. On me?

Two more guards were standing at another wooden door. That door swung inward and I was ushered through to see a pale little girl laying in a bed that was way too big for her and she was hooked up to way too many machines. *That bastard!* He said he wouldn't hurt her.

"Have you come to gloat, Edward?" Sarah Winfield was sitting in a chair beside her daughter's bedside. She looked like she had a rough couple of weeks.

I turned towards her. "Pardon?"

She held onto a small pale and fragile hand. "Have you come to gloat? Does it make you happy to see a child suffer?"

I looked down at the small girl. It wasn't right for a child to be so still. "No…"

"Mrs, Winfield, he had this on him." Sandra took the epi-pen from the guard. "What is this?"

"The antidote."

Sandra tightened her hand around the pen. "So, she was poisoned."

"Yes."

"And you did it." The tone of her voice was even. There was a hint of despair in her eyes, but right now, they gleamed with a mother's anger.

"Yes." I hung my head.

She got to her feet and stood beside Sarah's bed. She reached out and stroked her daughter's head, arranging the bangs across the pale forehead. "It was that scratch, wasn't it? That night at the Opera House, when I was feeling sorry for you having to endure that horrible kid. Did you laugh over it when you left?"

I crossed over to the still little girl. "Use the pen."

"Answer me!" Sandra screamed at me. I didn't bother trying to hide my wince.

"What do you want to hear? Was I punished? Hades gave me a concussion then I had to embarrass myself in public... again." I kept my tone low and respectful. I didn't have the right to feel any anger. I was not the injured party here.

"My baby girl is dying because of you, Edward. She's had seizures and fevers. The doctors have said that she is basically just an organ donor now. The light of my life is gone because of you and that want-to-be-Napoleon."

I ducked as she threw the epi-pen at me. It hit the wall and broke. "You're too late with your cure, Edward. My baby princess is gone." Sandra dropped to her knees beside the bed and held onto her daughter's arm.

I reached out and took her other small clammy hand in my own. Her life force was still beating strong. Her will was not diminished. Her heart was still fighting and would continue to fight. She was her mother's daughter.

Sandra never bothered to turn to me as she spoke. "I had my husband research you, Edward Xavier. I once had a mind to try and help you."

Princess Sarah Elizabeth wasn't supposed to get hurt, at least not by me. "Nothing can help me now."

"How did that evil man get a hold on you? How did he force you into prostitution? You once had an office job. You lead a normal life. You disappeared for so many months and you come back as what? His boy toy?"

The sound of the medical equipment filled the room. My voice was low. Was I trying to apologize? The guilt that wracked me now was like nothing I had never experienced before. "Why don't we just cut to the chase? I am Hades sex slave. I do what he tells me to do, because I am trying to protect my family. Just as you are trying to protect yours. I don't hurt children. I never would have done it, but he said it wouldn't hurt her."

"So he lied to you."

I rubbed my thumb over the soft skin of the little hand. I remembered her gentle smile as I kissed her cheek to get that damn rose back. A rose that once Hades had, he tossed into the corner of the limo and promptly forgot. Princess Sarah Elizabeth was dying because of a rose. A rose I gave her. I could be painted with the same brush as Hades over this.

"Do you want your daughter back?"

"She is in the hands of God now."

I shifted my vision and looked down at Princess Sarah Elizabeth. Her body was strong. Her mind… there was a bright ribbon still connecting her…was that her soul? I moved my hand and brushed it over her face. The ribbon fluttered in the makeshift breeze. It passed through my fingers but for a moment I touched it. It tugged at me like spider webs.

"Can I try?" I tried to pluck at it but my fingers past through the mirage.

"Try what?" Sandra glared at me. Color had returned to her face now that she had someone to hate.

"To save her. If I fail…she will not be worse off than she is now."

"What can you do, sex slave?" Her voice dripped with venom. She climbed to her feet and crossed her arms over her chest.

I closed my eyes. I deserved this. I gestured back to the guard. "Send them out."

I debated for a second once the doors were closed then decided to will out my white wings. Sandra might fight me if she knew I was a Vampire, but if she thought me as an Angel. Slipping off my jacket and shirt I shivered as the cool air of the air conditioning swept over my still over heated body. There was still a lingering weakness from the searing but it was nothing compared to what that little girl endured. I moved to the end of Princess Sarah Elizabeth's bed to make sure that I didn't knock into any of her medical equipment. Gritting my teeth I tried to keep from grunting as my wings slid out my wing scars. *Fuck!* My right leg collapsed out from under me and I had to grab onto the end of the bed. By the time I got back to my feet Sandra was sitting, stunned, on the carpet.

I lifted a finger to my lips. "Try not to scream."

I concentrated and burst into Healing Light. From the corner of my eye I saw Sandra bring her hands up to her mouth. Reaching out I laid a hand on Sarah's chest and her forehead trying to call that piece of ribbon, that soul tether, back to the fragile little body.

"It's not your time, Princess."

My fingers were engulfed in the blue healing light, as the flames danced on my arms, but this time when they closed on the ribbon, it was more substantial. From spider web, to string, to twine and then rope and then it turned hard... a metal chain. Gently I pulled on it, coiling it back to her body. I urged it and massaged that chain back and then suddenly it ripped through my fingers like a measuring tape retracting into its casing. I snatched my hands back.

I didn't know if I could bring her back; but, not trying would be something worse that I could live with.

The healing light extinguished and I dropped to my ass, a vampire marionette with its strings cut. I doubt that Sandra saw it but there was a bright white flash of light from the bed as the essential essence of Princess Sarah Elizabeth was absorbed back into her body.

Sarah gasped and sat up, opening her eyes. "Mommy!"

Sandra jumped from the floor to her daughter's side and caught her up in a desperate embrace that only mothers can truly give. "Sarah!"

That was the greatest sounds I have ever heard -- a mother and daughter reunion.

I lay flat on the floor, my wings cushioning my back. Weakness seeped at my joints but the lingering effects of sunlight were cured now. I needed blood. My fangs were beginning to tingle. I used my wings as a prop to get me up into a sitting position. Head rush.

Haley!

Sarah began crying.

"Edward?" Sandra cradled her to her chest and tried to look over the bed at me. "Edward!"

"Don't come near me...." My fangs were down. What did Father call it? Blood starved. I could smell both of them and they smelt really,

really tasty. I dug my fingers into the carpet to try and make sure I stayed where I was.

X...you need to come up here. I can't hold it. X!

Yes you can. Just concentrate on breathing through your mouth. You did good, Sexy. Don't fuck it up now. I'm here... I'm ready...

Xavier was so much stronger than me. I never thought I would do it but this time, I fell willingly into Darkness.

Little bro was right about how damned tasty the humans in this room smelled. Too damned tempting.

Haley...

I heard a commotion outside. "Let him in."

Sandra called out to the guards. "It's okay! Let him in!"

The door to Sarah's bedroom opened and Haley ran in, the leash hanging from his collar. He scanned the room then saw me lying on the floor. "Master!" Haley's golden eyes turned on the mother and daughter. "What did you do to him?"

"He turned into an angel and glowed blue." Sandra's voice was full of awe.

Haley dropped a hand to my shoulder and pulled me up against him. "Master, you showed them?"

"Get me up and down to the car." Haley picked me pretty damn easily and set me on my feet. Damn, I'm such a frigging lightweight. He paused as I willed my wings away again. This was a smart thing to show them. A vampire wouldn't have been appreciated. Besides who would listen to a mother sing the praises of an angel descending and saving her critically ill daughter. I swayed. Haley draped me over his shoulder in a fireman's carry.

"Tell no one." He almost growled at Sandra.

"Edward....I'll save you." Sandra's face was wet with tears.

"Hades will kill you. Just forget me...for your daughter's sake. Do nothing."

"I won't forget you, Edward!"

Haley carried me down the stairs. I could smell his warmth. I could hear the pulse of his life. My fangs descended further. I jammed my forearm against my fangs before I buried them into his back. He gathered my weapons off the sideboard in the foyer and then carried me out. The sun scalded me again until Turmoil got the umbrella over me. I closed my eyes and bit down harder on my arm.

Haley threw me into the back of the limo. I bounced on the carpet. He caught Turmoil and dragged him into the back. He shut the door and forced my bodyguard up against me. "Master needs blood. Give it to him."

Turmoil pulled his hair out of the way and I fanged him hard. He grunted and tensed as I drank fast and deep. I forced myself to pull back. Oh, god, I was so hungry. "More?"

"More." I saw Haley reach forward into the cabin of the limo. "No...not the driver. Never the driver. Take out."

Haley looked down at me, confusion easily read on his face. "I don't understand."

"People off the street." Turmoil gasped.

I grunted as Haley tossed Turmoil on top of me then opened the door and took off running.

"Lord Xavier?" The intercom buzzed to life.

"Follow him."

It took both our efforts to get Turmoil off of me. I had sucked him almost dry. I struggled to my knees and crawled to the fridge. I grabbed a couple of blood slushie packs. Slamming one on my teeth then stuck the other on my Loyal. My forearm was killing me. I had duel puncture marks through the meaty part of my flesh.

"You still alive?"

Turmoil was moving slow. "Yes, Sir."

"Can you sit up?"

"Can I lay here?"

"The pup will probably throw someone on you." I helped him get up on the seat, but he slumped over. I pulled out the last of the blood packs and slapped it on his face.

I was shaky. Two Healings in less than two hours. Note to self. Don't do that again. Who was I kidding? I would do the same thing again. Sex and I have a weakness for little girls.

"He's coming back. He's got a big guy." Riot called back into the cabin. That was all the warning we got.

Turmoil jerked his coat over his head. I pulled down my goggles and turned my face away from the door. The big man went oof as Haley shoved him inside the climbed in behind him. I couldn't keep a binding on him. He struggled to his feet. Haley growled and drove him back down to the carpet. This was going to be messy. I grabbed the big guy's forehead and searched for something calming. Oh my god....he was holding a newborn...No wonder he was fighting so hard. He wanted be there for his baby. I played that image back to him and he stilled. I tried to be as gentle as I could. I took only fifteen swallows.

I saw Turmoil's eyes. He needed more blood too. I pulled my fangs back and licked his wounds closed. I had more control. I altered the man's memories.

"Let him go, Pup. He's got something he wants to live for." Haley opened the door and let the man out. The pup came up to me and stared into my face with those pale brownish gold orbs.

"Master? Do you need more?"

I was weak, but the blood starvation feeling was gone. I shook my head.

The pup reached up and hit the partition. "Home."

"Thank you, Haley."

The Lycan pup eased me back on the seat then climbed up beside me. I let my arm fall down on his waist and he signed and pressed back against me. Again, nothing sexual...just a pack thing. "You showed your wings, Master. Are you supposed to?"

"I had to, pup. I put her daughter in danger."

"Now you're in danger."

"Maybe." I sighed and pressed my face into the back of his neck. The urge to fang him was gone. "I still had to do it."

"I will be your *Zsigmond*, Master. Do not worry."

I growled low at him. He smiled and turned to look back at me and gave a yip. "Later, Pup. Right now, I just want to sleep."

"I will watch over you, Master."

I yawned and lay down. God it wasn't even noon yet and I almost died twice. I slept.

Chapter Five: Liam

Something was tickling my face. I brushed it away but it came back again. This time trailing over my mouth. I went to roll over and felt weight across my hips.

Shade, get off me.

I'm not anywhere near you. I could image the twitching of amused whiskers on that feline face from the tone of her Silent Speak.

What?

I opened my eyes and saw familiar blue irises staring down at me from a heart shaped female face. I glanced down and…yup, female breasts. "Uh, Baroness, what are you doing?"

Claudia had my wrists pressed to the mattress on either side of my head. She was dressed in tailored slacks and a crisp white shirt. I was conspicuously aware that I was stark naked under my blanket.

"I have been trying to get a meeting with you for the past five days. I stalked you to your mother's farm, for heaven's sake and I got ignored -- as you got married to that big guy. You couldn't even bring yourself to say boo to me."

"That doesn't explain why YOU'RE SITTING ON ME!" I would like to say that I could have easily shoved her off me but I was still feeling weak as a kitten.

"Wow, you really can be a sourpussy when you first wake up." Well I knew who she'd been talking to if she was calling me that. The pear doesn't fall far from the tree, eh, Claudius? Like father like daughter.

"Get off me." I arched my back and bucked my hips to try and dislodge her only to slump back on my pillow defeated. Claudia was an irresistible force and an immovable object all in one feminine package.

"No." She said it so simply but let me know that she could back it up by leaning forward, pinning my wrists firmly above my head and resting her ample womanly assets on my chest. All the while catching me in that deadly stare that all women, human, hellcat or vampire have

79

that lets you know in no uncertain terms that you've crossed the line. What line? You know it and if you don't know it you better find out fast because the longer it takes you to figure things out the worse the fury is. Only problem was that I really had no clue why she was pissed and holding me down on the bed.

I stilled. "What?"

Her eyes narrowed. "I'm not my Daddy. I don't jump just because you tell me to."

"I assure you that Claudius has never jumped because I told him to. I know for a fact that I would get slapped down if I tried that shit with him."

"Language."

"It's my bed. It's my house. I can curse if I want."

Claudia shifted and I got knee pressure in a very sensitive area. I stilled and shut up real quick. A tight smile exposed her teeth and I noticed her pearly whites were a little more extended than mine which meant she was pissed. "Don't mistake my gender for weakness." I relaxed beneath her. She was going to say what was on her mind whether I liked it or not.

"See, you can listen to reason." She slowly sat up right, lifting her bosom from me but settling her haunches firmly on my hips.

"You've met my mother and sister...and you probably knew the Grandbitch. I'm the last one who would think that a pair of breasts limits your appetite for destruction. I flicked my eyes down to my crotch. The little bit of morning, er, afternoon or was it evening now, wood had disappeared when that knee tried to press it back inside me.

Claudia smiled sweetly down at me, but I could tell that she had gotten Claudius's spine o'steel. "We both know that if there is going to any procreation between us it's going to be sperm in a cup. You're my Daddy's mate for heaven's sake. It's just too....ick."

"If I'm ick, what are you doing on top of me?"

"It seems like everyone else is doing it." Was a note of censure in her voice?

"I am not a slut." Each word was pronounced and enunciated with enough precision to make a linguist proud.

"I never said you were. Project much, sweetheart?"

The lingering weakness that had clung to me at waking was sloughing off as I started to get angry. Bucking my hip forward, Claudia felt the loss of her upper hand even if she never let my wrists go. "Get off, or I'll make you."

"One simple question, Lord Emperor Intended."

"What?" I barked back at her.

"Why are you getting married?"

"To you?"

"Don't be insulting. I'm getting married to you to stop the possibility of a full scale war."

"So am I."

That must have been the right answer because she let me go and gracefully climbed off the bed. She wasn't wrinkled or even mussed up. That elegance thing must be a genetic trait from Claudius because it didn't transfer through secondary bite. Those arctic blue eyes nailed me with a searching question. "Is that the only reason?"

"I'm gay, Baroness. You don't have anything I want. Not that what you're displaying isn't appreciated I'm just hardwired a different way."

Shade sauntered into my bedroom followed by a thin gray wolf. What the hell? I was getting dominated and they were bonding by sniffing each other's butts? *Thanks for guarding me while I slept, guys.*

Silent speak rattled around inside my head. *I'd smack you for that tone of speak, but I heard Hades cracked your melon open this morning.*

Lycan intermingled with Shade's grousing. *She was in your limo when we left the farm. I thought she could be here.*

"Not in my bed."

Claudia stared at me. "Lycan? Daddy never said you spoke Lycan."

Suddenly there was the light of academia in her eyes and the only reason I knew it was that I'd see my Dad get that same look when a rare magical scroll ended up in his hands. "Can you read Lycan? I've got ancient scrolls rescued around the time of Sigmund's reign that need translations...."

I growled at her. She stopped mid-sentence and blinked those big blue eyes at me. Haley climbed up on the bed and edged his way carefully but insistently between her and me. Better late than never.

Pup, you're the blood of a vampire sandwich! Shade was in that humorous frame of mind and was enjoying having a straight man. Ha ha.

"Your Majesty, could you please escort the Baroness to the Great Hall. I'll formally receive her there." I said that at the same time to Claudia and to Nightshade in Silent Speak.

Claudia closed her mouth and bowed. "I shall await you there, Lord Emperor Intended."

Ooooh, this one's a live wire,

Shade, just...fuck off.

The Baroness is very observant. You are a sourpussy when you first wake up. Get dressed, Hans will have food ready for you. There was a long dramatic pause. *Sourpussy.*

I picked up a pillow and whipped it at the swaying, red tail. It never made its destination as Claudia plucked it out of the air, smoothed its surface then laid it gently on a chair by the door. I flopped back down on my bed. With a bed shaking sigh, Haley transformed back into his human form then pressed his naked self against me.

"She is your Alpha female?"

Oh, crap. I never thought of this High Council forced marriage. "She's going to be."

"I like her. She's strong. She will keep your pack in line."

I had a sneaking suspicion that she was going to keep me in line too. I closed my eyes and draped my forearm across them. Weakness clung to me like the odor of sweaty feet in old running shoes. I needed a mug. Chesterton walked in as if on cue. He carried a tray with a travel mug of blood and some grilled cheese sandwiches. Hmmm, sandwiches. That man knows me like a well thumbed book.

Chesterton's voice dropped to that commanding tone that got the staff a-hopping. Hell, he got me hopping. "What did I tell you? If you are in human form, you put clothes on." He placed his hands firmly on his hips.

I blinked at how quickly Haley calmed down at that British accented command. Then again Chesterton knew the boys a whole lot longer than I did and he's seen Armor all bent out of shape over the smallest thing and handled the chaos just fine. Haley was about five foot seven so he really didn't qualify as a small thing as he towered over the man facing him down. My guess was that Chesterton was trying to keep the status quo and doing an excellent job of it.

Haley whined and looked at me with puppy dog eyes. What was the saying, never piss off the cook? My motto was don't cross Chesterton...ever. Marcus did and look what happened. The whole staff quit on the same day and walked out. The fact that the manor was in a five alarm blaze helped out too.

"Do what he says. He runs my House." I kissed Haley's temple then sent the little pup on his way.

"Do you plan on adding any more pets, Lord Xavier?" Chesterton asked his voice back to normal.

"Oh hell no, Chesterson. A Hellcat and a Lycan is more than enough mayhem for one household. Speaking of mayhem, have you seen Armor?"

"No, Sir. Master Marcus is still here."

"I need him to be here."

"Master Armor can be stubborn."

"Duh. If you see him in your travels could you ask him to make an appearance as soon as possible." I had a slight headache so I gingerly laid back down, blocking the light by hiding my eyes in the crook of my elbow. "Can you kill the lights, Chesterton?"

"Of course, Sir."

"Wait a minute. Come here."

Chesterton approached the bed and he looked rather puzzled. I caught him by the back of the neck. He stiffened but couldn't do anything. I kissed his forehead. "Haley has told me that you're part of my pack--a very important member. I'm sorry if I haven't shown my appreciation in the past."

"Well, you have refrained from killing me on a number of occasions, Sir." There was a hint of wry humor in his tone.

"Thanks for looking out for me. Bigger thanks for taking Haley in hand."

"He has bonded to you rather quickly."

"I think it's the nature of the beast." I flopped back down with my arm over my eyes.

"Speaking of the Lycan, I better track him down and see what he is doing, Sir." Chesterton bowed, paused to lower the lights and shut the door softly behind him. I was hungry but my headache was a little stronger than the gurgle in my stomach. I should have asked for aspirin when he was here. Never mind, it was too much energy even just to turn over. I closed my eyes. I'll just rest for bit and then get up.

Jeez, Claudia was just like her Father. I'll have to find out how old she is. With age came strength and I didn't need her smacking me around like Father did. Okay, he only did it when I was pissy, but still...my mind was whirling...just relax. A few more minutes and I'd get up.

I was on a beach. The sand was warm beneath my back and the rays of the sun were balmy, gently warming my face, upper body and legs. I wasn't burning and shriveling into a dried out sponge which was a vampiric worry. Pulling my arms way above my head and pointing my toes into a stretch like a hell kitten felt good. It felt really great; which was strange because my entire life I had the redhead curse, I usually burned to a bright tomato red after being in the sun for ten minutes. Although, it had regularly gotten me out of cutting lawn when I was kid.

I turned over and let the sun bask on my back. Sunning my buns. Hmmm, naked. Now I know that this is a dream because I would never be lying naked on a beach anywhere, anytime. It didn't matter if I was supermodel status. Internally, I'm still the fat kid everyone made fun of and I would never ever consider coming to a beach to show off my body no matter how buff it was.

Big hands touched me. I relaxed further down into the sand. The touch was firm, massaging my shoulders and back, slowly working down toward my ass.

"Armor…" I sighed.

"Not quite."

I snapped my eyes open. That wasn't a voice I knew. I tried to turn over and found a large body draped on me. He pinned me down in the sand. I struggled against him for a moment then realized that he was naked…and aroused.

Shit. I was having rape dreams? What the fuck is up with that?

"No, my little Lord Emperor. You're not having a dream. This is very much a real thing. You've no idea how long I've been waiting to get my hands on you." This stranger's body was warm and huge. He felt bigger and heavier than Armor. Not good. So, not good. I stiffened as the stranger's hand cupped around the side of my sand clad chest then slid down my waist and hip until thick fingers paused at the hollow of my groin.

"You have me at a disadvantage." I twitched my hip away from that touch. "I don't like people taking liberties with my person, at least without an introduction."

My hair was pushed forward across my face. It was my long lost red hair. He chuckled and placed a kiss at the bare nape of my neck. I had to be in the Darkness but I don't remember this. Wait. Didn't Azrael say we weren't alone in there?

"You know my name."

Teeth scraped lightly down my neck to my shoulder. I shivered, not in a good way. "I don't think so. Get off."

"I have your permission?" I didn't need to see this jerk to hear his amusement and feel his cock riding the crevasse of my ass.

"What?" My would-be rapist hoisted my hips up in the air with the hand he had splayed along my pelvis and leg. My fingers made grasping motions in the sand but they did little to help me get away.

"To get off?" He ground his hips against me, making the double meaning way too obvious. I really struggled like hell to buck him off now then grunted as he drove us both back down into the sand. It went up my nose and coated my tongue. It's hard to fight when you're snorting up a sandstorm .

"You're strong. That's why I chose you. But little boy, here, you are just a human. No wings, no fangs...definitely no Phoenix attributes either." His hand snaked around my waist; then he moved it lower, he grabbed toward my cock. What little erection that had started with the massage was long gone.

Spitting out sand, I snarled at him. "Who the hell are you?"

"Liam." His hand closed around my length. "We've met before out in the real world."

I wracked my brains. I've never met a Liam.

He began stroking me, and pushing his hips against me. I tried to get up again. He kissed my shoulder. "Get off me! Stop it."

"This is a big part of your charm. Your will is like an eternal flame, little boy. You draw people to you like moths to the light. Right now, you've got your light sheltered, but when you open the shutters, you will burn them alive and they will gladly throw themselves into your fire."

I gritted my teeth. "I'm not Hashmallim."

My attacker let go of my cock, grabbed my hip and flipped me over like an egg on a spatula. I didn't have a chance to move before he was back on me, now driving our cocks together. I shoved my arms between us, forcing his chest up off me. White hair hung down around me, pooling on my chest and neck. He was big...for the lack of a better word, he was like a frigging stereotypical Viking from days of yore. Gray eyes, the shade of a cold stormy sea, stared down at me, the corner of his eyes crinkled as he grinned. He might have been handsome but I've had enough rapists to know to quit falling for the handsome face that came with the rest of the package.

Then he said something that froze my heart, "Of course you're not Hashmallim, I am."

I fought him. I fought as hard as I could. I got a leg free and tried to twist to knee him in the family jewels. He rose up, pressing his hips down hard, securely pinning me under him then he wrapped one huge hand around my throat and slammed my head and shoulders back onto the sand one handed. I grabbed at his forearm.

"Are you done?" I made my voice sound bored instead of panicked while I tried to pry his arm off but it was as if it were a stone monolith, solid and immoveable.

"You can't win against me here, little Lord Emperor. This is my domain. I have lived here long enough to command everything. I thought you would have liked the beach. No matter, we can do this anywhere, how about in the great wide outdoors."

I grimaced as pine needles bit into my shoulders and a pine cone tried to embed itself into my spine. We were now in a forest. Sand still clung to the side of my face and grated in the crack of my ass. The scent of the forest was all around us. Still didn't change the fact I was at a major disadvantage.

"I've already marked you as mine, little Lord Emperor. I gave you my hair. I thought that, that would be enough of a sign for my Honey Bee to begin making preparations for my return, but… it seems that I'm going to have to make him remember."

Honey Bee? Honey Bee. Oh my god. I supposedly blurted out the name Honey Bee when Hades was ringing my chimes. That is why the horny teenager freaked on me. "Hades is Honey Bee!"

"I knew you weren't stupid." Liam rested his hip between my legs settling his weight right on my man berries. I think I squeaked.

"Relax, you are only hurting yourself." There was a glint of amusement in his gray eyes but the pressure on my neck never changed.

I gave one more cry and gigantic effort, succeeding in straining my back muscles and shoving the offending pine cone even further into my spine. I was panting and damn it, tears were forming in my eyes.

"You truly are beautiful, Xavier. You were worth the wait. He already desires this body." He nodded down at me. "Our reunion will be sweet. My Cillian made a good choice."

Silly on? Did he call Hades, Silly? I twitched as fingers stroked my cheek, brushing sand off my skin. "Why me?"

"If I remove my hand, will you behave?"

"Define behave."

"Just be submissive until we are done with our talk. This is just our first official meeting so to speak. I figured it would be a firecracker of an event. You didn't disappoint, Red."

I swallowed under his hand. I couldn't do anything flat on my back. "Okay."

Liam cocked a white eyebrow at me. "Why don't I trust you?"

"You're not so stupid either."

He laughed, leaned down kissed my cheek then let me go, standing up over me. Suddenly he was fully dressed, in a black t-shirt and jeans. I had on leather shorts. What the hell? These were German or Bavarian or...what the hell?

"You could be naked."

I rubbed my neck and brushed the pine needles off my back. "Am I in a coma again?"

Liam shook his head sending white hair cascading down his broad shoulders. An image of that romance novel model came to mind, I almost smiled at the absurdity of it. "You're just in a deep, deep sleep."

"So, I can wake up any time."

"You'll wake up when I let you wake up. This is my domain, little Lord Emperor."

Liam didn't bother to look, he just tossed his ass backwards and landed in a chair...no, it was a padded throne that materialized from nowhere. I thought the chair Frederick had rented from the nearby church was gothic and regal looking but it had nothing on this one. It was large enough to make this giant of a....man? Vampire? Thing? Look average. I glared up at him as he gestured to me then patted his thigh.

I clenched my jaw, then climbed to my feet and went obediently to sit on his lap. I was just going to end up there anyways.

"Armor has taught you well. I was going to say broke you, but that is something he never has truly accomplished. Is it?" I sat like a good little pet with my hands clenched and my mouth shut.

"And you have learned to pick your battles. Good boy." He stroked my hair, laying my bright red tresses over my bare shoulder.

"Enough with the little Lord Emperor comments." My head tugged sideways as Liam began braiding a length of my hair.

Liam shrugged then nodded. "Ask your questions."

Crossing my arms and throwing a hissy fit would get me flat on my back again. I could play the adult when necessary and the way my mind was racing trying to figure out how to wake the hell up was more than enough to make me want to keep him talking. "Why are you trying to take over my body?"

"I have left my Cillian alone too long in the world."

No, not Silly on, Killion. "This is Hades you're talking about."

"So, he has called himself. He is my child. I made him. I loved him. I died for him. I have resurrected for him time and time again. I have loved him across the centuries, and I love him still."

I furrowed my brow, "Wouldn't it be easier for you if he was dead? I could kill him."

I winced has Liam grabbed my hair and jerked my head back so I was looking at him with my forehead pressed sideways on his chest. "If he was so easy to kill, I wouldn't have had to watch him wander around destroying everything he touches. No, little Lord Emperor. You can't kill Cillian. You're not strong enough." I was pretty sure I heard a silent "yet" in that statement; something to keep in mind. "Besides, I have plans for you and this gorgeous body."

I tried to push his hand away as it slid down my chest. It was like trying to push over a parking meter. It just wasn't happening. He caught my nipple ring. I stilled. That's all I needed was for him to get the push button start going. "I could have taken you a long time ago except for this."

89

He flicked the ring with his finger then gave out a hissing breath. "He gave you rings along with his heart. They were of no consequence. He gave you clothing along with his passion. And again, of no consequence. But this..." I gasped as Liam tugged on the nipple ring. "He merged his soul with yours with this. Because of this little token of affection, we are now having this conversation."

I grabbed at my nipple, trying to protecting it. "What do you want from me?"

"Everything. You don't remember who I am, do you?"

"You're the destroyer of nations." I hissed that out as he twisted the ring.

He sighed and sat me upright, however he didn't take his hand off of my ring. The budded flesh pressed up into the warmth of the palm of his hand. Slowly he began circle it. "Been there, done that. I set up how the Blood interact with each other now. It's not as bloody and territorial as before. I'm happy with it."

"But the Lycan prophecy..."

The brute actually snorted. "Prophecy? Those were all written AFTER I had destroyed nations, and rebuilt them into what they are today. Well, a little tweaking might be in order. This infighting is weakening each Blood Nation."

"Who are you then?"

"I have been called many things in different ages. Hashmallim was one. Alexander was another. I call myself Liam these days. That still doesn't answer your question, does it?"

Liam tightened his hold and dragged me back against his chest. One arm came up across my chest, rubbing his arm hair on my sensitive nipples. The other hand slipped down into my leather shorts and skimmed my flesh, the fingertips gently brushing my cock. He brought his face close and whispered in my ear,

"I am your progenitor, Little Lord Emperor. I am the first of our Blue Lineage. I am the First Lord Emperor. When my physical form wears out, I am reincarnated back into our Nation, back into our Line to rule again and again. I have been female. I have been male. I have given birth. I have laid my children in the grave. I have guided our House and our Nation throughout the centuries…until Sigmund. He was a crazy bastard. Magnificent on the battlefield but unstable."

"So I've heard."

Liam laughed. "Oh yes, you knew his bitch. Thank you for killing her. She caused more trouble than she was worth - out of unfounded jealously. Sigmund never looked at anyone else but her. He had bad taste in women. As it was I barely had time to get the Blue Line Houses into hiding. Getting my line, the Royal line into a family of Hunters was a stroke of genius and more than a little luck."

I shivered as he dragged his tongue behind my ear. He took me in hand and began to stroke me. "Stop it."

"It's just a wet dream, Xavier."

"Fuck it is. What the hell do you want? Let me go."

"Temper, temper. Like you, little Lord Emperor, I am in love. It is a never ending one. I carried it beyond my physical form. I see my Honey Bee in pain and I want to ease it."

"Hades…"

"I have been waiting for centuries to return to him. I tried to merge with Sigmund, but he was a fruit cake. All the power that I gave to him cracked what little sense he had. He crowned himself Emperor of all the Blood Nations and started a war. Then stupid ass got himself killed just as his bitch collaborated with the Blue Cull by the humans. Ever since then I have been waiting for a son to be born to the Royal line. Yes, I've been waiting for you, Xavier."

He opened his legs, which meant I opened mine and that also meant my ass touched his arousal. I am not getting raped again. Fuck no. I struggled and twisted in his grasp. He wasn't expecting it and I slipped off his thighs. I got out of his hold and took off running. I had no plan. Anywhere but here.

"Where can you go, little Lord Emperor? This is my world." His voice hounded me as I ducked into the woods.

I dodged trees and winced as the roughage of the forest floor bit at my bare feet. I was running in a blind panic. I dived into some underbrush and tried to control my breathing…and shaking. Holy crap. I listened carefully. I didn't hear any pursuit. Still, if he made this…illusion, he could pop up anywhere.

His voice began echoing around me as if it were being broadcast over a huge stadium PA system. "I have waited for a son to be born back into the Blue Line. I have protected you all your life, Xavier. Your mother would have made you into a Regency hunter. That would never do. I couldn't have you possibly harmed so I made your vision fade. Your depression at going blind worked in my favor. You were unhappy, it made you a compulsive eater to compensate for your depression, loneliness and helplessness. It kept you pure. I wanted you innocent when I came to you. Then Honey Bee went and fucked up with the Black Death. He took my attention from you. When I finally settled Cillian back down, Claudius's broken spawn had you. I don't agree with his methods, but his results are amazing. You are truly spectacular, Xavier."

Gack. A hand reached down and snagged me by the hair at the back of my head. Liam jerked me to my feet. The scene changed and we were back at the beach.

"Less places for you to hide, little Emperor." His other hand came up and caught the front of my face. He tilted my chin up until I was staring up at him green eyes to gray.

"Sadly, you're about as virginal as Queen Elizabeth the First."

I was more than a little angry about the announcement that he was the bastard who took my sight when I was kid. Medical science could do nothing because they didn't understand how it could be happening when there were no indicators that it should. "You fucked up my life, you prick!"

Liam lowered his head until we were forehead to forehead. "You were doing a magnificent job of that on your own. You have no patience, Xavier. I would have brought my offer to you. I stopped protecting you at twenty-one. You were of age then but you went downhill so fast. If Marcus had not taken you as his, you would not have made it to thirty. For that, and that alone, I will let that boy live."

92

He let go of my face and yanked on my nipple ring. I grabbed his wrist as he twisted it. My mouth opened in a gasp of pain and I found myself in a deep French kiss. The hand tightened in my hair as he kissed me. It was rough, but it gentled. It coaxed. He twisted my ring again.

No!

"You cannot stop me, little Emperor." He tripped me and I fell back into the sand again. He pressed his entire length on me. "You are powerful and so influential with the young ones. You have come into it on your own, without my help. You are stronger than Sigmund and he was a terror. Marcus divided you but that somehow that has made you more stable. You already have my Cillian's attention. Together, we can remove the curse I left on him."

That stuck in my head. '*You have come into it on your own.*'

On my own.

My powers were my own.

Liam didn't give them to me. Armor turned me into a vampire and helped me become what I am today. Not this…guy.

The hated ever present lower back heat was there. If he was oh so omnipotent and the Wizard of Ozzyland he would have taken care of this little burn problem. Concentrating I began gathering the Phoenix wings for a controlled burn.

"Get off me now, or I'll make you."

Liam burst out laughing. "Sigmund didn't have this steel core. When we are one, we will make this Nation strong and stable again."

"I said get off."

"What are you going to do to make me, little Lord Emperor?" He was taunting me, the big jerk!

"What did I tell you about calling me that?" I screamed in pain and rage as my Phoenix wings burst forth. Liam hissed in surprise and jerked his hands away as my flaming wings seared his flesh. The moisture trapped in the sand began steaming up from under me. I forced the wings wide and up to encircle me. The Father of my Line pushed himself off and scrambled away in a damned hurry. I used that fire wall to get back to my feet. The leather shorts burnt away, no loss. I opened my wings and glared at the huge Vampire. He dropped fang as he looked at the back of his burnt hand. I could see the skin was charred and pulled back from the surface. It had to hurt like a bitch. Those gray eyes flash fired into a very familiar blue flame. Liam held his hand up between us and I was mildly horrified that his third degree burn was erased like a zit in Photoshop. I had never healed that quickly. Flexing his fingers he stared passed them pinning me with his gaze. I went from mild to frighteningly gobsmacked when his fangs came down. They were as massive as the rest of him. He was like a sabre tooth tiger; my own fangs were like a kitten's.

He roared at me.

Serves you right, you fucker.

Liam pulled a Hand of Light sword out of thin air faster than I could blink. It was also twice the width and almost double in length of anything I ever made. He swung at me. I brought my left wing up. Fuck…crap…damn it! That sword cut into my fiery wing and it hurt like a bitch. I danced backwards angled my wings and lifted off the sand. I watched in ghastly fascination as huge white wings sprouted from this giants' back. Apparently although his great-grandkid had lost the ability of a standing take off, Liam had no problem with it.

Damn it, I couldn't let him get to me. I tilted my wings and rose higher trying to put more distance between us. It would be useless to try and match swords with him. I concentrated and fashioned a long bow out of Hand of Light. I was better with firearms, but I used to be good at archery. I caught a chortle in my throat. That used to piss big sister Shayne off to no end. Baby bro could hit what he aimed for the first time.

I pulled back on the draw string. An arrow of blue flame appeared nocked and ready to fly. I sighted his shoulder. There was no way I was going to bring him down in one shot, but I could slow him down. I let it fly.

He didn't expect it and my blue fire wings must have camouflaged the bolt. The arrow slammed into his shoulder. He veered off to the right spiraling out of control. He recovered fast. *Shit.* I notched another arrow. He dodged that one. Damn. I flapped frantically and started to pick up speed. I glanced back down. Where the hell was he? I scanned around below me.

I flipped onto my back and brought my arms up just as he smacked into me from a dive from above. He hit with the force of a car, a big one. The bow disappeared from my hand. His newly healed hand closed around my throat. Frantically I reached out and grabbed onto the arrow still sticking out of his shoulder ramming it deeper as hard as I could.

He grunted and spun away trying to keep his wounded shoulder out of my reach. The centrifugal force snapped my wings back away from him. I thought he was going to break my neck. At the last moment he let me go and I tumbled out of control. The horizon revolved wildly and I was approaching the ocean hard and fast. I couldn't....get....control. I hit the surface of the water and skipped across it like a stone. Each blow was like running into a cement wall. The third hit, my wings flickered out. The fifth, I began to flicker out. The sixth hit, I sank. My head hurt so much...too much stress on my newly healed skull. I think it broke again.

I was jerked out of the water by the back of my hair. My brains were rattling around in my skull. He transferred his hold to my shoulders. I was vaguely aware that Liam was carrying me while he flew back to the beach. He dropped down to the sand and I fully expected him to finish the job. He laid me down on the sand. I blinked up at him. God, he looked like he was eight feet tall from this position. His face grimaced as he pulled the Hand of Light arrow from his shoulder.

"You're a fucking delight, Xavier. Life's never boring with you around." He knelt beside me, his white wings folded back gracefully.

"You are brave, little vampire. You are strong. You could be this generation's Hashmallim, and I know that the world you would make would last for a millennia. But, I have waited so long to return to my Cillian. I can't make him wait anymore."

Gentle fingers reached out and pulled wet strains of hair off my face. "I would have been willing to wait for your children. I wouldn't have minded being reborn to a Father such as you would have made, but that can never be now."

My ears were full of water. It was hard to hear him. "What?"

"My Honey Bee fucked you over, Xavier. You've been poisoned with hemlock. It is only through the sheer force of your personalities banding together for support that you survived, but Cillian has wronged you."

Liam picked me up off the sand and cradled me against his chest. "You are now sterile. Any hope of the Royal Line continuing now falls to your nieces."

I tried to shake off my weakness. "Leave them alone."

He crooned in my ear. "Don't fret, little Emperor. They fall under my protection now."

My anger was as volatile as a wet bottle rocket. "No! If what you did to me as a human is your protection…don't do that to them. Leave them alone."

"I will have my Honey Bee. You can fight me all you want, little Lord Emperor but you will not win. I am eternal." He kissed my temple. "I like you. When I come to you again, show your respect and you will not be injured. Go."

I cried out and sat up in my bed suddenly. I collided with a body and knocked it backwards. Every injury I got in…where ever the hell that beach was, screamed in my physical body now. My head hurt so much. I brought my hand up to my face and caught the trail of blood seeping from my nose. Fuck. Both Sex and Azrael were fighting to get loose. I slumped over sideways half falling out of bed.

Soft hands caught me and I found myself dragged upright.

"What the hell?" Claudia caught my head and looked into my eyes. "You've got a concussion, Xavier. Maybe more. Help! HELP!"

I heard footsteps running in the hall. "You're free." My voice was barely a whisper.

"What was that?" She brought me to her chest and pressed my head gently against the side of her neck. She smelled of ginger and something floral. My blood dripped down ruining her shirt.

"What the hell is going on here?" Armor's voice washed over me. He came back. That was good… really good. Then, there was sweet blessed nothing.

Chapter Six: Insight

It was like the rumble of the ocean...or a train. It started off in the distance but gradually got louder and louder, until it was so loud it shook your entire core. I opened my eyes to a comedy of errors. Armor and Claudia were yelling at each other. She was not backing down even though she was half his size. Haley was almost running in a panicked circle around them adding to the commotion with long drawn out whimpers. Chesterton was trying to get by the barrier of flesh with first aid kit in his hand over to the side of the bed. Shade sat at the foot of the bed in sleek housecat form but her tail was flipping back and forth in agitation.

"EVERYBODY OUT NOW!"

I winced at that loud voice. Claudius stood at the door and glared at everyone. He took the first aid kit from Chesterton then stepped aside to usher everyone out of my bedroom.

"Armor." My big monkey turned and came back toward the bed. Claudia stopped at the door. Father pushed her out and shut the door behind him.

My head was killing me. I lifted my arms and Armor gently gathered me up. Oh thank god. I rested my head against his chest and hung onto him with desperate strength. "Little One? What happened? You were not this injured when you came back from work this morning."

"Thank you...thank you...thank you." I whispered into his chest.

His hand came up against my back. "For what?"

"For loving me. You saved me...again. Oh god, I've been targeted since I was a baby..." I pulled on him tighter trying to drive our bodies closer. I never wanted to let him go. I've been played for a putz since I was born, since the conception.

"X." I felt his breath in my hair. "X? Loosen up, you are hurting me."

Huh? I blinked and released my hug. There were white lines around his mouth as he tried to keep from grimacing. I'd gotten stronger?

"Xavier…" Claudius sat on the bed beside me. Gingerly I turned my head toward him then he took my face in his hands. Those blue irises stared into my green eyed soul. "You seem to have another mild concussion. How did you get it?"

It was an effort to string sensible words together. "Liam played skip rocks with my skull."

"What?" Armor stroked a hand down my face. "Who?"

I caught both of them glance up over my head and lock eyes that promised severe retribution on this mysterious Liam.

"I met Hashmallim." I felt Claudius and Armor share another sharp look. "I'm not fracturing again."

I closed my eyes. "But I do think my head is splitting apart."

The bed shifted as Claudius sat down behind me. Armor urged me back against Father. Claudius lifted his wrist to my mouth. "Drink, my son. You are weak right now. Take what you need then call on your Healing Light. Then take what you need from Armor when you are healed. We will talk when your pupils are the same size."

I dropped fang and leaned heavily against Father. There was a steady throb at the base of my neck. I closed my eyes and must have groaned out loud. I felt fingertips dance along my forehead. I had to blink several times to keep Armor's face in one place it was swimming in and out of focus. Claudius lifted his wrist, fanged it open himself then pressed it back to my lips. I attached myself like a leech and let his blood pool in my mouth.

"Only you can get injured lying in your own bed, Little Blue."

Each clovey swallow eased my thirst, calmed my fears and anxiety. The fact that Armor was stroking my left foot grounded me in the here and now. I pulled my head free, arching my neck back and taking a deep shuddering breath.

"Heal yourself."

"Let go."

"You are fine where you are. Heal yourself. Armor…"

I found myself in the middle of a vampire sandwich again. Claudius was plastered to my back. Armor crawled up and pressed against my

98

chest. He kissed me. So gentle. So sweet. So lovingly. I burst into blue light and engulfed the three of us. Claudius pulled my hair back, exposing my neck. Armor trailed kisses from Sex's heart pendant back up to my ear. I gasped and sighed as everything soothed and calmed and returned to way it should be. Almost. I turned my head and offered my neck.

Armor licked my pulse and placed a sucking kiss there but kept his fangs to himself. I brought my hand up to the back of his head and pressed him back against my flesh. I felt him strain against me trying to pull back but I just tightened my hold and offered my neck again.

"He cannot, Xavier. Not until we know why your blood is changing…you cannot share."

The healing light flickered out. Armor easily pulled away then gathered me up from Father's arms and pressed my mouth at his neck. I shook my head. "X, you need to feed."

"I don't get fanged. You don't get fanged."

I cried out as Claudius buried his fangs in my shoulder.

Armor pressed my face back to him. "Now, you are fanged. Drink. Xavier."

I turned my head away. Claudius reached across me, sandwiching me tighter between his chest and Armor's throat. Claudius finger nailed him open. Blood poured from Armor's wound. The scent of my sweet apple orchard filled my senses causing my still exposed fangs to tingle with a Pavlov's response.

Claudius slammed my face up into Armor's neck. "Drink."

No use crying over spilt blood. The scent of my orchard was driving me crazy anyway. I latched onto Armor and sucked like there was no tomorrow. He groaned and winced as I dug my fangs deeper. My bite wasn't as wide as Claudius'. When I pulled back and began licking Armor's wounds closed, he had a strange bite pattern, four puncture marks: Two smaller ones set inside the dentition of a larger set.

Claudius sucked and licked my shoulder wound closed.

I felt my crystal vision snap down. I brought my nose into his sable hair and inhaled. It went straight to my groin. "Pretty…"

99

Armor grimaced as he turned his face back toward me. He saw my blue flame and his own eyes narrowed. "I want to love you, Pretty."

Claudius pressed a kiss to my now healed shoulder, "Xavier, we need to talk."

"Thank you Father for your help. Please leave now." I found my chin caught between two fingers and my head was pulled back. I squinted my eyes.

"Open." I opened my eyes and looked at Claudius upside down. He let out a big breath of air.

"Xavier. Have at it." He tipped my head back upright and climbed off the bed. "Doctors have the results from your medical tests. They are coming over at six. Be done by then."

Claudius grabbed up the first aid kit on the way out the door. He opened the door to the hallway and had to fight his way out the crowd that was still there. "Move it."

I turned my attention back to my big monkey. He had his face lowered and his eyelids were almost closed. "Armor?"

"I made all kinds of promises to you, Xavier. I swore to be there for you, and the first test comes along and I fail you."

I was too far along in my flame to understand him. I watched his mouth but I really wasn't listening. "Let me love, Armor...I need to love you." I crawled toward him. My eyes never wavering. "My orchard. My apple. My Armor."

"Xavier..." His beautiful face was framed by that sable colored hair as those perfectly shaped lips moved drew me in closer and closer. I knew what they felt like skimming across my heated skin. My hand actually quavered as I brushed against his knee. Finally I brought my gaze up to his own. Those limpid pools of rich brown mud widened even further. "What has gotten into you?"

"Your love has saved me." I reached out and let my fingers trace his cheek. "You have no idea what you have done."

"Why are you..."

I laid a finger across his lips, "Unless you're going to say 'love me long and hard, X'. I don't want to hear it."

100

"You were just ill."

"I'm better now." I leaned forward and pressed my lips against his. I flicked my tongue out and let it trace along his upper lip. I inched forward just a bit and nipped the end of his nose. "I love your scent. I smell apple shampoo; I get a hard on."

I kissed my way to his ear. I let my tongue trace the shell of his ear starting at the inner swirl, letting my tongue run around the edge of flesh until I could suck his lobe into my mouth. "Give me your consent, Pretty. I need you so much, I'm going crazy."

"We will talk…"

"Later."

I gasped as I found myself flopped over onto my back and that warm familiar weight pinned me to the covers. "Beautiful."

I caught him by the back of the head and pulled his lips down to mine. I just had more than my fair share of blood essence from him, I shouldn't fang him. I sucked on his bottom lip, pulling into my mouth. He moaned into my mouth. That was so sexy. Our tongues came out, twisting and twirling. Apples and Cinnamon…cinnamon and apples. My vanilla was gone. Who I was, was gone. Because of this man. I fanged his tongue. Armor caught my head and pulled me tighter, sharing his small bloody cut with me.

I was naked. He wasn't. I dropped my hand down and pulled at his shirt. The back of my knuckles rubbed on his stomach. I snaked my other hand under the shirt hem and scratched softly at his right nipple. His whole body hitched on me. "X…I have never seen you so horny."

"You have a problem with it?"

"Hell no." Armor looked down at me his eyes glowing red with passion and desire. I used to be terrified of his red flame. Now, I wanted him in nothing but that red flame. He had too many damned clothes on. "Xavier, give me your consent. I want to hold you in my arms and make you see the stars."

I growled up at him. He furrowed his brow and stared down at me. His hair fell in a curtain around his head, around my face, locking up in a moment of privacy. I yipped.

Armor slapped a lip lock on me. Vampires rutting, gloriously exciting. Armor still had too many clothes on.

I shoved him back and he actually moved. There was surprise in his eyes but I didn't give him a chance to say anything. I climbed on his hips, caught his hands and pushed them back on the bed. I yipped again.

I heard an answering call from the other side of the bedroom door. I snarled toward the door. There was no other sound calling back. I was with my mate. My Lycan would guard the door. There would be no interruptions. I looked down at my captive lover.

"I never thought you could be more sexy, but your Lycan is driving me…" He bucked up his hips. I rode his erection through his pants.

"Yip for me, Pretty." I reached between my legs and unbuttoned his waistband.

A slight dusting of blush colored his cheeks. It looked marvelous. I never thought to make him blush…he looked good in pink. "Yip for me…"

His voice was low with desire. He yipped. I bit back a smile. It wasn't "fuck me now until I howl my release". It was 'feed me, I'm hungry." *Oh my big vampire, what do you want to eat? Me?* I laughed and pulled at his shirt. I took a good hold of it and ripped it down the center exposing that wide muscled chest. His dark brown nipples were pebbled with excitement.

"Give me your wings, little one. Be my Angel of Desire…my love."

I laid my hand on his cheek and brushed my thumb on his lip. "As you command, my Pretty." I willed my wings out prepared for the searing pain that usually accompanied it. They were up and out like a pop up umbrella. There was no pain, nothing like ever before. I didn't even have to try hard to get them to form.

"Are you... ugh." I leaned over and sucked a brown nipple up into my mouth. Armor's hand was in my hair. For a while he just let it lay on my head, then he tightened as he tried to get me off his little sensory overload button. I held it lightly with my teeth and lashed my tongue back and forth over it. He groaned and twisted his chest.

"Uuuhhhh, X….too much….too much."

I let my lips slip off his nipple with a pop. He opened his eyes and glared down at me. He flashed his fangs and arched his head back then sat up. I slipped back right onto his cloth covered erection. "Naughty, naughty, Little One. You know what that means."

I arched my eyebrow. "You'll fuck me unconscious?" I had just enough hope in my voice that Armor laughed as he brought me close for another kiss.

"What am I going to do with you?"

I let all kidding fall away. "Love me. Love me forever, Armor. God, please don't walk away from me again." I felt tears burn my eyes. "You are my inner strength. When you are weak Armor, lean on me. Use my strength. Don't run to Marcus. Give me a chance to try and be there for you. Let me try and save you for once."

Armor caught my neck and pulled me to his chest. He set his chin on top of my head and hugged me tightly. "You have saved me, Xavier. I walk in the dim light of this world just for you. I fight off Marcus, just to sit with you. I will move the heavens and earth just to lay with you, just like this."

I had said we were Vampires rutting. I was wrong. We were Vampires loving…cherishing, demanding and receiving. We were soul mates and because of that, I was here. I was here with my big monkey. Not Hashmallim. Not Liam, me. I was going to sear that on my soul. Armor and Xavier, together forever, XOXO.

I helped Armor shuck his pants then I took his hand pressed my lips to his knuckles, opened his palm and placed a kiss there. I could feel his red eyes watching me. I sucked two of his fingers. I let my gaze match his as I wet his digits. "Love me, Armor."

I took his wrist and pressed his hand down at my ass.

"Thy will, will be done, Little One."

I groaned as those fingers began to play with my hole. Teasing it open one agonizingly delectable inch at a time. I shivered. The white wings rang with the sound of hundreds of glass chimes. I licked my dry lips. Armor groaned beneath me. I arched backwards as he sank one finger deep. My gasping moan was accompanied with more ringing tinkles from my wings. It reminded me of rainsticks with just a little harsher tone. He began to move his hand back and forth. My torso fell forward. I caught my weight with my arms. My white hair fell forward landing in his face. I flipped my hair in a mimic of his porn star move.

"Beautiful." A whisper could say so much.

I closed my eyes and just felt. His hand reached up and brushed my cheek. I could feel a flush on his skin, on my back, on my chest and a definite burning in my face. "I'm here."

"I know." He urged me down for another kiss. I opened my mouth and his tongue invaded. At the same time, he added a second finger. His teeth scraped along my bottom lip. I twisted my head slightly and ran my tongue along his. I jumped when my nipple ring was flicked. I arched my neck backwards and my mouth hung open. Armor latched onto my sensitive flesh, kissing and licking his way from Father's pendant to my ear.

"When you are away from me, this is the picture of you that I have in my head."

"A wanton whore?"

"A sex god who chose me to have his pleasure with." He began to thrust both fingers in and out of me. My hands tightened on each side of the blanket he was laying on. "The other image is of you sitting at your computer the first time I saw you."

He hit my prostate. My wings chimed again. I grunted. My elbows quivered. My ringed nipple was pebbled already, the second nipple hardened into its own small erection. My chest throbbed with the pulse of my blood. I panted. He hit it again. My face screwed up with sensation. "I was fat."

"You were beautiful. I saw you, Little One. You are more than just a body to me. You should know that by now. If you do not, I will have to try harder. Take me inside you, my pale angel. Open your eyes. Let me see you."

I reached back behind me and found his hot pulsing bar. I stroked the shaft. The head was slick. My thumb spread the fluid around the tip; coating it. I matched flame to flame as I pressed the cock against my portal. A groan was caught in my throat as I moved my hips back against it. My mouth dropped open as the head slipped inside. I stilled for a moment at the slight pain. Deep panting rocked my chest. I let out a low growl and sank back fully.

A howl rose from the outside the door. I gritted my teeth to keep from answering the call of the wild.

"Damn, wolf." I cried out as Armor jerked up into me.

The crimson flame in Armor's eyes glowed as he watched me. "You are my mate. He can sniff around all he wants, but you are mineHe urged my knee up off the bed so I was sitting fully on his erection. He slipped deeper and touched that special spot. My own erection jumped and pulsed.

Armor began to rock into me. Driving deeper, touching that pleasure zone over and over again.

Huh…huh…huh…ooooohh.

Armor's huge hands caressed my biceps then urged my arms up over my head. His face rested along my cheek, his lips tickled my skin. "You feel wonderful, X."

I tightened my hold around his cock. He groaned low in my ear. That sent a shiver down my body. The hair on my body stood on end. He sucked a hicky into my neck. I couldn't stay still. "Harder."

"Thy. Will. Will. Be. Done." I was going out of my skull. My wings jingled with the force of each thrust. Bringing my right wing up and around him, I urged him to lay almost flat on me so the weight of him kept me anchored.

I survived Hurricane Armor…just barely. He did everything right, at the right time, at the right angle, varying the speed and intensity to send me off to the stratosphere. I was glad he had me pinned to the bed, my big monkey of love. I would have just twitched off him onto the floor when my orgasm hit me. As it was I was off in lala land, getting hit with waves of prostate pleasure when that telltale hitch in his breathing told me to tighten up. I clenched as hard as I could around him. My wings acted like baby bumpers that kept my Pretty from sliding off the bed. He slumped on me. His head was buried into my shoulder, his warm breath on my neck. He was still inside me.

I didn't want this moment to end.

Haley howled outside the door. The rough translation, "Fuck, yeah!"

I brought my hand up to the back of Armor's head and stroked his sweat wet hair. I howled back. Armor chuckled and lightly nipped my neck. I never thought I would miss getting fanged. He made a move to get up. "Please...stay here."

"I am too heavy."

"I can handle it, Pretty. Trust me, I'll tell you if you do something I don't want." I traced a finger down his nose where once I defied him and tried to rip it off.

He lifted his chest off me and looked down with his warm...hot brown eyes. He remembered it too. His hand came up and ran across my neck from my ear to my shoulder. "I am grateful that I never scarred you."

I brought both wings up and wrapped them around our bodies. "Oh, you scarred me, Armor." He stiffened. I tightened my wings around us to reassure my lover with the fragile heart. "If you didn't, I have no doubt in my mind that I would be dead by now. Or something else."

Armor's tone turned serious. "I agree with Father, only you can get injured laying in your own bed. What happened, Little One? You said that you met Hashmallim? Where?"

I stared up at the ceiling. I still wasn't exactly sure myself...but it explained a lot. "I'm not the Destroyer of Nations. This body was supposed to be the host for that... soul?"

Armor pushed against my hold to look into my face. "I was asleep. Liam, as he called himself, took me to a beach and tried to have a conversation – which seemed to involve him fucking me." I heard Armor's jaw snap shut; his began to grind his teeth.

"You know what it's like when you try to make me do something I don't want to do."

"You fight like a Hellcat with his tail on fire. These are your injuries?"

106

"If I can believe it, he said he's guarded me since the day I was born. He took my sight to keep me from being a Hunter. He liked it that I got bitter and fat because that would keep me pure. He watched me intently until…."

"Until?"

"Father and Hades had their falling out."

"What? What has this got to do with anything?"

"Apparently this Liam…this Hashmallim claims to be the First Lord Emperor. Ever. He told me he has been reincarnated back into the Royal line over and over again. He made Hades and he wants him back."

"Through you? I thought you said he gets reincarnated."

"You want to bet that Grandma and Mom and the rest of the Regency Council laid down spells of protection on me before I was born. I'm the first male in two hundred years in our family line. Maybe he couldn't get to me as a baby…"

I stilled.

"Xavier?"

Oh. My. God. Ohmygod. Ohmyfuckingod.

I glanced up and found Armor regarding me worriedly. "Xavier?"

"He said we had met in the real world." I pressed the heels of my hands to my eyes.

"Little One?"

"I used to have an imaginary friend I called Mr. L. That bastard. He's been around me since the beginning." I recalled my imaginary playmate. A frigging white haired gentle giant who always had time to play with a lonely little boy. He would come when I called and kept the darkness and fear at bay when I learned so early that there were monsters in the world and that they were real. I remember he kept saying that we would meet one day. BASTARD with a capital ASS. As a kid, I remember looking forward to it. The first thing my imaginary friend does when we meet again is try to fuck my ass.

I turned and kissed Armor gently on the temple. "If it wasn't for you, I'd be his by now."

"I do not understand."

107

"You're obsession with me was not part of his plan. When he finally started looking for me again, you had me. He decided to leave me with you because you building your 'sex god' but he didn't expect you to give me your soul. I don't know if he can take over, but your gift is making it hard for him."

I ran the back of my hand down on Armor's cheek, tilting his chin up toward me, kissing him with all the tenderness I possessed. Tears were forming in my eyes. I was sort of feeling sorry for myself but anger and determination were slowly over taking it. I am not a puppet. If the love of my life couldn't make me into a mindless drone…the Father of my Line wasn't going to either. I was not Sigmund—the deadly fruitcake.

Liam had said some interesting things. I don't think he realized how much information he revealed. Hades was running amok. I was, for the lack of a better word, tainted with another's soul. I was sterile so Liam's reincarnation as my prodigy was out. He had left a curse on Hades. A curse that could be lifted. Lifted by someone of the Royal Blue line. Someone with the Healing. What made Hades powerful? Age. That was natural. And Hemlock, hummm. Why would Liam call Cillian, Honey Bee? He cursed his young lover with a poisoned touch. That would be one way of keeping his heart pure and body untouched. No wonder Hades cracked my melon open when Liam had called him honey bee with my voice. Maybe, Liam could make contact with me, but he couldn't stay. I have no doubt if he could take me over, he would have a long time ago.

I gathered Armor in my wings and hugged him tightly. His hand stroked my side, gently brushing my nipple. He wasn't gearing us up for round two. Which was good, cause, damn, I was sore down there.

I closed my eyes. It could easily be so complicated but I had a flash of insight. I don't get them often so when I do, I pay attention.

It came down to Cillian or me. Sex was right back then. Hades had to die.

Chapter Seven: The Prognosis

It was surreal…sort of. I was down twice today, no, three times. Once by my boss; once by my guilt; and once by a soul sucking, eternal, grandfather type, former imaginary friend. And after all of that, I'm still standing. Luck, stubbornness, sheer force of will and a love so pure it hurt my chest were the only things that kept me here in this world. I'm not arrogant enough to believe I could have had withstood any of this on my own.

People were flocking to me. I didn't know why. I couldn't see what they saw. I got a finger ping between my eyes.

"Hey!" I blinked and looked up at my brown haired love monkey.

Armor finished straightening my tie. "You are thinking too much." He leaned forward and kissed my booboo better. "You clean up nice, Xavier."

I was in a pale grey suit, crisp white shirt with a pale pink tie. Armor tucked the matching pink hankie into my breast pocket. So what? I'm gay. Besides, I looked like shit in dark colors now. I had opted for the tailored suit, mainly because I had the stuffing knocked out of me today. I may have looked okay, but I felt bruised and more than a little fragile inside. So, it was power suit time with my Docs. I would never compromise on footwear again. I didn't have to play frying bacon on a car hood a second time to learn, tread is good. I frowned. Crap. I never paid for Father's limo.

Armor had seen me getting into my suit and skipped the casual clothes he had laid out and pulled out a nice camel colored suit. When I called him on it, he just called me his princess and dodged my thrown pillow. Once he was dressed and coiffed, he came up to me with a soft sable brush. While I was enjoying my grooming and was basically playing boneless chicken, he whispered into my ear. "I refuse to be labeled your boy toy, Little One. You dress up. I dress up."

I glanced at him out of the corner of my eye. No one would dare call him a toy. At least in earshot. I would make sure that was the last thing said about my mate. There was a whining at the door. Jees, that Lycan was worse than a kid.

"Come on in Haley." He opened the door and stuck his tawny toned head in. What ever was on his lips just died. He had on a red mirco fibre t-shirt that clung to him and white jeans. He was barefoot. I think he was barefoot most of the time anyway.

"What?"

He pulled at his neckline. "I don't have any suits."

"We'll pick some out when we got shopping again. You look fine."

"Was there a reason you came looking for us?" Armor snapped. *Jealous much, big guy?*

I reached behind me and went to grab his hand. I grabbed his crotch instead. He wasn't expecting it and jumped. He didn't squeak…well he did, but I wasn't going to tell him that. Haley grinned and crinkled his nose.

"Claudius said to get you because the doctors are here. Are you sick, Master?"

"Just a little."

"We hope." Armor added.

Haley was an open book. Whatever he thought was on his face. He bounded at me and caught me up in a hug before I even had a chance to get my arms up. "I don't want to lose you now, Master."

"I'm not dying…" I glared at Armor to make him keep his mouth shut. I ruffled Haley's hair and tried to back away. He finally let go. His pale golden eyes were shiny with unshed tears. He wiped at them and sniffed. I patted his shoulder in reassurance, "Now go tell Claudius we're on the way."

Haley also moved at one speed. He tore off out of the bedroom.

I turned on my heel and crossed my arms over my chest as I looked at my big Monkey. "What is that about?"

"I am not used to sharing your attention or affection."

"He's just a kid."

"He could be a parakeet and I would feel challenged."

Holy crap, babe. "What's going on inside that melon of yours?"

He snagged me and I got dragged back to his chest. "My emotions are all over the place when it comes to you. I am trying to be…cool. But, that little Lycan comes around, I get territorial. It is just as bad with Claudia."

I stilled in his arms.

"X?"

I tapped his forearms lightly and he released me back to my feet. I sent him a wry smile. "I'm going to want a second opinion but there just might not be any need to get married to the Baroness."

"Xavier?"

"Liam said I'm sterile. He said he would have liked to have been my son but that wasn't going to happen now. Considering he wants nothing more than to be jumping on his little Honey Bee, I'm a little glad about that." Armor hugged me closely.

"I am sorry, Little One. I watched you with your nieces. You would have made a good father."

"You would have let me have kids?" My voice slipped out a little more incredulous than I wanted it to be.

I got hugged tighter, "Truthfully, it hurt to come to terms with your marrying to have children. But once, I accepted it as fate, I was looking forward to being an uncle."

"Technically, you are an uncle."

"Stepfather then. I would protect your children with my life, Little One. You would not even have to ask. Do not take this Liam's word at face value, X. We will get a second opinion."

"I honestly thought you would be jumping for joy."

"I am an ass; but, I am not that selfish." He nibbled my nose. "There is a difference between choice and having none at all."

I got another sweet appley kiss. He gave me a smile. "Maybe you can still be a father. Let us see the doctors."

I used to think there were idiots out the world who knew there was something wrong but didn't go to the doctor in fear of finding out that there was something wrong and then finding out that it could have been cured if only they had come forward sooner.

111

I didn't know I was that idiot.

Thank God, Armor had my wrist in a grip of steel because I would have run off in the other direction. I actually pulled back on my arm a couple of times. Armor jerked me forward and put me in a headlock. Damn it. I pushed against him.

"Ssssh, Little One. You're messing up your hair."

Haley came loping around the corner and skidded to a halt with his bare feet. He paused for a second unsure of what to do. Armor just kept marching me forward. "Bring up the rear, pup. In case he gets away, you will have to tackle him."

Mikey was playing door man for the night. He looked shocked as our little threesome rounded the corner and approached. "Are you going to try and run again, Little One?"

"Let me go, you ass."

I popped upright. I got one breath in then Armor propelled me none too gently forward. Mikey got the door opened and I was able to walk into the Great Hall without looking like a plush toy being dragged along behind a toddler. I got the evil eye from Claudius. He didn't see what was going on but he knew that something had. I deflected it off to where it was deserved but all I got was the dreaded eyebrow arch. Armor actually smiled sweetly as he walked in. I wanted to kick him in the shins.

Haley wiggled by me and gave me a low laughing growl. I smacked his ass gently as he hurried back towards Claudius. The black haired Vampire reached out and scratched him behind the ear.

There was a gaggle of unknowns standing around together around a....wow, a flowing fountain of blood. Chesterton, I didn't know you could do that.

Nice you see you vertical.

Hey, Shade. Nice to be vertical.

I felt a disturbance in the force. By the time, I got to you, the Baroness already had you in her arms. What's going on?

My life has been all one big orchestrated opera. Right from day one. Maybe from even before day one.

I could tell Shade's concern was real. Are you still suffering from brain damage? I'm not following a thing you're saying.

I met the legendary Hashmallim, a little too up close and personal. He makes Hades look like a zit when I thought he was a volcano.

Oh....and...

He told me many interesting things. One of which was that he had merged with Sigmund and that pushed grandfather's instability off the mountain of reason. Liam, as he calls himself, has been 'protecting' me from day one. Making me go blind was his idea of protecting me.

So why were you injured not so long ago?

I was just my plain loveable self.

Eh? I'm surprised he let you live.

This ain't over yet, Your Majesty.

"Lord Emperor, Xavier Von Drachenfeld." Chesterton bellowed from beside the door. The entire gaggle turned toward me. Armor had wandered over to Claudius and Haley. Father, Lover, and Pup dropped down into reverent pose. I glanced over at the doctors. There was a momentary pause then one by one they assumed the position.

I would have face palmed but I got an eyebrow arch from dark and deadly. "Thank you for coming into my home to deliver my medical news personally. Please rise."

Claudius gestured at the chair he was standing behind. Armor took up position on the left. Haley motored off to the blood fountain. I sat in the chair feeling anxious. Claudius reached out and laid a hand on my shoulder. Haley came back with a crystal goblet of blood. I gave him a smile and took it. He dropped at my feet and leaned against my knee. We must have looked impressive because the low key chattering that was going on between the physicians screeched to a halt.

"Dr. Maxwell." Claudius spoke easily. I tensed under his hold. His hand tightened and he pushed down making sure I was anchored in the chair. He must have seen the dragging headlock to get me in here.

There was a knot in my stomach. I was going to throw up.

Dr. Maxwell stepped forward and bowed his dark blond head again. He looked like a doctor...from WWII. His posture was rigid almost

113

militaristic and if he gave me *that* salute there was going to be hell to pay. He cleared his throat and then stumbled over his words as I stared at him. "Ahem, Lord Xavier. We ran the physical tests while you were under our care earlier today. Basically, all our tests indicate that you are suffering from post burn hypermetabolism due to your...altered...physical state."

What the hell does that mean?

"When we say post burn hypermetabolism we mean that your metabolic rate has increased your glucose production and utilization..."

I zoned out. I had no idea what the hell he was saying. I doubt asking them to dumb it down a bit would have helped. Haley wrapped his arms around my calves hugging me tight.

"...and because of all those indicators that I just mentioned we are starting to see considerable loss in muscle mass. In order to stem this physiological symptom you will have to increase your caloric and protein intake well beyond what a normal vampire's diet would be."

Huh? I need to eat more?

Claudius picked up the slack, "Dr. Maxwell. Are you saying that the Lord Emperor's ailments are the same as a burn patient?"

I frowned. Didn't everyone know by now that I got myself Sigmund's aliment? A bathroom had to be converted to a huge kiln and vented through the roof. All those destroyed buildings and public pools. Hell, I was in a coma for almost a month with an uncontrollable need to burn every five to eight days. If these doctors, the heads of the vampire medicine, didn't know...well damn, those Loyal took their oath seriously.

"Which we cannot figure out. There is not one flaw on the Lord Emperor's skin that shows any indication of being burned."

Claudius dropped his voice and whispered to me, "How is your lower back, Xavier?"

Armor piped up, "Is it wise to let them know?"

"I do not think we have a choice. Your Little One, is wasting away before your eyes, no matter how much he eats or drinks. We need medical advice on how best to proceed."

I whispered to both of them as I sipped on my blood, "It's not bad. Once I show them, it's going to get out all over the Nation for sure."

Claudius squeezed my shoulder, gently. "I think we have been lucky that your....special talent, hasn't been leaked to the Nation prior to this."

"Lord Du Bussey?" The doctor asked from across the room.

"It is up to you, Xavier." Armor stroked a finger across my temple.

"Come with me, Doctors." I stood up and then wondered briefly where to leave my goblet. Haley popped up from the floor and took it from me. I patted his head and he grinned. It didn't take much to make the pup happy. "I'll show you how I burn."

While I was in my hemlock induced coma, Armor had taken over my burning. He monitored my temperature and when I started to get into the danger zone, he would take me to the bath and leave me there until the phoenix wings would reach critical mass and burst out on their own accord. He had altered the burn room so I wasn't left there alone. There was a tempered viewing window installed now so he could monitor my progress. I left Father to organize the doctors. Armor stood silent as he took my clothes and folded them as I stripped off.

"Are you all right, Little One?"

"I think we'll find out after the Doctors decide what the hell to do about this." I looked down at my arm. "We should have figured out that there had to be some sort of side effect."

"This must have happened to Sigmund."

My eyes narrowed. "Liam happened to Sigmund. He said I was stronger than my great, great, great grandfather."

"Should you take this Liam's word to heart, X?"

"I don't think he has any reason to lie, Pretty." I blushed. My face got hot as Armor wrapped my blooded kilt around my waist. His hand lingered on the soft skin of my stomach then he leaned forward and kissed me.

"I'll be just through the glass."

"So maybe once this is figured out, I can get fanged again?" I arched an eyebrow at him.

"You have no ideal how hard it is to keep from fanging your neck when you offer it." His fingertips brushed against the soft, tender, erogenous area of my neck. I grinned then walked around into the blast shield.

I looked up as the roof retracted. The light of the late summer sun seeped in through the opening but it wasn't enough to fill the chamber. "Front or back?"

"The back, Xavier." Claudius called out.

I turned my back to the window and closed my eyes. There was almost no effort to get the Phoenix wings out. The rising heat of the air was like slipping into a bathtub of warm water. I flicked them wide, allowing them to curl around the enclosure and reach skyward. I didn't need a long burn; my lower back wasn't that hot. I felt the elastics in my hair disappear and my white tresses swirled skyward. I turned slowly allowing the best doctors Hades could blackmail or buy see the entire extent of my burn. Finally facing them, I willed the wings away. The tiles glowed a bright orange with retained heat. I looked at the glass. I now know what an aquarium fish feels like. They were staring and pointing and talking amongst themselves.

I came around the barrier. Armor waited with my business clothes in his hands. I shook my head. I wanted to go hunting. Well mostly dancing. Last time at the club while in a suit, I got my ass kidnapped. Hmmm, the candy twins. I wonder if they still hung out there. I got goosed. I twisted around and Armor looked at me with one arched eyebrow. "No, I cannot read your mind, Little One, but I can read your face and you were not thinking about me."

"You remember the little blonde Hottentot that was all over you that time I got kidnapped?"

"Not particularly. I had other concerns at the time."

"He tasted like a candy apple you get at the carnival. His brother was like cotton candy. I wouldn't mind going into some sugar shock right about now."

"You want to go hunting?"

116

"Well they said it was just burns. Now that I know what it is, I'm not so freaked. Nice headlock by the way. Don't do it again."

"I think it is a little more complicated than that."

Sure enough it was. The doctors were in the middle of a heated discussion when suddenly they remembered the patient in question was standing behind them listening, and said patient was the unofficial Lord Emperor of the Vampire Nation. Said patient was also First. I cleared my throat.

"So, what now?"

"More tests. We will have to draw fluid from your back where you have the heat pool. For now, we will start basic burn therapy. You cannot drop any more weight – it is really muscle you are losing."

I frowned, "So what do I so do now?"

The doctors turned and started nattering amongst themselves again. I heard things like Benedict's formula and hypermetabolic rate and calories and a twenty four hour period.

Huh? "Guys can you dumb it down a bit?"

Dr Maxwell came forward, "Lord Claudius has informed us that you have started to eat at a human interval. Keep doing what you are doing. The meals should be balanced. We will have to have a conference with your chef. In the meantime I will prescribe a low carbohydrate and higher fat content blood shake. Lord Emperor, you require solids every hour based on the initial findings and what we just witnessed. How often does that burn occur?"

"Every five days."

"At the same intensity?"

"Greater."

"Maybe you should try smaller burns, daily. Diffuse the heat, control the burn. Shorten the length. The labs will get on analysis. Maybe we might be able find a way to inhibit the reaction. We will not know until we run more tests."

"This affects the blood intake as well?" Claudius asked with a touch of concern.

"This affects everything. The body is desperately trying to heal itself after each and every burn. I did not know that the Royal Line had this problem."

Armor spoke quietly, "This is not a Blue thing at all." I felt the heated gaze of my elder vampires meet over my head.

Dr. Maxwell paused. "How…ahem, how did this happen?"

"The Lord Emperor was captured by Ocanlov demons." Claudius crossed to me and stood off to my right side.

A look of alarm crossed the Doctors face. His eyes darted to mine. "I thought the Ocanlov were extinct."

Armor spoke up, "They are now."

Claudius took over as Dr. Maxwell found himself to be at a loss for words. "Apparently this also happened to Lord Emperor Sigmund…before he started his erratic behavior. Councillor Armanita called them Phoenix wings. You can see our cause for concern."

Dr. Maxwell cleared his throat. "Lord Hades has placed you high on our priorities list. I'm moving you to the top, Lord Emperor. Can you come to the offices tomorrow so we can run more tests?"

"I have duties to attend to in the morning; I should be free in the afternoon."

"We will be ready for you, Lord Emperor."

I got the synchronized bows. I nodded my head in acknowledgement then waited for them to leave. Chesterton, the ever present and ever useful, butled the doctors out of my hair. For now.

I sighed. "I've come full circle."

"Little One?"

"Once was I trying so hard to lose weight. I'd starve myself but everything I ate while doing that just made me bigger. Now, I got to eat because I'm underweight. What is that? A chocolate bar every hour?"

Claudius reached out and cupped my chin, "You are not eating junk food. There is nothing worse than a Vampire that has to gum his victim."

I blinked at him. I couldn't tell if he was serious or not. The silence went on. Finally he burst out laughing. Damn it. I like the sound of Father's laughter, but lately it's been at my expense.

"So what happens if you lose a fang?"

Armor wrapped me in his hug. "You die. You cannot take in the amount of nourishment you need with just one fang. You starve to death. Not a pleasant way to die."

I frowned. "Is that why you dragged that dentist down to the Manor when you cracked my tooth?"

"That and guilt. You won again and I lost my temper or I should say, I lost my temper and you won."

"I kept you on your toes."

"You still do."

Claudius came closer and pressed a kiss to my temple. "By your leave, Lord Xavier."

"What are you doing tonight, Father?"

"Just me and the piano."

"Come hunting with us."

"All right." That swath of black hair cascaded over his shoulder as he bowed his head.

"Do you still have that black-patent-leather-spray-painted-on outfit?"

There was a dramatic pause and another eyebrow arch. "Yes."

"That one will do nicely. Do you want to meet up here first or at the club?"

"At the club." Claudius leaned over and plastered a kiss on my lips. His tongue coaxed my jaw open. Armor stepped up and plastered himself on my back. Fingers twisted in my hair, I didn't know whose hand it was.

"Later, Little Blue." Claudius turned and headed straight for the elevators.

"I think Father needs Sex."

Armor chuckled into the back of my hair. "You made a funny."

I laughed out loud. I guess I did.

"Dinner is served, Sirs." In the hallway entrance Mikey bowed.

"Care to join me? You can watch me eat."

Armor's fingers skated along my skin just above my waistband. "I can feed you."

"We're not having a rehash of the sauerkraut incident."

"There would not have been an incident if you just did what I told you."

"Since when have I done what you told me?"

"True. There is always a first time." Armor moved beside me and offered his arm. "Come husband. You can sit in a chair if you want, but my lap is better."

"A chair would be safer."

"But not as much fun." He smiled down at me. His warm chocolate orbs were molten with indulgence and desire, but he was in control of his flame. There was no hint of red anywhere.

"Sit anywhere you want, Little One. I'll be close by."

I laid my hand on his forearm and we walked out of the room. I had spied a couple of black bags being carted off to our bedroom when I was leading the gaggle to the bath. I just might have my big red monkey back tonight. My wide variety of fuck me now clothes that had hung in the Du Bussey manor was gone but while Armor was off chasing Haley down in the racks, I pulled something together real quick. I think he'd like it.

We had to pass the long narrow corridor of erotic delights. I felt a flush on my cheeks as that memorable filled my thoughts. I paused and stared out at the moon that was rising against the pink twilight of the fading day.

"X?"

I just stared out the window. Seeing my reflection materialize as the light faded from the sky, made me a little introspective. I'm Xavier. I'm a Vampire. Armor came up and draped an arm across my shoulder and down to my stomach, urging me back against him. I'm loved. I'm cherished. That was worth fighting for. I reached back and tangled my hand in Armor's sable hair. He was worth fighting for. He was worth killing for. If it came down to it, he was worth dying for.

I took a deep breath and laid a hand over his. Our wedding bands glinting in the dying of the day.

I'm Xavier, Lord Emperor of the Vampire Nation.

Armor is my chosen Consort.

I'm the head of my House and I'm the First of Assassins. Woe be it to anyone who dares fuck with me and mine. I narrowed my eyes and watched as my eyes flared blue flame in that tempered glass. A small deadly smile crossed my lips. It was only a matter of time.

Tick tock, Hades. Tick tock.

Chapter Eight: Sensei

We weren't heading out clubbing until 11 pm, so I figured I better get my ass in gear and start taking care of business. From what I could figure out on my own the Master of the Territory was a blend of a small claims court judge and a military hammer of death. Armor's coven rampage had basically taken care of that for probably another fifty years, so I wouldn't have to worry about it. Which lead me up to all these different scrolls of parchment, books and post-it notes that were the basic laws of the territory. This was all fine and dandy for Claudius and Marcus, they had a kind of corporate memory to draw on. Armor had followed me into the library that I used as an office took one look at the mess and said *adios*. I was going to have to organize this into something I could use.

It must have been at least six months since the last -- what the hell do they even call it, Mastery? Court? Circuit Court of the Territory? I pinched my nose. I was getting a headache and I haven't even started this yet. I was going to have to create a database, and then organize this into a workable library and probably a website. I was going to drag this Nation into the new millennia. Kicking and fanging if I had to. I shoved my chair back and got up to get a coffee. I took one step sideways and fell over Haley. Somehow the silvery gray wolf managed to get under me so I landed on his bony carcass instead of the tiled floor. Enough of this.

"Human form. Now."

It was still a creepy little freak show to see him change from wolf to naked youth. The transtition was fast but I could see how his bones altered and his muscles flared stretching out his flesh. It was the bone cracking stretch of the middle of his face that turned into a muzzle that sent shivers down my spine. The muzzle returning the other way was just as freakish.

Haley's flesh was red from where I landed on him. "Sorry, Master. I had my eyes closed."

"I'm pretty well safe here in my own house, Haley. You don't have to hang around me."

"But I like being with you, Master."

"You are in my personal bubble."

Haley's eyes looked around me, "Bubble?"

I held my arms out from my sides. "This is my bubble, the end of my finger tips. I don't want anyone inside of it until I decide I want someone there. This means you, Haley. This means Father. There are times I don't want Armor inside my bubble."

Haley looked away. Now I felt like the school yard bully again. Damn it. I yipped at him. His sad face turned into a genuine smile and he jumped at me. I caught him but was off balance. I hit the table and sprawled across it. Haley was on me like white on rice. His tongue was out and licking everywhere like a wild and crazy puppy in human form. We ended up rolling off the table. It was funny, what were the odds of me ever playing with a naked boy, much less a Lycan pup? I flipped him over and pale legs kicked in the air as he went oof. I latched onto his ear and growled lowly. He stilled and whined. His hand came up and he brushed my hair with the back of his hand. He asked again. "Dominate me."

I let go of his ear and he rolled into position. He looked back at me with those golden eyes. "Dominate me, Master. Comfort me with your strength."

Crap. Crap, crap, crap, crap, crap! *Sex or work.* I was leaning way towards work.

"You promised later in the limo. It's later." He shimmed his hips.

"Haley..." I reached out and touched his back. "I'm not a Lycan...I just can't..."

"I can prepare you." I also never thought I would be pushing someone's face out of my crotch in a panic neither.

"Haley....enough."

He stilled and dropped to the floor. He pressed his face down on my foot. "I'm sorry Master. I'm sorry."

124

"Sssh." I reached down and touched his head. "Sssh, little pup. I don't know your ways."

Haley sat up, tears running down his face. "But Master, you are from the Hunter family. Every Lycan knows of the Regent Hunters."

"I…" I just slumped. "I never learned anything, Haley. I wasn't supposed to be a Hunter."

"You were supposed to be a vampire?"

"No. I never really had plans to be anything. Others made plans for me. Only now, I'm trying to make my own plans."

"What are your plans, Master?"

"One step at a time. I'm Master of the Territory. I have to learn how to be that. That's what I'm doing here. I need to get my head around this."

"I'm not helping, am I?"

"You have been through a lot lately. It is understandable you want to be in a pack. That is what you know. I just don't know how to be your Alpha. I don't know what you need."

"Master….you just protect us. You just continue to be our Father." I blinked as my chest constricted. This was followed by my throat tightening up. I must be having some sort of delayed allergic reaction to something. Yeah…allergies.

"I've been the one who needs protection."

"I saw you. I saw you in the night. I saw your power and your anger. You might have needed protection as a fledging…but not now." Haley's voice was low and full of awe. For me?

"Those Alphas have killed countless Lycan. I knew I was dead that night. When I heard their cry, I knew I was dead - I just wasn't going to stop running. I saw your wings. I felt your fire. I saw the pack die. If I can offer any protection, Lord Emperor…it is nothing to what I owe you."

"I offer my submission when I ask for dominance. If you accept, it shows me that I'm worthy of your protection."

Oh, Holy Crap.

"Master?"

125

"I...I...I can't dominate you like before. Haley, sex shouldn't hurt."

"This is not sex."

I stroked his back gently. "I can't rut."

Haley's face showed his confusion.

I needed help. *Shade?*

You're coming in loud and clear, over.

What?

10-4 good buddy. The roads are clear and the smokies are at the donut shop.

What the hell are you doing?

I've been watching old movies. What do you want?

Armor there?

Do I look like your babysitter?

What the hell are you on?

I'm high on life, little buddy. Besides, I'm licking a drug toad.

I was stunned speechless.

I heard laughter. *Oh my god, I wish I was there to see your face, Xavier.*

Er...okay. I'm looking for Armor.

I think he was down in Marcus' room.

Can you get him and send him down into my office?

What's up?

Got a little dominance problem.

I'll get him moving.

"Come here, pup."

Haley looked at me. "You spoke to Queen Nightshade."

"You heard?"

"It was just murmurs."

"Good to know."

I pulled Haley to me and just stroked his hair. He leaned into me giving me a low whiny chuff. "Alpha."

"We need to wait."

"Master?"

How the hell was I going to say this? "What do you know of Vampires?"

Haley looked down at the floor. "You drink blood. If you are trapped in the sun, you will die. You will die if you get your head cut off. You will die if you get a silver stake in the heart."

"I get the picture."

"Vampires are not considered allies."

"The pack you just joined is unlike anything in the Nation. At least, as far as I know. I really don't hang out with other vampires other than the Du Bussey House. The big guy – Armor is my mate. He is also my maker."

"Your father?"

I grimaced and hissed, "Sort of. Armor made me. Claudius raised me – I call him Father."

"What do you call Armor then?"

Armor's deep voice sounded from the doorway. "Asshole, Stupid Fuck. Pretty."

I sent a sneer in his direction then added the latest endearment. "Beloved."

"That is new. I like it." Armor walked in and looked at us on the floor. "You could have done it and I would never have known."

"But…" I closed my hand over the pup's mouth.

"Hush, Haley. This is between my mate and me. Don't interfere." I pulled the pup closer to me for him to be on the safe side.

Armor stood looking down at us. His face was blanked but his eyes were in turmoil. He had said his emotions were ragged when it came to me and regarding him now, I could truly see it. "I'm not out to hurt you, Armor. That's the last thing I want to do. But, I won't live like this under your reproach and scrutiny. I didn't understand what I was doing when Haley and I rutted that first night. You coached me through it but you didn't tell me why…and I was too naïve to ask you."

We matched stares, green to brown. His shoulders dropped from the stiff horizontal line of anger but it didn't drop enough to show that Marcus had taken over.

"I felt fear when the pup asked me to dominate him. Fear. Armor, you made me this way. You've made sure I won't stray, didn't you? Aside from getting blood from someone if anyone else approaches I'm terrified even if I hide it well. You did this so you can't get all territorial and pissy on me, now. I won't allow it."

I watched as he turned on his heel. "Don't you dare walk away from me." My voice was cold and my tone was harsh. "Come and face the mess you made."

"I love you, Little One."

"Then fix me."

His face twisted as he turned around and really looked at me. "I don't know how. I put that fear in you, Xavier and I…am sorry."

"Then give me your permission." I hugged Haley tight as I whispered.

"Xavier."

"My Lycan has asked for acceptance. That's what dominance means to him. To belong to the pack he finds himself in. I can't do it because of - what happened."

"Fuck him." Armor turned on his heel again.

"Beloved." I called out softly.

He stopped.

"We have to fix this. Some how. Some way. I don't deserve to live this way. I shouldn't have to live in fear. You shouldn't want me to live in fear. It diminishes half of who I am. Do you only want half a love?"

Armor turned and walked back up to us. He knelt down and slowly brought his hands out until they were buried in the hair of each of us. He pulled us forward until we made a triangle with our foreheads. "No one in this family should live in fear. Marcus knows what that is like. I am sorry, Little One. You do not need my permission, but if you need to hear it, fuck who you want, Xavier. Just love only me. And you, pup, your Master does not like hurting anyone while having sex. He cannot rut. Do not make him. It hurts him more than you know."

Armor pressed a kiss to Haley's forehead. "I get territorial. Remember that, pup. I have worked my way into the Lord Emperor's family. I will not give up my position. Challenge me if you feel you can take me, but I will not step aside."

He tightened his hold and held me up to get a kiss on the lips. "Some how, some way. You will not fear any more, Little Beloved. Should I stay, or should I go now?"

"Haley?"

"It is up to you Master. I would get dominated in a room full of Lycan. I feel no shame in others seeing my Master, my Alpha, claim me. I am proud to wear your collar."

I ducked my head behind my hair and whispered in his ear, "As I said, this is unlike any pack you've ever been in." I raised my voice, "I do believe we are a 'pod', isn't that right Armor?"

The big man's chest rose with a deep sigh. "I am never going to live that down am I?"

I looked up, rested my chin on Haley's head and regarded Armor carefully. I never considered him as fragile as a china doll. But that is what he was, and I could see the crazing in the glaze façade now. What had Father said? Armor was only out in the real world for about a year before I came along. He was like Marcus. He lived that hell. Physically he was tougher. But emotionally, he was like a little kid in the sandbox and I was his one specially loved toy that he wasn't going to share or let go of. But he was trying. I didn't need to mind fuck him to know that he wanted to do nothing more than rip the pup away from me and scent mark me as his own. To claim in me in front of the pup, to show Haley that I was his and his alone. That is what he wanted to do. He climbed back to his feet, trailing my long white strands of hair through his fingers. He was going to grit his teeth and walk away. He was growing.

"Love me?"

"Always." His reply was easy and full of promise.

He moved to turn away. I caught his pants. "It's your turn. Ask me."

"Love me, Little One?"

I made sure our eyes were connected. It was easy to recite these words because they were emblazoned on my heart. "I will be your sword.

129

I will be your shield. I will be your protection and I will be your light throughout the upcoming days of darkness. I will keep you safe. I will make you feel that you are loved. Be happy, Armor. Lean on me when you are weary. Let me bear some of the load. Let me stand with you." I lifted my hand up to him. "You're not alone. Not anymore."

He stood still. So still. Oh crap, did I break him again? The pup went flying as Armor grabbed me by the back of my neck and hauled me to my feet. He had me in a headlock embrace.

Humph....

"Just when I think I know you...you do this."

Air...air..I need to breathe. We got knocked over sideways. I ended up sprawled across his waist. Haley was plastered to my side and half on Armor as well. The tawny headed pup popped up, "You stay out of Master's bubble unless invited."

I started laughing. Haley was about a full foot shorter and about half as wide as Armor and he attacked to defend my personal space. And, he was naked as a jay bird. I reached out and caught the pup's head and pulled him to me for a kiss.

"I did not come here to be a bed for you two."

I scraped my human teeth along Haley's jaw. I pulled back and looked over at Armor. "Why can't I fang him?"

Armor flopped his head back to the floor. "I want you to fang only me."

I sat up slightly and stared down at him. "What the heck is going on in there?" I pinged him between the eyes.

"Oh, Little One. I do not want to become as obsessive as Marcus. But I find myself being so possessive. Even over a little scrawny pup. Don't call me a stupid fuck, I know I am."

Haley glared at Armor. I reached out and scratched behind his ear. He made a low groan in the back of his throat. He asked for dominance again. "I need your help, Pretty. Start me up."

I sat up wiggling on Armor's warm body. He urged me back to front on his lap. A hand came around my waist, snaking under my shirt and rubbing seductively on my skin.

"Pup, come here."

Huh?

Haley scooted closer. Armor reached out and cupped the back of his head. "If you want dominance, you will have to get your Master ready. Vampires need more than just scent. We need touch and sight and taste." Armor shifted and I found myself propped against Haley who now was the meat in this vampire sandwich but I had a feeling that I was the one about to be eaten. His smaller hand laid under Armor's on my stomach. *Holy tutor.*

"Uh….guys…"

"All you need to do is moan, Little One." Armor kissed my ear.

Moan and groan and yip and dominate. Armor passed his sexual secrets on to my Lycan. Or is it my sexual secrets? I was a quivery mass of flesh and desire. Armor ran his fingers down from my left ear to my neck resting in the hollow of my shoulder. Lycan lips and tongue followed that path.

"You're driving me crazy." I shivered.

"Ssh, I'm teaching."

Oh my god. I was hard and my blood was rushing in my ears. Armor's hand twisted one nipple. Haley twisted my ring. I screwed up my face and growled. Roughly translated, "I'll fuck you now."

"Master." Haley licked around my ear. "You are fine-looking."

"Let him touch you, Xavier. He has never done this before."

I stilled. Of course, he was a minor Lycan. He would only have been taken. He might have challenged younger werewolves, but it didn't look like he did that. My Lycan touched my cock. I glanced down and got harder still. Armor's hand was over his, stroking me, gripping me tightly. I moaned and threw my head back. Armor shifted me and I lay back on Haley. I opened my legs wider and leaned back letting both their hands work on me.

Yip. Who said that? Oh, that was me.

I opened my eyes as Haley set me up, moving from behind me moving into position to offer himself with lowered shoulders and ass

131

lifted high. Armor maneuvered me into position behind the Lycan. "Prepare him, Little One. He is your pet. Don't hurt him."

"What will you be doing?"

"Grading your performance. Don't worry, it is a pass or fail, and trust me, you will know if you passed." Armor handed me a warm tube of lubrication. My face must have looked funny because he leaned over and gave me a sweet gentle soul melting kiss. "I carry it always."

"Because I'm such a slut?"

"No, because I am. See to your pup, Xavier. It is getting late and we have to start getting ready. If you stand Father up, I am not going to get in his way when he comes looking for you."

Haley wasn't kidding when he said that he was used to domination. It didn't take much preparation to get him ready. He was a talker. He was a cheerleader. You couldn't get complacent fucking him. Being called his alpha rut master gave me a gentle thrill. The fact that Armor was laying on the floor beside us, watching intently, a slight red flame dancing around his eyes. I could barely string two words together as I stroked into Haley. Armor was telling the pup to do this, and that and when to tighten, like right now.

I cried out as Haley squeezed me hard. I lost it and jutted hard into him. He yipped back as I howled. I slumped over his back breathing in that unique scent if his...a blend of wet dog and merlot. Bizarre combination but right now...nothing smelled finer. Apples mixed in. I opened my eyes and Armor reached under and began stroking the pup to completion. I moved to back out of Haley but Haley's hand around and rested on my back. "Stay, Master."

"Yes, stay Master." Armor grinned at me momentarily then began concentrating on what...or should I say, who he was doing.

"Speak, Lord Emperor."

I narrowed my gaze. He did something and Haley just tensed. I groaned. Haley yipped and Armor just laughed. "You're a lucky pup. Everyone in this pack likes you. Father liked dominating you. You should hang around him a bit more. He misses his mate."

"I like...tall human." *Yyyyip.*

Chesterton? I started laughing. I moved involuntarily on his back and inside him. Armor did whatever he did before and this time Haley howled. What the hell? I howled with him. Both Haley and I started as Armor joined in with his own howl. Haley looked over his shoulder at me, his golden eyes still glazed with desire but there was a smirk on his face that he could barely contain. I didn't both trying to contain anything. I started laughing and fell off of Haley's back. Armor looked over at us and frowned. "What?"

"Don't tell him." Haley begged then broke off laughing.

I rolled onto my back and stared at the ceiling, tears streaming out of my eyes. The view of the ceiling as replaced with Armor's brown hair and warm but puzzled chocolate colored eyes as he peered over me. "What?"

"You said, "Oh god, help me I'm constipated!"

Yip. Haley rolled over and launched himself at Armor. He caught my big monkey around the neck and they both tumbled off me. "Thank you, teacher. Thank you for showing me how to please, Master."

"No problem. Get off me. What the hell did you say then? I thought it sounded the same."

"Rough translation, "fuck yeah." You okay, Haley?"

I got a faceful of Lycan. He growled and yipped right in my face then pressed a kiss on my lips, jumped up and disappeared out the door. Jeez. If Armor was a hurricane; Haley was a tornado. You're still left naked and reeling, hanging upside down in a tree.

"Does this work as somehow or some way, Xavier?" Armor leaned over me, arms on either side of my head. His face was that hated impassive mask he could pull on, but his eyes were dark with questions.

I reached up and pushed his hair behind his ears. I howled, "Fuck yeah." His face broke into a warm smile and he picked me up off the floor. I'd prefer bridal pose over ass over tea kettle any day. I played with his hair and sucked on his ear as we headed back to my bedchamber....our bedchamber. "I never thought of you as a sexual sensei."

133

"You inspire me, Little One." Inspiration continued in the privacy of our shower. For some reason, we did better in running water.
Ahoooooh!

Chapter Nine: A Night at the Pheasant: Part One

We were ten minutes late getting to the Golden Pheasant. Partly because Shade decided that she was coming along for protection. Nothing like infiltrating a hopping nightclub with a full grown black panther leading the way. Finally, Shade and Haley had some words, purposefully out of earshot then Haley came running back at his usual first gear stage. He had a tell tale red stripe across the side of his head from a hellcat tail. I glared over at Shade. She blinked back innocently.

What did you do? I knew what that look meant and with Haley's welt I knew what she had done.

Shade stared off with an imperial tone to her voice which belayed how angry she really was. *Your little under nourished pup has informed me that my services are no longer required. He has also the cajones to tell me that you are now under his protection and to stay out of his way.* There was a long pause before she started up again, this time back in her normal chiding big sister attitude. *I like him.*

Now I was confused. *So why did he get smacked?*

It wasn't because of territorial issues.

Shade? Haley tucked himself up against my arm.

She let out a big sigh. *He stuck his nose up my butt.*

Yeah, he does that.

Then he had the nerve to tell me I smelt like a nice little tabby cat. Tabby cat! I am royalty, damn it!

I tried to keep it in but I busted out laughing. *Someone's got her panties in a twist.*

I don't have my panties in a twist. I don't wear them and if I did, I would have you strangled with them by now.

Temper, temper, shady tabby.

Shade stamped all her paws on the floor and fuzzed out even more. *I'll smack you so hard, your winglets will be dizzy if you ever call me that again.*

I gestured everybody to the elevator. I was the last one in. "See you later, tabby." The elevator doors closed just as Shade got into the foyer. I snickered. Haley pulled on my shirt sleeve.

"I'll let her smack you."

I frowned down at him, "I thought you were supposed to be my protector?"

"I am. I will. Queen Nightshade is your protector, too. She is bonded with you, but she's scary."

"You got that too, eh?" Haley nodded with really wide eyes.

"Okay, here's the deal," I said, smiling at his expression, "I will not call her Tabby and you will keep your nose out of places it doesn't belong."

He yipped affirmative. I patted his head. Armor just shook his head as if he couldn't believe what was going on in front of him.

The elevator door opened on the main floor and I found myself backed in the corner as Armor then Haley formed a human...er, blood nation shield. The Loyal got out and scouted the entryway and lead the way to the limo. The Lycan tore out after them, passing and then running around the limo. I glanced questioningly at Armor he just shrugged. He offered his arm and ushered me in the car. Another set of Loyal followed up behind us closing the door when Haley dived in. I thought it was overkill but just like the staff of Von Drachenfeld, the Loyal are going to do, what the Loyal are going to do.

Haley was sprawled out on the front seat. "Why did you run around the limo?"

"Checking for explosives."

I stilled. I never thought of that.

"Your sense of smell is that good, pup?"

"It's better in Lycan form. I only need to smell something one to recognize it again. I could track Queen Nightshade now. The same with you, Master and you, Sensei." Armor's expression was absolutely precious. Somewhere along the line, Haley had his snout up his teacher's butt. I covered my smile with a cough and the back of my hand.

136

"I tried to get Chesterton's scent but he smacked with me a newspaper." I broke out laughing and fell over on Armor. The mental picture was killing me. What the hell was it going to be like when Haley went and asked Chesterton to dominate him?

"You are in a festive mood." Armor brushed my hair back off my face.

"I feel good." The mysterious need to eat every day was explained, well at least explained well enough for me to stop silently freaking over.

"I love to hear you laugh, Little One. It lightens my heart."

I glanced up at my big red monkey of love. Frederick had come through in a big way. Armor could be so delectable in suits and ties, but damn when he painted something on….yowzah! It was a warm summer night, a little too warm for leather but when he got out of the shower I had the Joker's Wilde big and tall line spread out for him. Red leather pants, a black tee that had tribal tattoos swirling through it. It was something like that shirt that I had way back when but it looked so much better, or it would when he filled back out. There was a long red duster that went with it with a funky scoop neck line but it was too damn hot for that. I thought it looked good lying on the bed; it looked better on him while he was lying on the bed.

I was tempted to skip going to the club then I remembered that I had invited Claudius. I knew that he would have no problem leaving the club when he realized that he got stood up and come over here and kick some manners and etiquette in me.

I had tossed together my own little fuck-me-now outfit. In celebration of my monochromatic look, I picked out a shiny white microfiber tee and heaven forbid a white leather kilt. As people continued to shove their hand down the waistband of my kilt - I really hate that fucking photograph now, every time I had it on, I was not traditional, meaning I had bike shorts under it. However, I wasn't wearing this kilt for others; I was intentionally wearing it for Armor. From the look red ring of flame encircling his eye, it was working.

He flipped over on his knees and crawled toward me. My throat dried up as his eyes began to burn redder. "Uh…remember that Father beats on you worse than me so we better not be late."

Armor let out a big sigh, "Up. We stay in here; we are both going to get worked."

Haley tore into the room and launched himself on the bed. I narrowly avoided him by dodging to the right. Armor rolled out of the way. "Pup, there is a door for a reason."

Haley was in a pair of desert camo pants and a tight beige undershirt. He was barefoot again. "Sensei. The car is ready."

"You need shoes, pup. They will not let you in barefoot."

"I don't like them."

Armor added with a no argument voice. "Then you cannot go."

Haley's face screwed up and I thought he was going to cry. He jumped off the bed and tore out of the bedchamber. "He's going to break his transmission if he keeps red lining at that pace."

Armor looked over at me and cocked an eyebrow, "Car references really do not work well with me. Let us go."

Haley and his shoes were back with us before the elevator came to our floor. The back door was closed and the car began to pull away from the curb when the pup pounced from the opposite car seat and landed on me. Okay…that's got to stop. I pushed him to the floor by his face. I held my ribs where he landed. "You're killing me, pup."

"I'm sorry, Master."

"If you want to wrestle, do it with Armor here."

"Hey…" My love protested quickly.

I made a cutting motion with my hand to keep this from escalating. "Listen carefully, Haley. I will not dominate you in public. Don't ask me to. I will allow you in my bubble and I will hold you. That will be my way of showing you in public that you are protected and cared for. Is that understood?"

"Yes, Master."

"Then come here, there is something I want to try with you. If it hurts you in any way, tell me and I'll stop."

Haley knelt in front of the seat, his tea tinted golden eyes looking at me in expectation. I didn't know if this would work. I only thought of it when Haley was explaining that he could track. "I'm trying to find two people. I fed off them before and I liked their blood. I want to know if you could find them at the club if I give you their image. I want to try and put their faces in your mind, Pup."

"You are not kidding about your sweet tooth." Armor stated sitting up straight, interested in this experiment.

"What are you going to do, Master?"

"I'm just going to touch your forehead. Don't fight me. I know it hurts if you resist."

He nodded and closed his eyes. I fixed the candy twins image in my mind then reached out and touched Haley. He twitched but didn't pull away. As I mentioned before, you get what you get when you go tripping through someone else's mind. Haley viewed me as a creature of light with blue wings of flame. I was an Angel. I was merciful. I was powerful and I was his perpetual protector. I was held in such high regard, I almost didn't leave the candy twins images as I backed out of his mind.

"Haley?" I hope I didn't fry his brain.

Haley blinked a bit then tilted his head slightly. "Twins?"

"It works, Little One?"

"I call them Candy Apple and Cotton Candy."

"If they are in the club I will find them for you, Master."

"Right now I would eat a whole cake all to myself. I just crave something sweet. Where's a cinnamon roll when you want one?"

"You're cinnamon, Master."

I stilled and looked at the little Lycan. Armor pulled me to side and wrapped his arms around me. "There is nothing else, just cinnamon?"

Haley cocked his head and looked at us, unsure of our mild distress but knowing that he somehow caused it. "I am sorry, Master." He ducked his head down.

Haley, come here. I opened my arms and Haley crawled up against me.

139

I deliberately kept my tone neutral even if my insides were clenching. "There is nothing but the scent of cinnamon on me?"

"You have Sensei's apple scent on you, but the under scent, your pure tone, is cinnamon. There is nothing else. Should there be?" Innocent eyes looked up at me. The pup didn't know the distress he caused by that simple affirmation. I was changing into something else.

"I used to be vanilla." I thought I was keeping it together but Armor's arm came over my shoulder, leaning me into him.

"Is this because you are sick, Master?"

Armor kissed my temple. "Yes, little pup it is because he is not completely himself right now. But I still love you, Beautiful. I did not pick you because you tasted like vanilla cake. Your core, the part that is essentially you, is strong. Do not forget that, X."

I patted Haley and stroked Armor's forearm. "Thanks…both of you."

The limo came to a halt and I looked out the window at the Golden Pheasant. My first killing ground. The place where I learned to flame. The place where I found out that I was a different sort of vampire. Haley scrambled upright and pressed his forehead to the door's glass.

"I had to sneak in with Derry the last time we were here." Haley sounded sad. I blanked for a moment then I remembered the petition that had gone missing.

"If you don't want to go in, it's fine. We can get Father and find somewhere else to go."

Haley wiped at his eyes and sniffled a bit before sending me a lip trembling smile. "Why would we want to go somewhere else. Derry and I danced until they kicked us out. We couldn't get served because we looked so young but this is the last place we were happy."

"Let's dance then." I sat up and straightened my kilt as the Loyal opened the door. My Lycan bounced out. Armor slid his red clad ass out of the car and I bit my lower lip to keep from groaning out loud. Damn, he was looked scrumptious in red leather. My own sexy devil incarnate. He turned and reached out a hand toward me. I looked up into his warm eyes and smiled, he smiled back at me and I melted. I took his hand as he jerked me out, stumbled and hit his chest. He caught my other hand and laced our fingers together, band to band. "I want you to know if you see something you want take them. I will keep myself under control. This I promise...just remember, Beautiful, save the last dance for me."

He gave me a soul stealing kiss. When I finally came up for air, there were cheers and jeering from the cue behind us. I blinked at Armor in a sexual stupor. *You bastard. You do something like this now, when I can't jump you and send us both to Vampire bliss.*

He ran his fingers through my hair starting at my temple and ending at the small of my back. "I can be a tad bit slow, Little One. I don't need fear to keep you with me. I just have to keep you so satisfied that you never want to leave."

I opened my mouth. He brought a finger up under my jaw and closed it. "Let's dance."

He turned keeping our hands linked by the wedding bands and led me into the Golden Pheasant. The doorman opened it at our approach.

"Have a good time, Misters Von Drachenfeld."

I grinned and followed Armor into the club. About five paces in, I remembered why I had debated about wearing white. I glowed under the black light effects. I was a frigging beacon. Damn it. There won't be any hunting for me tonight.

Claudius had commandeered the chaise lounge at the far end of the dance floor and was elegantly sprawled across it in that same mouth watering black patent leather , approach-me-and-die-but-it-would-be-so-worth-it, outfit. Sex perked up -- in more ways than one. I started getting hard. I caught a groan in my chest or so I thought. Claudius looked up as we approached. Haley jumped forward. Father lifted one arm and deflected the Lycan off to the vacant part of the couch without as much as a hair being disturbed. Haley bounced once on the cushion then was back on his feet his face puzzled as he tried to figure out what happened.

Father reached out, scratching Haley behind the ear. The pup closed his eyes and dropped back on the seat, leaning into the touch. When

Father let go Haley almost slipped off the couch in a boneless slide. Sex knew what that felt like. *Down boy.*

Claudius sat up as the Loyal deployed around us discreetly except for one. I glanced at Winter. Since the snafu at my parents farm and his discipline, the Loyal had given him the option of death or death. Death that night or death in the service of his Lord Emperor. Since that time Winter couldn't even look me in the eyes anymore. He was my front line, my man in black, my secret service to take a bullet for me. The rest of the Loyal blended in. Only Winter stood out from the rest of the Loyal. He was the obvious distraction to draw attention away from me.

"Another five minutes and I was going to leave, Little Blue." There was no mistaking the warning that was there in his voice.

"Sorry, I was trying to reason with a Hellcat. You know well that doesn't work all the time."

"And how did you get away from her Majesty?"

"Actually, Haley laid down the law." I leaned over and pressed a quick kiss to Father's cheek. I moved past him and flopped down against him. Armor nodded at him as he plopped down beside me. I found myself hauled up on my big monkey's leather clad thighs, his arm looped around my waist. I glanced over my shoulder. "You know there is more than enough room for the three of us on this lounge. I really don't have to sit on your lap."

Armor snagged Haley's collar dragging him down between Claudius and us, ending the argument of there is room-enough. "No, there is not."

Claudius easily wrapped an arm around Haley's narrow shoulders. "What was the argument about?"

Haley grinned from ear to ear. "I told Queen Nightshade that I was Master's protector now. She wasn't needed."

A dark eyebrow went up. "I take it that went well."

Haley pouted. "I got hit with her tail. That hurt."

"Tell, Father why you got hit with the tail." Armor's hands were curved around my hips but he was being good and not getting all touchy feely while we still were the center of attention of the whole bar.

Haley looked down at his hands, "I sniffed her butt."

142

Claudius blinked and looked down at the tawny haired youth as he explained. "Lycan have an acute sense of smell."

"Have you sniffed, Father yet, pup?"

"Not yet."

Claudius eyes narrowed, "Define, not yet."

"Somebody has had his snout where your tail should be. Almost everyone has experienced that." I returned with a sly smile.

Armor brushed my hair back behind my ear. "Except Chesterton."

Haley nodded. "Oh yes, Chesterton is quick with a newspaper."

A waiter approached us. Winter intercepted and quickly searched him. I could hear the human's squeak of surprise as he was quickly patted down then released when he was deemed harmless. He got up to us and leaned over to get our order then froze. Recognition flared in his eyes and he danced backwards. I frowned and then got a memory from Az. He nibbled on this one when he had the short, short hair. I snaked my hand out and touched his forehead. Jeez, the poor kid lived in terror since that night. He knew something happened but he couldn't remember the details, but my face was a big, big part of it. I soothed his fear, calmed that panic. I let him back away. He blinked at us then smiled and asked for our orders. Hmmm, I'm going to have to teach Az how to cover his tracks better.

"Master, I'll hunt for you now."

"Hunt?" Claudius reached out and snagged Haley's collar pulling him back effortlessly against him. Haley leaned back and looked up at Father, upside down.

"Master has a sweet tooth."

"I know. Hunting here?"

"I am just herding for Master. He is too bright to hunt on his own."

Claudius looked over and smirked. An actual smirk quirked his lips. "I can see that. Xavier is rather day-glo."

"Shut up." I groused.

A black eyebrow arched.

"Sir." I added quickly.

"Manners make the Emperor, Little Blue." I got a light smack on the cheek. "I am going hunting. There is a nasty individual over there in the shadows by the back rooms that has just been coveting me since I came in. It would be nice if I could have one dance with Sex before the night is over."

"I have a feeling that you'll know when he's out."

Claudius let Haley go with a ruffle to his short locks. "Go herd." Once Haley had cleared the couch Father leaned over and slapped a lip lock on me. It wasn't a peck. It was a frickin bushel full of lusty desire. His tongue stroked along mine. His hand came up and his thumb stroked along my jaw line. He urged my mouth open wider and sucked hard on my tongue.

Armor's voice was rather amused which was a little shocking. "Don't send him into Flame, Father. As you said, he is rather day-glo and there is nowhere to take him. Except the back rooms."

I twisted my head away, "I am not going to the back rooms."

Armor whispered into my ear, "I never said you were."

Claudius pressed his forehead to mine. "I thought for a moment you stood me up. I have never been stood up before. I did not like the thoughts going through my mind as I waited for you to arrive. If this is what I did to Sex, I apologize. I did not realize how much turmoil it causes in one's head and heart. From now on I will keep my cell phone with me at all times."

Claudius pulled back. I ran my eye up and down his body. "Where the hell would you put it in an outfit like that?" Little flesh was exposed but his leather bodysuit left nothing to the imagination.

"I do not object to carrying a man purse." Okay, only Father could get away with a statement like that. "As you said, I will know when Sex is here."

Father turned and walked away every muscle on his lean body rippling and being shown so gracefully in his patent leather outfit. Where the hell was the zipper to get out of that? Okay, Sex was here and wanted out now. I closed my eyes and leaned back against Armor. I wasn't letting him out in this place. I wouldn't have to wait for the back rooms.

"Little One?"

"Sex is trying to get to Father."

"Father does naughty well." I glanced up at him and he was watching Claudius weave his way through the crowd toward his interest lurking in the dark corner.

"You're not helping. Asking for assistance here. I haven't even nibbled yet."

Armor leaned over and whispered in my ear. "This is not your day, Sex. If you don't behave, you are not going to be dancing with Claudius later. You know I can stop you. We still have not settled our accounts from before."

I blinked. Sex was getting strong. Really strong. Which was a good thing...in a scary way. He still reacted first and thought about things later. But there at least there was a moment's hesitation. If I could react quickly enough, I might get him to slow down. Ha. So far that hasn't worked. Sex does everything in hyper drive but he was trying and that was all I could ask.

Armor shifted and whispered into my other ear. "I think it would be quite entertaining to see Sex and Haley go head to head."

I sincerely doubted that Armor meant that in a sexual manner. "He just settled down again, don't encourage him."

The waiter came back. I really checked him over. There was no sense of lingering fear now. Yup, I was going to have to talk to that younger brother of mine. I was handed a fruity drink with an umbrella sticking out of it. I had ordered a beer. "Compliments of the gentleman at the bar. The one in the power suit with the red tie."

What the hell? I was sitting on Armor's lap and someone was buying me drinks? Besides, who the hell wears a suit here after eleven anyways? Armor glanced over at his would be rival. He snorted. "You would eat him up for breakfast and still be looking for seconds."

Armor waved him closer.

"What the hell are you doing?"

145

"Haley was right, you are too bright to go hunting. So be the spider and let the flies comes to you." Armor brought my hand and drink up to his lips and took a sip from the straw. "Well it is sugary sweet. Not my taste. I am going hunting in the shadows, Little One." He slid me off his lap, pulling my kilt up into a micro mini. "Set your trap, Beautiful."

I yanked the kilt down past my knees. I didn't need to advertise because I was having too much success as it was. Winter inspected power suit then glanced back at me. I nodded and he let the man by.

"I know you." He sat himself down brushing thigh to thigh.

"Thanks for the drink."

"May I?" There is something to be said about manners, but the feeling I was getting off this man was that I wouldn't want to be alone, anywhere with him -- even as a vampire. I changed his name to creepy suit.

His finger traced a small pattern across the hem of my kilt then began stroking with his middle finger along the inner skin of my knee. Ooohh, this was just nasty.

"I offered you a seat, not a feel." I pulled my leg away.

"Don't be like that, precious. I can't believe that your friends just abandoned you. Someone as innocent..." He stared into my eyes and licked his lips, "...virginal as you left to fend for yourself. This is a dangerous bar."

Virginal?

I didn't even wear white on any of my wedding days. Did that line work at all? I reached out and gently touched his forehead. *Eww. Eeew Eww EEEEwwwww.* Creepy suit had a wife and four kids, and...two lovers, one male one female...and he wanted to add virgin me to the mix. I don't think so. I hastily implanted, get the fuck away from me, and left the drink on a small round table. I can't be bought for $4.95.

I gestured to Winter. "Get him the hell out of here asap, but nicely. No notice or hassle."

I didn't have to watch as creepy suit got the bum's rush toward the exit. I shivered. My fangs actually shrank away from him.

146

Haley bounded up with a pretty young thing in tow. "See I told you, I knew Sex, the supermodel."

"Oh, wow. I mean oh my god. You're....hair's white? It looks so cool. You should dye it blue. It would look so cool blue...the lights in here make it look sort of blue but a dye job would..."

What is this?

No Candy twins, sorry. He's sweet. Pink Bubblegum.

"Pink might do too, naw, it should be blue."

Does he shut up?

No.

I stood up and offered my hand. "Pleased to meet you...?" I let my voice rise up in inquiry.

"Oh, Derek. I'm Derek...oh my god, I will never wash this hand again. You're shorter than I thought you would be...but you're still amazing. I mean, I told my hag that if I had your looks I would head right into making pornos."

"Derek."

"Hmmm?"

"Shut up." I pulled him close pressing a kiss to his lips. I didn't have to worry about him running away. He actually melted against me. I distracted him with an image of him being a porn star. Haley watched with the intensity of a research scientist as I flipped my hair, covering both of us then I nuzzled my way to his throat. Derek's hands rested on my hips. I fanged the kid. He arched into me moaning. Haley was right. He was pink bubblegum. I took five deep swallows then licked his neck closed. He hung onto me dazed as if I had just slipped him a Mickey.

"Thank you, Derek. No, I won't be going blue. I'm too old to have hair color outside of the possibility of nature." I covered the wound with a hicky.

"But you would look so hot...wow you can kiss. I came in my pants. I've never done that before. Well not since I was fourteen..."

TMI. I reached out and brushed his forehead. "Go home now. You've had a long night. You can dream about me as your porn star."

Haley took his arm and lead the boy away. I signaled the waiter and ordered a beer. I felt self-conscious sitting alone on the chaise glowing like an escaped radiation test subject. Note to self, no more white under black light.

I spied on Father. He had his target leaning into him as if the man were menacing the black haired cat suited man. Didn't he know how deadly Claudius could be? A shy smile crossed Father's face as he ducked his head allowing his long black hair to fall forward. As if any one could play shy dressed like that. The other man fell for it. He reached out and touched Claudius, stroking him through the leather, tracing a hand down his pecs and over his rock hard stomach. I could see Father's red eyes from here. The man leaned in and gave Father a kiss, it was just cursorily as he moved his hands down the leather clad body toward pay dirt. Claudius tilted his head and his midnight curtain fell between them.

Haley bounded up and tossed his upper body across the back of the chaise. "What are you looking at, Master?"

"Claudius. I have never really paid attention to how he works a room." I snagged Haley dragged him over the furniture back and pinned him up against my side.

"You remember what this means?"

"Yes, Master."

"Thank you for the boy. Did you get him on his way?"

"I put him in a cab. You want more?"

"I'm good."

"Where's Sensei?" I still had to smile at that. Sensei Armor, sex monkey extraordinaire.

"Wanna dance?" A brown-haired man asked wiggling his eyebrows as he leaned over the arm of the chaise. Haley reached across and punched him in the face. Whoa. I grabbed the Lycan pinning him against me.

"He's in your bubble."

Oh crap. I'm going to have to watch what I say around him. "... uh, in a public place, my bubble is a lot smaller. As long as people aren't holding onto me, it's fine."

"Oh..."

I glanced over and saw one of the Loyal was leading the man away, a hand on the back of his neck altering memories. Haley huffed. "I want a beer."

That would be a big mistake. The pup was fast and unpredictable now, what the heck would he be like with a few brewskis in him? I've never met a drunken Lycan, and I don't think I'd like to. Still...one shouldn't hurt him. He was forty-five years old after all.

I went to hand over my beer and the waiter magically appeared and snatched it out of my grasp. "No underage drinking. We can lose our license."

I snatched it back. ID wasn't something I thought to get him. That would be the first thing on my list tomorrow. "Fine. No drinking." I took a big mouthful then gestured at Haley. He moved in close as I caught his chin and pulled him up for a kiss. As soon as our lips touched, Haley opened his mouth wide and accepted the cold beer from me. A trail leaked out the corner of my mouth. Haley swallowed the beer then ran his tongue long along mine, he lapped at the beer trail on my neck down to my shirt neck. "Any regulations about kissing?"

"Hee hee, yeah, how about that." He shook his head and turned away from us.

"It has a hot aftertaste."

"I think that's me." I sighed slightly, "You want some more?"

Haley wrinkled his nose and grabbed my hand. "No, Master. Let's dance."

The pup was like a snowplow. Dancers got shoved out of the way as he made for our destination which was smack dab in the middle of the dance floor. Once we got to our objective, Haley whipped around and wrapped his arms around me, pressing his head against my throat. It was a surprise to say the least. The music was thumping hard and people

149

where jumping all around us, but Haley just hung onto me and we swayed slightly.

Derry would have liked you, Master.

I am sorry that I never met him.

You did. The time we gave you the petition.

I brought my arms and pressed him closer. *We both know that, that was not me. Just the like this morning at the little girl's house, that was someone else.*

He tightened his hold. *You smell the same.*

I'm different, little pup. So is Sensei. If you plan on staying with us, you'll eventually meet all of us.

Why are you different, Master?

I stared across the dance floor in to the shadows towards the left corner. The same spot Claudius first had me pinned when I fanged my lip open. My vampiric vision allowed me to see Armor as clear as day as he seduced another hulking man. I felt a spiral of desire descend from my stomach right to my groin. Armor leaned forward, his hair falling forward as he pressed a predatory kiss on the man. No one else except a vampire would know that the gasp of desire was really a cry of surprise as Armor fanged him.

I started as Haley ran his hand along my neck. I glanced back down at him. *Why are you different, Master?*

Both Sensei and I survived some very horrible things, but we couldn't do it alone. Others came and helped and how they are a part of us. Of me. I call them my brothers. We may smell the same, we may taste the same, but we are different. This morning you met Sex briefly. You are kind of like him.

I smiled down at the Lycan and petted his head, "You both seem to have only one speed. He has a good heart but sometimes he just charges ahead without thinking."

That's bad?

Not really but sometimes it can be dangerous. Just be aware of where you are, Haley. Of where we are. You want to dance or just get dominated?

Haley bit the underside of my chin and jumped back with a happy yip. We danced. I lightly fanged those who approached. I was feeling really, really good. I turned and saw Father and Armor sitting on the chaise chatting away easily. That looked good. There were times I wondered if they got along, but then again, until now they never had the chance. Armor averaged two days a year outside of Marcus until I got here. And even then, it wasn't a full twenty four hour period when he had been out.

Haley jerked on my arm and pointed at a shiny crystal punchbowl being hauled up to the small stage across from the bar. "I want that. It could be my water bowl."

I opened my mouth to say something then just snapped it shut again. He looked human, but he wasn't. While his situation was hellish right now, he knew who and what he was. He turned back to me, his gold eyes flashing. "Please…"

Jeez, he was just as bad as my nieces. I was already wrapped around his little paw. I tapped the dancer nearest me and yelled into his ear. "What is that about?"

"Dance contest. The winner gets it. They do this every couple of months. Don't bother, they already got the winner picked."

That wasn't fair. "Well, what is the criteria?"

"That you can dance, be sexy and look good while doing it." The boy shrugged and turned back to his partner.

"I don't think we could get it if we tried, pup. It seems the fix is in."

"Not me, you and Sensei."

"Our type of dancing isn't appropriate here. I mean…it's too old fashioned."

His face just dropped. The pup turned and looked at the bowl and whine/cried. "Oh, alright. Go ask Father if he wants to enter the contest…and don't knock people over getting over there!"

Haley, sedately for him, took off toward the chaise. I watched him carefully, so I didn't even have a chance to tense up until someone's arms came around me and pulled me back to soft squishy breasts. "Are you my own private stalker, Baroness?"

"If you would keep your meetings, I wouldn't have to track you down like this." I got a kiss to the nape of my neck. I shuddered slightly.

I looked over my shoulder at Claudia and had to do a double take. She was just like her father. She oozed sex appeal in a black leather spray on Chinese style dress. There was a large scoop cut out at the décolletage and she filled it admirably. It was sad that she did nothing whatsoever for me. She took my hand and hauled me off behind her toward the bar. I could feel six pairs of eyes, okay sixteen pairs of eyes, on us as she towed me behind her little a little kid's toy tugboat. I glanced over and saw Claudius as he laid a hand on Armor's shoulder and pulled him back down on the seat.

"You do show up in the most unexpected places, Baroness."

"Claudia. And don't expect me to call you Lord Emperor every hour of the day, Xavier."

"You can call me 'X'"

"We need to talk."

"Maybe not. What are you having?"

"Martini." I ordered her a drink, got myself another beer and stared out across the sea of humanity. "I told you, you were free, Claudia."

"I don't understand you."

"I'm getting a second opinion, but I believe the first diagnosis. Why are you marrying me, Claudia? We both know that Sex loves your Father."

"The Council commanded it."

"You're only doing it for the Nation right. You're doing it to provide Blue Line heirs."

"Yes…"

"What do you get out of it? You do not strike me as a corporate wife type, if anything, I think you should be looking for a corporate husband."

"Been there, done that. I need something more than pretty and vacant. Eventually, you have to get out of bed. Diagnosis?"

I leaned forward until my lips touched her ear. "I'm sterile. It wouldn't matter if I was built differently. There will be no children for us. You are free to walk away."

Claudia wrenched her head back and stared at me. Her face was totally unreadable. Her eyes were too. It was amazing that they were the exact same shade of blue... and no one knew that she was Claudius' daughter. "You...ass!"

I blinked as I looked at her. "This marriage represents hope and stability. Kids are a bonus. If you are sterile we can always do what Father did. The Nation will blame me for producing reds. Gaw..."

She downed the martini in one gulp and stared me down. "So pretty...I didn't think you were vacant too. I would never have thought that Daddy would have settled for a toy. There will be an engagement party at Von Drachenfeld in five days. I'm having it at your house, so you can't avoid it. Free to walk away. Gaw..."

She turned on her heels and stormed away.

No wonder they used to name forces of destruction in nature after women -- there I was hanging upside down in a tree, again. At least I wasn't buck naked.

Haley stood at my elbow, "Your Alpha is mad."

"In more ways than one." I picked up my beer and gestured him back to the chaise.

"What did you say to my daughter?"

"I told her I was sterile and that we didn't have to get married. She didn't take it well."

Armor dragged me onto his lap. Why do I even bother sitting on furniture? I took a drink of my beer and watched the dancing crowd. I was getting tired. I leaned back on Armor. He pressed his cheek against mine. "Are you okay, Little One?"

"Why wouldn't I be?"

"She is your intended." Claudius piped in.

"Yeah...but no offense to you Father, I really don't want to think about her right now." I heard a whine. I opened on eye and looked down at Haley.

"Can I have a drink, Master?"

I filled my mouth with beer and leaned over. Armor kept me anchored on his lap. He watched intently as Haley kiss sucked the beer from my mouth.

Armor commented with all the emotion of a nature program narrator. "That reminds me of how penguins feed their young."

Ewww. Bad imagery.

"I signed Claudius and you up for the contest, Master."

I looked over at Father. "You said I could dance with Sex."

Sex was jumping around inside of me ready and willing to get out there and shake his groove thang. Oh crap.

The music suddenly cut off. "It's the witching hour, and time for our latest dance off. Clear the floor."

I leaned back on Armor and watched the dancers. Apparently, they had no idea what kind of music would be played and had to freestyle something up on the spot. Some of the contestants were good. A couple of dancers were so bad I couldn't watch it. I kept penguining Haley and he was giggling now. He was beginning to sound like "Muttley" with his low snickering so I cut him off.

He climbed up on Father's lap and transfixed his gaze on the glittering crystal punch bowl. I guess I'd have to buy him one.

"Get off the floor. That was embarrassing for everyone. Our next contestants are X and Amour."

I stilled. What? Armor slid me off his lap and took my beer from me. "What are you doing?"

"We...are dancing." He took a good hold of my wrist and dragged me toward the dance floor.

"Wait...wait. We can't dance out here without looking like fools, not with the music they've been picking." I felt the shift. It was momentary, and Armor was back in less than a heartbeat. "What did you just have Marcus do?"

"Impressive. I didn't think you would feel that."

"Armor...hey, he called you Amour."

"You think I want to use my real name if we fall on our asses out here?"

"What are we dancing?" Armor lead me out to the middle of the floor then spun me out in a presentation. I pushed my hair out of my face and looked back at him.

"What do we do best?"

I was going to say the horizontal bop when the strains of Enya started. My heart melted. We were going to waltz. *You just keep surprising me, you bastard.* The world fell away. We weren't going to win and I didn't care. We did a Viennese waltz in the small confined space. We may have danced a little quicker than humanly possible, but I wasn't touching the ground to begin with. Armor maneuvered us into the center of the floor and began spinning in a clockwise motion. I was starting to get motion sickness when he stopped, and we began spinning counter clockwise. Contrary to popular belief, spinning in the opposite direction doesn't make your stomach any happier.

Armor slowed us and stopped just as the music drifted off. I stared up at him through my cloud of white. He tenderly touched my forehead and brushed my hair off my face. He caught my chin and tipped my face up to his. He tasted of sweet wine and apple. His tongue stroked mine, I probably tasted like a mulled beer. Was there even such a thing? "I love you, Little One."

Screams and applause broke our little bubble. I blinked myself back to reality. "I love you too, Pretty."

"Clear the floor. Clear the floor. Hey, wake up. We have one last group. Let's welcome 'Noctural'."

Armor took my hand, kissed my wedding band then stepped aside, revealing Claudius. "You cheated, Armor, please ask Marcus to do the same for us? Pussycat Dolls, please."

I opened my mouth then snapped it shut. Pussycat dolls? "How the hell do you know about the Pussycat Dolls?"

"Sex left me his mp3 player. I listened to what he likes. That was the least offensive to my sensibilities. Please, may Sex come out to play?"

155

X held the curtain open for me to slip past as we exchanged places. "What do you mean least offensive? I listen to your longhaired crap all the time."

Gorgeous reached out and laid a finger across my lips. "This is a vertical expression of a horizontal desire, Fallen."

I grinned up at him. "How vertical do you want to get?"

The music started slow and seductive. Something about buttons…and them coming off.

Claudius whispered this softly in my ear. "Dance for me, my harem boy." I watched him take a couple of steps backwards then lower himself to the ground, lounging like a sultan. His blue eyes gleamed with…mischief. Did he think I couldn't do this? Wait a minute. He spoke to me in Russian.

"Sex?"

"Harem boy?" I returned with an arched eyebrow. He grinned that I answered him in his native tongue.

Okay. Let's wind this up. I raised my arms and began undulating my stomach and hips in a temptingly sensuous belly dance. This was going to be hotter than that strip number I had to do for Hades; mainly because it was for my mate; my black-haired master assassin; my light in the darkness. I let my hair swing around me as I twisted slightly. I did one complete spin and screeched to a halt facing my sultan of sexual delight my hair swung over my face, but I kept my eyes locked with his. A shimmer of red flame flashed across his icy blue orbs. I straightened up slowly swinging my hips in a wide arc, offering up my groin if only he reached out to touch me. I lowered my arms until my hands were in my hair then pivoted on my toe so my back was toward him now. I pushed my ass out and barely bit back a squeak as he jumped off the floor and plastered his groin to my backside.

"This I remember." Gorgeous trailed one hand up my side, pressing lightly on my nipple ring as he brought his fingers up my chest, to my neck, stroking my chest and finally tangling in my white hair. He tightened his hold and jerked my head sideways. His lips grazed my temple. His other hand splayed across my stomach dipping into my waistband, then…then he started his hips rocking in that glorious figure eight.

He ground himself on my ass. He was hard as a rock. I was getting there myself. Claudius maneuvered us into slow sensual samba rolls. Our hair mixed together, black and white when we stretched forward, Claudius's weight pressed heavily on my back. I arched backwards and rested on Claudius for the second half the roll, lifting one hand up to catch his hair. He caught my hand and pressed a kiss to the palm. His tongue flickering out on that surprisingly sensitive patch of skin. I gasped out loud.

I twisted in his arms and brought one leg up, catching him around the waist. I brought my hand up to the nape of his neck. He brushed my cheek with the backs of his fingers then dragged me forward on one leg. Somehow, we segued into an Argentinean Tango. Our eyes never left each other. Our legs intertwined as we moved to the music. Finally, Father caught me by the back of the neck and dipped me to about six inches off the floor. My hair fell back and pooled underneath me. I didn't care where the hell we were. I offered my neck. Claudius snapped his eyes shut as his eyes burst into red flame. Thankfully his black hair hung like a curtain around us.

His words were an agonized whisper. "Oh Sex. It is not our day to run."

"I know…maybe…"

"No, do not ask." Claudius lifted me up gracefully and then pressed a chaste kiss to my forehead. He opened his eyes. His flame was mastered. I was ready to explode. Then I realized that it was silent. I flipped my hair out of my eyes. The DJ hadn't started any other music. The crowd was still. Claudius looked at me puzzled. He elegantly bowed and waited until I was upright and lead me back to where Armor and Haley were waiting.

The crowd finally erupted into cheers and applause.

"I did not think it was that bad." Claudius stated as he got close to Armor.

"It was like watching you make love out there, Father, Sex. Hotter than hell."

I turned around and pressed myself back against Father. He brought both his arms up and wrapped them around my chest. I saw the little Lycan looking at me puzzled. I lifted my hand to him. He sniffed at it then returned his gaze back to my face. "Sex?"

"Hello, Haley. We'll see if we got you that water bowl."

I smirked. There was a hell a lot of frontal adjustments going on.

"And the winners of the dance competition are: Frank and David."

Boos rose up all around us. Fix. Ripped. Boo. Fraud.

"I guess, we'll have to buy you a bowl, pup."

"You won it." He took off right for the stage. I could have caught him but Father was in the way.

"Damn it." I pulled away from Father and trailed him up to the pre-determined winners. He got to them before I could slow him down. He wrenched the bowl out of the blonde's grasp and turned back toward me. The bowl dropped and shattered on the floor. There was sheer terror on his face. "Haley?"

Lycan.

I grabbed him close and pivoted on my heel. Sex faded back quickly. I scanned the darkness but didn't see anything out of the ordinary which told me that they were in human form.

"Hey, we won that!"

"No, you didn't." I snapped back at him.

How many, Haley? Haley? He cowered in my arms speechless with fear.

"MARCUS! I need information!"

I dragged the pup away from the center of the floor. As soon as we got out of the spotlight, I returned to my day-glo color. Damn it. This was just like a bull's-eye painted on me. Marcus stepped up, "Lycan...how many and their location."

Marcus' brown eyes dulled for a moment. "Six. Right now, they are in a tight pack in the northeast corner."

158

The blonde dancer came tearing up after us. "Hey, you broke our…" His voice squeaked as Armor caught him by the throat.

"Go away." He dropped the man and shoved him backwards.

"Maybe they didn't sense us yet."

A lone howl rose up over the crowd. Holy Crap, we were found.

Chapter Ten: A Night at the Pheasant: Part Two

The Loyal closed ranks and somehow Haley and I got to be the monkey in the middle. The humans around us didn't really know what was going on but they backed off after Armor tossed the blond portion of the dance champion aside as easily as a mini beanbag.

Lycan? I called out to the strangers.

There was a start of surprise in the mind that I touched. *You're not a bitch. You're not Lycan. How can you use the Pack Call?*

Who the hell is calling who a bitch? *It's a gift. What are you doing in Vampire territory?*

Smug arrogance came across really well in this Silent Speak/Pack Call thing I had going on. The voice was low but there was a slight rise at the end as if his real tone would have broken like a teenager almost at the end of puberty. *We're out for a run then we scented someone who is sorely missed. We've come to take him home.*

On yeah, that sounded really sincere. *Come forward and we will talk.*

No talking. Just send the pup over to us.

I'd call that response barking like a dog at an intruder but it was more like a grunt and rather rude. *Not happening.*

You think the room full of humans will stop us?

Arrogance? Really? One of us was going to have to take the high road and it looked like it was going to have to be me. *It's the sign of a poor leader if all you want to do is rumble first and ask questions later.*

It's a sign of a weak one if all they do is talk when fur should be flying.

...and youth. Not a good combination.

"No.... let's go, Master. Let's go home." Haley tugged on the hem of my kilt.

"Too late for that, little pup." Armor let his hand fall over Haley's head and gently ruffled his hair.

Who am I talking to? The Lycans were on the far side of the bar but there were still too many people about to get a good look at them.

Emmet... And you, non-bitch? Enough with the bitch comments.

X.

Just a letter?

"Father what are the chances of you getting Haley out of this club without the Lycan's giving chase?"

'Slim to none, Lord Emperor." This was all said in Russian. Holy smokers...we really were going to have to look into this language transfer thing once we got everything moved outside.

Glancing back to across the crowd I knew that I was going to have to try and be diplomatic. Vampire and Lycan relations were strained at the best of times. All out war.... especially if I started it; since I'd already been officially warned off, it was not going to be a good thing.

An almost abandoned catwalk above the dance floor caught my attention. It would do. *We meet on neutral ground. Catwalk up above your head. You approach from the left. I'll take the right. We meet in the middle.*

...and the pup?

He's good where he is.

Haley's eyes widened and he dug his hands into my arm. "No...no. Don't do it. He's a new Alpha. You would be his first kill. Don't..."

I pushed the pup at Armor. He snagged Haley and dragged him back to his chest. He squirmed against that hard chest but I knew from experience that he wasn't getting out of Armor's hold. He was stronger than I was as a human but I never could get free no matter how much I raged even as a new fledgling. I was counting on Armor to keep it consistent.

Claudius looked over at me, "What is Haley talking about, Lord Emperor?"

Damn I forgot that nobody else could hear what was going on. "Opening round of negotiations. I'm going to talk to the leader up there."

Father reached out and grabbed my shoulder. "At least, arm yourself. The Hand of Light should only be the last resort." He knelt and pulled a small broad blade from his ankle. He clipped the holder to the back of my waist, so it settled in the small of my back. "You should be armed at all times, Lord Emperor, no matter how skimpy your attire."

Skimpy? Who the hell was grinding into my ass less than two minutes ago? Not the time for that…

Haley grabbed at my elbow. "Master…don't go…"

Emmet's tone of arrogance seemed to be even stronger. I could only think that he got a good look at his opponent. So not wearing white to a club again. *Agreed, X. We shall meet up on the catwalk.*

Arrogance and overconfidence will get you dead quick, Lycan.

"Master…" There was a hint of panic in my pup's voice now.

"Sssh, Haley. They can hear you."

Haley shut up but he twisted violently in Armor's hold. He was going to hurt himself. I reached out and touched his forehead. *Sleep.*

He slumped in Armor's arms. "Keep him safe. I've left him defenseless."

Armor reached down and gathered Haley's legs up to his other arm into the infamous bridal pose. "No you did not. You left him with me. Be careful, Little One. Lycan are not known to be honest in their dealings with Vampires."

"I've dealt with Lycan before --as a human and as a vampire." One ended in tragedy; the other was a successful campaign due to surprise. Even I knew enough that one on one with a full grown Lycan was not conductive to getting another year older. I glanced up at the catwalk. There was nowhere to run if things went bad. I would have to drop over the side. The landing was going to hurt, but I could roll away from it.

I pulled the back of my t-shirt out at the back of my waistband to make sure that my added weapon was completely hidden. "Claudius, I can I leave this floor in your capable hands?"

All I got was a sharp little head nod and then the former First of Assassins took over the situation. "Move to the shadows, closer to the exit. Haley is a priority, but nobody takes their attention off the Lord Emperor." I took his barking orders to the Loyal to be a yes.

163

I was really wishing that I wasn't glowing in the dark. I could see the smirk on the pack's face from way across here. I went to move forward, and Winter blocked me. "Sir."

He stripped off his dark jacket and handed it to me. I guess I was glowing a little too much. When I grabbed the coat I almost dropped it. He had a handgun in the pocket.

"Thank you." I slipped the jacket on and turned back to the pod to discreetly check the clip and flick the safety off then headed for the stairs. There were a couple of humans getting acquainted on the metal steps. I chased them off with a low Lycan growl of warning. Winter followed up with a menacing, "Get the hell out of the way."

The atmosphere of the Golden Pheasant had changed from light and fluffy to sinister in less than five minutes. I took the stairs two at a time, the weight of the gun hitting me in the hip as I climbed. Emmet was already at the center of the catwalk by the time I got there. He was a big brute, but rather young for an Alpha. Then again Haley was almost fifty and he was still considered a pup. I glanced down at the rest of this pack of six that was milling around below us. The whole pack was young. These were probably littermates that banded together to keep from getting decimated by other established packs. There was even one pup amongst them.

"I'd offer you a smoke, Vamp, but I don't have my lighter." Vamp wasn't meant to mean vampire. Apparently this Lycan didn't have a clue that the kilt was still all the rage. I held out my hand. His pale-yellow eyes flicked over to me. I knew what I looked like. He probably thought he could snap me like a dried twig. Too pretty. Too skinny. Besides he's wearing a skirt. I didn't need to mind fuck him to pick that up. In that one respect Emmet was just like Haley, his emotions and thoughts were all over his face. He pulled out his cigarettes and handed me one. I motioned for him to take his own.

I stuck the cigarette in my mouth then touched the end with one finger. I didn't even have to concentrate to get a small amount of heat generated to light my smoke. I took a few puffs to get it going then reached out and touched the end of his cigarette. He puffed, and I watched the expression on his face change from confidence to wariness.

Emmet chewed on the end of his cigarette as thoughts flitted across his face. I leaned forward on the railing of the catwalk and looked down at the undulating crowd below us and the flashing colors of lights. It was almost hypnotic.

"You are in a clearly marked Vampire feeding ground, Emmet."

He joined me at the railing. He was close to six feet six inches and had the shoulders of a linesman. He wore baggy clothes, but his forearms were hard as rock. The rest of him probably was too. He'd clean my clock if we tried to duke it out like humans. He knew that too even though I startled him with my little parlor trick.

"As I mentioned, X, we were out just cruising around when we caught the scent of someone who is missing and sorely missed."

"I'd have Britta know that Haley wasn't as missed as she thinks. That pack chasing him almost did him in."

"You use Den Mother's name rather freely for a Vampire. She is our leader. She deserves respect from someone beneath her."

"I'm not beneath her." I took a long drag. I haven't smoked much at all since I woke up to the eternal nightlife. Not as satisfying as I remember it to be.

That gave him pause for all over half a second and his voice rose with anger, "Who the hell are you, Vampire?"

"From what I can figure out, I'm her equivalent--for now." The thoughts of Liam, the original Lord Emperor, and grandpa fruitcake, Sigmund, danced across my mind. I didn't plan on crowning myself Emperor of the Blood Nations but there was a boatload of people wanting to do it. Well, I didn't plan on Emperor's wings, Phoenix Wings or Lord Emperorship either. The plans of mice and vampires...

"X...what does that stand for?" I could see the wheels turning as he tried to place me.

"You've never heard of me. My name wouldn't mean anything."

"Still..."

I took another long drag on the cigarette, surprised I wasn't hacking up my lungs up on the grating we were standing on. "It's Xavier."

"You're right, it means nothing." Oh score two points for that little dig.

It seemed that straight forward and blunt was the way to go. "Take your pack and leave now."

"Or what, you'll make us?" Emmet glanced down at me with a full on sneer.

"If I have to."

"Give us the pup and we're on our way."

"He's mine now. He's not going anywhere."

"Vampires can't own Lycan."

"I don't own him. He is part of my House. He's family."

"You cannot keep a Lycan. His only family is his pack. His own grandmother wants him to come back home."

I stubbed out the cigarette on the railing and tossed the butt over the side. "His own grandmother branded him and his littermate and sent then out to die. I can't see her concern as anything else than her attempt to finish the job."

"Do you know what happened to the Alphas that were trailing him?"

"They're dead."

Emmet popped upright from the railing. His yellow eyes gleamed with anger and disbelief in the dim light of the walkway. "You lie."

"Do you think I would have the pup if that Alpha pack was alive?"

Emmet sputtered. "You're arrogant for an albino vampire."

That insult hurt my feelings. "I'm not an albino. I'm just...color challenged right now."

Emmet made his move and pinned me hard against railing. Considering Vampires and Lycan really didn't get along that great, he had a hard on for me that he ground into my back. He brought his arms up on either side of me, the knuckles of his hands curling around the railing. His nose snuffled my hair right behind my ear. I shivered and not in a good way. "I'm giving you three seconds to back away from me. One."

166

"What can you do? All your body guards are down there." Grind. Rub, Thrust.

I was going to elbow him in the throat. "Two."

"I've never fucked an albino anything before. I'd turn you, if you were human. You could be the pack's bitch." He cried out as I fired up my small hand of light cigarette lighter and ground it into the tender fleshy part of his hand, between his thumb and forefinger. I brought my elbow up and rammed it into his jaw as I turned around. He staggered back a few steps. That was enough to get me and my coveted ass out of arm's reach.

"As lovely as the invitation, my ass is over claimed all ready."

Emmet sucked the injury in his mouth as his eyes narrowed. "You just sealed your death, vampire. We were just going to kick you around a bit and then take Haley back to the Den Mother. She will have a great reward for us."

"There's a bounty on the pup?"

"The right to be in her new Alpha pack. If deemed worthy enough, I could be chosen as leader."

"This is your last chance to walk away from here, Emmet. Take your young pack and leave."

"I challenge you."

I blinked. "What?"

"You and me, we fight for the right to take the pup."

"Why would I do that? I already have him, and I know for a fact that he doesn't want to go back."

"Put it this way, albino…we are going to have…. what did you call it, ah, a rumble for little Haley."

"There's no need to be insulting. Back alley behind this place. It's secluded."

"Be there. If you run…" He sniffed the air, "I'll find you."

I wanted to laugh in his face. I've already had one Lycan nose up where the sun don't shine and basically Haley said that it was the best way to set someone's scent. This air sniffing was just for show. The light merriment I had faded as Emmet barked and growled down to the five remaining Lycan. "We are heading out back. Kill them all. We'll take the pup when the vamps are all dead."

Big, tall and furry was a little slow on the uptake. If we had been conversing in the Pack Call – a Lycan female trait, why would he think I didn't speak Lycan? "One on one, eh?" I said in regular speak, I wanted to confirm this little betrayal.

"To the victor goes the spoils." Emmet turned and walked away.

Bastard. Fucking lying Lycan bastard. I glanced around. No one was watching so I tossed myself over the side, lightening my weight so I landed without snapping my ankles. I walked over to the 'pod' and watched as the six pack, ha ha, left the bar out the front door.

"From the expression on your face, negotiations fell through." Father reached out and brushed my hair behind my ears

"On the surface, everything went fine. Until he started speaking Lycan to his pack. It's an ambush out back in the alley. Haley has a bounty on his head. Grandma wants him back. Why? I don't think it's out of maternal love."

"We can just leave." Armor added.

I shook my head. "He knows my name. He knows this place. He has confirmation that Haley is with us. I gave them the opportunity to walk away and he lied to my face. The pack has to go."

Claudius agreed with me, whole heartedly. "They have to go down hard and fast."

"Damn, I wish I had my daggers."

"Winter, go to my limo. I've got a set in the back." The vampire booked off at top speed. Father turned and regarded me with an imperial arch to his expressive black eyebrow. "Why do I think you're going to face him on your own?"

My time to shine, bro.

You really want to do this, Az?

What did I tell you about shortening my name?

Sorry, Azrael.

You gave them the chance to walk away. It's my turn to show them the error of their ways.

168

X fell back into the Darkness. I let a slow lazy smile cross my face as I stretched every inch of my body. All that dancing had limbered me up pretty good. It's not that big bro can't kill, I'm just better at it. Youth, arrogance and under-estimating the foe should be met with a swift and quick kill. Those pups shouldn't be made to suffer because of their leader's stupidity. "I agree with X. It's time for a little bit of mayhem to be unleashed. That Lycan doesn't know I can understand him."

Father clicked in immediately. "Azrael." I knew that I would never get the drop on him again.

"Hey there, Pops." I turned and looked at Armor. He was carrying Haley in the dreaded bridal pose. I approached slowly. That time trashing Du Bussey Manor was fun in a brutal bone crunching, agonizing way. Armor and I would have to do that dance again, soon. I reached out and touched the sleeping Lycan pup. Elder brother really knocked him out with that mind fuck…or it could be the amount of beer they were sharing. "I like this little menace."

I glanced up, "Can I see my Puppy?"

Armor's eyes narrowed, "Now is not the time."

Normally I don't like backing down, but this was not a normal situation – or it better not be the beginning of what was defined as normal. I needed intel and I needed it fast. "I need locations."

"This is just a trick to get Marcus here."

"No, I really do need locations." Winter came back with two bundles in his hands. I shrugged out of the jacket and gave it back in exchange for the bare blades. I kept Father's other blade strapped to the small of my back. "Tick tock, Amour."

If his glare was stony before, it just got icy. "Armor."

I liked needling him. "Where's your sense of humor? Oh yeah, you don't have any."

"Boys…" Father's voice was sharp.

"Hurry up. I need to know where they are, so I can get into position."

"Don't piss him off." Marcus sighed. His eyes glazed slightly. "They are taking the long way around. No weapons. Arrogant young Lycan idiots."

"I'm going through the back rooms and wait for them. The rest of you come around from behind. They can't leave here. Puppy..."

Marcus looked down at me then smiled. I crooked my finger at him and he leaned over. "I need my sugar fix."

I gave him a tongue lashing. I held him roughly by the back of hair and sucked hard until he moaned into my mouth. I jerked his head to one side and fanged him deep. He closed his warm soulful eyes and leaned into my sucking kissing. I circled my head slightly, opening his punctures so I could get more apple essence in my mouth. My lower half sprang into action. I licked him closed. X might have a ban on fanging. I didn't. I licked my lips. Hmm mmm good.

"Damn, Puppy, you just keep tasting better and better." Haley moaned over being crushed. "You better let Armor keep him safe."

I slapped him on the cheek lightly and winked at him. I pointed at Winter. He just looked surprised. "Come on, Winter. It's time for some redemption." I looked over at the other Loyal still with us. "He makes it back; the sanctions are over. Agreed?"

"As you command, First."

"No, decide this amongst yourselves. I don't need someone who's only reason for getting up is to die for me. Makes for a very strenuous day for everyone." They didn't seem too keen on it. "Think about it."

I gestured for Winter to follow and I took off at a run toward the back rooms. Not a nice place, the black rooms. There were times I wish I had less sensitive sight, hearing and smell. With relief I broke out into the night and the alley. Winter side stepped and blocked the exit so no unwary humans wandered into our melee.

I could hear the pounding of the feet turning into the alley. I picked up a stone and smashed the light shining above our heads. It wouldn't give either side an advantage, but it would keep prying eyes a bit less sharp.

"Got a question for you, Winter. Answer me truthfully or I can find out, the hard way, for you."

"Sir?"

"Have you got somebody to live for?"

"Sir?"

"Simple question. They don't have to know that you exist just for them as long as you know."

Winter's voice was low, "Yes, I do."

"You don't have to tell me, if you don't want to." I listened as the running Lycan got closer.

"I had a son and daughter when I was human. They had babies. Their babies had babies. I have been there for every birth. When they are old enough to get into college, I give them their education. If I can help, I help—even if it is only money."

"A guardian angel."

"No, Sir. I'm an assassin."

"So am I. I need to you think of those who need you when we fight, Winter. I want you to live for something. It makes death a hell of a difficult thing to accept."

"I can't believe I'd forgotten."

"Now you remember. I'm taking the leader first. I'll break to the left after that. Take the last on the right. Leave the pup, Xavier has plans for it."

"After that, Sir?"

"I should be done with the rest by then."

"Sir?"

"They're just punks. Incoming, Winter, we meet them full tilt."

I readied my daggers in both hands. Winter dropped his jacket to the ground and pulled out his guns. "Now."

I started running full out at them. They weren't expecting it. They thought were going to be coming up at us from behind. I let out a full Lycan Alpha hunting howl just as I got close to Emmet. The younger ones stumble-started. Emmet growled and rushed at me, changing faster that I expected. I dived to the pavement and rolled making a hacking slash on his hind quarters as I passed by then popped back to my feet. I sliced his Achilles tendon, twisted and sliced deep across his hamstring. The Alpha crashed to the ground with a shocked yelp.

I pivoted on my heel and slammed a dagger through the Lycan's throat. Blood poured out coating my hand. I lost my grip on it and when the Lycan dropped it took my left dagger with him. I changed my hold on the other dagger wrapping one knuckle around the cross hilt with my palm still on the hilt. I jumped to the left and grabbed at the approaching Lycan's head. This threw him off balance; I brought my dagger up under his soft flesh of his chin. It buried itself into the brain. The Lycan dropped like a stone. Off to the right, I heard the small explosions of a silencer going off. I caught my arm under the corpse when he dropped. Damn it.

I glanced up and saw the pup on his stomach, his hands over his ears. The last Lycan jumped at me. In the dimness of the alley I saw the left side of the Lycan's head explode. I let go of the dagger and rolled out of the way. The Lycan was dead before he hit the pavement, half landing on the corpse of his pack mate I had been momentarily trapped under.

The pup was whimpering. "Don't move. Don't look up. If you do, I'll kill you." I growled at him.

Winter had his guns trained on the maimed Alpha. He glared at me as I approached. I stopped and retrieved Father's daggers. "You speak Lycan." He growled at me.

"Well Xavier used…what did you call it the Pack Call. You would think that he could do other things too. It was just bad manners to enter negotiations then to tell your pack to kill everyone. You give werewolves a bad name."

"I am not a half breed werewolf. I am a pure blood. All my pack were pures, no drop of human blood."

"You do know you're going to die."

"My pack will…"

"All you have left is the pup and I've already dominated him." I squatted in front of him and showed him the blood daggers. "We are

172

going to have a talk. Why is Britta so desperate to get my pup back? Does she want to kill him herself?"

"I will tell you no…" He howled as I cut his pinkie off.

"What was that, Emmet? I couldn't hear your answer over the screams."

"You fucking…." I rammed Father's dagger through his wrist, pinning him to the pavement. He howled again. I tilted my head and looked down at his face of agony.

"Screams are beautiful to me. Not so much to my friend here. Not really helping your Pup either." I showed him the other dagger with the blood of his pack dripping from the blade. Actually, I think that was brain matter.

"This kind of a public place so I don't want hang out here too long so…. I'll be cutting off more things at once if I must repeat myself. Why does Britta want my Pup back?"

Emmet gritted his teeth. I sighed, knelt forward and cut the last remaining fingers off his hand. He screamed and jerked, then howled as he pulled against the pining blade. Blood poured out on the pavement. "I don't know. I don't know. She just sent out a call."

"So, we were just a lucky find?"

"Yes…"

"Why did she brand him in the first place?"

"Rumor is, he went against her direct orders and talked to a vampire about internal matters."

"Okay." I stood up and pulled the dagger out of the pavement. He groaned and pulled his mangled hand to his chest. His left leg was hanging behind him useless. He was maimed in human form and as a Lycan. I nodded at Winter. He stepped up and pressed a silver bullet into Emmet's brain.

I looked over at Winter. "Isn't it nice to have something to live for?"

"Yes, Sir."

"Don't fuck up again."

"I won't Sir."

The rest of the 'pod' came running up.

Chapter Eleven: A Night at the Pheasant: Part Three

So much for the fun night out of carnival, tasting blood and dancing. Here I was again standing out in the back alley behind the Golden Pheasant surrounded by body parts and general carnage. After all the killing that just happened here there should have been even more blood. I raised my dagger and saw the dark liquid clinging to it. I licked the flat of it. Hmmmm, apparently Lycan blood doesn't match their scent. Or else, I just had too many different samples on it. I looked over the narrow alley where four dead Lycan lay. Another was nearby still in the process of dying...ah, not any more. The smallest Lycan of this young and foolish pack had transformed himself back into human form. It didn't take a vampire's heightened sense to feel the pup shivering behind the garbage bin even though the night was warm and rather balmy. I watched him carefully, he was terrified. He was hovering between the fight or flight mode and knew that either choice lead down a dark path. So far, he was staying in one place.

Good. I glanced back over my shoulder at X's Lycan pup. He was shivering just as badly as the other one. I raised my hand and gestured him forward with my fingers. He hesitated, oh so briefly. I let the back of my hand brush his face and stroke his short tawny, caramel hair back off his face. I pulled him into my chest and he buried his face against my throat. I'd allow it - this time.

"Puppy." Marcus turned towards me, but his eyes were scanning the darkened rooftops.

"Master?"

I nodded skyward jerking my jaw line up to the rest of the roof tops around us. "Check the area. Make sure we have no more surprises tonight."

Watching Marcus carefully, his presence vanished briefly into the ether, metaphysically was rather a turn on. His eyes sparked crimson when he was done and back to himself. "Clear."

"Now, Haley." I peeled the pup's face from off my throat and gently stroked the back on my fingers down the side of his cheek. "You know better than I do that this is what happens when packs fight for territory. One pack wins; that's us. One pack loses; that's them. Now, the only difference in this scenario is that the territory we were fighting over is you." He tightened his arms around me and whimpered.

"Should we kill the last pup over there?"

The smaller Lycan in question heard that and started crying as he backed himself in a corner. He was young. Very young.

"But I need to send a message to your bitch of a grandmother. Well, the first pack that X took out was a message, but Britta ignored it. This one, she can't. She won't. I won't allow it." I hooked a finger under Haley's collar and peeled him off me. His golden eyes seemed brighter with unshed tears.

"Subjugate that pup, Haley. You are a part of Xavier's house now and this was a direct attack against him. You claim to be X's Zsigmond." I looked down at the diamond studded X hanging from his collar. "Brother has even given you an expensive tag marking you as his."

I stepped around behind Haley and made him look down at the Lycan I killed. "I need you to send Britta a message. You need to hammer it home on that little pup. When you are done, I'll let him go. If you can't, I'll have to kill him."

I traced the silver scar on Haley's shoulder from the branding his own grandmother had ordered. "They are not your pack anymore. They ceased to be when they burnt your flesh and sent you running to be hunted out in the woods. They had their chance to kill you, Haley Dennings of Von Drachenfeld, they failed. My brother has taken you into his House and, whether you are weak or strong, his pack will not desert you."

The little Lycan looked up at me uncertainty in his eyes. "Who are you?"

Marcus came up and draped himself across my back. I reached up behind me bringing his head forward to rest on my shoulder. "Tell him, Puppy."

"This is Azrael, First of Assassins, also known as the Angel of Death. He is the Lord Emperor's younger brother." Marcus nuzzled against the side of my head so I pushed back against him.

"You are not Master." Haley looked at me then leaned in and took a sniff at my neck. "You smell like him but you're not."

Marcus extended his hand like a boy would when meeting a strange dog. Haley snuffled him. "You're not Armor." It was a statement of fact not an inquiry.

I introduced my light of my life. "This is Marcus." Tilting my head back so I could look into those warm brown eyes, "You belong with me. Right?"

"Yes, Master." Marcus said it so naturally it made my stomach all buttery inside.

Haley's forehead was furrowed and he stared at us knowing there was something different, not seeing it but still knowing something wasn't right. I used my index finger to clean more blood off my blade and offered it back to Marcus. He sucked my finger into his mouth swirling his tongue around my digit, cleaning all the Lycan blood off it. "Can you taste individual essence?"

"No."

"Me neither." I turned my attention back to X's shivering pup. "Do I kill him, or will you subjugate him, Haley?"

I was a little taken aback when Haley snarled. "Kill him, Azrael. His pack as been defeated. He will be torn to shreds if he goes back. He is too young to try and survive on his own. With his pack defeated, he would never be allowed to join another."

Marcus stood upright, well as upright as he got. "Could he be absorbed into ours?"

I found that kind of funny to refer to the family as a pack. Better than a pod. Haley shook his head again. This time when those topaz eyes met mine there was a spark of determination there. It was easy to

177

forget how much dedication he had to defy his pack leader then run for his life for so long. "You are the enemy. You decimated his pack. He would never accept you as his Alpha. He would try and kill you the first chance he got."

Haley turned his gaze away from me and stared at the shaking pup across the way. "I'll do it."

Claudius approached from the end of the alley when all of a sudden he coalesced into view through the paleness of his face and hands. There was a reason he was called the Black Death among other things. It was rather freaky how he could blend into the shadows. I had to get him to show me how he did that. "A cleaning team is on its way. We should be moving quickly. It is never too good to stay in an alley with so many bodies."

I nodded in agreement. "I thought X would just burn the carcasses?"

Claudius shook his head negatively. "We need to limit the burning, Azrael. You've heard what the Doctor's have said. Your metabolism gets kicked into high gear every time Xavier does a burn. That is placing a lot of stress on your system. It is best to keep everything low key until the Doctor's can find an effective treatment."

I stroked Haley's hair. "You need to do it then pup. Be merciful even though they wouldn't have shown us the same regard."

Haley nodded and began stripping off what was left of his clubbing gear. "Your hunting clothes are ruined, Master." I looked down at the former white leather kilt and white mirco fiber tee. I looked like I was in the front row of a messy performance freak show and was now blood splattered. Damn it. I guess there had been enough blood to make a mess.

"You looked hot in them. An angel on the dance floor. White on White." Marcus buried his face in my hair catching strands in his mouth. "You taste different now, a warm spice kick."

"Ssh, Puppy. Keep a brain cell on X's pup. I don't want to push him too far. Tell me if he can't do it."

Haley changed back into a grey wolf. The pup stalked toward the younger Lycan who had shifted back into its form, lowering himself to

178

submission -- rolling over on his back, extending his throat. I leaned back into the warmth of my Marcus. Haley refused the pup's offer of submission. There was a growl and then an all out dog fight...or wolf fight ensued. X fought to get loose as soon as the sounds reached my ears. He almost dropped me to my knees. Marcus changed his hold and dragged me back to his chest. *We didn't start this, Big Brother.*

Stop him. I could feel Xavier's distress for the pup. He really could be a bastard but there was that marshmallow inside that might be the end of us one day. But it wouldn't be today.

Those Lycan are coming for him. They will keep coming for him. Let him stand on all fours.

He's just a pup.

He's older than you, brother. How many have you killed?

It's not the same. I could tell that Xavier was getting frustrated with my off hand attitude. However, this incident would affect everyone.

There was a sharp bite of anger when I snapped back at him. *He's a Lycan. A werewolf. Tell that to your sister's dead husband.*

Shut up. That was low. A big sigh echoed around me in the darkness.

I started again this time with a little bit more evenness in my tone. *Xavier... let Haley grow. His own grandmother sentenced him to death. He is exiled from his kind. He will never mate. Killing is natural to him...it should be. This might be as close to being a true Lycan that he gets.*

There was a long pause before Xavier spoke again. *I don't want him hurt.*

I cast my gaze across the alley easily making out the two feral forms in the night. *That little pup won't offer any resistance, he won't even defend himself. Haley's doing him a favor now because he won't survive without his pack. Dominate Haley when he's done. He's going to need it. I'll let go when it's over, X. Don't listen if you can't handle it.*

The alley fell silent. I looked over at the spot where the last Lycan had been. A form the size of a large dog lay still on the dirty, trash strewn concrete. Haley was naked on his hands and knees leaning over

179

the corpse. He was shaking and staring down at his first kill. X was just beside himself.

I laid my hand on the warm, strong forearm beside me. "Brother's coming out. You know how much he likes you, Marcus."

His grip tightened on me. "One more day."

I turned my head and kissed my puppy long and hard. "One more day. Get Armor. We need to secure the area and get the hell out of here."

I felt the shift to Armor and I let go, feeling X breeze passed me. *Haley, come here.*

The pup was still over the wolf corpse. *HALEY!*

He popped his head up. Blood was caked on his face, around his mouth, chin and nose. His chest was smeared as well. Even though the distance between us was more than a human could easily see them, I saw the glistening trail of tears streaming from his eyes. It cut a gruesome mask of clean on his bloodied face. Quick and merciful. Haley could have drawn out that pup's death as revenge for the killing of his friend Derry, but that wasn't in this pup's heart. I lifted my arms in wide welcome silently offering him a home. He bounced over his fallen brethren faster than I expected and was glad Armor was backing me up because Haley hit me full force. I grabbed onto him and returned the strength of his hug. He began crying in earnest. I brought my hand up and cradled his head against me. "It's all right, pup. It's all right."

Armor tightened his hand on my shoulder...wait! Marcus leaded over and whispered in my ear. "We're not alone. Left corner, upper roof. Lycan...a strong one, an old one."

Well crap. What the hell was that saying? A good defense is a strong offense? Well I could be offensive. "It's not nice to crash a party then not introduce yourself." I called out loudly.

The Loyal turned and located the interloper.

A voice deep and rich came back. The pitch was Barry White, low and smoky but it matched the hulking silhouette that stood up on the roof. "It's not every day, I see a Lycan as a pet to a coven of vampires."

180

"Pod." Haley sobbed into my neck. I held him tightly to me. This strange Lycan didn't need to see all the blood on my pup.

"Sssh, pup. Get behind Armor." I pushed him back so I could face our new guest full on. "Why don't you come on down and join us."

"I think it's safer for me to stay where I am."

"Now what are you going to do?"

"What can I do, the pack was young, stupid and trespassed in clearly marked vampire feeding ground. I was sent to gather them up, but I am too late. What are you doing with the carcasses?"

Claudius stepped forward, "We will clean the area."

"We can clean up after our own."

"As you pointed out, this is a clearly marked Vampire zone."

"It would be a sign of good faith…"

"The pack attacked first." I had enough.

And who did they attack that that pack needed to be totally decimated. They should have been taught a lesson then sent on their way. This was asked in Lycan and directed at Haley.

As you said, this is well defined territory and those pups weren't just out looking for a little bit of harmless fun. I returned in Lycan.

I could feel the surprise of the unknown Lycan. "There is only one group of Vampires that would have a Lycan pup as a pet. The ones that killed the Elder's Alpha pack." He returned in Lycan. *Our Den Mother wants him back.*

Britta threw him away. I found him. He's my Zsigmond now.

That silenced the stranger. I guess the offering of *Zsigmond* was a pretty big deal. A very big deal based on the amount of anger that was rising off him.

This Johnny come lately snarled down in Haley's direction. *How dare you offer up that sacred oath to a Vampire!*

I'm not just any Vampire. I growled back at him. *Tell your Den Mother, that Haley is mine now. He wears my collar. I will not tolerate any more actions toward him. This little party is nothing compared to what I will do to any other Lycan that comes against my House. Now speak human; you're in my territory.*

181

"Who the hell are you?" The Lycan's voice held more than just a touch of annoyance and anger. It seemed that Lycan emotions didn't need to be tempered or reined in. I knew exactly where I stood with him.

"Who are you? You're the interloper here." I returned not so emotionally controlled because my insides were quivering -- with more horror, probably, than rage. Azrael did what had to be done.

"Bruce, Alpha of the Northern Pack. And you, Vampire?" Alpha...not an Alpha pack. So did this mean that he was Britta the Elder's right hand mutt? Okay, so that should mean Bruce should be talking to my right hand man.

I nodded my head up to the rooftop. "Claudius, can you tell Bruce of the Northern Pack, who I am?"

I watched as Father stepped out of the crowd of Loyal to stand alone before me. I'm sure that the symbolism wasn't lost on our dark hulking shadow. "You are addressing Xavier Von Drachenfeld, Lord Emperor of the Vampire Nation."

There was silence again. "So, it's true. The Blood Emperor has returned. Do with them what you will." Bruce gestured at the body parts still littering the alley.

"Stupidity is not rewarded in the Lycan Pack." Bruce called out to Haley. "Any message you want to send home."

"I'm already home." Haley returned strongly. Bruce had nothing to say to that.

"I will deliver your message to Britta. Do you know what happened to the Alpha pack that were trying to retrieve Haley?"

Claudius held up two fingers. "There were two pups - Haley and Derry."

"Of course..."

Claudius laid it out plain and simple. "The Alpha Pack were killed."

There was a long pregnant pause before Bruce started speaking again. "By which group?"

"Why would you want to know?"

"Their names would be recorded in our histories as valiant foes. It is not often our highest pack is taken down in its entirety."

Claudius crossed to me. "This might not be the best thing to do, Xavier. You have already been warned off about getting involved in Lycan affairs."

The asphalt of the alley was slick with dark pools, and bits and body parts were strewn across the way. I was already involved in Lycan affairs. "Do you think it might get me a meeting with Britta?"

"It would definitely get her attention, possibly not in a good way."

"The option here Claudius is, do I go big, or do I go home? I'll take your advice."

Claudius paused. Even in the deepest shadows, I could see those cool calculating wheels a-spinning in his noggin. "Tell him. Go big, Little Blue."

I don't know how imposing I can be drenched in blood while still wrapped in a once white leather kilt and vacuum-formed micro tee shirt. "You want a name to record into your histories. You can write down Xavier."

"You! Alone?" The disbelief in Bruce's tone was rather insulting.

"They trespassed. They killed mercilessly on my territory. I would have two pups in my care now, as it was, I was late and lost Derry. I will not fail Haley...ever."

This time the Lycan's tone was a little less incredulous, but only by a smidge. "You, Lord Emperor, killed six battle hardened two hundred pound plus males."

"Yes, I did." Gesturing to the carnage scattered around me, "I killed these here as well."

"Is it wise to make an enemy of the Lycan Blood?" Bruce offered me a genuine warning.

"As long as the Lycan continue to attack me and mine, there will be death between us."

"I have no doubt you will be hearing from Britta. Losing fifteen Lycan to a single Vampire is something that cannot be ignored." Bruce shifted and began to move back to the crest of the roof.

I called after him. "Sixteen. Haley will not be returning. Seventeen, Derry will definitely be not returning."

183

"Seventeen it is. By your leave, Lord Emperor. We will meet again." I watched the hulking shadow bound away over the roof tops.

Finally Marcus gave us the all clear, "He's gone."

I was shivering internally. Holy crap. Crap, crap, crap. "Everybody back to the cars. We're getting the hell out of here. Father, I want some of the Loyal with you."

"Not necessary, Lord Xavier."

"This is not a request, Father. None of us wanders alone until Britta and I get some stuff hammered out." Claudius paused for a moment then nodded.

I turned and saw Haley hanging on to Marcus. The big guy was hunched forward a bit and crouching slightly to give Haley a good purchase to hang onto. "Thank you for your assistance, Marcus."

"Do you know how you speak Lycan, Xavier?" There was a hesitation in his voice almost as if he wasn't going to say anything but decided to face the dragon.

"It's a surprise to me that I'm speaking it at all."

Marcus vaguely gestured in the air towards me. "There is like a small stream of light, not continuous, that you seem to draw on when you speak to the Lycan. It is almost like you are reading their mind, or their soul. It's almost as if a faint tendril reaches out for you. Actually everyone here has these faint...spikes of light and they pull toward you. It is almost as if you are a magnet."

"So I'm magically learning languages?"

Marcus nodded once. "Speak to Haley in Lycan."

I rumbled at my tawny haired pup. He whined and twisted reaching out for me. I gathered him close to me inside my personal bubble and hugged him tight. He was trembling.

"It did not do it for him. Maybe once you get the language down with an individual you have it retained. You should search out other Bloods and see if you can pick up their language."

A Loyal called out to me. "Cleaners are here."

"Head out!" I didn't have to yell. Everyone seemed to be hanging on my every word.

184

Marcus faded back into whatever they called their separation and Armor stepped up, gathering Haley up in a bridal pose. "Sleep little pup. You did well. Your Master is proud of you."

"I have to protect, Master."

"This is what our pack does. If someone is in need, we help out each other. You are weak right now, so I will step in and protect, Master. Rest, the danger is over." Armor walked past me, "Come, Little One. Let the cleaners do their job."

I waited until the cleaners began to pick up bodies. The first one they picked up was Haley's first kill. How did the night get so fucked up? It was just supposed to be some nibbles and dancing. I pinched the bridge of my nose as I felt a headache coming on. Can't anything be easy?

I sat in the limo with a whole pile of Father's wet thingies and wiped the blood off of Haley's face. He was still shaking but not as much as before. I tilted his head to the left and to the right to make sure that I got all the visible splatter. I ripped my shirt off and gestured for him to get rid his. He stripped off his bloody shirt and I helped him into my less marked one. He whimpered low in his throat…so low I doubt Armor heard it. I opened my arms and he crawled up on the seat and buried his face in my neck.

Armor picked up all the bloody bits and pieces laying on the floor and shoved them in a plastic garbage bag. He reached out and dragged both of us to him. It felt good to lean on him. His arm came around the pup too. Haley shifted slightly so he could bring his arm around Armor's waist.

"Sex and Claudius should have won."

I patted his head. "Hey, I didn't think we were so bad."

"You were…something to strive for. Sex and Claudius were something to be lusted after. You were ripped off."

185

"It was just a contest."

Haley sighed and leaned heavily against me. "It's the way of the world. You do something good…you get punished for it. I didn't mean to get you in trouble, Master; Sensei."

"You may not know it, but I'm always in trouble, Pup."

"Grandma will send out the female Alphas now. She will tell them I am held against my will and they will rip your house to shreds…even the tall thin human."

Armor stroked my hair and said nothing, just providing that silent block of strength we both needed. I spoke comfortingly. "You are mine now, Zsigmond. You are part of my House, a part of my Family. I will fall before they get to you."

"And I will make sure that they don't get close to you to begin with, Little One." Armor rumbled from his chest.

The limo ride home was short. The elevator ride was shorter still. Haley paused outside my bedchamber. I dragged him in with us to get a quick shower. I watched red swirl down the drain; we had gotten bloodier than I thought. I quickly stripped and pulled on my purple pj bottoms. Armor got into his champagne silk pjs. I gave the pup my pj top. I fell into the middle of my bed, Armor climbed in on my left and rested his arm against my stomach, his fingers dipping slightly under my draw string. I yipped lightly at Haley. He climbed on the bed and settled in my arms. I folded him close to me.

He cried himself to sleep in my arms.

"You should be a father, Little One. Hades stole that. I will never forgive him."

I leaned back and rested my head in the hollow between Armor's shoulder and arm. "Don't go looking for trouble, Pretty. There's a freight train coming our way as it is." I closed my eyes as his lips dusted my temple. Jeez, I had to go to work in the morning. Nothing like a healthy dose of hemlock to kick-start my day.

Chapter Twelve: A Proposal

I hung on to Haley, matching the strength he used to hold his body against mine until he drifted off to sleep in my bed. My big sex monkey was snoring into the back of my head but his hand was on my stomach: his thumb would stroke my skin occasionally; it was comforting. I closed my eyes. Again, we all could have died tonight.

Thank you, Azrael.

Azrael's voice was gruff and he was still hanging around the veil that separated who was in control. *You know you can count on me, Elder brother. We both know you couldn't have done it.*

I wasn't about to argue with him. *No, I couldn't have.*

No more talk of me being expendable. His tone was hard and cool.

He was holding a grudge. I did owe him an apology. *You pissed me off when we were trapped in the Darkness. Sex looked like he had dragged his sorry beaten ass across hundreds of miles to get to us and you attacked him like an owl on a wounded mouse. He couldn't even defend himself...but there was no call for me to get on you like that.*

So give me more face time with Marcus.

You know...

Fifteen minutes early. That's all I'm asking.

All right.

Go to sleep, you're exhausted, X. You can handle this.

Haley whimpered in his sleep. I shifted and curled around him and he snuggled back against me. I laid the side of my face on the pillow and breathed into his hair. Relaxing an inch at a time until....

I was on that goddamn beach again. Fuck!

I scrambled to my feet searching for the elusive Mr. L. That's when I noticed I wasn't naked. I had on surfer baggy shorts and a bright multi-patterned Hawaiian shirt. A ratty canvas hat with a floppy brim that would hang over my eyes lay on the sand where I had woken. Apparently, Liam wanted something other than a fuck toy today.

There was a touch of humor in that gravelly voice. "You are not a fuck toy, Little Lord Emperor."

I pivoted on the sand and stared at the most garish looking tacky tiki hut I have ever seen. It made the Hawaiian shirt I had on look like it had been washed 80 times and faded to pastel. The white haired giant was sprawled out on a beach lounge and was dressed just like me...or probably more accurate, I was dressed like him. He held up a coconut with some fruit and a couple of straws sticking out of it, topped off with a little decorative drink umbrella. "Grab a seat, little Lord Emperor. We need to talk."

I bit back what I wanted to say, which was – "what the fuck do you want, you lying manipulating son-of-a-bitch." I snagged the hat off the ground and trudged over toward the plastic monstrosity that seemed like commercialism at its worst as it sat hunched over in the sand. "What is this?" I gestured toward the hut and then my outfit.

"My way of greeting you. You don't like?" If this...scenario was an attempt at an apology over the last time I ended up here, Liam was far from being sincere.

"What's not to like?" And, oh yes, there was a day-glo orange plastic palm tree beside the hut, aglow with blinking white fairy lights. I was wrong. You could take this even further into tackyville. And everyone hated my bowling shirts?

He raked me over with his piercing eyes which told me my sarcasm wasn't appreciated. "You know I could have just brought you here, left you naked and pinned you to the sand with my naked body. I can still do it, if that is what you prefer."

I took the coconut from his hand and flopped down into a matching lounge. I didn't have a natural knack for diplomacy so I figured I might as well do my usual bull-in-china-shop routine. Straight forward and to the blunt point of the matter. "I've got to work in the morning. So can we make it quick?"

"This won't take long." Liam leaned back on the lounge and covered his eyes with his hat. "Or do you want to play Lycan and Master? Guess which one you would be."

"Pass."

"Don't pout, Xavier. It ruins your stunning looks."

I stared down at the drink then shook it from side to side. "What the hell is this?"

"You need work on your language, Lord Emperor. I can understand your need to reach out to the common vampire, but please…good grammar and wording is a must. That..." he nodded at the coconut "is whatever you decide to make it. I mistakenly told you last time that you were a helpless human here. You have proven that you are not. Make your drink whatever you want it to be."

"I really need to be sleeping now."

"Your body will be refreshed when you are returned to your regular time frame as long as you behave here." Liam made a big production out of drinking from his coconut then lying back as if recovering from its orgasmic effect. Drama Queen.

"I'm not having sex with you." Might as well lay it out in the open right away.

"I haven't asked you to. You are so twitchy, relax. I can hardly remember a time when you weren't twitchy, or rather stressed, all the time. Take this moment to relax and recharge."

Liam presented me a pose of complete and utter relaxation but if I believed that, I would buy a bridge in Brooklyn first chance I got. Even with a straw hat over his face I could feel his gray eyes burrowing into me. I stared at the coconut and wished for a pina colada. I took a sip. Damn that was good.

When I was twitchy all the time? Ah… "Well Mr. L, apparently you've been around me for a while."

He raised his hat to face me. "Ah you remember. Yes, I've been around you since you were conceived." Mental shudder. I set the coconut down, nestling it firmly into the sand so it wouldn't tip over.

"If you could have had your way I guess, I wouldn't even exist."

"If I could have, I would have possessed you in the womb. Your soul would have been sent to another newborn. You would exist somewhere in the world, little Lord Emperor but not as the person you

189

are now. You would have had different parents, a different life; a less stressful future should have been what awaits you in the years to come. Your life would most likely be a little less dramatic."

"Shoulda, coulda, woulda."

The big man gave out a loud sigh. "Xavier...you push when you should yield. I would have thought that the first thing out of your mouth would be - What do you want?"

I obliged. "What do you want?"

"Conversation."

"I figured that out when I wasn't naked."

"You are such a delight. Lay back and enjoy the sun."

"It's not real?"

"Of course it isn't real. We'll both be shriveled husks of vampires...well you would, I've got solar immunity. Sssssh...lie back and relax for a bit, just pretend that this is real for now. Honestly, your life is more enjoyable to watch than TV." He kicked off his sandals, crossing his ankles.

I laid down as suggested, or more like...ordered, picking up my coconut drink and resting it on my chest. I don't know where the hell we are but I know I can only manipulate a hair's breath of it compared to what the jerk next to me can do. I'd beaten him last time because I caught him off guard. I was pretty sure he was more than ready for any of my tricks this time. I was there until he sent me home. I grabbed my hat and plopped it over my eyes.

It wasn't real...but it felt good. I missed the sun. Not the burn. Definitely not the burn-to -a-crisp death but the physical warmth, the sun on my face, radiating red through my eyelids, the over all drowsiness of lying in the sun soaking up the rays. That's one thing I noticed about being a vampire, well aside from the sun suddenly becoming the enemy, but the lack of heat. A chill was always hovering around the corner. It was still comfortable but there was a possibility of it going arctic. But then again, that was before the Phoenix wings. I pulled my shirt off and leaned back into the pleasure of faux sunbathing. Liam was going to do, what Liam was going to do. The best I could do, if he started something, was stab him in the eye with my drink's decorative umbrella fruit pick. Drinkers beware. I relaxed with a low groan.

I must have been in stasis. I don't think you can sleep, while you are sleeping. Maybe you can, I don't know. Or it could be that when you were sleeping in this world, you were really awake in the real world or was it that I was sleeping in the real world or...was I in a coma again? Could that be what was giving me a headache? I lifted my hand to pinch my nose and hit something. Ah, not something, but some-fricking-one, Liam was leaning over me blocking out the faux sun while intently staring down at me. My hat was gone and he was stroking my long red hair. "You are so frail...yet you have created your empire so quickly."

Huh? I blinked at him. My empire? *What you talking about Willis?*

"You have a devoted army at your fingertips. That Loyal you redeemed last night, will do anything for you. He would have gladly died in your service. He'll die for YOU now. You have Generals in your lovers. You have allied with the Hellcat Nation. They are savage hunters and killers, yet they are lining up for you to take their essence. You have a member of the House of the Yellow Moon of the Lycan Nation as your personal body guard. A royal male at that. And, you have done this without my help. You are truly remarkable, Xavier Von Drachenfeld. May you reign from now until eternity." There was a hint of something in Liam's voice. What? Awe? Admiration?

He slipped off the lounge and elegantly lowered himself into reverent pose. Even bent over, he was bigger than me. I stared up at him stunned, this was kind of scary, this creature of darkness, of promised future chaos was bowing to me. I think I would rather have been naked and fighting him off me. He lifted his head, his gray eyes level with mine.

"I want Cillian with me, little Lord Emperor."

"What does this have to do with me?"

"Cillian is powerful. Too powerful for the Vampires around here. He is still too powerful for you."

"You are not joining with me."

He reached out and caught me by the back of the hair. "Were you listening the last time we spoke?"

He flicked my nipple ring. "Your soul is already merged. No, this would be simple possession. With your permission, I would take over your body and give you the strength to take him down. I need physical form to do this. He will not come to me willingly. I fear I have hurt him too much this time. It will take years to coax him back to me. Until then, I will have to hold him by force. I will have to have his body protected while I have him on this plane. You would be an able caretaker. I would return here with Cillian. He will love me again, I'm determined that it will be so; I just need to get him here first."

"What guarantee do I have that once you have Hades that you would leave me alone?"

"Have I lied to you?"

"You've manipulated me from day one." I reached up and pushed at his arm. He resisted for a moment then allowed me to get his hand out of my hair. "Why did you disappear when I needed you most as a kid?"

Liam rose up and gingerly sat himself on the edge of my lounge. He leaned over me blocking the sun, resting one huge hand beside my head, "I accidentally told you something that someone of your young years shouldn't have known, I had hoped that you would forget but you were way too intelligent for your years and one day you mentioned it to your father. Your human Hunter father figured out that your imaginary friend was not so imaginary and set up wards and spells of protection around you. They were designed to keep my energy from you. Those spells ended when Claudius' broken child…"

I really hated it when my lover was referred to as strange or special or broken. "You mean Armor and Marcus."

Liam nodded his head in acquiescence. "Yes, when Armor and Marcus turned you. The spells of your childhood were broken but that Battle Mage still managed to bar me from direct contact. I kept watch over you but I still could not contact you. What I was able to do did keep those away who sensed the dormant blood line within you, Little Lord Emperor until you were finally able to protect yourself."

192

He reached out and touched my upper arm. His fingertips traced the spot where I had been clawed. "One Lycan got past me."

The scars from that mauling were gone now, healed by my first Healing Light as a newly formed vampire. But for the longest time, I lived in fear of the dark, of the moon, of going outside...of everything. Nine years old and terrified beyond my wits. Too young to realize that real monsters lived in my world. Too young to know that Mom and Dad killed the things that attacked others. Nine years old and everyone expected me to be so strong...wait a minute.

"Did you say I got mauled by a Lycan?"

"Your Mother killed it."

"I thought it was a dog."

"It was a Lycan."

"Why was there a Lycan on our property?"

"I'm not omnipotent as you so violently pointed out on your last visit. That is a question you will have to ask your Father.

"Claudius? What would he know about...eep!"

Suddenly Liam's face was right up in mine as his hand tightened on my hair at the nape of my neck. "Stop being so cute. I have been without my Honey Bee for centuries and I am at my limit." Liam snuffled in my hair. "Nothing. You are lucky you aren't scent marked by him."

"Why am I here now, Liam?" I pulled my arm away from his touch.

"My Cillian..."

"Hades."

"You can give him to me. It would free your broken brother. It would free your Father."

I glared at him, "You're not possessing me."

"You cannot beat him, little Lord Emperor. He's far too strong."

"Hemlock is his curse. I'm assuming his natural essence is honey."

Liam nodded.

"How did you do it?"

"Gradual build up over decades."

"You systematically poisoned your son."

"My lover…my love."

"That's selfish."

Liam sat up and stared out across the sea. His long white hair fluttered from under his beach hat. "A candle that burns twice as bright burns half as long, little Lord Emperor. The vampiric body I was in was failing. I was already past my prime in that form when I found Cillian. I hung on as long as I could to stay with him. He was a total innocent. He was absolutely pure. He was acknowledged as my Royal Consort but he was young, barely able to control his fangs and when my time in that physical form was over he would be defenseless. So I tried to protect him from beyond the grave by giving him unusual strength and that physical warding, the essence of Hemlock to make him untouchable."

Liam turned and sat on the sand, his fingers dropping to the beach then allowing the fine grains to seep back down. "My essence burns my host quickly. I can average two hundred to two hundred and fifty years per vampiric body. Those times together, my Honey Bee and I were happy, Xavier. I would die, leave him until a suitable host was conceived or discovered and I would rejoin him…"

Liam slapped his hands together brushing the sand off. "Sigmund was a disaster, as you know. He only had a daughter and his daughter had daughters and more daughters and more daughters. While I waited for you, Xavier, my Honeybee changed. He's gotten hard and cold. I never meant to sentence him to such loneliness. When I return, I remove the protection I placed on him, however he's had it now for almost four hundred years. My protection, my love has turned into a curse. He doesn't deserve this."

If Liam, the color challenged giant, was expecting sympathy from this little baring of souls he was mistaken. "Claudius didn't deserve Hades. Sex doesn't deserve him either. How many others has your precious Honey Bee fucked over?" I let my anger fill my voice. "As you said, I'm sterile. Your Honey Bee fucked the royal line over. That means, you fucked yourself over. There will be no more Blues to suck souls from."

"There is a way, little Lord Emperor." He continued to stare out to sea ignoring my outburst.

I stilled. "What?"

"It would be a one time thing. If I have a host, if I...become one you on this plane, you will take my pure immortal essence into you and carry it to the real world." Liam turned and leaned back over me. His finger came up and traced the side of my face, "In the physical world, you will have one try to have children. It can not be sperm in a cup, my potency will dissipate quickly so it will have to be deposited in the tried and true way. If you want a child, you will have to have sex with the Baroness."

"What do you mean, Host?"

His finger traced my lips. His gray eyes gazed down at me indulgently, "I would share with you. Just you Xavier. The brothers will have to go."

"What?"

"I would merge you back into a single being, Xavier. Then I would have the room to live within you. The sensation would be like you share now with your brothers."

"NO."

"You were born as one. You came to the Blood as two."

I jerked my head away. "NO fucking way, I'm not dumping my brothers, they saved me and kept me sane and safe whenever I needed them. And you want me to thank them by destroying their existence in me just so you can take...fricking Honey Bee to your own personal love nest and have make-up sex for however long it takes to win him back?"

Liam climbed to his feet. I scrambled off the lounge and tensed ready to defend myself. "You cannot win against my Honey Bee."

"Don't know until I try and if I have to, I'll figure out how to make it all of us brothers against one asshole teenager."

"Stubborn. Go back to sleep, little Lord Emperor. Oh, give up the pup. Britta is an old she wolf but don't mistake her fragility with weakness. She only needs to blink and Vampires die. You do not need a war with the Lycans before you even take over the Vampire Nation. Don't fight a war you don't have to."

195

"Haley stays. Unlike you…I don't abandon my family."

His moved so fast I didn't see him. He wrenched me by my red hair and jerked my head back. "Don't push me, little Lord Emperor. Remember, if I keep you here, you don't wake up in your world. If I kill you here, you die in your world."

I matched gray eye to green eye stare. There was enough distain in my voice to let Liam know that I wasn't impressed. I was scared but not impressed. "So you're telling me that if you fuck me here I'll have kids if I jump on the Baroness as soon as I get back. Does that line ever work or am I privileged?"

He dragged me forward like a rag doll and pressed a kiss to my forehead. "It's not a lie. It is an offer of atonement. It's on the table. The decision is yours. Go."

I closed my eyes.

A groan reached my ears. Wait that was me. A spike of pleasure ripped through my body. Opening my eyes and glancing down, a tawny toned head was suckling at my nipples as one hand stroked my hardening erection. What the fuck? Haley?

"Pup….uuuuuuh. What are you doing?"

"Preparing you, Master." Haley makes hard suck kisses on my sensitive nubs. I arched off the bed with the sensation he was ripping through me. I clenched my fists into the bed sheets and turned my head, gritting my teeth. The pup learns fast. Oh my….uuuuuhhhh.

"Haley….Haaaleeeey…."

"Please dominate me Master. Protect me."

I closed my eyes and shivered as his lips began trailing down to my erection. There was still a quiver in his voice. I brought one hand down to stroke his hair.

Haley whispered. "I was having a nightmare, reality is so much better."

Armor caught my free hand pressing into the mattress; he leaned over me, kissing my temple. Haley settled back on his haunches then regarded his sensual sensei as if asking permission to continue. "You are doing good, Pup. You want me to help you, or just watch?'

"Help me, please Sensei."

Holy….help me please, Sensei. Armor slid behind me, propping my back to his chest and set his chin on my shoulder. His brown hair hung forward tickling my arm and chest. Haley took me in his mouth. I gasped in surprise then pleasure as Haley showed me how Lycans get their groove on. I panted with mounting pleasure. Armor started scanning the band with my nipples, tweaking and twisting with just the right amount of pressure to make me crazy with lust. I think I shrieked. My body arched backwards until my head rested on his shoulder, turning my head, his neck was right there.

I remembered the taste of him from Azrael's bite at the club. Why was I denying myself? I dropped fang. I brought my free hand up pulling his head forward. Armor resisted for all of one or two seconds then I scraped his flesh with my fang. He did that porn star hair flip, giving me direct access to that pulsing vein that ran down the side of his neck. I sniffed along his neck, ahhhh, the scent of my orchard. I opened wide and bit him gently but deep.

He was apple cider. I let his blood pool on my tongue, slowly fill my mouth. I swallowed. His hand came up and stroked my throat encouraging big swallows. I did it five times, starting to feel drunk on his essence.

Haley invaded my portal with his finger. I grimaced and came off Armor's neck with a gasp.

Armor growled. "Take it out, pup. You're hurting him."

"I'm sorry, Master. I'm just…"

I fumbled at the nightstand drawer. Armor shifted me a bit and I was able to drag out a tube of lube. I gasped, "Use this."

"Sensei?"

"You have Master's permission. Coat your finger. Rub around his asshole…gently. Tease him open. You can never have enough lube, pup. You can always wipe off the excess. Listen to his breathing…when you hear it change, stop or you will drive him over the edge before either of you will want him to go."

197

Listening to this was…dirty. That's it. I was naughty and dirty listening as my lover told my Lycan how to fuck me. Oh…..uuuuuhhhh. Haley was invading my ass, stroking my insides with liquid desire. His mouth returned to my cock, his tongue swirling around my head. "Can you hold it?" Armor whispered. Huh? He twisted my nipple ring. I spasmed. My hips jerked up and drove my cock deep into Haley's throat. My portal gripped his finger. It felt as my body was glowing red hot. I gave out a low throated growl. "I'll fuck you now."

The pup gave me one last sucking lick then let my cock fall from his mouth. His eyes flashed feral gold as he turned to present himself. Armor maneuvered me like a doll until I was draped over the Lycan's back. I reached for the lube. I couldn't hurt him even if he said it was fine…causing him pain just wouldn't work for me. He question yipped as I rubbed at his asshole with the slick ooze. I bit the back of his neck then pushed his shoulders to the bed. His knees opened wider; he wiggled his ass at my groin.

I took myself in hand and pressed at his opened gate. I groaned as I sank into his depths. The pup yipped back in pleasure. I began thrusting forward. Armor's hands stroked my back. His thumbs ran along my spine down to my flanks and right to my bullseye. "Oh, yah!"

I hitched forward hard into Haley as a one of Armor's digits disappeared inside me. I flipped my hair to the right. His lips came up to my ear. "X, I think you're so sexy right now. I want you. I want to be in you."

I shivered. "Haley….Sensei wants to play…" I think my eyes rolled up into my head as Armor hit my prostate.

The pup yipped back and wiggled back into my groin, forcing my cock deeper. I held onto his hips and stilled as Armor prepared to mount me. A threesome, I'd never done this before, not this way anyway. Armor must have felt my sudden tension. His lips came back to my ear. "This will be nothing but pleasure, Little One. I'll do all the driving…you stay in the passenger seat and just enjoy the view."

Driving scenario…haha…ohmygod. Ohmyfucking….. I shivered. I shuddered. I trembled. My arms gave out and I landed heavily on Haley.

Then the sex sensei started to move. A whine started at the back of my throat…a whine of intense pleasure. When Armor drove into me, I drove into the pup. When he pulled out, he pulled on my hips controlling the Lycan's fucking. I screwed my eyes closed, panting heavily. I couldn't do anything else. The sensations were overwhelming.

Yip. That was the pup. Rough translation, 'yeah.'

Yip. That was me. Rougher translation, 'oh hell yeah.'

Some semblance of sanity returned to me. I reached under the pup and caught his cock. I jacked him in time with Armor's rhythm. I don't think I did a good job of it but it didn't seem to matter to Haley. I was in the middle of a slut attack and he was reaping the benefits.

Yip. Yip.

Armor gave that hitch in his breathing. His hand transferred off my hip and twisted my nipple ring. I spasmed again. I tightened up unbearably on his shaft as I threw back my head for a deep throated howl. I jutted into the pup in five lurches then slumped forward, boneless and devoid of any coherent thought. Armor laid on my back, wrapped his hand around mine, the one that was still on Haley's cock and began stroking the Lycan to completion. His howl of fulfillment wasn't long coming either…. then the bed broke.

The upper left corner of the box springs crashed to the floor canting the bed down to the floor. Since the mattress was one of those pillow-top ones that had a princess and the pea effect so it was higher than normal from the floor, so the slant downward was acute. Armor was pitched off me. His arm was wrapped tight around my waist as he dragged me with him. Haley bounced forward ending up sprawled half off, half on the mattress. I was sprawled on my sex monkey. I catalogued the devastation, made sure everyone was intact, and then started laughing.

I don't think my bed was designed for Lycan/Vampire three-way relations.

Haley crawled off the debris field and propped his head against my stomach. I tangled my fingers in his hair. "Are you okay, pup?"

He kissed my stomach. That sent another shiver through me. "I'm taking that as an okay."

His grin was wide and pearly white. "I am good, Master. Thank you, Sensei. You dominate well."

I snorted, the combined result of snorting and chortling at the same time. Oh yeah, Armor knew his way around my body. I leaned back against him and closed my eyes in contentment.

I felt a quick kiss on my lips and looked up to see Haley crouching before me in all his Lycan human form splendor. "I will go to my room now. Thank you, Master." He took off at mach two, totally naked. A howl of satisfaction trailed along behind him.

Armor stroked my hair back off my face. "And how are you, Little One?"

"We'll just have to tell him that I would like to be awake before he starts preparing me. He needed it though. I'll let it go for today."

"Your sleep was restless."

I stilled. The bodily sensations I was subjected to make me almost forget my lovely little visit with Liam. "I have to sort some things out up here…" I tapped my temple, "before I can tell you anything, Pretty."

It was comforting to know that my big hunk of vampire seemed to instinctively gather my emotional rollercoaster and offer a stable and safe haven. "Are things that bad with Hashmallim?"

I kept my tone light. Claudia was never a good topic to bring up and I was damned if I was going to add her to the mix while we were lingering in a post-coital daze. "If I had some bones in my legs right now, I'd be running around in circles screaming. It's nothing bad…. but…"

"Work it out first then, Little One. What are we going to do about your bed?"

"You broke it, you bought it."

"I don't have any money. Besides, we broke it."

Huh? Shifting to my hip I sent him a glance over my shoulder. "What do you mean?"

Armor sat me up and wrapped his arms around my chest pulling me against him. "I told you, I came to your house with just these." He opened his empty hands. "Everything, I ever earned was in trust to the

House of Du Bussey. Even Marcus has no resources left. Technically, I'm your sex doll, X."

I got indignant. "That's not fair. You earned that money. They can't just take it away from you!"

My whole body heaved as Armor let out a huge sigh. "It was part of the sanctions by the House of Assassins. All personal accounts and investments were forfeit to pay for the damages and expenses of tracking Marcus down. Until Marcus or I start getting assignments, I must rely on your good will for shelter, food and support." Armor laid his head on my shoulder. "Just because the physical punishment is over…does not mean that the punishment is over."

"I'll get this straightened out." I don't know how the hell I was going to do it, but I would. This was more than a simple pound of flesh.

A shiver ripped down my ear canal and merged with my spine as warm lips nibbled on the curl of my ear. "I do not mind being your sex toy, Little One. It is actually refreshing to have a vacation."

"You know what? I have a job for you. Data entry into the database I set up for the Master of the Territory. You'd be able to cross reference stuff it's taking me hours to track down."

Armor stilled. "Well, technically you know it would be Marcus who has that information."

I stroked the back of his hands with my fingertips. "Well, then we use Marcus. I need to get that database up and running before the Council calls me on the carpet for shirking my duties. With everything that's been happening lately, I need to keep under the radar as much as possible. Keep Haley with you today. I'll leave some credit cards, get him a new bed. Buy him a flashy water bowl. He wants some suits. What do you want?"

"You."

Ah, the warming cockles of my heart. I leaned over and kissed him then bit his nose. "Well I'd like to shower first, but my legs don't want to work."

Bridal pose it was. Armor carried me to the shower and we proceeded to get clean, then dirty again and clean once more. He lounged naked on the cantilevered bed watching as I tied my tie. "You clean up nice, X."

"You're not too shabby yourself, Beloved."

He rolled off the mattress and caught my chin, pulling me toward him. He kissed my lips gently, lightly scraping a fang along my bottom lip. "Let me be in your thoughts today, Little One." He caught my hand and pressed it against his warm, naked flesh. "When you do, I will feel it here." He opened my palm over his heart. There still was a slight indent there from Armanita's spike.

My eyes teared up. The weepy assassin is on his way to work. "Oh yeah, Azrael is coming out early today."

Armor set me back from him. "What does that bastard want?"

"I owe him for yesterday. He's coming out at 11:45 tonight."

Armor's jaw tightened slightly but he nodded. "Thanks for the warning, Little One. You better start moving. You don't want to keep Hades waiting."

I patted Armor's ass then turned and walked out of my bed chambers. Hades wait time was just about up, anyways. Tick Tock.

Chapter Thirteen: Fucked up – Big Time

I debated all of two seconds--Hall of Records or Hades. I hopped off the elevator on the twelfth floor and scurried my ass down to the huge depository. I had a plan…well the inkling of a plan. I needed a plan or someone else was going to plan my life for me. Claudia popped into my head. She was scary--Claudius scary. The apple didn't fall far from the tree with that one.

I came through the frosted glass doors and deflected a Glock that was starting to aim into my face. I reacted without thinking. The poor security guard was down with my foot on his neck, one hand twisting his wrist back on itself and his own gun cocked and ready to end his life.

I heard running, so I yanked harder on his wrist pinning him to the tile as I twisted the Glock around and held it in the face of a startled librarian. She squawked and skidding to a halt as the barrel whacked with her forehead. Big brown eyes went cross-eyed as she stared down the dark opening of the barrel.

Her voice was a high-pitched squeak. "Oh my…apologies, First. Please let him go."

I pulled the Glock back. Her eyes rolled into the back of her head as she dropped like a stone. I let the guard go and snagged her before she smacked her noggin on the floor. I knew what the hell that felt like…far much too often. The guard held his neck and slowly sat up.

"Sorry…you surprised me." I offered up a weak apology.

"Records isn't open until nine a.m." The guard looked up from his position and I could see awareness click into place.

"I'm out of here before nine. You got somewhere to set her down; she's not as light as she looks." I can fly, I can heal, I can mind fuck someone to death, but I can't lift a medium sized girl. Someone was having a big assed laugh at my expense.

The guard pointed to a chair. I set her down then propped her up slightly when she shifted sideways. He disappeared for a moment then came back with a glass of water that he handed to me.

I looked down at it puzzled. She couldn't drink it. "What do I do with this?"

"On her face." The guard gestured at the woman.

"Are you sure?"

"Yes sir."

I threw the whole glass into her face. She sputtered and gasped.

"I meant sprinkle it on her face, idiot...uhuhh, Sir." He slapped his hand over his mouth when he realized who he just called an idiot.

I shrugged. "It worked. She's awake."

The librarian coughed and wiped at her eyes.

"Are you okay?"

"Thank you, FFF...First." She stuttered then coughed and sniffed. I don't know who was more embarrassed, the guard who was now as red as a garden ripe tomato, the woman who now resembled a wet rat or me for scaring the crap out of everyone.

Wincing slightly at the welt on the librarian's forehead, I knelt beside her. "I don't want to appear like a total ass, but I really need access to some information really, really...I mean really quickly." I opened my eyes wide and blinked at her. Please...blink, blink, blink. She got a slightly glazed look in her eyes. Wow, it worked. Mom would have just shoved me out of the way with a hand to my face if I tried that look with her. "I really need to have all the information you can find on the previous Lord Emperors."

The librarian started to speak then turned away to give the daintiest cough I have ever heard before turning back to me. That was so adorable. "Most of our database can be accessed on-line. Only the most ancient of documents are stored here. We do have those available as PDF but they are not accessible online. Normal genealogical researchers are restricting to using those materials here; however, you're the Lord Emperor. I can down load those to a flash drive."

The guard had a blank expression as the lovely librarian and I chatted. Don't let "geeks" get together 'cause we'll go off about dpi and gigs and a sundry of other things. Camilla, my bookish new wet friend, allowed me to take a minor ancient document written in the old Vampiric tongue. Who the heck knew there was a special language of the Vampires? Claudius never mentioned it. Again, the vampires I seemed to hang around with never wrote anything down, case in point that damned Master of the Territory database that was hanging over my head. So, if what Marcus said was right I just needed to show this document to someone who could read it while I did my mind fuck maneuver and I should be able to soak it up like a sponge. Downloading knowledge right to my noggin a la "the Matrix." Cool but invasive.

Camilla handed it to me in an acid free manila envelope. She said something about gloves and oil or bloody fingers ruining it and I nodded attentively. Glancing at it seemed to show that it was a simple list. As far as she knew the one who could read it was High Councillors Rothchilde and Thomas. Well, one was dead, and the other was on my don't-interact-with list. Rumors of the Empire's return didn't sit well with the current ruling class. Camilla was apologetic that she couldn't come up with other Ancient would might be able to read that list. The oldest fart I knew who might be able to decipher these glyphs was....

Ah crap, Hades.

I bowed to her and her whole face turned crimson. I kissed the hand that gave me the flash drive then pivoted on my heel.

The guard was in my way again. "I apologize for calling you an idiot, sir."

"We're even, I stepped on your neck after all. Your name?"

"Milton, First." He bowed at me. Well that was better than having him get on the floor.

"Keep her safe. I just may have pissed someone off getting this info. It'll get back here eventually. Tell them I overpowered you and I punched her in the face." Which I might as well have. She was already getting black eyes. "I'm sorry."

The guard looked over his shoulder and widened his eyes in alarm at the librarian. Okay her wet shirt was now see through. "I really am sorry." I turned away covering my eyes then narrowed my brows as the Milton continued to ogle. "Ahem."

He snapped to attention and turned away from her as well. "I'll be better prepared next time, sir."

"Good stuff." I clapped his shoulder and tucked the flash drive in my inner breast pocket then the manila envelope down the back waistband of my pants and made sure than my jacket hung smoothly over it. Safe and invisible. I glanced at my watch. I still had five minutes to get up to Hades office. I got to the elevator as a trio of white coats came running up to me.

"Lord! First!" What? I turned and looked all innocent of any clandestine doing as the lab rats surrounded me. They were all red faced. What were they doing, running the entire building? "We've been looking for you since you signed in."

They had been running the entire building. "What can I do for you?"

"Dr. Maxwell wants to see you as soon as possible regarding your treatment." The elevator opened. I was pulled into it and they hit floor twenty.

"Why didn't you call my cell phone?"

It went off as I said that. I glanced at the display. Oh great. I flipped it open. "First."

"I am getting pretty tired of having to track down my number one, Xavier. Where are you?" His voice cracked with annoyance. I forced back a shiver. Four hundred years of puberty squeaks and pitches. If he wasn't such an asshole, I'd feel sorry for him.

"My elevator has been hijacked by the 20th floor."

"Ah, Dr. Maxwell has made a breakthrough. Come up when the good Dr. releases you."

"I need to run something by you." I could feel the hard edges of the envelope pressing into my shirt.

"Yes, I have something to discuss with you as well, Xavier. I have received an unexpected invitation."

"Got to go." I hung up. That creepy adolescent voice. I shuddered.

"Are you chilly, First?"

"Someone just walked on my grave." The lab rats looked everywhere but at me. What the hell?

The elevator doors opened, and they hung back waiting for me to exit. I stepped out and Dr. Maxwell flagged me down. The lab rats scurried out and disappeared. I frowned. What the hell was going on? The only ones not bowing and scraping to me or scurrying away from me were the librarian I cold cocked with a Glock and a security guard I made eat linoleum.

"Lord Emperor?"

"It's nothing. You were looking for me?"

"Yes, please come this way." Dr. Maxwell gestured me forward. "We have made a breakthrough."

Then one of the doc's associates proceeded to glaze my eyes as he launched into a scholarly diatribe. He nattered on about Insulin resistance and elevated levels and glucose. I really tried to follow him, but these lab rats were making assumptions that I was smarter than my kilt poster. I was, just not Mensa medicine level. There must have been an interested expression on my face because they just kept talking and throwing up medical terms of about fifteen syllables at a time. The only thing that really alarmed me was the statement that "occasionally burn patients can suffer massive organ injury and organ failure."

What?

Dr. Maxwell finally came in for the rescue. "Take these twice a day." He handed me a pill bottle.

"If you feel any swelling or have difficulty breathing or swallowing or if you faint. You call me immediately -- day or night." Dr. Maxwell handed me a card with his personal cell number on it. "Oh and stay away bananas."

"Bananas, er.... okay." Then to add to the rest of the confusion, Dr. Maxwell handed me a piece of paper with my physician approved training schedule on it. As if running wasn't a total joy to begin with, I now had to follow a Terminator body building schedule.

Dr. Maxwell tapped the schedule. "You should have come to the labs sooner, Lord Emperor. You've lost five percent of your muscle mass since we've started treating you. You need to rebuild that and maintain it."

"Now…" He cleared his throat and looked at the rest of the doctors. They suddenly found better patients to harass and disappeared down halls and through doorways. "… about that other matter. We ran the tests several times. Lord Emperor…"

My shoulders sagged. "I'm sterile."

"Yes…I am sorry." Dr. Maxwell really didn't have a convincing patient comforting vibe.

"Is it possible…?" My words trailed off. Was I really going to say this? Really?

"My lord?" The doc canted his head and peered at me.

Taking a deep breath, I blurted out. "Someone made an offer to cure my sterility."

Maxwell shook his head. "Not within modern medical possibility."

"This is more of a spiritual thing."

"That is not an area I am competent to comment on."

I nodded. "So, I take my pills, eat regularly, drink my shake and work out. Who thought being dead was so hard to maintain."

"I would like you to keep coming in regularly for monitoring once a week for at least the next six months, my Lord. You were lean to being with. You cannot afford to lose any more muscle." In my mind's eye I could see him and his lab coat cronies poking at me with sharp sticks.

"Thank you, Doctor." I offered my hand and was surprised that I received a hearty handshake.

I picked up my pills, tapped my back to make sure that my sample of ancient Vampire writing was still there and headed back out toward the elevators. So, I was a walking symptom of a burn victim. Well at least we verified what the problem was. I pushed the elevator button up. Armor was going to have fun keeping me to this the body building schedule. I really hated working out. I could just hear him, one hour lifting weights or one hour on my knees. I smirked. On my knees any day. Okay, that was not going to be an option anymore, well at least for exercising.

The elevator doors opened and there was Billy Envoy sitting there all in white yet again. I waited for the Hallelujah chorus to start but it didn't so I hopped out before the doors closed. Billy got to his feet as I stepped into the foyer. "First, Hades has asked that you wait here."

My forehead furrowed. I looked at my watch. I was only forty-five minutes late and I had the teenage bastard's permission. There wasn't another chair, so I sat my ass on the edge of Billy's desk. You think I was doing something a little naughtier the way he reacted. He sat down and gave me that 'I hate you' glare.

"You love him."

"What?" There was a moment of pure startle in his expression before he composed himself quickly.

"Hades, you actually love him, don't you?" I was just making conversation.

"I don't know what you are talking about." Billy turned his head away from me and became engrossed in a letter.

I crossed my over leg over the other then pulled my pant leg down a smidge. "I watched you in the limo that time, when Hades was playing horny toad on me. You wanted it to be you. I don't want to be his sex toy."

"Hades is a great man."

"He's not a man. He's a punk."

Billy jumped up. He was older, but I had caught up to him in strength and I surpassed him in speed. He found himself slammed back first on his desk. I had my hand on his throat as I leaned over him. He hissed up at me. "You will show your respect to your superiors."

"Didn't you hear? I'm the Lord Emperor of the Vampire Nation. Even Hades as acknowledged that." Billy tried to arch off the desk. I forced him back down hard. I matched gazes with him. "You love him."

"I…" Billy mouth gapped like a fish as he tried to compose himself.

"Tell him."

"Let me up."

I let go but stayed sitting on his desk.

Billy tucked everything back into perfect order on his desk, then sat ramrod straight staring directly ahead at a god-awful modern splatter painting. When I made no move to get off his desk he started talking.

"I've worked for Hades for one hundred and thirty years. I was only forty when I started. I don't even know when I fell for him, but he had Claudius as his partner. Claudius never loved him. He's like you, Claudius tolerated him. It makes me sick to see Hades turn to those so unworthy of him."

Billy smoothed his tie. "Hades and Claudius, if you can call it a relationship, were stormy. They would be on and off. One hundred years ago, during one of their off periods, I made my feelings known. I knew I was young and reaching beyond my abilities but one kiss from Hades put me in the hospital for six months. You're a yearling…how can you be with him?"

I didn't say it in a way that meant Billy and I were finding common bonding ground. "He put me in a coma."

"…. after he treated you like the whore you are."

Asshole! I turned and glared at him. "Like I want him."

"Hades is a brilliant mind. He can speak twelve different human languages. He can speak all the Blood languages. He is a student of history. You only need to engage in conversation with him to learn that."

Why the hell was Billy trying to sell me the cow? "Hades has no interest in 'engaging in conversation' when I show up. You've seen him."

"You are the only other one that he can touch." I thought that Billy would be screaming at me at the top of his lungs, but his voice had dropped down a low hissing whisper.

Folding my arms across my chest I kicked the front of Billy's desk with the heel of my shoe. "Harassment. That's what this is, sexual harassment."

"He's lonely." Billy's attention turned to the closed door of the inner sanctum. I didn't need mindfuck ability to see the deep yearning in his physical stance. He truly loved that little teenaged bastard. If Billy had confessed to Hades and Hades had put him in the hospital…

I narrowed my eyes and bit back the rest of the comment of why the hell was he jumping me every time I blinked my eyes? "What would you sacrifice if you could be with him?"

210

"Who?"

For some reason I wanted a cigarette right now. I snatched a pen from the desk and tapped it irritatingly on the wooden top. "Hades. Would you give up your eternal life, to have one day with him?"

Billy looked at me with absolute distain. "Why would I want to do that? That would just leave him alone again."

I pointed the pen at Billy as if I was a prosecutor winding up my argument. "How about if you could stay with him for 200 years?"

"Don't toy with me…" I could see the physical effort it took for the receptionist in white not to swear at me.

"Yes or no. Simple choice here."

"If it were possible, yes."

I shook my head. There was more than simple agreement in that 'yes.'

"I really don't understand why. Maybe Hades shows you a side of himself that he doesn't show me. Well, he only shows one side to me and that's more than what I want to deal with." I glanced over at Billy as he regarded me with suspicious eyes. "How did he get to be the dink that he is?"

"What?" I wasn't trying to keep Billy off his feet, but my changing gears was throwing him for a loop.

"I know how fucked up Marcus is, and I know why. I know how Claudius got to be where he is. I know this because I care for them and I took the time and effort to find out."

Billy wrenched the pen from my fingers and set it back strategically in the pristine order of his desk pad. "I won't follow this train of discussion any further."

"You don't know." I shrugged.

"I know."

Leaning back on one hand I swiveled so more of my leg rested on the desk top. "Well, spill it. What is this side of Hades that you know, that I don't?"

"He's over 900 years old."

"I know that."

211

"Did you know that he was a Royal Consort? He was made by a Lord Emperor."

I turned and looked at Billy. "So, we're related?"

That stopped Billy cold in his tracks.

"Who was it? I'm starting to investigate my family history. The only one I know something about is Sigmund and I'm less than thrilled to be directly related to him with everything I am finding out."

Billy closed his mouth tightly until the seam of his lips turned white with pressure.

I sighed. "It doesn't matter. I'll find it out eventually."

"Lord Emperor William. His reign was rather short, only about two hundred and fifty years but in that time, he organized the Vampire Nation into the thirteen Houses that they are today. From what I understand, before this reformation everything was based on loose clan systems who were caught up in never ending blood feuds. With the creation of the Houses, the Vampires were able to rise above the other Bloods who were still killing each other over petty differences."

"So, what happened to Hades when William died?"

Billy suddenly turned to his computer screen not even trying to look at me. "I don't know. I just know that there is something about Hades that appeals to Lord Emperors. As far as I can tell, he has been chosen as Royal Consort three times."

I grunted. Well, crap. Liam wasn't lying. He would come back and claim his Honey Bee over and over. Why the hell did Cillian allow it? Setting himself up for heart break every two hundred years must be destructive.

"William, eh? Any idea who very first the First Lord Emperor was?"

"Records are sparse, and the older ones are written in ancient glyphs that are even older than Hades. I doubt few could read it now."

I pulled out my envelope from my waistband and pulled the scrap of document out from my folder. "Glyphs like this?"

Billy's eyes widened. "Where did you get that?"

"I asked nicely to borrow it. You think Hades could read it?"

I pulled the list back out of his reaching fingers. There was no telling what Hades' little loyalista would do if he knew what I wanted it for. "This is far older than him."

"Well it never hurts to ask." So, I hoped. I tucked everything back into the snugness of my pants. "Who's in there anyway?"

Billy leaned back and crossed his arms across his chest, "A Lycan representative."

Crap. I popped up off the desk and looked at the door.

Exasperation hung around Billy's words like a shroud. "What is this, the second Lycan pack you've decimated in less than a week?"

"Er...yeah."

"You don't do anything by small degrees do you, First of Assassins?"

"It looks that way."

I tensed as the outer door to Hades office opened. Bruce, Alpha Lycan of the Northern Pack walked out flanked by two smaller Lycan. Smaller? They were almost twice as wide as me and taller than Armor. The Northern Pack knew a little bit about intimidation. Bruce paused when he laid eyes on me.

He bowed his head in my direction, "Lord Emperor. We meet again."

How do you address a Lycan Alpha? No clue. "Bruce." I returned his polite head nod.

Billy got up and pressed the elevator button. Once again, ever present and ever useful.

Bruce called out, his back to me as he waited for the elevator, "You have gotten Den Mother's attention, Xavier. I don't know if that's a good thing in your case."

"You had no clue that I worked here, did you?" I could feel the danger waves emanating back to me and the elevator doors were polished enough that I could see his telltale yellow Lycan stare reflected in them.

He turned his face sideways towards me but still didn't turn around.

"You thought you could come here and buy a contract on my life."

213

"We did not know that you were First of Assassins, Lord Emperor. And for the record it was not a contract for your life, it was for a lesson to be taught in meddling in affairs outside your concern."

"Hades turned you down. So, what now?" I wasn't crowing but Bruce was representing a pack that tried to kill defenseless pups and almost succeeded.

"There are diplomatic channels we can follow. We go to the High Council. Den Mother still wants her grandson back."

"Well then, I'll see you Tuesday."

"Tuesday, Lord Emperor?"

"That is the next time the High Council meets. I have a seat there."

There was a loud ding as the elevator announced it arrival. "You seem to be everywhere, Xavier."

"Yup, seems like it."

The elevator opened, and Bruce and his entourage stepped into the car. He turned and looked directly at me. His eyes flashed feral gold. "You are far smaller than I thought you would be, Lord Emperor."

"I'm not short."

"I never said you were. You just seem to be too small for the size of the cajones you carry around."

I really wished I had a smoke right now. "I hadn't had any complaints. If there are any problems, it's that I have too many lined up for my attention. I'm sure, as an Alpha you've had that problem."

"Yes, subordinates always seem to need reassurance."

"Dominance has to be done right for everyone to benefit. I have to keep my *Zsigmond* content."

If anything, Bruce suddenly got a little bigger at the mention of that. Just like a puffer fish blowing up at the first sign of danger. His eyes burned a deep feral gold. Yup, a *Zsigmond* was a huge freaking deal. Pup and I were going to have to have a sit down.

"See you Tuesday, Lord Emperor." He gave me a thin grin, briefly flashing fangs, nodding his head in a quick acknowledgement as the doors closed.

"Xavier, you get your ass in here right now!" Hades bellowed from his inner sanctum.

Billy turned and looked me in the eye, gave me a smirk that made me want to punch him in the fangs, which he must have seen because he returned behind his desk quickly.

I gathered up my blue bottle of prescriptions then headed into Hades office. I got further than I thought I would before I got my expected reprimand. I got to his desk before he moved and blindsided me. I saw him this time and I could have blocked but…then that would ruin the surprise.

I staggered sideways then changed direction as he slapped my left cheek. He held nothing back what so ever. I dropped to my knees. I blocked his kick with my forearms then kicked out with my right leg. He wasn't expecting any retaliation. I caught him full on the shin and he dropped on his hands and stomach. Twisting I lashed out at him again, Hades easily countered. My bells were ringing from those two slaps. I shook my head. That gave him enough time to end up sitting on my chest with a hand around my neck. I stilled.

"I have NEVER met anyone like you before." His usually well coiffed flippy do was all over the place, curls in disarray, hanging in his eyes. But his eyes burned with anger. "I can't turn around without hearing what else you or your brothers or your lovers have done. Xavier. Stop it and sit still for a while."

The pressure on my throat let up so I took it as my chance to try and offer up my side of the story. "That pack started it. I offered to let them go."

"What are you still doing with that Lycan pup anyway? A royal pup at that? The Den Mother's grandson!"

"She threw him out with the trash. He's mine now."

"Give him back."

"No, he doesn't want to go back to the Lycan."

Hades tightened his grip on my jaw then rattled my head against the floor for a few heartbeats then stood up. He looked down at me with an unreadable look in his eye, "You are one stubborn ass. Lycan relations

215

are not that stable. We work under an uneasy truce. Your shenanigans are jeopardizing that Accord. As it is there is a renegade group of Vampires running around out there slaughtering werewolf safe houses."

"I know." When Hades stepped over me I slowly sat up.

He turned and glared at me. "What was that?"

"I know what those vampires look like. I got their faces from the first Alpha pack I killed." I could tell Hades was upset from his Lycan visitation because after knocking me around, he didn't yank the elastic out of my hair.

"When were you going to share that tidbit, First?"

"I didn't know I had to."

Hades walked back to his desk and pulled out a pack of smokes. Agitation? What the hell could shock the oldest vampire? I guess the oldest Lycan. Hades lit up his cigarette and tossed the pack back on his desk. "Aside from assassinations which are the bread and butter of the company, we deal with other areas. R&D is another major area – beneficial drugs, weapons of mass destruction. The other big thing we do is police the Nations when requested, however we keep the internal peace of our own also, Xavier."

I rolled back up to my knees. "So, we are the High Council's *Komitet Gosudarstvennoy Bezopasnosti*."

"The KGB? Really Xavier, we are not so cut throat. Who are they— these vampires that are stirring up so much trouble?"

I climbed back up on my feet then made a production of rearranging my clothes but made sure to re-tuck the envelope. Pissed Hades might not be all that cooperative now. "I just have an image. Nothing else. Just a Polaroid picture."

"How did you get that image. Is it reliable?"

"I mind fucked a dying Lycan. He had no reason to try and lie."

"You sink right to the gutter don't you?" A big waft of smoke drifted in my direction.

I fingered the small USB drive in my pocket making sure it hadn't gone flying when I got knocked over. Now I tugged on the sleeves of my shirt trying to appear nonchalant. "Speaking of gutter…I met a mutual friend of ours."

"I sincerely doubt we travel in the same social circles, Xavier. The Golden Pheasant is not my hunting ground."

Well fuck you too, you little prick. "No, he definitely knew you. He called you something else…Cillian."

Hades froze. Every inch of him stiffened with alarm.

"He asked me to pass on a message, William says, he'll see you soon."

His eyes were wide and wild as he snapped his head around to pin me where I stood. "You lie."

Picking my pony tail up and smoothing it over my shoulder I watched for Hades reaction. "He said that he gave me this monochromatic look as a sign for you to start getting ready for his return. You know him: big guy, white hair, gray eyes, with a huge god complex."

"No…it can't be him. Not after all these years…"

I could feel myself getting angry. How dare Hades play shocked and amazed at this information? I stalked up to his desk. "Apparently Liam's been hanging around me from day one, Hades, from the moment of conception. When he couldn't get in and hijack my body he decided he was going to be my protector in my human life and he 'protected' me by making me go blind! All to get back to you. He's been fucking with my life just for you." I leaned on the desk, glaring at him with all the anger and distain that had been swirling inside me since my last little visit to the beachside bungalow. Hades had drained right down to cadaver pale. A light sheen of sweat beaded on his forehead.

"Every step I thought I made of my own free will has been influenced by this…. giant, this First Emperor. Everything he's done to me, to keep me safe has only been to get back to you." Throwing caution to the wind I reached out and grabbed Hades lapels. "How the fuck do you think that makes me feel? I'm his puppet! All this time I've been dancing to his tune…I've been dancing to your tune. The tune he makes you dance…"

217

Hades shoved me off him as he stood up. "No…I can't do this again."

"Oh, Honey Bee." He backed away as I stalked around the side of his desk. "You're just as fucked over as I am. Liam is tired of waiting for you." Hades hit the back wall and I leaned into him, my one knee coming forward spreading his thighs and I laid one hand beside his head and pressed our groins together. I breathed in his scent as I ran my nose along his neck. "If you were a switch hitter, your Lord Emperor would have been back on you in a blink of an eye, or should I say as a Lady Empress. This curse of his…" I trailed a finger down from his ear, to his neck around to his shirt collar and down his tie. "…would have been lifted long ago. You must be beyond so fucking desperate right now."

I didn't expect this type of reaction from Hades. He trembled. He was purely terrified.

"All those growing boy hormones yet so deadly to touch. You must have got tired of jacking off by yourself probably in the first one hundred years. You must have been overjoyed to find Father. Somebody you could touch and not kill. You made him sick though, didn't you? You took his small remaining piece of good heart and froze it."

"Shut up…"

"Truth hurts doesn't it, Cillian. My brothers are not dying for you."

Hades snapped his eyes to me. The terror that had struck him to his core was mastered now. He grabbed my throat, twisted and I found myself face first against the wall now. His body pressing against me hard but this time his cock wasn't a bar of steel poking me. He was still freaked out. "Explain."

It's hard to talk with my cheek rammed up into the wall. "Liam wants to merge me back into one single identity. Once he does that, he's coming for you through me and he said I had a choice, but I don't think he's going to wait anymore. He's coming through me whether I want you or not."

Hades shoved himself off me. I turned and looked at him as he sat heavily on his desk. "That's not fair."

Fair? What the hell does this little teenaged prick know about fairness? "What's not fair is the fact that because of your little hemlock punishment session with Sex, I'm sterile."

Hades stilled again. "You've killed the blue line, Honey Bee. You've forced Liam into my fucking corner."

"Don't call me that."

"Every fucking horrible thing that has happened in my life comes back to you." I clenched my fists. I had a tremor in my hands I was so damned angry.

"That's not my fault."

"You've waited for Liam to come back."

"I have not."

"Then why the hell are you 900 years old? When it was clear Liam wasn't coming back, why did you hang on? After the first two hundred years of this isolationist hell you should have known he wasn't coming back."

"I didn't wait for him."

"He said he was getting tired of watching you fuck up everything you touch."

"You can't blame a stalker's action on the victim."

"Victim? You're calling yourself a victim? You raped Father. Sex consented but it was just as bad as Father's was...it was worse...little brother just laid there and took it. He didn't even fight you because he made a bargain with you."

He didn't expect it. That's all I could think of to explain it. I moved from the wall and shoved him as hard as I could. I saw his legs go flying as he flipped off the desk on the other side. He popped back up and slapped my face. I staggered and dropped to one knee.

"What the hell is going on!" Billy Envoy stood at the door with four security guards backing him up.

We must have been a sight. The First and the CEO engaged in a slap fest. Blood filled my mouth. I stood up, wobbling slightly. "I've had enough of playing puppet for you and your star-crossed lover, Cillian."

That last slap knocked some of my hair out of the ponytail so I made a show of smoothing it back, straightening my tie, tugging on my cufflinks then straightened my shoulders so I faced blond and curly head on. "Hades, I challenge you."

You could have heard a pin drop.

"What?" Billy gasped from the door.

Hades' forehead furrowed. "Challenge? Challenge me for what? You're already First of Assassins."

"You were First. Now you're Head of the House of Assassins. I challenge to be Head."

Hades waved away my words with a flick of his wrist. "I've been appointed to this position."

"You set the precedent. You moved from First to Head. I'm making a formal challenge for your ranking, Cillian."

"My name is Hades." Ice dripped from his words.

"Cillian." I was being an ass and I knew it.

"Stop it!" Billy's voice rang out strong as if he was auditioning for the role of town crier. We both turned toward him. "A formal challenge has been received before witnesses. Hades, do you accept?"

Hades shook his head while keeping those watery blue eyes intently. "I'll kill you. You know that. You're barely two years old. You don't stand a chance."

A laugh of self-derision erupted from my throat. There might have been a tad bit of hysteria in it, but I snapped it back under control quickly. "The way I see it, it's a win/win situation. If you're dead, Liam has no reason to try and come through me. If I'm dead, he can't. Because of the both of you, I've lived in fear since I was nine years old. I'm tired of it."

"Don't be stupid, Xavier."

Hades had no idea just how stupid I could get but I was about to show him. "Cillian aka Hades, CEO of Shadow Incorporated; Head of the House of Assassins and former Royal Consort; I, Xavier Von Drachenfeld challenge you for the right of rank. Accept and we will battle. Refuse and I take your rank before these witnesses."

Hades shook his head, "You sign your death certificate, Xavier. I accept your challenge. When and where?"

I glanced over at Billy. He pulled out his planner and looked down at it. What was it with these older vampires and tactile things? Preferring pen and paper when there were wifi and tablets. "Sunday, 2 p.m. at the Warehouse."

"Weapons?" Hades crossed his arms as he turned on his heel and stared out the large picture windows that made up two walls.

I propped myself up against his desk. "Your choice."

"Daggers." Hades kept staring out the windows. "You're going to die, Xavier."

"Then everything will finally be peaceful, won't it?" I moved past him and picked up my pills up off the floor as the envelope crinkled along my back. So that meant I had to get my ass moving on getting the database done. I pulled the crumpled manila envelope out and retrieved the ancient document. "Oh, this was the reason I came up here to see you, Hades. I need you to read this out loud."

He finally turned back to me, glancing down at the piece of parchment. He held his hand out, but I stayed against the desk, not out of a play for superiority, but because I wasn't sure my legs were going to hold me up. He let out a sigh as he stepped forward taking the writing from my hand. His brow furrowed again. "Where did you get this?"

He was going to find out anyway. "I literally brow beat the librarian for it down in Records. You actually might want to send down someone from Floor 20 to check on her."

"Really, First." Hades peered down at the parchment. "One bag of grain. Three casks of mead..."

I snaked my palm out and laid it on his forehead. He was startled by my lightening strike and for just one moment the mental shield he had around himself shivered. I glanced down at the glyphs and concentrated on its meaning...and suddenly the glyphs were as simple to read as English. Just as quickly as my hand shot out, I pulled it back. Billy and security never had a chance to move before it was over.

Hades gave me the stink-eye look. He knew what I had just done but continued reading the glyphs out loud as if to give me time to make sure I knew what they said. "One slave girl. Four ingots…"

Hades handed it back. Yup, I could read it.

Since my business here was done and I wanted to get the hell out of his office as quickly as possible I looked for the daily assigns. They were scattered across the floor. As I gathered them up I ended up pausing as Billy handed me a couple that were out of immediate scoop range.

I bowed to the Head of the House and moved toward the exit. Hades' voice called after me. "First! You can still stop this challenge right now. Once, you leave my office your words cannot be recanted."

I didn't bother to turn around. "Xavier is taking tomorrow off. Sex will be taking Sunday off. See you at 2:00 p.m. Don't bother contacting Claudius, he will be acting as my second."

I threw the parchment on Billy's desk hoping he would have the presence of mind to return it to records. I had to get out of here without running like the scared idiot I was. As I waited for the elevator it felt like it was taking forever to come back up. Finally, the doors slid back and I stepped in pushing the button for the garage.

Hades stood at the door of his office, his arms folded across his chest. "It doesn't have to be this way, Lord Emperor."

I could feel the side of my mouth rise in a wry smile. "You're not even going to admit you've done me wrong, are you?"

Hades stood there with purse puzzlement on his face. "I've never done anything to you, Xavier."

My laugh of disbelief broke the heavy silence. "You fucked with Father; you fucked with Sex; you fucked over Marcus so tell me how those things don't affect me? Give Marcus back his investments, he earned them. He still should have something left after paying penalties and repairs. He shouldn't be a pauper because of one single lapse in judgment."

"That can be done."

At least that was one concession that was worthwhile. The elevator doors began to close.

"About the Lycan pup…" Hades started again.

"He's family, end of discussion." The doors closed. I stared forward for about three floors then noticed the security camera up in the left corner of the car. I jumped up and ripped it off the wall. My papers went flying everywhere but I could have given a rat at this moment. My legs collapsed under me and I crumpled like a marionette with cut strings. I held a hand over my mouth as a wail started in my chest, but it had to battle with acute hyperventilation. I closed my eyes and pressed my forehead to the floor.

Oh God. What the fuck have I done?

Chapter Fourteen: Carnage

I'm sitting on top of the world, looking down on creation and I think I'm finally drunk. A gust of wind came up and knocked me sideways. The bottle went clink on the girder. No not just drunk, I'm hammered. My feather wings chimed like thousands of little glass...well, chimes. They sounded soothing reminding me of lazy summer days. I lay back stretching my wings out under me like a downy blanket but not so soft...actually rather lumpy and they kinda pinched where they came out the back but was better than being on cool painted steel. I was finely able to close my eyes and savor the little bit of peace I found.

I just had to get away for a bit. The drinking...well, that seemed like a good idea at the time. Same with the smokes in my pocket. I lit up a cigarette with a controlled flick of my finger and took a drag letting it fill up my lungs. It wasn't as if I was going to be dying of cancer any time soon. I couldn't talk to Angel Reggie because the memorial statue I commissioned would be the first place the Loyal would look.

The metallic creak of the Ferris Wheel cars shifting as they spun on the axis around me was a comfort now. I had a shield around me, *don't look this way, nothing unusual here, just an albatross.* Unless someone was damned determined or they were winged, no one was going to bother me while I was perched on the axle of the giant wheel. A strong gust of wind rattled my empty vodka bottle.

I felt a light kick to my shoulder. I opened my eyes and saw Azrael standing next to me staring out at the beautiful sunset. What the hell? The bastard kicked me. I groaned as I rose up on my elbows. We watched the water glisten and dance with the changing light of day as night impatiently waited to take the dance floor. Then it hit me, what the hell was Azrael doing standing there?

Azrael didn't leave me hanging long. "You passed out, you lush. Our body was vacant at the moment so we moved in." He didn't even look at me when he said this.

Oh crap. "Where's Sex?" My head was starting to hurt. Already? This sped up metabolism was giving me my well deserved hangover already? Wait, if Sex was in the physical why did I...Azrael gingerly held the front of his forehead as well...we have a hangover?

"You got the wings out. I asked him to take over so we don't get blown off our wonderful perch. Nice view though."

"You're pissed." I sat up, squinting out across the orange tinted bay.

"Fucking right I'm pissed. Since you forgot, I'm supposed to be getting married tonight. How the fuck am I and Marcus going to accomplish that now?" Azrael tightened his jaw. "Now I see where Sex gets it from. God, elder brother...when you fuck up...you really fuck up."

I didn't go up into Hades inner sanctuary with the intention of making such a grandiose challenge. Things just got the better of me. For all I knew, it was Liam's influence again. No, not Liam's, this was my own making. "I got so angry."

"You bitch at Marcus about control yet, when push comes to shove, you have the emotional control of a three year old, X. Great place to hide too. You've got first degree burns from the sun. Alcohol and the sun don't mix well with the Vampire in us, brother."

I reached into my pocket and shook my little bottle of blue pills Dr. Labcoat shoved on me. "This will take care of it."

Azrael smacked them out of my hand and grabbed me by the hair. Damn...that hurt. "Get your suicidal tendencies under control. I'm not fucking dying out here." Azrael dropped to his knees and I found myself caught in a headlock. "I've got someone to live for, Xavier. Sex has someone he lives for. You got so mad at Armor for fading when he was shaken...and then you go and do the same thing, but you're taking us down with you."

"He's going to kill us." The liquor didn't take the quaver out of my voice. Did alcohol ever?

The pressure around my head lessened as Azrael turned it into an embrace. "Hades is going to try. Death is not easy to accept when you have something to live for, brother. Who do you have to live for? Tell me. Tell me who do you live for?"

My voice wavered then completely cracked as I started naming off those individuals and those people who had taken residence in my heart. "My House. My whole damn house; Armor, Father, you, Sex, Marcus, Haley, Chesterton...."

"Okay, I don't need the whole list. The point is, X, you want to protect them; you want to shelter all of them. You can't do that if you're dead. You can't protect anyone if you're drunk. You can't run every time something doesn't go your way. And...if you answered your cell phone at all today, you know damn well that there are those who care about you." Az pushed me back from his chest and carefully tucked my free flowing hair behind my ears. "I'll forgive you this little lapse in faith, but you better get your section of our headspace in order or Hades really will hand us our asses."

My head was pounding. I cradled it in my hands. Another brilliant idea I shouldn't have run with. Spur of the moment impulse didn't work for me. Jeez, I've just screwed myself over as an assassin. This Lord Emperor crap was never my gig anyways. Oh, God, now I'm feeling sorry for myself. *Shake it off. Shake it off you idiot and get it together. Azrael, for god's sake, is giving you shit.*

The brother in question answered in a long suffering tone. *I can hear you, elder idiot.*

Azrael backed off a few feet. "I hope you can find some useful information in those files you got from the archives, X. Honey Bee was Liam's Royal Consort off and on for about six hundred years. He'll know everything we can do and he probably knows what we can't. Hell he probably knows what we should be able to do because he's been sleeping with the source. We need to find some new tricks."

He let out a bit sigh and stood up facing the water off in the distance, "I'll forgo my day with Marcus."

I lifted my blurry eyes towards Az...er, Azrael. His short red hair rippled in the strong breeze. He was all in black again this time with a "Punisher" graphic tee. He always dresses so cool.

"Thanks for coolness points but don't shorten my name. I'm having enough trouble with Sex as it is."

227

"I'll talk to him."

"You feeling better, Elder Brother?"

"Yeah. You keep your time with Marcus. We don't have to go to work this weekend. If you just give me a couple of hours during the day when Marcus is sleeping...I should be able to tell if I have anything useful. There's less than a hundred files here. I don't think it'll take that long to go through them."

"You did pick a pretty spot to have your breakdown."

The short red hair flamed in the dying of the light. No wonder everyone was lining up for...ahem, me. My stomach was upset. Too much alcohol in too short a time span. "What do you want to do aside from get married?"

A wild look of glee grabbed his face for a moment, "I'd like to rumble with your sister...our sister."

"What?"

"Wailing on Armor in the manor was fun, but I bet if Shayne let go, she might hand my ass to me gift wrapped in a basket." He glanced down at me and gave a genuine laugh, "Don't fret Elder Brother. Hades doesn't know it but we're going to win." He said it with such confidence that I had to close one eye to focus him in.

"We're gangbangers." Azrael turned his face over his should as he gave me a sly grin.

"WHAT!"

"Three against one, Elder brother. Maybe Hades knows the Emperor's gifts, but he's only met each of us, one-on-one and he's only sees Sex as a toy. We cycle through depending on the situation, we're golden. Fool picked daggers. Didn't he see Sex cut Father? Nobody has come close to cutting Claudius as far as I can tell. Each of us has overlapping skills. Some are better handled. Some aren't. Me and healing power is a bitch for some reason."

Claudius is here...and holy crap, steam is coming out his ears. We both heard Sex cry out.

I rolled over and fell against Azrael's leg still highly lacking in coordination. I was hammered. Azrael pat the top of my head not so

228

gently. "You're not a pretty drunk, X. You better not let Armor see you like this."

"He loves me just the way I am."

"And do you realize how fucking lucky you are to get that?"

"I know, little brother. Yeah, maybe we should clean up our language. Doesn't sound that refined for the Lord Emperor."

"Step up, brother Emperor. I think Sex better take over until our body gets back inside the Ferris Wheel car. You're not in full control of your facilities."

My body grew cold as my throat began to tighten. "I'm not feeling too well."

"Get moving, Sex. Elder brother is going to hurl!"

The transition was quick and I thought I felt a soft brush of a hand on my shoulder before Father's hands bit hard into my forearms as my body swayed. My feet hit the floor inside the car and I lurched forward through the opened door. I blinked a few times to get the double, blurry Claudius into focus. The slight breeze from the opened car made his long black hair whip tendrils across his face but he never let go of me. "Again, only you go somewhere no one else can get to, my son."

"I....I..." I threw up on Father's shoes. Oh god. I barfed again. My knees collapsed under me but Claudius tossed me onto the seat so I didn't land in the mess I made. I got sick again as the Ferris wheel lurched into a swinging and dropping motion. The door swung closed under its own motion. When I finally stopped embarrassing myself I noticed Father was holding my hair back at the base of my neck even if it meant I threw up on his lower pants leg.

"I'm sorry...." I tried not to. I really tried not to but I started crying. "I'm...."

"You have done more harm to yourself than what I was going to do, Xavier." The car slid backwards and my stomach decided to return to its messy sport. This time when I was done making honking noises, Father was on the cell phone. "I have found him. Bring his suitcase from the limo. No, he is not injured. My son is not a drinker."

"I'm sorry..." My words were still slurred.

229

"You already said that, Little Blue." Claudius's calm voice stabbed at me more than if he would yell at me.

"I'm sorry I ruined your shoes."

The car was filled with a big sigh then he stroked my hair back off my temples. "Honestly, you ruined my day, Xavier. Let us let down on the ground and get you cleaned up."

"I'm sorry…"

"I am thankful that you are not a mean drunk, Xavier." Father took a hold of my upper arm easing me back on the seat.

"I don't drink…"

"You are doing a great imitation of it right now."

I could real the sob in my voice. "Shit. He's going to kill me…."

"Ssssh. Let us just get you cleaned up."

"I…" I wasn't a mean drunk but a whiny one is worse.

"I said, shut up." Father's voice was soft. That made it ten times worse.

Ride management was less than enthused with the state of their car when the door was opened on the ground. The girl's face was priceless as she shut the ride down to grab at a hose that was off the base stairs between two venues but when Claudius held out his hand she quickly handed it over. Not only did I throw up on his shoes, but in them. He sprayed down his lower legs then moved to his feet. I had the presence of mind to hand off my flash drive to one of the waiting Loyal before Claudius turned the hose on me. Father hosed me down entirely from my head to my foot. I staggered sideways until I hit the guardrail and hung on before I fell down. He finally took his shoes off and rolled his pants up.

"I'm sorry…"

"I said, shut up, Xavier. What I want to say to you cannot be said in public." I held my forehead up with my hand. He jerked me to my unsteady feet and my stomach lurched. "Are you going to be sick again?"

I waited in anticipation. I felt like shit. I shook my head. Oh…big mistake. I hung my head over the rail until I got down to the dry heaves.

In the middle of the amusement park Father stripped me down to my underwear taking my holster and sheath and wrapping them in my splattered jacket. I made one noise of protest but it dried up in my throat when I saw how cold his eyes were. This was now Carnage. I actually made two steps before Carnage snagged my wrist and twisted my arm behind my back.

"You have pushed me beyond my limits today, my Lord Emperor. It is in your best interests to be a good obedient son right now. Is that understood?" I stood shivering in my underwear, miserable and immune to the snickering of the crowd. I didn't care much that people were staring at me.

"This isn't what I wanted…" The acrid aftertaste in my mouth left me breathing deeply to try and keep my stomach inside my body.

"But this is what we now have to deal with, Xavier. Now, shut up and get moving." The platform rattled as a Loyal dragged a suitcase full of clothes up the metal staircase. Carnage dragged a black t-shirt over my head and gingerly pulled my dripping hair free from the neck. I struggled into a pair of camo grey and black multi-pocketed shorts. I hadn't changed the sizes in the suitcase and everything was exceptionally baggy.

I held my hand out and the Loyal began to give me back the flash drive but Carnage snatched it. His jaw firmed up as he glanced at it then dropped it into his pants pocket. I opened my mouth for just a second then snapped it closed.

"Finish cleaning the area." Carnage pointed to the black limo at the entrance to the park. I started to bend over to get my wet shoes. "Leave them."

"But.."

Carnage caught my wrist and squeezed hard on it. My knees buckled and I gasped in pain. My alcoholic mist was blown away by the pain. "Get to your feet, now, Xavier, or I will drag you to the car."

"You're hurting me."

"This is nothing compared to what I really wanted to do to you when I got a call from Hades this morning." Apparently I didn't move fast enough. Carnage started off to the limo. The pavement ripped into my knees as he dragged me behind him. I twisted and got my feet under me and lurched up to my feet behind him. Oh yeah, I was on my way to sober really fast and the hangover was moving in.

Carnage never let go, yanking me in behind him as he climbed into the limo. I was pushed to the floor facing the front partition, and pulled back between his knees as he settled on the seat.

"Father...."

"You need to be quiet, Xavier. I am trying to control my rage right now. That is one emotion I never have had trouble with because I have never attempted to rein it in. Just stay where you are and...for once listen to me."

I brought my battered knees up and rested my chin between them. I could smell the alcohol seeping out of my pours. I buried my face deeper and tried to keep from crying. Damn it. I brushed at my eyes. I was startled as a brush began working through my damp hair, carefully working out tangles.

I didn't have the courage to turn around.

"Home, Walker."

"I should..."

Claudius jerked on my hair, wrenching my face off my knees and staring up at him. No, it was still Carnage. "You will sit still and keep quiet. If you get sick in my car, I will make sure you regret it."

He shoved my head back to my knees and let the oppressive silence fill the back of the limo. I lifted my hand to my ear and got the back of the wooden brush hard across my knuckles. "Sit still."

I jerked my hand back and curled it into my stomach.

For once I got absolutely no enjoyment out of getting my hair brushed. I was too busy trying to convince myself that I was not going to be sick. I thought I had done an admirable job until the limo lurched to a halt. I scrambled for the door and jerked it open. I threw up in the gutter as I half hung out of the car. I wanted to die.

Afterwards I was physically hauled back into the limo. Carnage handed me a couple of wet thingies and I cleaned off my face. "You should stick to beer, Xavier. Hard spirits does not bode well for you."

I closed my eyes. I was done with alcohol. I got the shakes now…but I couldn't tell if it was the booze or the act of stupidity I engaged in earlier this morning.

By delivery of the last assignment, it was out all over the House of Assassins. The seventh ranked assassin Smother, I had thought Scope was a bad name, looked at me and shook his head. He was tall, lanky and bow legged reminding me of a wild west cowboy and like most of the ranked didn't care for me.

Smother didn't bother mincing his words. "I heard about you, First. No one has ever come close to taking down Carnage and I don't think you beat him fairly. I guess it doesn't matter; Hades is going to crush you like a beetle. You're insides are going to splattered all over the training room." I kept my mouth shut, handed over my envelope and left to head right to the nearest liquor store.

Now, I lay on the floor of the car not really caring that Father was lightly jerking on my hair as that brush continued moving. 100 strokes and counting.

"Up." The wooden side of the brush tapped my shoulder hard enough to get my attention.

Walker opened the door and I got…well not jerked…but not really allowed to meander at my own pace either out of the limo. I swung back and forth behind Carnage like a water tube out of control and at the whim of the rogue wake. The lobby of Father's condominium looked really elegant from what I glimpsed of it. I'd never been to this place before, Father would drop in when he wanted to see us. This looked pretty exclusive. The doorman/security looked at us unsure of exactly what to do as I skidded to a barefooted halt behind Claudius when he stopped to check in. My legs suddenly dropped out from under me and I landed hard on my skinned knees. I still wasn't sober.

"Do you require assistance Mr. Du Bussey?"

"I have it, Reynolds. I do have it, right, Xavier?" I didn't need to see the iced gaze in Father's eye because the chill in his voice was effective enough. I think I left a streak of blood on the Italian marble lobby from my re-opened knees as I clumsily imitated a new born foal's attempt to stand.

The elevator opened and I didn't have the chance to make a second attempt to get to my feet because Father caught me by the back of my shirt and dragged me in the car on my stomach, tossed me in the corner of the elevator without a backwards glance, then pressed the floor button. The security guard came out from behind the desk as I oofed when I hit the back of the car and fell over on my face. Apparently this was an abnormal event for Claudius.

"Wha…." My protest dried up in my throat as a single finger lifted and pointed at me. The floor tile was cool and soothing so I simply laid there, pressing my temple against it.

"Get up." The elevator had stopped; Claudius was standing in front of the door to keep it open. I pulled myself up to my feet by the wide metal railing accenting the rich mahogany of the elevator's décor then staggered out. My head was pounding.

Claudius lead me to a door, opened it and held it open so I could get in. He gestured to a room. "Wait there. There is a bathroom connected to it if you are still feeling under the weather. I need to shower and change. If I have to hunt you down again, Xavier…you will not have to wait for Hades to kill you."

"Yes Father."

I staggered to the bathroom. I wasn't feeling too fresh either. My baggy clothes were still damp but clean of vomit. However, something died and was rotting in my mouth. *Stupid, stupid, stupid. What the hell time was it? Oh god. I wondered what the hell Armor was doing? Did he also hear what I did? He was still a little off from a couple of days ago. Oh crap, this wouldn't push him off the deep end again, would it?* I splashed my face with cold water then rummaged for some mouthwash. Where the hell is my cell phone? Probably still in my ruined suit.

I came back out of the bathroom and took a good look around the condo. *Holy pack rat, Father.* It was filled floor to ceiling with books, parchments, scrolls and magazines. I'm sure there were several bookcases in there somewhere. I walked in and twisted around the other collection and piles of junk. I didn't expect this. Actually I never thought of what Claudius's house looked like. I thought maybe more Japanese zen type concert piano kind of thing. He had so much crap in this room, if he had the rest of the place like this no wonder he kept his piano at Von Drachenfeld.

I wrapped my arms around myself. I pissed Father off and...Oh jeez...Carnage hunted me down. At least I still had the survival instinct not to fight him. I made my way over to a window and opened the blinds. It was officially night. I wasted a day. A day I could have been planning or researching or practicing. Oh God. I barfed all over Father. I ran a hand down my face. Could this entire day get any worse?

"Xavier. Front and center."

Oh yeah, it was going to get worse. I turned around but didn't see him amidst all the clutter. "I'm by a window. Where are you?"

There was a long heavy silence then a light turned on in another room. Gingerly and with a hell of a lot of concentration I shuffled my way towards it. When I finally broke free of the hoarder jungle I found myself standing in an abnormal clear zone – the kitchen.

Claudius was leaning against the counter dressed in a white dress shirt and black trousers. His arms were across his chest in a deceptively relaxed pose but I knew better than to poke the resting tiger. "Do you have a cell phone?"

"Yes, Sir."

Those blue eyes zeroed in on me, pinning me in place. "When it rings, you pick it up and you talk to whoever had taken the time to call you. Especially, when your precious youngest son has got himself into a death match."

Father's voice was very calm. He turned his head away and a curtain of midnight black slipped from his shoulder hiding his face. When he tucked it back behind his ear I was able to making myself look into his eyes and was taken aback at the pain there. I think I preferred the icy cold blue. I had hurt him. "I know Hades can make someone lose it with just a well timed eyebrow arch. You are a baby compared to him and I do not mean just in years. You are not a match for him. You know that too. I would not have to put up with vomit and excessive heights to retrieve you if you were confident in your abilities."

Claudius reached out and lifted my chin. "Hades called me. I have never heard him this upset. He told me that he gave you a number of times to recant, to withdraw your challenge. Why did you push him, Xavier? You pushed him into a corner in front of witnesses. He does not want to kill you. You are his Lord Emperor. Tell me why?"

"...I..." My voice cracked. Damn it.

Claudius pulled me into a hug. "You reek of alcohol, Little Blue. Heal yourself. Burn that poison out of your system now. You will think clearer once this is done. I have ordered food for you."

Claudius did a quick glance around then pointed back down the narrow corridor left by towering boxes of...boxes and I ended up back in front of the elevator. Better to be safe than an arsonist. A mere thought of will and I burst into Healing light. Father watched from the room as the blue light cast shadows around the area. Once the alcohol was gone...the flame went out. I set my hand out and steadied myself on the wall. I had just flambéed like cherries jubilee. I made it back to the kitchen under my own power as Father walked up and presented his wrist.

"I don't deserve...."

"Drink, Xavier. You will need all the strength you can muster in these next few days." Father pulled my back against his chest as he offered his wrist again to my mouth. I dropped fang and bit, tasting the spicy clovey goodness that invaded my mouth. Father offered more than just the bond between a father and son; he gave me his strength. I pulled my fangs free. I started sobbing. I twisted in his arms and hugged him hard.

His hand came up and rubbed a circle on my back. "Little Blue, what are we going to do?"

"I got to talk to Armor...he's probably freaking out."

236

"He does not know. When you leave for work, Marcus comes out. All this broke while Marcus was in control. I spoke with him and we agreed that Armor should be left in the dark--for now. We need to deal with one problem at a time."

"Marcus?" I pressed my forehead up against Claudius' throat.

There was an electronic whistle that startled the hell out of me. "Your pizza is here."

"I'm not really hungry." Claudius moved his arms and gave one jerk on my pants. They slipped off and pooled around my ankles. "Okay, I'll nibble."

"You will eat it all." There was still that hard edge to his voice. Okay, I'd choke it down if I had to. "Then you will give me a full explanation of why you did this, Xavier."

I nodded and let my hands drop. I don't think Father wanted to hear it was because of terror and anger. I reached up and loosely braided my snow white locks into a single braid down my back.

I was like Pavlov's dog. The pizza box went by and my stomach started growling, feed me, feed me now. I really wasn't up to eating after all the extra activity it had been doing, but Father was right. I had to keep my strength up. I remember when I was still human and morbidly obese I had fleetingly wondered if I would have to be buried in a piano case cause I had gotten so fat. Now? Who the hell heard of an anorexic vampire?

I followed the pizza box into the kitchen. Well if he's anything like he was when he lived at the first mansion he probably doesn't use it much. Father started getting out plates and silverware. I waved him off, grabbed a paper towel and started eating out of the box. It wasn't like he was going to eat with me. While chewing on my first slice, he went and got himself a coffee mug and a blood pack. He nuked it then poured it in his mug. I was impressed that he was competent in the kitchen.

He watched silently and sadly as I finished my second slice. "Xavier..."

I interrupted him. "What can you tell me about the very First Emperor?"

237

"The First Emperor? Nothing really…"

"Did he have a name?" Bite. Chew, chew, chew. Swallow.

Claudius shook his head negatively.

I made a drinking motion with my hand. I should have known that damned pomegranate juice would be stocked in the refrigerator. Why would he even have it? It's not like any of us had ever come here before. Then again, it fit the Claudius's personality. The quintessential vampiric boy scout – prepared for anything. "What can you tell me about Emperor William?"

"Just the basics…he organized the Vampire Blood Nation into the fifteen houses, unified the Nation under one banner and raised us up as the pinnacle of all the supernatural bloods."

Pizza and pomegranate did not taste well together. "Did you know he made Hades?"

"Hades was his Royal Consort?" Claudius gave me a simple eyebrow arch of surprise.

"I take it you didn't know that Hades has been Royal Consort three times in the past 900 years."

Claudius shook his head. A frown appeared on his face. "What does this have to do with your challenging Hades for rank?"

"I've met him."

Claudius shook his head in exasperation. "Met whom? You are speaking in circles, Xavier and this is not explaining why you challenged Hades."

I wiped my greasy fingers on the napkin. "Do you remember if Sex saying something about the Darkness? When one of the brothers is in control I wait in something like a staging area – in the dark. I thought that was all there was waiting for me, but there was someone else. I met Hades' maker. He also happens to be the Progenitor of our Blood line."

That got Claudius's attention. He leaned forward with his eyes seeming to crackle with energy. "What? What are you saying?"

"He calls himself Liam. He was named William when he made Cillian…that's Hades real name by the way. Liam regenerates every two hundred and fifty years, either by stealing a newborn's soul or by merging with a vampire. He has this thing about nobody messing with what it is."

I could see that Claudius was not catching on. "He laid a curse of untouchability on his little lover thinking he was going to come back to him in a short period of time. To keep his little consort pure and untouched he tainted Cillian with a toxic poison that only he could remove." I caught Father's look and returned it, staring him right in the eye, "We both have experienced Hades. He will do anything to be touched, so we both know that this hemlock curse is not done with his consent."

"When did you meet this Liam?"

"I think he was there in the Darkness with all of us when Hades put us in that coma. Sex said something about getting thrown into the circle of light where we were waiting. I met him again in his own little staging area, which he has control over because we were on the beach, then the forest then he re-cracked my skull open and sent me back to my bedroom." I laid my hands flat on the table feeling emotionally unstable again. Fear, anger, and more than a little bit of intimdation were battering themselves against my stubborn resolve. "Liam wants to kill my brothers. He wants to remove them so he can move in."

"I'm not understanding you, Xavier. What does this have to do with this challenge?"

I closed my eyes and I could feel my hands clench on the table. "Liam wants to come back to this physical world and reclaim Hades. To do that..." My voice caught and I had to swallow down a frog in my throat. "...to do that, he needs a body and I've found out, he's been trying to get mine since before the day I was born."

The sound of Claudius' mug slamming down onto the table snapped my eyes open, "How would he do this?"

"I don't think he needs my consent. He's been waiting for the next Lord Emperor to be born. That's not the kicker though; he offered me one chance to have a child because of Hades sterilization oopsies. If I submit to him, where ever the hell it is he takes me, he will implant spiritual essence which would give the Vampire Nation one try to get the

239

Royal Line back in business." I stood up and wrapped my arms around me because I suddenly felt chilled. The pizza was sitting in my stomach like a lump of lead.

"Xavier?"

"He's going to try and trap me there on that beach, wherever it is. He's going to take my body as his. He'll reclaim Hades, whether Hades wants him or not. He will become Lord Emperor and he has already told me that he would become this generation's Hashmallim. He wants to tweak all the Blood Nations to fit his idea of what they should be and you know that means full scale war."

"Fight him!" Claudius jumped up to his feet.

"That's what Sigmund did. I can't prove it, but I know Liam forced himself into Sigmund. I think that is why my grandfather went crazy. He was trying to get Liam out. When he realized he couldn't he went out into that battlefield and committed suicide. Sigmund the deadly fruitcake...he saved us all and history remembers him as a megalomaniac."

Father's voice was quiet, "Are you trying to follow Sigmund, Xavier?"

"No, I'm trying to remain here. Azrael pointed out I got people to live for. Sex doesn't want to leave his Gorgeous. I don't want to leave Armor all alone. Haley still is targeted by the Lycan Nation. Azrael wants to get married."

"So why challenge Hades?"

"Liam is doing this to get to him. If there is no Hades...there shouldn't be a reason for Liam to possess me. If Liam isn't here; there won't be a new Hashmallim."

"And if you can't kill Hades?"

"Then Hades'll kill me...so Liam can't get here again. If that happens, to make sure he can't take over -- ash my body." I thought it would be harder to say. To tell a loved one to make sure that my body was dead if I wasn't in it.

Father got up and caught me in a hard embrace. "Why have you been dealing with this on your own?"

I felt my eyes burn and tears started to stream down my face, "I'm the Lord Emperor. Isn't that what I'm supposed to do? Protect the Nation. Shelter my House from harm."

"And who protects you?"

"You?" He pressed his face along my cheek.

"It does not matter that I am not your true Sire. You *are* my son. A father's goal is to see his children surpass his dreams. He does not want them to die before him. It does not matter if he is Human, Vampire or another Blood." He tightened his hold on my chest. "If Hades has to die to keep you and your brothers safe…then Hades will die."

"You'll be my second?"

"You need not even ask. Carnage will back you up completely." Somewhere in this mess of Father's rat packishness was a grandfather clock. It chimed ten times. "I take it Azrael wants to go home and get ready for his wedding to which I was not invited, by the way."

I shook my head. "It's a private affair for two."

Claudius reached up and wiped the tears from my cheeks. "You are forgiven for making everyone worry. You are not alone. You do not have to handle this alone. I will discover Hades weaknesses." He shifted and held up the flash drive he had taken from me. "What is this?"

"I'm hoping it will give me a clue if Liam has any weaknesses."

He handed it back to me. "Eat your pizza, Little Blue. When you are done, I will have Walker drive you home. I know you might not understand, but keep this from Armor as long as you can. You know what he will do if he feels you are in danger." He stroked my cheek with the back of his hand. "Which is not a bad thing…but I have no intention of losing either of you to Hades. Promise me this, Xavier."

I nodded. If Armor wanted to go off half cocked, he was going to go dragging me behind him. "Loose lips sink ships. Come for Sex at your regular time, Father."

"I will be there. Tell Azrael, I wish him well for his special day." Claudius let me go and lead me back to the table.

"Father, can I ask you one question?" An eyebrow arched which I took to be an okay. "What the hell is up with this?" I gestured at the clutter.

There was a loud sigh and a dramatic drooping of shoulders. "I was dirt poor growing up, my son. I coveted everything I saw. Now I can have everything I covet…I have always been like this. Katrina hated it too if you must know. If I have a room, I fill it." A wry little self decrepitating smile crossed his face.

"I never expected it from you, but I like it. It makes you more…approachable." I grabbed up another slice of pizza and tore into it.

"I remember meeting you, Little Blue. Armor had already started the change. You were naked and bloody. You were just a pretty thing…until you opened your eyes. Your defiance and courage and strength of will shone in your lovely jade green eyes. I feared you at that first instance."

I blinked and stopped chewing. Huh?

"Both Marcus and Armor lied to me while they reformed you that year. Marcus has always been an open book to me, maybe a little hard to read and slightly tragic but I always knew what he was doing. To go to such lengths to keep you secret, there had to be something else going on beside physical intimacy. At that moment, I knew you were going to take my beloved son away from me and that was when I thought you just a Red. I knew you were going to change both our lives, now, I thank you for it." He rose to his feet and closed the pizza box. He handed it to me. "Go be with my son, my youngest, cherished one."

I stood up. Claudius reached out and traced the gold chain down to the locket. I assured him, "I haven't taken it off since you put it on."

"I know." He breathed softly. I thought I was going to get Sex's usual lip lock. He bent my neck forward and kissed the top of my head. "Go. I need to start looking for a way to get to Hades."

"Thanks for coming for me. I don't think I could have gotten off of the Ferris Wheel by myself."

"You are not by yourself, Xavier. You are never alone. Do not forget that."

I bowed and took my pizza, heading for the elevator. I stepped into the car and took one last look back through the pack rat's corridor. Father was standing silhouetted against the night sky, his shoulders squared and his hands clenched in tight fists at his hips.

The words were low, barely audible but I thought I heard Father mutter. "I am not giving you anything else I cherish Hades. I will kill you this time. You are dead."

The doors closed in my face. That was Carnage again. This time, I felt comforted. *Thank you Father.* The elevator opened to the lobby and the doorman eyed me and the pizza. He opened the door with a straight face but there was a smirk in his eyes. The cool evening breeze hit me in the face. I took a deep breath. Oh…crap. Marcus was taking Azrael's virginity tonight. A sly smile streaked across my face. Yeah, Marcus fucked me over but as Sex said, it was nothing but pleasure. Walker opened the door as I approached the car. Azrael was in for a treat tonight. Poor little topper was going to find out what it meant to bottom.

"Sir?"

"Take me home, Walker."

Chapter Fifteen: Brotherly Love

I stopped in the foyer with the last slice of pizza hanging out of my mouth as Armor stood there with his arms crossed looking his intimidating best. My heart went donkie donk. He was spectacular when he was miffed.

"I said, where have you been?" Oh my god I felt like a teenage girl trying to sneak back into my room after a night of innocent fun. *Yah, right. Tap dance. Tap dance. No, he can tell when I'm lying.*

"I was with Father at his condo. You never mentioned that he never met anything he didn't like."

His brow furrowed. "What?"

"You never told me that Claudius keeps everything. His place is well on its way to needing a hoarder's intervention." I wiped the side of my mouth free from pizza debris and chewed on the congealing cheese.

"I could have told you that. Why do you think the Manor was so big? He just kept adding floors and rooms as he collected more and more junk. I think it almost killed him when he moved out and had to start all over again. He has a warehouse now aside from his condo." Armor opened his arms and gestured me forward. I eyed him warily. He had that gleam of mischief in his eyes. Which usually meant trouble for me...or if I was going to be honest, it meant some serious snuggling leading to some mutual carnal indulgences.

"You cannot have candy, but Father buys you a pizza."

I stuffed the rest in my mouth and wrinkled my nose at him. I glanced at the clock. Azrael was going to be coming out pretty soon. I still needed to shower. I tried to duck past him to get down our corridor but he snagged my shoulder and I was pulled back into his embrace. His nose settled into the space between my ear and hair.

"You smell like pepperoni." That came out as a sexy growl.

"Well that's nice." I needed a shower, a quick rinse with the Ferris wheel hose really didn't give me that fresh feeling I desperately wanted.

However, I did snuggle back into his arms. "What do you do when you're home all day by yourself?"

There was a moment of stillness as if he were debating what to tell me. Really? I can't tell any fibs, but you can? "Armor?"

A sigh whistled by my ear. "I have nothing to do when you leave since we are still under sanctions, so Marcus comes to play his violin or he paints. He has been painting a lot lately. Come and see it." Armor grabbed my hand and dragged me after him. I'm not a small man but damn…these vampires must enjoy dragging my ass around behind them. Armor let go of me just outside of Marcus's room. My stomach muscles tensed slightly in spite of what I had told myself.

"Should we even be here?" I don't know why I was whispering. It wasn't as if Marcus was going to step out from his room.

"Marcus never said you could not look at it. It is almost complete anyways." Armor urged me in front of him and then dropped a paw of hand across my eyes. "Take five steps in and I will turn you in the right direction." I got the bums rush into the room, wrenched around on my heel until finally Armor dropped his hand.

For a moment I thought I was looking in a mirror then I blinked at the canvas. Oh. My. God. I was standing in front of a huge canvass with a painting of the 'pod' all in life size. I was seated in that brown leather wingback chair from the Great Hall. Marcus had me in my pale gray suit, crisp white shirt and he had changed my tie from pink to a shade close to my eye color. I took a few steps forward staring at the artist's rendering of me. My hair was long and crimson, cascading over my shoulders like a waterfall captured in a still frame. He had caught me in a smirk…no, not a smirk -- a smile of satisfaction and indulgence. I was lounging in the chair; one leg was up crossed at the knee. My right hand held a goblet, it wasn't shown but that wasn't a cabernet in it. My left arm was folded up and back, laying over top of a hand that was laying on my shoulder. I followed that arm up to see my Armor standing there behind the leather chair. I knew it was Armor because he was standing upright and his shoulders where squared. He was in a taupe suit with a crimson tie. His sable hair was tied back loosely. I spied a flash of gold and found our bands painted onto the fingers of our left hands.

My eyes trailed along the bottom and there was Her Majesty in all her crimson glory looking as if her image could walk off that painting. Her tail up was at the ready to do damage. Marcus was lounging on his elbow, one hand on her back. He was in leather…red leather pants and a black silk open neck shirt. His hair was loose and fell off to the left with rich sable toned waves. He was leaning back against Azrael. How did he…. how did he get my red hair color right? How did he know that…oh, yeah? Mindfucked. It looked like the short-shorn hair actually shimmered in the paint. Azrael was in black leather with a dark burgundy silk shirt on. One hand was gripping Marcus by the shoulder while the other was laid possessively on the red leather hip. Staring out of the painting was the same jade green eyes but the expression was harder, a little more dangerous – purer Azrael

The right side of the painting had Father and Sex. Wow….smoking hot. Claudius was in a dark dove gray morning suit with tails. He was tucked slightly behind the leather chair. One hand gripped one of the architectural wings, the other was around Sex's waist as he plastered himself against Father. Sex had the full head of white hair and he his head on Claudius' shoulder. Strands of it cascaded down Father's arm. The green of Sex's eyes was darker and smoldered with erotic promise. But it was Claudius' eyes that got to me.

They were happy.

I found my hand was against my mouth. Marcus did this? How did? I…

"It's not done?"

Armor came up and slipped his hands around my shoulders and pulled me back gently. I smiled as he folded his warmth around me. He pointed to a spot down by the chair. "Haley cannot sit still long enough for Marcus to finish."

"It's beautiful." I was stunned.

"Marcus has made it for you, Little One."

"For me? Why?"

247

"He is Marcus again. Everything is nice and calm up here." Armor took my hand and laid it against his temple. "This is a gift for allowing us…Marcus and myself to live with you…to be a part of your House."

"Yourself?"

"I give Marcus part of my time with you to paint."

"It's beautiful. Speaking of Haley, where is he?"

"He's sleeping now. Chesterton wore him out, today." I shifted my weight to one side and stared at Marcus.

"Chesterton did what?"

Armor looked down at me puzzled then understanding dawned on his face. He threw back his head and laughed. "No. The pup asked Chesterton to dominate him and I thought Chesterton was going to faint. He politely declined the offer. The pup asked this in his usual fashion."

"Pants off and bum up in the air."

"Yes, in the kitchens."

I think my eyes must have bugged out. "You are so kidding!"

"It caused quite an uproar in the kitchens. As I understand it, Chesterton has declined sexual congress, but he said that he would groom the little Lycan every day. They disappeared for half the day, apparently Chesterton found an exotic pet groomer – which is something like a spa and took him there. I do not think Chesterton meant to do it, but he has a Lycan pup for a tail now."

"What? I've been abandoned?" My tone was fake indignation and I even waved my hand dramatically in front of my face.

Armor pinched my nose lightly. "Would you rather be tripping over him?"

"As long as that boy's happy. He's had too much tragedy in his life. That is if Chesterton doesn't mind it." I gestured to the canvas. "This is a work of art, Armor. Thank you for allowing Marcus the time to work on it." I gestured Armor down to my level and kissed his cheek. "I've had a long day and I need a shower before those two get together."

"Take your time, Little One. Marcus has asked me to speak to Azrael before this night starts."

I looked at him with alarm. "What?"

"This is between Azrael and me. Don't worry, it is not anything bad. Just a little naughty."

The thing was that Azrael's version of naughty was nowhere near my version of naughty. Armor must have seen this on my face. He took his hand put it on my head and twisted me until I was facing the corridor that would lead to me to my shower. "Go, Little One. It is time for Azrael and Marcus to celebrate their style of love."

It worked for them. I forced back my shudder as I walked toward the bathroom. Azrael and Marcus. Master and Servant…or better yet, Master and Puppy. It made them happy. I just didn't want any memories of whatever kinky freaky stuff they were going to be getting into.

"Incoming Azrael." I called out to my younger brother.

I blinked as Elder brother faded back twenty minutes earlier than I thought he would. So instead of fifteen minutes, I got a full half hour. Oh yeah, I needed a shower and I needed to brush my teeth. Drinks after effects were bleck.

While soaping up, I checked myself over completely. At least Father had let X heal. I didn't want to be suffering with the after affects of X's ill planned drinking binge, not when I had Puppy waiting for me. Damn that was a nice painting. Marcus looked so hot. So fuckable. My Puppy had talent. Why wasn't he out there sharing his gifts? What did Armor say, Marcus was calm again. I'd better leave things alone at least until we got the progenitor out of our hair. So we'll just stick with the play time and a little hardcore romance I had planned for the day.

I shut the taps off grabbed a towel and fluffed myself dry. I wrapped a warm towel around my waist and used another towel to dry my hair. When I walked back into X's room Armor was sitting on the bed. I arched an eyebrow in his direction. "Yeah?"

"Azrael? I was expecting Xavier."

"He decided to head out a little early. Considering the shit, you put him through, he's very vanilla and he's a little twitchy with the freaky deaky. There is nothing wrong with that. He's happy with it. He's happy with you."

"Thank you."

"De Nada. Marcus wanted you to talk to me? About what?"

Armor pushed himself off the bed and rose up to his full height. "You will be joined with Marcus tonight. You offered up a very precious gift. Are you still determined to give it to Marcus?"

Who was testing my resolve? The love of my life or the bane of my existence? "Who's asking?"

"Just answer the question."

"Yes, I'm giving Marcus my virginity."

Armor nodded. "Marcus has an agenda set from midnight to six a.m. to deal with this gift. I have been asked to get your consent."

"Sure…"

"Listen up. If you agree to this, you will accept anything and everything Marcus does. You will have no voice until 6:01 in the morning."

I blinked at this. What has my Puppy planned? I felt myself get excited and a tinge of alarm.

"Do you agree, Azrael?"

I met Armor's eye squarely. "I do."

"Bring out your wings." I tossed the towel I was using on my hair onto the floor. The last time I called on the feathers they stuttered out of the wing scars almost as if they were fighting my command and they stung like a bitch and I ended up on my knees panting as if I had just run the 100 meter dash. This time the feathers came out easily and quickly. No pain at all. I let them stretch and flutter for a moment then folded them across my back.

Armor rose from the bed crossing to the nightstand where there was a tray that held a set of black leather cuffs and a strip of black silk to be used as blindfold. Armor held a rag in his hand and a dark brown bottle. I frowned and looked at him. "What is that?"

"You have agreed to Marcus's demand. I have promised him to prepare you. Kneel down and bow your head."

A little frisson of fear rippled through me. I lowered myself down crossing the trailing edge of my wings behind me. I heard Armor move closer then crossed behind me. "You look good on your knees before me,

Azrael." I popped my head up. He pressed the rag against my nose and mouth. I stiffened his hold then what ever fumes he had in that rag overtook me. Everything spun for a moment then started to get dark. He whispered in my ear with a low dark laugh, "You are going to be sore in the morning, little big man."

Consciousness came back slowly.

Oh crap. What the hell did Armor drug me with? What the hell was he doing drugging me to begin with? My head throbbed with the hangover I thought I had avoided when X flambéed the alcohol out of our system. I opened my eyes. I opened my eyes…. wait…oh yeah, there was a blindfold. I was hanging like a side of beef. My wrists were aching, and my hands were numb. That was going to hurt when blood got back up there.

I got back to my feet. At least they were free. I shivered as a blast of air conditioning hit me from above. And, I was naked. A little bit of alarm hit me in the chest. What the hell had my Puppy planned?

Violin music started up again. I thought I had been dreaming it. Marcus…what is going on in that pretty head of yours? My wings pealed as I shifted my weight trying to get some circulation into my wrists. The music stopped. I listened but I couldn't hear him moving around.

Hands snaked around me from behind; one at my waist another across my chest, under my left wing with a fingertip resting on my nipple ring. Hot breath caressed my neck as he pulled me back against him, stretching my arms out above me even more. "Hello, my beautiful little pet. Finally awake I see."

That voice sent shivers along my spine and my wings chimed again. "Are you frightened, my angel? You shouldn't be frightened. I've finally found you."

He kissed that spot just behind my ear and where my neck started. He left a sucking kiss there. I got weak in the knees. "You don't know how long I've been looking for you. I've got you now. I'll never let you go."

251

He had a vocal binding on me. I couldn't talk…I inhaled sharply as he bit my ear but any moans or cries were silent. He was missing out on the best part; listening to Marcus' sweet cry of pleasure pain and the way his voice quivered as he came.

"I'll let you ask one question. Think carefully."

I gasped and twisted in his grasp as he pinched my unadorned nipple.

"Ask me now." How the hell was I supposed to think when he was doing that?

"Marcus…"

He ran a hand down from my wrist, trailing the backs of his nails against my flesh running it down to my very sensitive pit, stroking there for a moment then moving on down to my hip and back long my flank. "Ask your question, my captured angel of death."

I cocked my head then turned my blindfolded eyes to the direction I thought he was standing. "Do you love me, Marcus?"

He stilled. "With all my heart, Azrael."

"Then I trust you with my body and soul." I pushed my hips back into his groin. I bit my lower lip and shook my money maker.

"Damn you." Marcus hissed in my ear, shoved my head forward and backed away. I stumbled forward but was brought up to a halt by my chains. The binding was back on. I could fight it and I could break it…I don't know how, I just knew that I could. I didn't try.

Then I heard it. Marcus was crying. I twisted my head toward the sound. I couldn't do anything thing. I pulled on my arms. I just hurt my wrists. If I burned, I could get free…but I had no idea where Marcus was. The last thing I wanted was to set my Puppy on fire. He hit me with his body. His face buried itself against my stomach, his arms wrapped around my upper thighs. The only thing I could do was bring my wings around in a loose embrace. I heard something smash to the carpet.

"Even like this…you own me, Azrael. I can't win with you. You're not even competing with me…and I can't win. This time…this was supposed to be the night Armor stole you from the bar. I was going to take your virginity the way it should have been. I would calm your fears.

I wanted to awaken your body to pleasure. You should not have had that year of horror. I wanted to tame you with kindness; not with terror."

Tame me? I started laughing. That was strange with no sound. I laughed even harder.

Marcus dropped the binding. My laughter filled through room. I blinked as the blindfold came free. Marcus rose up and looked down at me. "X isn't tamed, Puppy."

"Then why?" Unlike Armor, Marcus seemed to lack some emotional control; or it seemed that he just couldn't when he was around the brotherhood.

"This is our night and you drag Armor and X into it." I looked up into his tear glistening brown eyes. "We are different, Marcus. Alone, we are lost and we are weak. Together…together we are good. Touch me."

I groaned as he handed his hand down between my legs. I was hard as a rock. "I don't mind this. Do you like it?"

Every hair on my body stood on end as his low whispered worship skipped along my navel. "You should always be displayed this way."

How could I get harder than I already was? "Do what you want to do to me."

Marcus took a handful of my hair and jerked my head back, exposing my throat. "I want to tame you…" He ran his fangs along my extended neck.

"You want to gentle me?"

He lifted his head and kissed around my mouth. "Just to my touch. Just to my desires…" He licked my lips. "Would you be mine, Angel of Death?"

"Yes, Boss." I could feel his smile as he licked his way back to that spot behind my ear.

"Would you wear my ring?" I arched into him as he ran his hand down my spine, stopping at the curve of my ass. "Azrael?"

"I will wear it." I got a kiss to the nose then the blindfold was pulled down over my face to puddle around my neck. I opened my eyes and spied the ring he was talking about. I let a smile cross my lips. "I will wear it with honor."

"I commissioned this for you, my Angel of Death. A pure red natural diamond is a rare and precious thing – so rare that few have seen it's like that that is why I wanted it. A diamond is the hardest substance known and this color of red is the rarest of all. That is what you are to me. Hard and unyielding. Cold yet burning with inner fire. Beautiful…so beautiful that sometimes just looking at you makes me want to cry. Yet, you see me. You see me, and you want me for what I am."

Marcus pushed the nipple ring into his mouth; keeping his eyes locked with mine as his fingers closed around my cock and began to stroke. My hips began to arch up to his stroke. He pulled on the back of my thigh pressing it up around his waist.

"Up." I pulled myself up by the chains from the ceiling and Marcus caught me by my lower back. He pressed me hard up to his stomach as my legs wrapped around his supple hips. My unadorned nipple was at face level. Marcus suckled me. I threw back my head and arched up into his mouth. If there was a binding I would have broken it when my voice cried out in sweet agony. Marcus bit through my flesh. His talented tongue worked the ring through my new hole. I gritted my teeth as he began sucking on my stiffened nub. His other hand spread wide and a finger began sweeping passed my asshole. I bucked up against him.

Finally Marcus raised his head, a small trial of blood eked out of the corner of his mouth. His eyes were red with his Flame. I let my own blue Flame loose.

"With this ring, I thee wed." I whispered to him.

I stiffened and let loose a scream as Marcus drove himself into me. So much for gentleness. I closed my eyes and threw my head back. I cried out again as he continued to work his shaft in and out of my ass. I claimed my Puppy in the alley with the blood of seven men. I wing fucked him in the limo without his consent to show him that he was mine. I bit my lip. Now, I truly was his. He raped me. No, we had made agreements and I wanted this from him. This wasn't rape. He needed me. He needed the master who could keep him safe and he needed a place to release the darkness that I knew it was within him. I drummed my heels against his ass urging him forward. I endured. I wanted it to end...and I didn't. I needed to be all he could ever desire...so I had to endure. I had to. Pain lets you know that you're alive.

"Azrael...Azrael....my Angel of Death...my love...you are mine. You are mine...forever. Ever...lasting...love."

Marcus wrenched my head sideways and fanged me hard. I groaned in joy. I missed this. Suck, fuck, suck, fuck. I was lost in rough pleasure. I came on Marcus's stomach from the mutual friction. My abused ass fluttered and tightened. Marcus roared, lifting his fangs from my neck as he jutted into me.

Somewhere within the penthouse, a grandfather clock rang out four bells.

Marcus rested his forehead against my throat. He breathed heavily and I was moved with each motion of his body like a dinghy on the ocean. He was still hard and so deep inside me. My wrists should be bloody and raw but those huge talented hands cupped my ass, using the strength in his body to keep the chains slack and my arms hanging loose around his shoulders. Gentle caring violence. That summed up my vampire to a tee.

"Azrael?"

I moaned in pain as he withdrew. My void still felt like a warm iron bar was deep inside.

The scent of cinnamon and apples wafted around us. "I've...drawn blood."

"Don't you fucking apologize, Boss." My throat felt raw. Everything was raw. This body wasn't virgin. Thank god for that. I didn't think I'd survive this stint of raw passion if that was my first physical act of love. I felt my eyes burn with true tears. The red flame of Marcus's gaze was nothing but a glowing ember as he reached out and brushed at the tears streaming down my cheeks. Carefully, he untangled our limbs, got up and moved out of my line of sight.

I hung from my cuffed wrists and slowly spun in a lazy circle. Marcus ratcheted me down quickly. My legs wouldn't support my weight and I half collapsed to the bedroom floor slamming my knees hard on the carpet. The concern on my vampire's face was something I would cherish forever. He honored me by showing me what he had hidden from Claudius. This had been engrained in him from birth and it was all that he had known until he was rescued by a shadow as dark as night, who took him from a nightmare that his birth father had called love. My Puppy walked in the light but this darkness would always be with him. To him, this violent surrender would always be true love. The chain dropped more and I ended by slipping off to the side of my hip. So be it. I wanted to give him music and roses but he needed whips and pain then I would be the vampire to give that to him.

This assassin loved an artist.

Marcus quickly unbuckled straps of leather gently massaging my red welts back to painful life. His hands wiped at the tears still running down my face then he leaned over me and gave me the most pure and chaste kiss I'd ever felt.

An artist loved this assassin.

"Azrael?" The uncertainty was back in his voice.

"You are the Boss until six am." My arms are numb. I looked down at my new ring. It sparkled in the dim light as if there were a brilliant hidden fire there. A red diamond. When Armor did this to X, I thought Sex would be the next one to get something foreign placed in our body. Who knew? I groaned and moved enough to lay face down. I probably should have asked first.

"I wish you could have kept your wings out." I heard him walk off, the sound of running water in the distance then I must had drifted because I jerked as I felt Marcus begin to clean me with the tender care that someone would take cleaning a masterpiece. I felt incredibly cherished. He cleaned cum off my stomach and privates. I crunched my eyes tight as the washcloth cleaned my back side. I hid my face in the crook of my forearm bur he must have seen the muscles in my back tighten involuntarily.

"Look what you made me do. I broke you. I can't play with you if you're broken. You can make noise, pet. You can cry out. You can moan

256

and groan. You don't talk. Understood? Clench these beautiful cheeks as a sign of yes."

I clenched my buttocks and was almost overwhelmed with the sensation of shame and a feeling of dirtiness. I lay pliant under his touch. He stroked my ass as he knelt behind me; his hands moved down the backs of my thighs, then trailed them back up the inside of them, pushing my legs wider. He ghosted a touch over my asshole and my whole body tensed up.

"Oh, pet, we can't have that. I'm going to claim you again. Before the clock chimes six a.m. you are going to know what it means to be mine." I gritted my teeth as he pushed a finger into me...slightly. It was still agony. "Show me you understand?"

I nodded.

"No, I told you how to say yes."

Oh my god...I squeezed my asshole around his finger. I gasped at the sensation.

"Good little pet. You continue to be obedient and I'll give you a reward. You'd like that, wouldn't you, my pet angel."

Tears eked out of my closed eyes. I squeezed again in agreement. Marcus pulled me up onto all fours.

"My saliva has healing properties, pet. I'll heal you since you can't heal yourself then I'll make you mine again."

I felt fragile. Marcus manhandled me easily as he used his tongue on the tears his extended possession caused. It didn't take long before I was writhing with renewed need. Marcus knew this body. No wonder X didn't stand a chance. I pulled at my weeping cock.

"No, my pet. I control your body now." He pulled my hands away then positioned me back on all fours and slowly, carefully worked himself back inside me. He bucked forward with little strokes until he was buried deep in me. I tossed my head back and groaned to the ceiling.

"So sexy. If others knew how fuckable angels were, they would be tearing you from the skies." I shivered as fingers raked gently up my spine. "Say yes."

I was too full. I just panted as I sat impaled on him. He took my wrists and pulled my arms behind me. He pressed his head close to my cheek. "I'll have to help you."

What? He tugged on my newest red diamond acquisition. I arched up and tensed my portal at the same time. He opened his other hand on my stomach and pushed me back down onto him. I moaned and quivered. Marcus kept me impaled but tugged on my sensitive nipples. Basically I was milking him with my ass. I hung my head forward and panted for all I was worth. My white hair hung everywhere masking my face. I was so close when his hand dropped off my rings.

"Finish me."

I tried to move my hips but he tightened his hand on my stomach. My chest heaved and my mouth hung open in a perpetual pant. I gritted my teeth and tensed. I was rewarded with a low groan in my ear.

"Yes, fuck me, my pet angel. Draw my offering out of my body."

Shut up. Oh shut the fuck up. I can't concentrate when you're whispering in my ear... or licking that spot. Tense. I groaned as he shifted under me. Tense.

"Do you need help?"

I nodded.

"How do you say yes?"

Tense. Marcus didn't need a second invitation. He grabbed my right thigh and pulled it up, opening my legs wider and changing the angle of his thrusts. He hit my prostate with every jerk. I couldn't have been quiet if my life depended on it. My body was stretched out and taut. He caught my lobe with his teeth and tugged on it as his hard bar of flesh stroked into me. He hit that deep spot again and I screamed in ecstasy as my eyes rolled up in my head when my cum spurted. I hung off Marcus's hard driving cock as he held my hips and fucked me hard and fast. He would hit my prostate again and I would shiver. Both my nipples were diamond tipped and throbbed in time with my hard racing heartbeat. Finally Marcus groaned his completion.

We breathed heavily in time with each other. In time, Marcus slipped out of me. I could feel his offering trailing down my leg. To my horror, my ass pulsed with hunger. He chuckled lowly in my ear. "I've made you my special pet, my needy pet angel of death. Don't worry; no one else will ever know you so intimately. They won't hear your cries of release. You're mine."

I had turned my face away, hiding in my hair. I got a special thrill to hear that. That is what I felt when I was in charge of my Puppy. I was glad he knew my joy of ownership. I cried out as he pushed two fingers inside me and began massaging my special spot. I was reduced to panting and squirming and getting hard again. It was getting to be too much...I turned my face toward Marcus and suck kissed his throat. "Just one more time, pet...and I'll let you rest. Open your eyes, I want to see your Blue Flame."

Marcus pushed the hair off my face and stared down at me. I looked like shit. My face was flushed and I stank of sweat and sex...and fear. I was close to release again. I felt that lurch that preceded my orgasm. Marcus was waiting for it. I brought his hand up to the nipple ring he gave me and gently twisted it. I bucked my chest up to him.

"With this ring, I thee wed, Azrael, First of Assassins, my Angel of Death, my Master....my Heart." He turned his head and swallowed my cries with a kiss and a tongue lashing. I ejaculated in the air without any external stimulation. I had finally reached X's boneless chicken mode...I thought he was just being goofy when he named it that but....no that's what it was. Marcus lifted my arms off the back of his neck and lay me down carefully. I had no clue what time it was but I knew I was in the middle of the sexing of my young life, at least until the grandfather clock chimed six.

Marcus leaned over me and brushed my hair off my face. His melted chocolate candy eyes looked me over earnestly. "You can talk now."

I felt something poke me in the thigh. "What's up? You take those little blue pills?"

"Yeah." He pressed a kiss to my temple. "I didn't want to disappoint you."

I closed my eyes. I was in for a hard time. Ha...I made a funny. It just took too much energy to laugh. That tenderness that was essential

Marcus came through strong as he cleaned up our latest round of debauchery. I was drifting along in my own little bubble of contentment, pressed lightly across his stomach, my head resting on his forearm as he ran a brush through my hair. I felt like a kitten, sated, safe and warm. If I could purr, I think I would have been doing that. Then Marcus began to sing to me.

Lost in the darkness
Lost in memories
Of betrayal and heartache
Wanting no one to save me
I willed my light to stay shuttered and faded
But then you came along
My angel of darkness
Bearing a light
That burned so blue and so true
You offered absolution without any questions
You took what was faded and colored anew
You brought back the joys that were forgotten
I grew so scared...I tried to return

Lost in darkness
Lost in memories
Of music and colors
You wanted to save me
My angel of darkness
You brought back the light
That I'd stopped reaching for
So long ago.
You kindled a flame in my cold, cold heart
That burns now with the glory of you
You gave what I needed though it was dark and hurtful
You stood before me when I lost my way
I've never known this joy and acceptance

My angel of death...with you I will stay.

I let a smile cross my face. He had a beautiful voice. Well, I knew that from my big brothers, but now I got it first hand, it was even better.

"Boss?" My voice was raw.

"Yes, my pet?"

I took a long slow breath. "You gentle my darkness. I hope you know that. I scare Xavier as it is. Could you imagine how bad I could be if you weren't in my life? You make things better for me, you make me better than I could ever be alone."

Marcus was silent for a moment then I was shifted so he could give me countless Marcus specials. I could feel his body asking mine to flame again. I closed my eyes. I tried to get the Healing Light...nothing. His cock was reawakened and was knocking at my back door. This was going to hurt. I lay on my back and pulled my legs back to my chest. His face glowed with possession as he settled himself over me. I wrapped my arms around him and buried my face in his hair. I bit back my cry of pain as he slid inside me. Pain meant you were alive.

"I love you, Azrael."

I was so damn grateful to be alive. I'd have Xavier heal us when he came later today. Right now, it was about Marcus. I tensed tightly around him even as tears trailed from my eyes, "Take me, Boss."

This assassin was in love.

Chapter Sixteen: ...the blues

I was never so happy to hear the grandfather clock chime six bells. Marcus groaned one last time and spilled his seed deep in me. *Oh god. Get up, get off, get lost.* My asshole felt as wide as the Grand Canyon. Marcus carefully held his weight off me as he disentangled our limbs and uncoupled from my docking port. It's not that I didn't want to move, I couldn't. I understood it now when X said he'd been fucked over.

"Azrael?" Marcus ran his hand along my cheek.

"Give me a minute." I closed my eyes and dropped my forehead to the carpet. If this was any indication of what Xavier's first year would have been like if Marcus was the one to kidnap him, he would have been well past 800 fucks. I'm putting this down to enthusiasm on my Puppy's behalf cause...I really don't think he could carry on like this day in and day out. I sure as hell know I can't. I winced but bit back my cry as I tried to move.

"Master, did I hurt you?"

"A tad." *What the hell was a tad?*

There was that anguish back in his tone. "Why didn't you say anything?"

Damn, I didn't want that insecurity to come back to him so quickly. "I agreed to the terms. Don't worry about me." I pushed myself up on all fours. Okay, that was a mistake. I panted and waited for the pain to drop an octave before moving again. The next thing I knew Marcus picked me up like a sack of potatoes and dropped me on his shoulder. "What are...?"

"This was supposed to be mutual pleasure. Damn it, why didn't you tell me that I was just giving you pain." Angry Marcus was a novelty. He marched me into a bathroom. I don't even know where we are. I'm making the assumption that we are in Von Drachenfeld penthouse otherwise we would have been arrested for disturbing the peace by the amount of screaming I did. He set me on my feet, turned the taps on to fill a tub built for two. That would be nice. I could soak my aches away.

263

My hands were numb, and my fingertips tingled. I flexed them; they worked. The little fear that I had about my hands being damaged faded. Maybe I just pinched a nerve or something.

Oh yeah, the warm water felt good. My personal floatation device felt even better. Marcus held me loosely against him to make sure I didn't drown. I started drifting off to sleep. Yah, it sounded so much better than passing out or fainting.

A finger curled a white tendril of my hair as he whispered to me. "I never meant to hurt you."

"Yes you did." I returned drowsily. "Be honest with me, Marcus. I'm not running away from your honest desires."

My whole body moved as my big man gave a huge sigh then silence descended around us. The scent of sweet yet tart green apples filled my nostrils and the warmth of the water eased the lingering aches. I could still feel his ribs under his stretched skin from his time wandering and starving out in the world after House of Assassins sanctions. Marcus was eating but who knew how long it was going to take to get him back up to normal size.

"I never thought you could be more beautiful, I was wrong…my pet angel." I think I moaned something out loud then let the beckoning hands of sleep faded me from my physical body completely. He didn't show Xavier this side of himself. He did all this for me. He was now truly mine. He showed me his darkness and I didn't turn away. I wouldn't say I fully embraced it but I didn't turn away, because I love him with all his faults and imperfections.

Only, at this moment, I didn't want him anywhere near me.

"You certainly are a strange one, brother number three"

X wasn't kidding when he said that this Liam character's voice was low and creepy.

I popped my eyes open. I was standing in the warm water of the ocean with a large body behind me that wasn't my Marcus. One arm was around my waist, the other across my shoulders pinning me back to his massive naked chest. What the hell? He tightened his hold on me before I even thought of trying to escape. The wind came up and blew my hair across my face. Red. I was a redhead again.

Emotionally I was a little rocky from the horror lovefest, but there was no way I was showing it this guy. "I take it you are Liam?"

"Humph. Interesting…Xavier told you about me?" Liam's body felt so warm as if he were running a hundred degree plus temperature, but the hard strength of his arms told me that he wasn't weakened by it. It might be the norm if he's burning out his hosts faster than normal.

"Well if anything affects the core, we get to know all about it. Is this really necessary?" I shrugged my shoulders as if shedding his touch. "Obviously I'm not going anywhere until you send me back from wherever this is."

"It's not necessary, but I like it. However…" He let me go. I walked toward the sand of the beach. I wanted to turn around and stare at him, but a little more distance was in order to get my thoughts working right. Observation one: I was walking without pain. Since I can't get in touch with the Blue line that deals with healing, either this behemoth healed me physically or he was blocking outside stimuli. I flexed my fingers; everything seemed to be in order. Of course, I was naked as a jay bird but as soon as I cleared the water I found myself dressed in black cargo style shorts and a tight black tee shirt. Better than a mini kilt, I guess.

I turned and watched the pale, white giant walk out of the water. It was like watching Poseidon leaving the sea. He was naked. Holy crap, no wonder Hades wanted nothing to do with him. He was a massive fucker in all ways.

"Language, little brother." I blinked, and Liam was dressed in baggy surfer shorts and had on a bright – blindly bright—Hawaiian shirt. He came up to me and I had to tilt my head back and squint to look into his gray eyes. He was almost half a head taller than Marcus. A finger reached out and touched the gold locket at my throat then it trailed across to Marcus's wedding ring.

"I didn't think it was possible."

I took offense to that. "That X could be loved?"

The look he gave me couldn't be interpreted any other way than 'don't be stupid.' "That, that broken Vampire could give away even more of his soul."

I could feel my hackles rise. "His name is Marcus and he's far from being broken."

"Interesting."

Why did that sound like a scientist finding something beyond his research parameters?

I narrowed my eyes and squinted because my hair kept blowing into my eyes. Liam lifted his hand and a la David Copperfield he snapped his wrist and suddenly had a black bandana dangling from his fingers. I took it and tied it around my head and presto instant pirate/biker.

"What do you mean interesting?"

"Your lover raped you repeatedly for six hours straight, but you still defend him…and you still hold him so preciously in your heart."

"Our love is different from others."

"I'll say." Liam snorted.

"It wasn't rape. We both walked into that room as consenting adults. Besides he's my mate."

I stilled as Liam's hand dropped on my shoulder and squeezed it gently. "What's good for the gander doesn't necessarily mean it's good for the goose." Liam walked past me toward the hideous bit of architecture that doubled as a tiki club house. The sand was hot beneath my feet. The water had been warm. This felt real.

"Oh, it's real, little brother. It's just on a different plane of existence."

I reluctantly trudged after him feeling the sand go squish between my toes. Liam tossed his big huge ass on a lounger and held up a frosty glass offering, tall and thin, dripping with moisture with pineapple hanging off it. I passed on that. I wasn't touching alcohol again for a long time. "What the hell do you want this time, Liam?"

"Blunt and argumentative. Is that any way to start this relationship?"

I gingerly sat on my own lounger, more than a little surprised that my nether parts weren't screaming bloody murder. "I consider it honest and to the point."

"So, I will return your honesty with mine, I can't let you fight Cillian."

"Which is fine by me since I'm fighting Hades."

"They are one in the same."

I cocked my head and looked at him. "If you can drag X and me here why don't you haul your precious honey bee back here to your wonderland of tacky?"

The giant turned his head and looked me over. "You seem a little sharper than your brother."

"Now, there's no reason to get insulting. I just ask the questions X won't."

Liam let out a sigh then took a drink. His eyes looked passed me to the watery horizon. "I can't bring him here, because I taught him how to shield against it."

"Bet your kicking yourself over it now." I let a wry grin cross my face.

"I like you, Azrael. Yes, I've been kicking myself, but he needed that protection as my Consort. He was so innocent and young when I had to leave him."

"Nothing like getting hoisted by your own petard."

"You've been hoisted yourself."

I lay on the lounger and looked out to sea. "Can't say I enjoyed it every moment of it either. But I survived."

"That shows your willingness to walk through hell to get what you want; which tells me, I have to guard my Cillian from you."

Glancing over towards the big man, I saw that he was regarding me with a deliberately unreadable expression. "Do you even know Hades?"

"They are one in the same."

"That's like saying I'm the same as X, or Sex. We both know that isn't so. Tell me who your Cillian was."

I was met with silence. Fine. I raised my arms and pillowed my head. Might as well rest while I could.

I was drifting pleasantly in my thoughts when Liam's voice floated over to me. "He is gentle concern and softly spoken love. His scent is sweet and pure. His emotions are easily read on his face. You know he is glad to see you because his smile lights up as soon as he lays eyes upon you. He is innocence personified."

The Hades we brotherhood knew was the opposite end of the spectrum. He was death personified now. "Where did you find him?"

"He was a shepherd boy. I was out hunting rogue Lycan when I spied this vision leaping from rock to rock carrying a tiny lamb. He had such grace in his movements. He had the body of a dancer, the beauty of a concubine all wrapped up in a fragile fleeting existence."

"So basically, you saw him and went schwing."

"Don't be crass. He was only twelve when I first saw him. Far too young to know what he wanted. I let him grow, but I kept an eye on him. I wanted him older before I came for him. But the whim of the Vampire Lord is nothing in the face of human war. It was the spring of his fifteenth year when I had to rescue him. Raiders wiped out his village and his clan. If I had left him in that village, he would never have survived on his own. He was still a child. I brought him back to my castle and made him a part of my household."

Pedo. I shuddered.

"My tastes have never run to children." Liam sounded offended.

I had memories from X from his time as a teenager. It wasn't a period I would want to experience firsthand. But Hades was stuck in that hormonal hell for eternity. For once it made me feel a little for the poor bastard, just a little.

"Everyone knew that boy was my favorite and his charming manner made him the darling to my servants. I spoiled him outrageously, but I'll have you know that he never took advantage of my generosity. He never asked for things he didn't need. I gave him gold and jewels, but he gave them to others in need. When I couldn't find him, I only had to look in the barns or in the fields to discover him tending to the animals. His heart was huge. I wanted to wait to see what kind of man this precious boy would grow into."

"But you couldn't wait." My words weren't an accusation it was a statement of fact. Hades was a teenager.

"Times were different, Azrael. Cillian was considered a young man. I left the decision in his hands and he chose me as his lover. The strength of his essence was like mead. I would get intoxicated from his kisses. When we made love…."

"Lalala" My fingers were over my ears. "Too much information."

Liam laughed. "You are decadent yet still prudish, what an odd combination. You are a mix of contradictions, Azrael, Angel of Death, First of Assassins."

"I'm not going to kill Cillian." I heard Liam shift on his lounger. I shifted my eyes out on the horizon. Liam was going to do what he was going to do and fighting him was going to crack my skull open and this time he might not care if the physical body he wanted to co-habit lived or died. "I'm going to kill Hades."

"That is not permitted."

"Cillian doesn't exist anymore except in your memories, Liam. There is no honey in Hades essence. It is hemlock. It is deadly poison. From what I understand from Elder brother, you created this monster by locking him in a poisonous shell then you left him in that prison for centuries. What survived has devoured your sweet innocent Cillian. Hades had to. You left him no option."

"Cillian is still there. He just…."

"What, waits for your touch? I've looked into his eyes. There is nothing sweet and innocent there. I've had his essence in my mouth…there is nothing but burning pain and death. He's a spider setting traps to suck his victims dry. Your possession ate him alive. It would be a favor to him if I did kill him."

"In the past when I returned he would…"

269

I sat up and pulled my knees to my chin. "You don't get it do you."
I turned my head and looked at the Progenitor of the Vampire Blood.
"You gave him a mortal wound and he has bled out over centuries.
What's left...what remains is anger, pain, desperation and loneliness. If
you truly love him...you wouldn't want him to live like that. You can't
even call it living. He exists in a solitary Hell."

I turned my gaze back to the sea. "Hades is a toucher. He craves
contact so desperately and he's killed so many accidentally from a
simple inadvertent brush. It's sad to see the lengths he goes for it.
Father...he took Father because he was strong enough to endure that
poison. Maybe because, Father was disassociated from his emotions at
the time...he couldn't feel that pain. But Hades crossed the line with him
and burned him out. Now, X comes along. He can handle Hades touch
because of the strength of the Royal line but it damaged him."

I had a light bulb moment. "You planned it that way. You made
Hades repellent to everyone except to the Blue line. Claudius is a
carrier, isn't he? Somewhere down the line, he carries the Blue gene."

Liam sat up and sent a menacing vibe in my direction. If he wanted
to start something I would bring it even though he would probably win.
"There is a brain behind those lovely green eyes and beautifully flawless
face. You are different from Xavier."

"He cares for everyone and everything. I don't; so, there are times, I
see things a little clearer than he does."

Liam stood up and moved back to the tacky tiki bar and began
mixing some concoction up. "Katrina Du Bussey had a mission. She
was like Armanita without the side benefits and craziness. She was to
gather our scattered Blue blood line. Fewer Blues were being born and
unlike the Reds who merely need to bite, we must procreate. We needed
fresh blood. Those candidates she found she brought back to the Blue
houses and they were married back into the bloodline. It was working.
We were having a resurgence in our upper houses' population. Then she
stopped in a Russian village on the steppes and found herself a black-
haired lover."

I turned my head and looked back at Liam. "His mother was nothing but a whore...but his Father...his father was one of ours. Just like men, Vampire males always have to spread their seed be it a she vampire or just a mortal woman. When a vampire mates with a human woman, if there is offspring it's human but it does carry our blood line in a dormant state. If that dormant gene is activated with a bite, well a high Crimson Flame for a Red is born. As with the Royal line that runs through your family blood, it carries forward with each generation. Claudius's father left behind a blue legacy. I sent Katrina there to retrieve him. I had a perfect mate picked for him already. Katrina decided to claim him as hers."

I laughed then rubbed my eyes. X got himself caught up in something that was in the planning, for only Liam knew, how many years.

"Ah, I see it now. Claudia is Claudius's natural born Vampire child. She carries the Blue line. She mates with X and...you are guaranteed to get the Royal Blood Line back in business. Hades must have pissed you off to no end when he sterilized X."

"I was less than amused."

"So, Hades really doesn't play a part in your kick starting your line back up. I should be able to kill him off without repercussions."

"I can't allow that."

I uncurled myself. I was about to get handed my head. So be it. "You don't love him. It shouldn't matter to you."

"I have loved him through the ages."

"No, you've possessed him...you've owned him through the ages. If you loved him, you would have done anything to get back to him."

"Like you?" I knew Liam was referring to my lovely little six hours of sadistic bliss.

"That's love. If that is what Marcus needs from me to ease his heart and truly know that I love him, I'll bite my lip and let him take me any way he desires. I prefer the keys, but I can step aside. You told X, you were waiting for the next Emperor to come along. Why? Why couldn't you have come back as a Red? Would your Cillian have been so disappointed if he couldn't be Royal Consort?"

"He didn't care about titles."

"But apparently you do. You left your Cillian twisting in the wind. You could have come back as a lesser vampire to ease his suffering, but you didn't. Even now, there is a Red that loves the mess Hades has become so much that he would risk being killed to get so much as a kiss from him."

I cocked my head to one side, "But you won't come back as anything less than Lord Emperor. If you did you'd be below Hades and you're not prepared for the hell, he would put you through."

Yup. That pissed Liam off. He cleared the tiki bar with one jump and I was able to take only a single step before I had to block a hand coming at me at lightning speed then another a massive hand closed on my throat. He squeezed and lifted me up at the same time. I kicked with my feet for a moment then found purchase on the lounger. "What do you know of love? You are just a fragment."

"Well this fragment has 2/3rds of his lover's soul. I have all the gentle emotions an emotionally stunted Father can give me. I have the knowledge that I am loved and cared for. You? You got sand."

His eyes blazed with intense blue fire then seemed to unfocussed. "What are you doing, little assassin? I can't let you do that." I had a feeling that he wasn't talking about me.

I went flying through the air arching for the ocean. "If you love your Father, stop him. Go. Now."

I came up coughing water in the tub. Marcus grabbed at me and pulled me hard to his chest. "What the hell just happened?"

I coughed some more then drew a shaky breath. Oh yeah, I was back in the real world. My body was in complete agony. I groaned and buried my face against Marcus neck. "Master?"

"We have to find Father...now." I couldn't move...*X, please...I need your help now.*

"Master?" Marcus wrapped his loving arms around me anchoring me to his slick skin. Apples filled my head.

272

I took a deep breath filling my lungs with the scent of my lover. It hurt to move but I pushed myself upright. "Marcus, have you ever known Claudius to do anything half assed?"

Marcus reached out and steadied my torso as he regarded me with deep concern. "Father does everything with full dedication."

"That's what I thought."

"Master, I don't understand."

"What time is it?"

"A little after seven."

"Please X...heal me." Marcus flinched as my body burst into blue healing light. Oh, thank God. *Thanks Elder Brother.*

"Father does everything full dedication. If he is Hades lover, he would have given the bastard his heart...or at least offered it because that was expected. Hades would probably have been living with the hope that Liam was coming for him and rejected Claudius. That's why Father only sees him as an employer."

The healing light faded. Oh, that was so much better. I climbed out of the tub still feeling a little fragile, but it faded with each step. Marcus followed me.

"Azrael what is going on?"

"Father knows that we can't harm Hades. He knows that Hades would probably kill me..."

Marcus shook his head in confusion.

Pivoting on my heel I caught up my hand in Marcus's hair, my thumb caressed the swell of his cheekbone. He needs more food. "Claudius is on his way to assassinate Hades. He's going to get today's assigns then he's going to try and take Hades down. Liam knows this, that's why he let me go. We've got to get there before Father tries anything."

"Call him."

"He won't answer. Marcus...I need to fang you. I'm healed but weak right now." My Puppy pulled his hair back and offered his neck without a second's hesitation. That's love. I fanged him hard and deep, sucking hard to cure the weakness still running in my body. It was like

273

chugging apple cider. I wrenched my head back breathing hard as his essence rushed through me. Oh, yes...I opened my eyes and he held his hand to his neck.

"You okay?"

"Let's get Father."

I held out my hand to him and he grabbed it without hesitation which was great cause I still had no clue where I was. In the back rooms of Von Drachenfeld, apparently. Marcus stopped to get Armor's tools of the trade. Then we motored down the halls back to X's room where I got dressed in black, got my tall doc's on and pulled on a long sleeve shirt. Marcus moved off to get the limo ready.

I was buckling the sheath on my forearm when Armor walked back into room. Yeah, he would be better for this than my Puppy.

"Monkey see, monkey do, eh?" He gestured to the outline of both nipple rings through the snug fitting shirt.

"Copying is the sincerest form of flattery." I slipped into my harness.

"Not impressed with your decision to keep secrets from me. Challenging Hades? Are you mad?"

"Ah, I wasn't the one doing the challenging. This all happened with X, Father and your inner brother. Bitch at them if you're going to come down on anybody." I returned quickly.

"I think we are going to have to limit Father's limit with Sex. He is acting like him, impulsive and reckless."

Armor pulled on a light jacket, hiding his own personal arsenal.

"We have to save him from his own stupidity first before we can put sanctions on him." I clipped the small dagger to the waistband of my pants at the small of my back. I slipped on a black windbreaker then grabbed for my goggles. I did a quick rundown. I had everything I needed.

"Tick tock, Azrael."

I slipped the goggles onto my forehead, flashing Armor a big wide smile. "Let's dance."

We headed out of Von Drachenfeld with one mission in mind. Save Claudius.

Chapter Seventeen: A rescue or two

The rescue mission was stalled. Armor looked at me, his jaw clenched and his eyes wary. I stared back at him then pulled my goggles down over my eyes. He pulled out his shades and slipped them on. "If we start melting, you just throw it into reverse."

"Yah…" I tightened my hands around the steering wheel. X had asked to have his car altered with the same specially coated, magically sealed glass that we now had in Von Drachenfeld. The only problem was that neither Armor nor me knew if it had been done. If it was installed, we were laughing all the way to Shadoe Incorporated. If not…we were just backing up into the building as fast in reverse as possible. Could you even do a burnout in reverse? We just might find out. I revved it, threw it into gear. Drive into the sun to test the glass like dipping a toe into the pool or cannonball in? I've never been a dipper. I floored it.

The brightness of the summer sun burnt into my eyes even though it was barely passed seven in the morning and I had my goggles on…but we weren't drying up and blowing away either. I waited a few more seconds just in case.

Armor nodded. "We are good to go."

We were driving ourselves because the limo was "conveniently" out of commission. Tires were slashed, brake lines were cut and all the vampire safety windows in the back was smashed out. I had one guess who did it. Wiley bastard. Father was an 'all in' kind of guy. I could learn so much…if Hades didn't kill him.

I floored it and the vampire version of Rescue 911 flew out into the street. Vampire assassin one and fourteen heading to the rescue of assassin number two in an 1957 Chevy Nomad station wagon. There was something more than a little odd about that.

"I did not know you could drive."

"I didn't either." I could feel his eyes snap to me. "I mean, you and Marcus must have some overlapping talents."

"Not really."

Okay. Hmm, how to put this. "Sex is the one that passed the test. I can drive pretty good. Don't get in the car with X."

"Stay within the speed limit. We do not need to be pulled over. Watch out for that car." I rolled my eyes. For someone who doesn't drive, Armor was going a great imitation of a back-seat driver.

"Shut up! You're making me nervous." I screamed at him but never took my eyes off the road. I knew I had a death grip on the wheel and Armor's advice wasn't helping me calm down.

"It's just that... WATCH OUT!" I saw his hand make an instinctive grab for the wheel but I slapped it away. I slammed on my brakes and yanked the wheel over to the right. We skidded, bounced, and then came to a lurching stop at the curb. "I'm new at this. I'm doing the best I can. Shut the fuck up and let me concentrate, all right?"

Armor turned and looked at me. "Did you get any sleep?"

I sat back and looked out the front windshield. "You know damn well I didn't."

Armor settled himself back into his seat. I noticed the stares we were getting from the everyday citizens. Screeching to a halt and arguing was bound to get us noticed by the police and since my fingerprints weren't purged from the last time, I didn't need to be run through the system, not now anyway. X wore gloves on the last assignment but as Marcus proved, nothing is foolproof.

Armor's voice was a little calmer. "I do not know anything of the sort, Azrael. Marcus hordes his and your time to himself."

Thank God for small favors. I put the car back in Drive and merged back into traffic. Armor never said another word, but he kept slamming his foot on the invisible brake on his side of the car with his hands fisted in his lap. The imitation of a nervous driving instructor was just as annoying as his co-pilot driving commentary.

Then from out of left field, Armor made the comment. "You seem to be walking all right from what I noticed."

I clenched my teeth and tightened my knuckles on the steering wheel. Armor was the last vampire that I wanted to discuss my betrothal night with. "I had X heal me."

"I thought so. My neck still hurt when I took over."

I winced a bit. I had fanged Marcus hard and deep almost at full extension. "Sorry, I didn't heal the fang marks."

"All I get from Marcus is peace and satisfaction...you must have done something right."

I clenched my teeth and brought the car to a stop at the stoplight. "I think I liked it better when you just grunted at me."

"Actually, I have never grunted at you. Our first meeting, we beat the crap out of each other. We never did finish that."

"Yes, we did. You submitted."

"Not to you."

"Doesn't matter. You submitted."

"We are going to have to finish it then."

"I look forward to it." I pulled the Nomad down into the underground parking. Security halted us as X's vehicle was a strange car. We had to use the underground lot. There was no way I was parking out front then running across the wide shade less entryway to get into the main lobby of Shadoe Inc., followed by going upstairs, taking on Hades if he wouldn't listen to reason and if he did, then trying to subdue Claudius without hurting him. I needed all my facilities about me. I didn't need a touch of sun sickness right now.

"First! Cipher. You're together?" The security guard looked like I could push him over with a feather.

Both of us at the same time said, "No."

"Carpooling."

"Giving him a lift."

"You have a designated parking area on the fourth level."

"I need to get upstairs to Hades, now. Can I just leave it and have someone park it?"

"Frank!" The man had a set of lungs on him. Another Vamp in black materialized beside the car. "Can you park this car?"

"We are not a valet service."

"Frank, Azrael wants his car parked."

You could see the color drain out of Frank's face. He glanced down into the car and paled even further. "Of…of course, Sir. Please." Frank opened my door and bowed. I bit back a smirk even as Armor muttered under his breath calling me a 'show-off'. Time was of the essence and besides if you got the reputation what's wrong with flaunting it?

I booked for the elevator to the lobby. Armor was breathing down the back of my neck as the elevator car took us back up to ground level. I didn't like him there behind me but there wasn't much I could do about it. I know damn well I can't take Father down my myself, well not without hurting him anyway. A finger reached out from behind me and flicked at my new piercing. I gasped and elbowed Armor as hard as I could in the stomach almost simultaneously. "Hands off the merchandise."

"Is it just as sensitive as the one I gave to Xavier?"

I shuddered. Oh, yeah, he put the other one in first. "It's enough to be a distraction I don't need right now."

"You took my gift to X off."

"Which I shouldn't have done. I apologize for that, Armor." That shut him up.

The elevator doors opened to the lobby. I wanted to run to the security desk but kept it under control. No one needed to know Claudius was off his rocker right now. I signed in and scanned to see if Father had beaten us. Nothing there. I moved on to the next check point.

"Is Hades still in his suite or has he gone to his office yet?"

The security guard looked down at whatever was there. "He is still at home. You are cleared to go up, Azrael. Cipher, you are not."

"Can you call Hades?"

"Sir?"

"I need Cipher with me. Give him a call."

It took all my strength of will not to tap my fingers impatiently on the desktop. Finally, the guard handed the phone over to me.

280

"What are you doing, Azrael? I assume it is you, because it is Saturday." Hades adolescent voice held pleasant surprise.

"Yes, it's Azrael. I have Armor with me. I need to see you. We need to see you now."

I could see him in my mind's eye staring down at us in his monitors. I turned and waved at the camera.

A slight laugh accompanied the action. "Cute. I thought your day was pre-booked by your mating rituals with Marcus."

"We multi-tasked. Everything's done now. We have to speak to you about something important. I cannot discuss it down here in the open."

There was a moment of silence then Hades capitulated. "Come on up. Cipher cannot bring weapons. He is still under sanctions. Hand me back to the guard."

I turned and looked at Armor. "Hand them over." The guard set a lockbox on the counter. Armor sighed and pulled out his guns and extra clips. They were set in the box, locked and Armor was handed the key to the gun safe. Once that was done, I was handed the brass key for access to the upper levels.

"Could you give us a heads up when Carnage arrives." I tapped the top of the desk with the key so it rang out.

"Yes, Sir."

"Just don't tell him we're here. It will ruin the surprise."

Once we got into the elevator, I fit the key in the slot then waited until the elevator stopped. I turned the key and the panel slid out. I pressed my palm against it and waited for clearance. We started upward again. I reached into my jacket and brought out my Glocks and handed them to Armor. I still had my blades. He slipped them into his holsters and I could feel the confines of the elevator get colder as both of us slid into Assassin mode.

Armor stared up at the elevator indicator numbers. "We got a plan?"

"Don't kill Father."

"That's it?" There was a tone of incredulity in that question.

"I'm not a big planner." I tensed the muscles in my shoulders and back then let them relax.

"I'm more of a bullet myself. Just point me at what you want dead and I'll kill it."

I shook out my arms and hands. "He's kicked our asses so many times."

"We'll have to take Claudius together. He gets to Hades, he's dead. There will be no mercy for Father. Let's not let it get that far." Armor was only stating the obvious.

I turned and made a fist and held it up. Armor looked at me briefly then did the same thing and we punched knuckles. It was either that or a hug. Armor is not the vamp that I wanted to hug. "You break right, I'll take left. I'll head for Hades. Keep an ear open for him. I wouldn't put it past him to take the stairs."

The elevator door opened, and we split up. I flicked my wrist and caught my dagger. I searched quickly moving my way deeper into Hades suites. Sex knew almost every inch of this place intimately. *Don't go there. Concentrate.*

It was before 7:00 a.m. so Hades was still wandering around his suite in pajamas and a dressing robe. He was in the middle of playing good host and was carrying a tray with three mugs of blood…and toast for me. He keeps food here?

"What brings you here…with a blade unsheathed?" His voice started out warm and got arctic before the last syllable left his lips. "I thought you were coming here to tell me that you've finally come to your senses and were here to withdraw your challenge."

I lowered myself into reverent pose then lowered my forehead to the Persian carpet. "I've come to beg you for mercy."

"What have you done?" Hades crossed his arms over his chest.

"Not for me." Armor made his way down the hall and came into the room behind me. He lowered himself down into reverent pose behind me.

"And Cipher is armed. What is going on, my First?"

"I swore an oath to you. I swore to protect you."

"Only because you were going to kill me yourself. Who's coming?"

I lifted myself up back into my knees. "Carnage."

The shock in his voice was real. "Claudius?"

"I beg for the same mercy you showed Sex when he came for you. He did it out of duty to his mate."

"Claudius is going to assassinate me out of duty to his mate?"

"He's doing it to save his stupid sons – all five of us."

"He has never won against me."

"I beg for his life."

"This is a serious breach. I cannot allow my Second to attack me."

"No one but us knows."

"Why. Tell me why a loyal…" Hades voice broke off and ran a hand through his messy curls. "This is why there shouldn't be factions within the House of Assassins, Azrael. You have turned a good friend against me."

"It was not intentional. He believes, I cannot beat you in the challenge. He's actually being a very good father."

Hades turned his attention back to me. "What do you offer, First? What do you offer me to show Carnage mercy?"

"What do you want?"

"Withdraw your challenge."

"I can't. I wasn't the one who issued the challenge, but I agree with Xavier."

"Azrael!" Armor hissed at me.

Hades snapped back. "Why not? What is so important about dying tomorrow?"

An electronic beep broke our little tête-à-tête. Hades picked a mug up then sat down on the couch before reaching over and picking up the receiver. He listened attentively for a second. I watched as his jaw firmed. "Carnage is on his way up. You haven't convinced me, First."

I matched his watery blue gaze with my own. I wanted him to know that I knew the truth and that I was speaking it as well. "William first saw you when you were twelve years old. You were jumping from rock to rock carrying a lamb that had wandered off from the flock. He came and rescued you after your settlement was razed by raiders. He brought you back to his castle and waited for you to grow up but neither of you could wait. Which leads to this..." I waved my hand over at Hades' eternal youth.

"You've fought beside and against him, Honey Bee...have you ever won? You're 900 years old do you think you win against him? I say no because you freaked out on hearing his pet name for you. If you can't win against him, how can I? I'm barely two years with the Royal blood line running through me. Do you want to be forced under his hand again? Do you think I want to play unwilling host to Liam's personality? Tomorrow must happen, for both of us. Ask for something else, Hades and I will give it."

"Sex...here with me until midnight." I didn't even have to ask brother. He was anxious for Father.

"He agrees."

"The same provision as when Claudius came to me. He draws my blood. He forfeits everything including his life."

"Agreed." I got to my feet and gestured back at Armor. "We have one chance at this. We have to get him off guard."

I pulled the elastic out of my hair and shook my white hair loose and free. Sex reminded me how damn painful it was to see Claudius on his knees in front of Hades. Even if he was only sucking blood from his wrist...it was a heart blow.

"Do you have a stun gun?"

Hades gestured to a credenza. Of course, he'd have one. Armor pulled it out and turned it on. There was also a telescoping baton. I pulled my jacket off. My wings ripped through my shirt. "Base of the skull, Armor. You remember how effective that was when Father used it on Xavier."

His face hardened. I needed that from him. If we couldn't incapacitate Father in one blow...we were so screwed. I sheathed my dagger and gestured for Hades to sit on the couch. I was more than willing to climb on Hades, but Sex made a good argument. Claudius would know the difference between us, even if he only looked at us from behind.

Don't offer if you can't do it, Sex.

284

I can do it. I'll get to Father before he gets to Hades. I don't want Claudius dead or hurt.

Make the change slow…we still need to surprise the bastard tomorrow.

I closed my eyes and counted to five before fading back. I followed Azrael's example and counted to five before opening my eyes and looking over at Hades. "Come here, Edward."

I licked my lips and nodded. I walked up to him and hiked my leg over his thighs, so I was sitting on his lap. My knees I wedged into the seat, so I could have some purchase if I had to leap up right away. I heard the elevator doors open. "You save Claudius, you're mine."

"Just for the day." I stretched my wings out, making sure to shield Hades completely. I leaned forward and speared my fingers in his hair. I kissed him. My lips began tingling and stinging. I let my mouth open and I slipped my tongue into his lips, teasing his mouth open. I ignored the pain. This was to save my lover. My heart. I looked into Hades eyes. "You've never seen me Flame, have you?"

"Hades, I know that Azrael is…." Claudius voice trailed off as he spied me sprawled on the CEO's lap. I flipped my hair and turned to look over my shoulder at him. "Sex…"

"Oh hello, Father…come to commit a little mayhem?"

Armor stepped out of the shadow and pressed the stun gun against the exposed neck, but Claudius shifted so quickly. He still tensed as the charge ripped through him with the entry point at his shoulder. Claudius didn't drop though. He turned and elbowed Armor in the face. I winced as the big guy's head snapped sideways but Armor hung on and zapped Father again. I climbed to my feet and turned positioning myself between Father and Hades, again making sure my wings were a barrier. This time Claudius dropped to one knee. He dropped his daggers. I jumped over the small table and kicked him in the jaw. One blade went twisting away. The other came up and slashed at me. I gave a cry as the edge cut into the top part of my wing. Claudius stilled. His eyes snapped up to me as Armor brought the stun gun up and this time hit that sweet spot. He twitched, and his eyes rolled up into his head. His dropped to the floor, his head smacking it with a melon thud.

Armor's face was a mess. Blood splattered every. He had a broken nose. My own wing was turning red from the deep cut. I stepped over Father and gestured for Armor to kneel. "I'll straighten your nose on three." He nodded.

"One." I wrenched it back in place.

He grunt-groaned and his eyes snapped open with a glare. "What happened to two and three?"

"The element of surprise. It hurts less if you aren't all tensed up besides; I have to keep you looking pretty for brother."

I called out the healing light and touched his head. I was still burning blue when I reached down and touched Father. He groaned and slowly pushed himself off the floor.

"Do you yield?"

Claudius was groggy and a little off balance for a moment, but he was growing stronger in leaps and bounds. He shook his head then gave me a gruff and disgruntled. "Yes."

I grabbed onto his shoulders and dragged him close, folding my wings around him. "You stupid, stupid, stupid…why didn't you tell me you were going to do this? I would have helped you." I whispered lowly.

"How did you know? I decided it less than an hour ago when I could not find a way for you to defeat him and Xavier refused to retract the challenge."

I rubbed my cheek on his slightly static hair. Black tendrils of hair reached out to me as if they had just been rubbed with a balloon. Well more like 50,000 volts times three which would be like rubbing your head on the Hindenburg. "Liam had Azrael. He made an educated guess that you were the little assassin that shouldn't be doing what he was planning. And I knew for once, that it wasn't me."

"Why did you stop me?"

"Because Hades would kill you, and I couldn't handle that." I closed my eyes, "And, I need you to get my sister pregnant."

286

He stilled. Armor's eyes got big as he stood behind us. I kissed Father's temple. "You carry a piece of the Blue Line as well. You get my sister pregnant and you become the blood father of Emperors."

"What are you saying?"

"If I die tomorrow..." Father caught me up in a desperate embrace and hugged me so hard I thought I heard my bones creak as I felt them groan inside me. "I said if, not when, the Royal line will continue with you as its Regent. This is the only way. Please...please say you'll do this."

"I love you...I don't want to be with anyone else."

"Promise me, Claudius. Promise me that you'll stay alive. You'll probably have twins. My sister and I were the exception. You could tell them their Uncle wasn't such a fuck up all the time."

"No. Do not tell me goodbye. I will not take a goodbye from you." Father began to struggle to get free. "I will not take a goodbye from you, Sex." I hung onto him desperately as I made my hand of light a stun gun.

"I love you Father. My Gorgeous. My Light in the Darkness."

"Fallen..."

I brought my hand to the base of his neck. He cried out and spasmed in my arms, my wings chimed as he shuddered then he dropped unconscious. He looked so vulnerable when he slept. He looked young and at peace. I dissolved my wings and Father slumped to one side. I held onto him tears brimming in my eyes.

"Take him home, Armor. Marcus has got a room set up at the back of the manor. You'll probably have to chain him up. Is that all right Hades?"

"You have fulfilled your side of the bargain. Take him out of here, Cipher. Leave Azrael's guns here, it will look odd to the security if you have them. Take Claudius in the north elevator. It will go directly to the parking garage. I will have my limo ready for you."

Armor picked up Claudius' still form and slung him over his shoulder. He reached out and grabbed me around the neck and dragged me close. His cheek rested against mine as he whispered in my ear. "I will not accept a goodbye from you either. I will have your car ready for you to come home at midnight."

"I got the Nomad downstairs. I'll drive home." I hugged my upper torso as I watched Armor walk away carrying my heart on his shoulder. Long strands of black hair hung down to the floor and swayed as Armor walked.

I stood there still staring down the hall long after they had left. Hades walked up and pressed a kiss to my shoulder. I closed my eyes and bowed my head. My eyes stung as tears fell from my eyes.

"Sssh, Claudius is fine. You saved his life today. He may not thank you for it, but he will be grateful, eventually."

I wiped my eyes dry. "I'm not crying over that…Liam's got everybody fucked over. I could be so happy here with Claudius."

"And with me?"

"I thought you were just an asshole, Hades. I realize that Liam's fucked you over worse. Only Nobility can touch you. Only Royalty can hold you. All because he only wants to come back stronger than you."

Hades stiffened and the hold on my shoulder tightened almost to the point of pain.

"He's been waiting for this body, this blood line. It's the only thing stronger than you…or could be. He knows he's done you wrong and he's fearful of what you could do if he were weaker. He left you in hell for four hundred years because he's scared of you."

"How the hell do you know this?"

"Liam's been taking us…one at time to his little beach paradise. He said, you know how to stop it – that Liam had showed you how to guard against that kind of attack. Could you teach me?"

"Blood your shield."

Huh?

"Cover your mental shield with your blood. Vampire blood has many properties, healing is just one of them. Protection is another. I keep forgetting how young you are." He swept my hair back from my head and neck. I grimaced as his lips burned me. "How beautiful you are."

288

"Make it go away...." I whispered out loud.

Hades lifted his head, "What was that?"

I turned in his embrace and looked into his cold blue eyes. He stared back at me puzzled. I took his head in both my hands and leaned forward almost kissing him. "Thank you for your mercy. Here is ours."

I flashed into healing light. Hades stood still in my grasp for a moment then he stiffened and stared to hiss. I grabbed him hard around the neck and dragged him in closer contact with my body. He started screaming and writhing. I closed my eyes, hung onto him with all my might. I heard crackling and steam. His body grew hot as my healing light engulfed him and burned from blue to white hot. He bucked up against me still screaming. We fell over onto the carpet and he tried to roll away. I wrapped my legs around his waist and buried my head against the crook of his neck. Finally, my light faded. I had the strength of a newborn. This time when Hades moved, I slipped off his chest and landed on the floor.

"What have you done?" Hades lay on the floor behind me, panting and staring up at the ceiling. "Sex, what did you do to me?"

"I got the poison out of Princess Sarah. I didn't know if I could get it out of you."

"I feel strange."

"Kiss me."

Hades shifted and leaned over me. "You can tell with a kiss?"

I raised my arm weakly and draped it around his neck. He moved forward and pressed his lips to mine. I licked at my lips and urged him down again, this time opening my mouth and inviting him in. I stroked my tongue along his then smiled and whispered to him.

"You're sweet...my little Honey Bee." Hades looked down at me, his eyes wary and tinged with fear. "What did Liam do to you, little shepherd boy?"

Hades rolled onto his back and laid a forearm across his eyes. "He made me love him. He promised to protect me. Then he never came back. I've been alone for so long."

The bastard started crying. Not just gentle sobs but the, I-don't-want-to-be-here-to-witness-this kind-of-crying kind. Hades curled into a fetal position away from me and wailed out four hundred years of soul stealing agony. I could barely sit up. I just had to touch his back and he grabbed me around the waist and buried his face on my thighs. This was sweet Cillian. He wasn't dead, just dormant. I dropped my arms down on his back and rubbed my hands in a gentle circle. The crying eventually ceased.

I heard an 'ahem' from the corridor. Billy Envoy stood there ill at ease, but his eyes were shooting daggers at me. I looked down at the blonde head and gestured Billy away. Hades or Cillian, neither one of them would want anyone to see this breakdown. Billy nodded and backed away. The teenager's breathing evened out as exhaustion took him down. I shook my head. After all of this – pain and torture, this sexy teenage bastard was still in love with Liam. I guess Armor wasn't the only stupid fuck in the world. I leaned back against the coffee table and closed my eyes. Damn, it wasn't even nine in the morning yet. This was going to be a long day.

Chapter Eighteen: Friendship

I was tired, hungry covered in carpet burns as I lay naked on the rug and was actually sick of sex. Azrael would have a field day with that one. Hades turned from a toucher to plastic wrap cling-on. I would rather trip over Haley every time I turned around. *Get off me.* I tried to disentangle myself but even half-asleep Hades just found another hold.

"I need to go to the bathroom."

He muttered not even bothering to open his eyes. "No, you don't."

Oh yes, I did. I'd had marathon Marcus the night before and just regular horny teenager all morning. "Hades…I'm not kidding."

"Come here, Edward."

"Get the fuck off me! And my name is Sex, not fucking Edward." Okay I've never claimed to be the brightest bulb on the Christmas tree. I found myself pinned on the floor; the watery eyes that were almost closed a second ago were wide open and tinged with red. Hemlock had nothing to do with his strength. Secretly I was hoping for a Samson like effect. Cut the hemlock, cut the strength. That didn't work.

"Shall we re-phrase that?"

"Master, I need to go to the bathroom."

"Better. What's your name?"

"Whatever the Master decides." I got my noggin rattled on the carpet for that remark.

"Again, what's your name?"

I turned my head away from him, "…Edward…"

It was safe to say his little breakdown this morning was long forgotten. He dug his hip into my groin forcing my legs to open. I reached down to shield my privates, but he grabbed me by the wrist and forced it back beside my head. He did the same with the other wrist. I stared up at him and tried to unclench my jaw. He transferred my wrists to one hand.

"Please…don't." He trailed his hand down my face, rubbing his hand along my jaw, his thumb pressing against my lower lip, bruising it, his teeth cutting the inside of lip.

"So beautiful…" I closed my eyes and turned my face away. His hand trailed down to my chest and his fingers flicked one ring, then the other. Even though my body was protesting it reacted to the stimulus. "My beautiful Edward…. tell me what you want."

"Whatever the Master desires."

Hades gripped my left ring and twisted it hard. I cried out and tried to turn into the pain to get it released. He used this to get his thighs against mine and pushed my legs open wider…then he pushed himself inside me. "Don't make me hurt you, Edward. Not now. Not today. Be honest." I lay under him, trapped, as he slowly began to piston his cock in and out of me.

"That's one thing I like about you, Edward. You were always honest with me…even if you despise what I was doing."

He laid his body on mine. Honey sweet kisses peppered my face and neck as his hips kept to his slow rhythm. "Tell me what you want, Edward. Be honest…I want you to feel good."

Tears were leaking from my eyes. He licked them from my face. I said nothing. He grunted then raised himself back up off me until the only connection was his cock in my ass and our thighs rubbing on each other as he stroked and his hand on my wrists. I thought it was bad before when he was all hemlock, but this was a different kind of horrible. My whole body rocked as he slammed enthusiastically into me.

"Do you like this?"

"…no…"

He stilled. He was still deep inside me. He rotated his hips slowly. "Tell me what you want, little boy."

"I want to go home." I whispered still looking away from him.

"What was that? I didn't hear you."

I turned my head up to him and opened my eyes. I blinked to get him in focus. "I want to go home. I want to be free."

Hades was silent. There was something going on in that head of his, but I didn't have the energy nor the inclination to do something about it...besides, my hands were still pinned to the floor. I couldn't mind fuck him even if I wanted to. And I'd never want to peer inside that dark and twisted skull.

"Withdraw your challenge and I'll set you free, Sex."

It could be so easy. I could tell Hades what he wanted to hear and I could go find Claudius and beg forgiveness. But in the end, it would mean losing everything. Azrael and I were born out of necessity, but that didn't mean I couldn't exist outside that horror. Both of us found something we weren't looking for. What we didn't know even existed for...what did Liam call us...fragments. Fragments found love. Even though Father would probably break my nose before welcoming me back...if he welcomed me back.

Blood my shield. It would prevent Liam from dragging us to whatever plane of existence he was perched at, but it wouldn't stop him from coming here. If we couldn't beat him, he would kill Azrael and me. There was no other way of putting it. Forcing us back into Xavier was just the same as killing us. If he took over X, there was no way Armor would be allowed to stay with him. It would be William and Cillian, until this body was dead. If Xavier's name was remembered at all it would be Liam's deeds.

Father, what would he do when his sons were dead, and their killer lived in the 'shell of the house'? He would challenge Liam. He would challenge with a wounded soul and a broken heart and he would die. The smiles he gave now, the joy Marcus caught in the painting that was there for me to see when we were together...all those precious things would be lost: there would be nothing left to show that I even once existed. No, there was that painting. Someone one would see it and know we were once happy. Marcus...he's unpredictable, emotionally unstable so he would probably be killed too. If he didn't do something crazy, then Armor would. X would be left alone with that monster.

Hades had to die. Or I did. Or Liam...but then he was dead to begin with and that is where all the trouble starts from. The consequences of Liam taking me over were just too costly to pay. I closed my eyes, gritted my teeth and lifted my legs, raising them beside his hips. I could leave at midnight. It would be Sunday anyways. Our turn to shine.

"Not withdrawing." I responded to Hades' tantalizing offer.

I fully expected Hades to go into Roger Ramjet mode as punishment for my defiance. I waited and waited. "Edward…" That name was a sigh in my ear as he began to slowly thrust into me. When Hades wanted to, he was skilled. I gathered my wounded soul and packed it in bubble wrap as Hades played my body just as skillfully as Marcus paid the violin. What is physical pleasure when your heart's weeping?

He knew I still wasn't with him. He tried harder. I came as his free hand jacked my cock, my body betrayed my heart. I arched skyward and Hades took that as a sign to ride me hard all the way to the finish line. I felt his offering coat my backside. When he finally slipped out, he released my hands and slumped beside me on the floor. I turned away from him and curled into a fetal position. I should be crying but my eyes were abnormally dry.

Hades spooned me. He dropped an arm around my waist and dragged me back to him. I felt his hand at my ass spreading his leaking offering on my skin like butter on toast. I closed my eyes and prepared to endure.

"You can't win tomorrow. You can't even fight me off you now. Do you want to die?"

My voice was thankfully toneless, "Master, may I go to the bathroom now?"

"Edward! Withdraw your challenge. You can't win against me."

"I…we can't leave X alone to suffer with Liam…"

"You honestly believe that William will try and take over your body. He's never done that before…he's always been reincarnated."

I stared off sightlessly into space, "Are you telling me that Sigmund never came for you?"

"Sigmund? Lord Emperor Sigmund?" I felt a kiss at the nape of my neck. I closed my eyes. "He came to me once, but he was crazy. He

294

tried to force himself on me, but I fought him off and then Rothchilde showed up and everything went to hell in a hand basket. Never come between a man and his woman, especially if they are both nuts."

"Sigmund wasn't crazy."

"What was that?"

"That was Liam. Sigmund only had a red daughter. There was nobody Liam was willing to re-incarnate with, so he took the next best thing."

"Are you saying the maniac that broke into my house in the middle of the night and tried to violate me was William?"

"I haven't heard that Sigmund swung both ways. He couldn't handle the women he was with as it was." My stomach roared and rumbled.

Hades sat up then slid off the bed. He seemed to be annoyed that I kept brining Liam up in the conversation. "Go to the bathroom and have a shower. It's after one. We need to get you, something to eat and we'll plan the rest of the day." I slowly sat up, wincing as my ass shot a spike of pain up my spine. Hades kissed my shoulder. "Find something else to wear. Azrael can pull off black…you can't."

"Nothing else fits."

"Nonsense."

Did he just use the word nonsense? I turned and looked back at him. "Nonsense?"

Hades threw open the closet door and gestured at everything hanging so neat and orderly. Even the shoes were lined up perfectly on shoe racks. "I ordered all those clothes in your size for all occasions. Pick something."

I didn't feel up to arguing with him. There had to be a belt or something in here. I could fang the leather to make more belt holes if I needed to. Plan the day? I thought it was going to be me on my knees all day. I yawned. I was tired I could sleep through his fuck sessions if he was gentle enough. Yeah, like that was going to be an option.

I set the water to a few levels below scalding and stepped into the steam, letting the warmth seep into me. Funny, I didn't know I was so cold until I got warm. Leaning my head on the warm tiles, my hair hung dripping in snow white hanks. My lower back was getting hot, not unbearably so but enough to tell me that X hasn't burned yet. Well…it would all depend on how tomorrow went. I leaned forward more and rested my forearms up above the shower head and let the water stream over me. Wash me clean, I ordered the shower head with my best imperious thought, as if it could really do that. Even standing in the water, I felt soiled. Remembering Father's face when I turned and looked at him after kissing Hades; he had looked…wounded. Analyzing my actions now, it was petty payback on my part. It had hurt so much when I thought he was servicing Hades…I pinched the bridge of my nose. My throat tightened, and I hugged my upper body as my tears blended with the shower, I hurt him. I kicked Father in the face and I Hand of Lighted him.

"Ssssh." Hades arms came around me from behind. I hung my head. I should have known that he would be in here with me. "If you didn't incapacitate Carnage, he would be dead by now. Kneel."

Oh god, what did he want now? Reluctantly, I lowered myself to my knees then the scent of mangos filled the shower as he squeezed something out of a bottle. Hades started washing my hair. Was nothing sacred? I fought the urge to slap his hands away, placing them on my thighs, clutching at them until my knuckles were white with strain. There were going to be bruises. I was the pampered miniature schnauzer again. You'd have to hand it to Hades, he took care of his toys even if they didn't want such personal attention. I stood there like a mannequin, his own personal anatomically correct Ken doll and let him play dress-up, pulling out clothes from that massive closet full of clothing for me to wear. Once dressed he finally saw what I had told him. I had to hold my pants up.

"You've lost that much weight? Get your black pants on. I'll take you shopping."

He pushed the intercom and Billy Envoy's voice came on. "Yes, sir?"

296

"Edward has some medical problems. Get Dr. Maxwell to send up his prescriptions immediately. Have my car ready, we are heading out shopping."

I put yesterday's underwear back on; I didn't wear it much anyways, slipped my black pants on and was lacing my Doc's to my knees when Billy came back to the bedroom. I snagged the pill bottle he whipped at my head. Jealous much, Billy?

"You're not worthy to be in his bed." That tone couldn't be taken as anything other than a snarl.

I didn't even care enough to spar with Billy Envoy. "You can take over any time you want."

"I would if I could."

I stood up and noticed he was staring at my bare chest. I could just see the thoughts flitting across his face as he saw that both nipples were now pierced. Yes, I'm a whore. The sad thing was, I was everything he wanted to be. "You can now you know. I've cured his touch of death."

Billy blinked. "You lie…"

He was going to say something else but remembered that I was more than just a whore, I was a royal blue emperor whore. He snapped his mouth shut and turned away.

Hades walked out dressed in jeans and a crisp blue linen shirt. He sauntered over up and stuck himself to my back like a burr on a shaggy dog. His arms came up and encircled my waist. "It's true."

He splayed his hand across my stomach and turned my head with the other towards him. He gave me a slow leisurely French kiss right in front of Billy. Was he being deliberately cruel? No, Billy had as much presence as a piece of furniture, Hades didn't even notice him.

Hades handed me a long sleeve purple t-shirt. The Goth look it was then. I slipped my small dagger into the back of the waistband and finished with my forearm sheath. I pulled the purple sleeve down and tested it. It dropped easily. I looked up and Hades was watching me intently. "What? I'm still your bodyguard until tomorrow."

"Your oath was to protect me, so you can kill me yourself?"

"Well that was Azrael, but I think we all agree to it now. Don't worry, you'll be safe with me until tomorrow. Honesty it can't come soon enough for us."

Hades gestured for the elevator. I lead the way. Billy trailed along behind us. When we got to the open doors, Hades rattled off some instructions for Billy to carry out then hit the ground floor button. Hades had his tongue stuck in my ear when the doors started to close. It looks like Billy got sucker punched in the solar plexus.

"What are we doing?" Getting my ear canal tongue fucked was not that exciting. Actually, it was just wet.

"We are on a date." Hades emphasized the 'we' in that statement.

I pulled away from him. "What?"

"We are on a play date. We, you and I, my friend are just going out to have fun."

"We are not friends, Hades."

"Yes, we are. You are my best friend." Oh my god, he believed it.

"Friends don't rape each other."

A hand was tangled in the back of my hair and I was pulled down slightly to his meet him face to face. Hades glared at me, his watery blue eyes flaring slightly into the red danger zone. "Remember how you got here, Edward. I consider you a friend. I like being with you when you are not being a prick or trying to kill me. If the truth be known, you are my only friend. I've called Claudius a friend, and still do, but he would rather spit in my face than shake hands with me and I've accepted that I deserve it. Still doesn't make it hurt less." The elevator doors opened, and I was shoved forward toward the waiting limo. "Now, get the hell in the car."

So, I spent the afternoon with a teenager; a 900-year-old teenager, a horny touchy teenager. I just had to grin and bear it. At least he wasn't in me…well his cock wasn't. I was getting *frenched* every other step but that was still better than staring at the ceiling. The effects of turning a chronic toucher into death was blatantly clear and the reversal of fortune just accented how young he was. He skip-ran everywhere dragging me along behind him like a reluctant pet. He stroked dogs. He cooed at babies. The feel of the wind was met with open arms and full exposure to the sun. I stood in the shadows of a building in new clothes – desert camo shorts and a long burgundy graphic tee. I had an Aussie style brimmed hat and my goggle glasses.

Hades was old enough to be able to withstand the sun. Ten seconds in it made me weak in the knees. Finally, we ended up at the same amusement park, X had barfed all over. I hung back for a moment until Hades grabbed my wrist and dragged me into the lengthening shadows of the afternoon sun. What the hell did we look like? A preppie and a punk hanging out together. Hades reached out and stroked the back of his hand along my cheek. Now, the preppie and the punk were gay lovers. I kept scanning the crowd waiting for the inevitable asshole to come up and start some trouble.

"Win me that." Hades pointed at the plush toy hanging from the carny booth rafters. I had to blink at that childish demand.

What? I turned around and lifted up my goggles. We were in deeper shadow along a row of games of skill and chance. Hades shuffled from foot to foot and he looked up at me with his pale eyes gleaming with…joy? Four hundred years of being the touch of death and now all he wanted as a black stuffed life-sized panther to lug around.

"I'm not carrying it."

"Did I ask you to?"

"We need tickets." I reached back for my wallet. Hades shook his head.

"Wait here." He spied the booth and took off almost running faster than a human.

"You make a cute couple." I turned and looked back and looked at the carny leaning on his counter. "It's refreshing to see young love."

I didn't need any Blue line abilities to see pervert written all over his face. I know I looked a little tougher than Hades dressed as I was, but I was actually offended by his wanton stare. "Your boyfriend's in trouble."

I turned and sure enough Hades was surrounded by four young men. I sighed and head over to save them from doing something stupid that

Hades would kill them for. I just got close when I heard, "How much for all four of us?"

"I can't leave you alone for a moment without you getting into trouble." I leaned over and kissed Hades temple and then draped myself across his back, wrapping my arms around his shoulders and tightening them.

"I can defend myself, Edward."

"Yah, butt out Edward." One of the college kids returned with a jeer. Did that work as a provoking statement?

I let out an Oscar winning dramatic sigh. "I don't need to spend the night in jail, again."

That statement paused the group. I pressed my head along Hades cheek, brought my fingers up in a kiss which I blew toward them then dropped my arm down and flicked my wrist. I caught my dagger and slowly brought it up in front of us. "I think you're leaving now." The group backed up slowly, turned and walked away; only one glancing back at us. Honestly, who wants to tangle with a knife welding maniac? I watched until the very discreet Loyal surrounded them and shuffled them towards the exit.

Hades let loose a sigh as he spied those assassins who worked for him but were dedicated to me. "You can be so thespian, Edward."

I hid my blade before it called unwanted attention.

Hades turned and bought about two hundred dollars' worth of tickets. I rolled my eyes. What did he think, I couldn't win anything? Sharpshooter here. Well that was X but I knew I could shoot. Sure, enough Hades chose a rifle shooting target game. Shoot out the center of the star to win. The sight was off, and I messed up the first turn. After that, I just kept reloading and shooting until the man threw the last big prize at me and told me less than elegantly to fuck off.

Hades picked up the black cat and then a husky dog and then tried to add a blue pig, but his arms weren't that long. I just stood there watched him struggle with it. "Help me."

"I said I wasn't going to carry anything."

"Fine." He threw the husky at me. "That is for your Lycan. He's probably used to sleeping in a pack."

"Yah, he always ends up on X's bed."

"What am I going to do with the rest?"

I gestured over to a group of kids being herded up for the end of the day. They looked a little underprivileged. "Hold this." I got the panther shoved at me and Hades headed over to the group.

There are moments when Hades did something that just didn't fit with the ass who basically was on my ass all morning. He gave away all those prizes to those kids. I gave the stuffed dog to a little girl with eyes almost the size of her face. She could barely walk with it because it was bigger than her. In the end there were three children left with nothing.

"Oh, for god's sake, give it up, Hades."

"But I want this." He whined crushing it against his chest in a hug. Did he actually whine?

"I'll win you something else."

I reached out and jerked it out his hands. I handed it over to a little boy. He jumped around and made kitty noises then dragged it off to his group. I turned and looked for another shooting game. Hades grabbed my elbow and dragged me backwards toward a "pop the balloon" game.

"This should be easy. Locate the large prizes." He opened his cuffs. I took the tickets out of my pocket and gestured for the carnie to come over. I gently brushed his forehead and lightly mind-fucked him.

"Yellow, upper left; green, third up from the bottom in the middle; red, two over and three down, from the right." I handed the man a handful of tickets and cleared his mind.

I think we were supposed to use the darts in the man's hand. Hades snapped his daggers down and threw them. Yellow and Green popped. I flipped mine down and threw it at the remaining red.

The man paled at the sign of the knives but did his job. "We have winners!"

Hades climbed over the counter and retrieved our daggers. He set his back in his hidden sheaths then climbed back on the counter, swinging his legs to the side swiveling on his ass. He held my blade in his hand as he gestured me forward. The carny handed over the three stuffed animals to the two little munchkins that had followed us to the booth. A red fluffy kitty cat was left. The kids went running back to the bigger group. They screamed and shouted back "Thank you".

"Edward."

He gestured me to him. I watched a little wary as he held my blade on his thigh. I walked up to him and stopped between his open thighs. The carny was still pale but finally found his voice as Hades pressed the tip against the hollow of my neck, just above Claudius' locket. Like the good little sex slave, I was, I dropped my eyes then lowered myself to my knees in front of him.

The carnie made up his mind against his better judgment not to get involved. "Get away from him, or I'll call the cops."

Hades stared down at me, "Withdraw."

"No, Master."

"Left hand." I raised my hand to him from my knees. He trailed the dagger up my neck, along the soft underside of my chin and finally flipped off my jaw. It left a burning trail behind like shaving without soap. He slid my dagger back into the forearm sheath.

"So beautiful. So stubborn. You don't have to die tomorrow."

I said nothing. Hades reached for the kitty and looked at it. "Here. It looks like her Majesty in kitten form. Keep it. Come." Hades kicked his leg over my head and walked toward the giant Ferris wheel.

I grabbed the stuffed cat and looked down at it. "Stupid, that's me."

"You love that ass?" I looked over at the Carnie.

"No."

"Then what the hell are you doing with someone who treats you like shit?"

"I made a deal with the devil's younger brother and now I got to live with it."

"Is the price you're paying worth it?"

I turned and looked over at Hades' blonde head chatting with the ticket girl at the entrance to the ride. Well at least it was small favors.

The operator that had to wash down my mess last time wasn't there. I was probably banned if he saw me.

"The one I love is safe now. I would do it again in a heartbeat." I waved the kitty back at him and headed over to the Hades. My stomach lurched as we got closer to the wheel. I held a hand over my gut. I wasn't going to hurl. I wasn't going to hurl.

The ride stopped, and the door opened on the car. Hades hopped in. Oh God, I was going to be sick. "Well aren't you a cute one." I looked at the girl. She smiled and winked at me. "Have fun."

Oh crap. It looked like I was going to join the 300-foot club.

"Edward!"

"Here." I tossed the kitty to the girl and trudged reluctantly into the car. The door shut behind me with the ominous thunk of a cell door as the wheel geared up into the motion. The sun was fading but the sting of the light was still there. I winced as it hit my face then ended up squatting down on the dubious clean floor, with my back pressed to the lower edge of the car to keep as much of me hidden from the light as possible.

"Still too much for you?"

"I'm only going on two years, Hades." Five more hours and I could go home. Hades flopped himself down on the seat and spread his arms across the back.

"I haven't gone out of Shadoe Inc. in decades just for myself. It was always business. Do you know why Edward?" He gestured me forward between his spread legs. I crawled over to him. He pushed my head down on his right thigh; he took my hat and set it on the seat. His fingers played with my hair. "Humans would accidentally brush up against me and they would die. Even if my flesh was covered, they would fall sick. I was the First of Assassins for decades because I can kill. It doesn't affect me much; but, that was killing with an objective. The casual contact, deliberate or not, made me into a plague carrier. People would drop dead behind me as if they were wasps getting sprayed with WD-40."

How the hell did he know about that? Hades fingers began stroking the curl of my ear.

"William did this to me. He did it before as protection for me when he had to leave but he always came back before too many years had passed. But this protection he gifted me with turned into a curse when he didn't come back. You're right, Edward. I'm waiting for him." Hades gave a sad hiccup of a laugh. "How pathetic is that? Four hundred years as walking death and I'm longing for the Vampire that did this to me. I'm waiting for his return."

The car shifted with the motion of the large wheel and I closed my eyes. *I am not going to be sick. I am not going to be sick. Tide goes in, tide goes out. Tide goes in, tide goes out.*

"I'm over 900 years old, little boy. I think the longest William ever stayed with me was two hundred and thirty-nine years and he fought to stay with me that long. You should have seen my William. I think he stayed long after the vampire form was used up until finally, the body just dissolved. The last words from his lips were Honey Bee. He turned to dust in my hands."

Hades fell silent, "When he comes back to me, he treats me like I'm a special treasure, like I'm his little shepherd boy still running barefoot in the glen. No matter what I've done since he's been gone he takes me back into his heart and I am warmed and cherished. Even now, I miss him. After all this, I miss him."

"Claudius…beautiful, cold and deadly. I've told you before, he is my biggest mistake. Just being with him brought some of that feeling back. I only thought of what I needed. Katrina was dead. Her husband was still young, and so beautiful. When he challenged for First, I knew I was going to have him…" Hades dropped his voice, "Whether he wanted me or not."

"I never thought he would come for me with daggers that I gave him. His core of duty is strong. He truly loves you, little boy. I'm glad. There is a glow of warmth in his eyes now." I stilled as his hand came under my chin and pulled my face sideways to look at him. "You've given my Black Death back his soul. You've stripped the touch of death from my body. Please, my Lord Emperor…don't make me kill you tomorrow."

I sat up then ducked back down slightly when I felt a searing heat in my scalp. I never knew sunset could last so long. "We're three. We endured hell to get there. We're not four and we're not two and X has made it clear that we will not be just one. Liam, your William, wants back and he's made it clear that he's coming through Xavier to do it. Azrael and I will be dead if we do nothing. Don't ask again, Hades. You won't like the answer."

We were in silence until the ride came to a halt. We were at the apex. "How much did you give her?"

'Three hundred for twenty minutes. Right now, they have suffered a mechanical malfunction." Hades reached out and stroked my forehead. "If we were human, and you saw me in a club…would you want me?"

I pulled back and looked at Hades closely. His eyes were guarded, and his lids were lowered. The sexy bastard was unsure of himself? Was this the Cillian side? "Sex, would you have wanted me?"

I narrowed my eyes at him. He knew my name. "If we met when we were human, I would have wanted you. You wouldn't have looked at me twice. Not the way I was, or X was. If Liam hadn't interfered, I have no doubt that X would have been a Hunter. Male hunters don't last long; that is a statistical fact. I probably would have been dead before I reached thirty."

Hades dropped a bomb. "I want you, Sex. I want to share with you."

I jumped to my feet then hissed and dropped back to the floor as the sun burnt me. I skittered back to the other seat. Hades looked at me shocked. "You've never shared?"

"X shared. It's not a good thing." Marcus at Armor's bidding mind-fucked X to get the IDs of the covens who kidnapped him back in our first year as vampire. That's how Nightshade the Hellcat Queen came into our household.

"Then they did it wrong. Sharing is a special gift between lovers…I would like to share with you as a friend. Your heart belongs to Claudius.

I'm not asking for your heart, Sex. Maybe this is my way of 'making it better" between us. It doesn't matter if you will agree or not, when we reach the ground, you are free." Hades got up off the seat then knelt before me. "I'm just standing in Claudius's way. In your way. Share with me…as a friend."

"I don't know how…" I really didn't want to. If I was going to Share with anyone it was going to be my Gorgeous…if he would even want to after getting zapped.

Hades voiced started with hesitancy. "I will show you…I won't force you…"

I rather rudely cut off his offer. "I'd rather share with Father."

Hades closed his eyes. His shoulders slumped. "I thought so. If I offered my body to you…you would decline as well."

"Cillian…" Hades eyes opened, and he blinked tears free. "We are not friends. I don't think we can ever be friends. You raped Father. You admitted it freely. I can't forgive that. I endure your touch because that is the bargain I made for my stupidity. I burnt the poison from you because I owed you for showing Father mercy." I rose up on my knees bowing my head towards him. "I'll let you fuck me now. Anyway, anyhow. I won't resist you…but I will walk away when this ride ends without a backwards glance."

"Honesty. I think I hate it right now." Hades took the back of my neck and pulled me up to his throat. "Drink. If all I can get from you is one last fuck…I want to see you in the sunlight. This should give you enough strength to withstand the rays."

I stilled.

There was a bark of a laugh. "My neck is not as exclusive as yours, Edward. Drink."

I dropped fang and turned my head to get a good purchase. I was conditioned to taste bitterness, so this sweet warm essence was a surprise. It was warm honey. I let it pool in my mouth. He was a hard candy honey drop and full of such strength. I took another deep swallow. One more and I was starting to get light headed. It was like getting drunk…. I laved my puncture wounds closed. Drinking, blood or alcohol, wasn't a good thing on a Ferris wheel. Been there, done that.

"You even drink like Claudius. Stand up."

I climbed to my feet and swayed slightly. My stomach was queasy, but it wasn't doing flip flops. I flipped my goggles down and turned toward the fading sun. It was a bright red fiery ball. There was a slight sting, but nothing more. "See, my blood offers protection. If you drank enough, you would eventually match my strength. But it would take a lot of blood and I would need something more than just an offer of friendship to do that. Take off your shirt. Hands on the glass. Look out at the world, Edward. Look out at the world that you could own as Lord Emperor, as I fuck you, as your Master instead of a friend."

My inner core clenched with fear as Hades whispered these words in my ear. I moved to take off my blade. Hades stayed my hand. "Keep it…hands on the window, little boy." His clothed arm came around and his fingers tugged on my right piercing. His other hand flicked open the button on my pants.

He pushed my pants and underwear down to my knees. In the distance I could make out a lone seagull flying in the still warm breeze, a speck of white in the pale blue sky. Hades yanked my hips back to him. I rested my forehead on the window, my hair falling forward blazing white in the rays of the sun.

Hades pushed into me without preparation and buried himself to the hilt. I grunted then gasped in pain. My fingers curled into claws on the glass. He set a hard-even rhythm. Holding my hips in a bruising grip he pounded into me. The dying light of the sun glistened like diamonds as tears filled my eyes. I listened as he grunted with each thrust. This could have been more brutal. I knew it. He knew it. This was a lesson. This is what happened when you spurned the affections of Hades, CEO of Shadoe Inc, Grand Master of Assassins. The Ferris wheel began to move again.

Hades shoved me up against the glass and started to push into me harder and faster. His breath blew my hair across my face. He groaned and jutted hard up into me, giving his offering with usual gusto…and without the condom that protected his partner from coma or certain death. I gave that to him.

He leaned against me for a few moments then the car rocked again. He pulled out of me and tucked himself back into his pants. I stood against the glass in physical pain and dealing with mental anguish. Even before…this…we couldn't be friends.

I moved to pull up my pants. "No. Enjoy the sunlight while you can, little boy."

His offering was beginning to trail down my leg. I pressed my hands flat on the glass. Anybody directly across from us could look in and see me practically naked. A blush turned my chest and face red. Finally, the car moved down into the shadows cast by the surrounding buildings. "Pull your pants up, Edward."

I'd survived worse. I could walk out of here. I'd crawl out of here if I had to. I reached for my shirt.

"Nope. I bought that for my friend. Leave it."

I straightened up and looked out the window. I could feel his eyes on me. There was a hint of regret in his voice, but a hint just didn't cut it. "It didn't have to end this way, Edward. Even without Claudius as a side benefit, I wanted you."

The car finally touched down and the operator opened the door. She had a smirk on her face, but it faded quickly as she felt the tension between us. I left the hat and shirt laying there. I stepped out of the car and then paused to let the girl get out of my way.

"EDWARD!"

I didn't turn around. "Would it be so bad to be with William and me? We are happy when everything gets calm."

"You said I was free."

"I release you from your oath, Edward."

"My name's not Edward." I started walking toward the exit. I could barely see where the hell I was going, my eyes were full of tears and my goggles were fogging up. I could feel his warm offering trailing down the inside of my leg. No, I couldn't kill a friend. I could kill an enemy and Hades had danced all over that line, but he ended up standing on the wrong side of it. I could kill him tomorrow.

Chapter Nineteen: First

I held it together damn well. Or so I thought. I mean, I was born out of rape. I knew that pain on a first name basis. The Loyal explained they could have a car for me in ten minutes, but I waved them off and hopped into the first idling cab. The taxi cab ride home was uneventful. Thankfully. Hades blood still coursed through me, so the remaining sun was just bright...not a killer. When I got home, the Loyal's umbrellas came out, the taxi got paid and I was shepherded into the building. Well, they probably thought it was Azrael staggering in half naked because it was still Saturday by another four hours. The elevator ride was nothing. I walked out into the entryway and spied Shade's long red panther tail flicking around a corner and I lost it.

My legs dropped out from underneath me and I curled into myself with a wail. Soft red fur was under my face before I really hit the floor. I clawed my hands into Shade's pelt and screamed out all the agony, frustration and horror of the day. I could hear murmurs from her, but nothing distinct. Maybe that's what a baby hears when it's in the womb - just gentle mumblings but with a soothing tone. Only X could talk to her.

My Lycan came tearing around the corner in wolf form at the sound of my cry. He didn't even take three seconds to realize I needed him. He morphed back into human form Haley and plastered himself on my back, hugging me with a desperation I needed. Everything...everything was just so bad today.

"Master.... don't cry."

"Don't call me Master, Haley...I don't own you." I stopped sobbing, but I hung onto the kitty warmth Shade provided.

"But...you're my Alpha."

"Then call me Alpha...I've had enough of calling someone Master...I don't want to hear the word."

"Alpha, don't cry. I'll protect you. Shade will protect you." Tears began streaming out of my eyes and matting the red fur.

311

Bare feet came padding up beside us. A stupid thought ran through my head, why was he wearing his pajamas? It was only about 8:00 p.m.

"I know that I'm not your favorite person. I can get Armor if you would prefer." Marcus crouched beside us looking at our little fur pile with such concern. "You look like you desperately need a friend right now, Sex. I'm willing to be that, if you will let me."

Sweetness and Light. He was finally the sweetness and light everybody had talked about. He reached out to touch my shoulder, but he pulled his hand back as it hovered over me. I turned and lunged at him. I caught him around the neck and hung on. He ended up falling on his ass with a shocked expression on his face. His arms came up, but he hesitated. "What did Hades do to you?"

I shook my head on his throat.

"Little One." Marcus's arms gently enfolded me under the baleful glare of the Hellcat and the watchful eye of the Lycan. Softly, almost as if it were a gentle breeze, his fingers stroked through my hair. Back in the Horror, when I would come and save Xavier...when he was at his breaking point; when all was said and done, Armor would hold me and call me that pet name. It was Elder Brother's endearment but to me, it was almost like payment for enduring. Oh, god I was so fucked up back then. I clung to any sign of kindness...even if it wasn't mine.

He picked me up without effort. "I'll take you to Father, but first, we'll wash Hades off of you."

"Alpha?" Haley's voice was unsure.

Marcus glanced back over my head. "Come on, Pup. I don't think Sex should be alone right now."

Rub a dub dub, two vamps and a Lycan in a shower. Thank god X was a hedonist and had an oversized shower. I hung onto Marcus as Haley scrubbed me clean...even down there. I was so messed up mentally that it didn't even phase me. Marcus hummed something in my ear. I had no clue what it was, but it was soothing and pretty. I moved my head and looked up at his nose. There was just a hint of bruising left around his eyes from the broken nose. He glanced down at me saw where my attention was then touched his nose.

"I have never had more abuse to my nose than since I met all of you."

"I didn't break it."

"Setting it wasn't a barrel of monkeys for me."

"This whole day wasn't fun. Father hates me."

"No, Little One, if Father hates anyone it's Armor right now which is one of the reasons that my younger brother is scarce."

Huh?

"Armor chained Claudius up in Angels Haven."

Oh God, they had a name for Az and Marcus's rape fantasy playroom.

"When Father woke up from the taze you gave him, he ripped the mooring post right out of the concrete. So, Armor knocked him out with the Ether we used last night."

I was alarmed. "Where is he now?"

Marcus gave a heavy sigh. "Armor chained him in the music room."

"What? Why would you put him there when he tore out of a torture chamber?"

"Armor chained Father to your piano. If he wants to get free, he can get loose, but he will destroy that red piano to do it. He's been quiet."

"You left him here all day?" I was horrified.

"I played for him for a bit, but he less than politely told me to get out."

I stumbled trying to get out of the shower. I landed on Haley. He gave a little yelp and held his chest where my elbow had dug in. "Sorry."

Marcus picked me up from the floor. "Father isn't going anywhere. Let us care for you, Sex. You have done so much for this family today."

He settled me on the bed. I lay on the covers and buried my face into the softness as Marcus looked down and gingerly explored my portal. He spoke to Chesterton.... *Chesterton*! I groaned. I didn't need to have all the staff looking at my ass.

"Most of this…damage is my fault, Sex. I had planned to heal Azrael but then everything happened so quickly. Hades must have fed you his blood to repair most of the tears. You…."

I didn't want to hear Marcus apologizing for giving Azrael, the twisted menace, all the joy and pain he could handle and more. The smarmy bastard was still on that high. "I healed Hades." I mumbled face down in the pillow.

"What was that?"

"I healed Hades from his hemlock poisoning."

Marcus stilled for a moment then went about rubbing something medicinal between my legs. My eyes teared up and I hissed at even his gentle prodding. "That is good then. You can touch him. A major weapon has been dismantled. Haley can you get his pajamas out of the drawer…no, the green ones. They make his eyes sparkle even more."

While Haley was off scrounging through my dresser, Marcus leaned forward and whispered. "When you go to Father it would be best if you are in pain. Everything is swollen, and you are bruised on your hips. I do not think you could stop Father again if he decided to continue his path. Make him focus on you. You deserve to be pampered for all you have done for this family, Sex." Marcus placed a brotherly kiss on the nape of my neck.

Marcus dressed me like I was spun glass. Maybe I was; I felt fragile. Maybe I was just tired. Maybe I dreaded going to see Father. Marcus picked me up in bride pose and started carrying me down the hall. "He needs you, too, Sex. His day has not been the best either."

Outside in the hall at the music room door, I shot my arm out and prevented Marcus from carrying me in. "Haley."

The tawny head popped up into my line of vision. "Alpha."

"Get a nice suit on and sit still for Marcus. We'll give Xavier that painting in the morning to hang on the wall in the Great Hall."

"It's hard to stay still."

I reached out and cupped his chin, "I know. That's what will make it special, because you gave the effort to get it done."

"I'll sit still." Haley's eyes narrowed a bit as if stiffening his resolve.

"Good boy." I tickled under his chin lightly.

"Are you hurt, Alpha?" There was real concern mixed with devotion in those yellow eyes.

"A little bit." It didn't feel right to even attempt to tell a white lie to the pup.

"Claudius will make you better?"

"Yes."

Marcus spoke up, "Go get your suit on, Haley."

Haley danced around behind Marcus then pressed a gentle kiss to my temple, followed up by a lick. Ewww. "Get better, Alpha. I like the water bowl you bought me. You still should have won."

Haley took off.

"I can walk, Marcus."

"You don't get it, do you?" I looked up at his face. "Father has been worried about you all day. Don't just stroll in as if nothing has happened. We both know what you've been through. Let him care for you, Sex. Give him that. Your body is weary. Let it relax. You will recharge faster that way."

Marcus held me in that easy pose until finally my body started to relax. The pain I had been resisting hit me full force and I curled my head up against Marcus' chest. Tears began to stream down my face. I could just hit me with healing light but that would only take care of the physical scars and bruising. Right now, I wanted Claudius to see how I was on the inside too. I don't know if that's right or not, I just really want him to show me that he cares.

"It'll be all right, Sex."

Marcus pulled the door open and stepped into the music room. I gave out an involuntary cry as I saw Father. He was sitting almost dead center beneath the piano, his arms were stretched up and wide, the chain itself wrapping around the red lacquer piano legs and crossing over the closed lid. Every time Claudius would move, the chain would rip into the finish. He was sitting cross legged, but the worst part was his head hung forward, his black hair trailing on the ground in front of him masking his face from onlookers.

"I said to get out." His voice was low and even and oh, so cold.

"I can leave, if that is what you wish, Father but if I do, I take him with me." I watched as the black head slowly sat up. He tensed, and the chains moved.

"Why is he so still?"

"You've been with Hades, Father. You know what he does. You know what he did. Do you want him here with you, or shall I just put him to bed?"

"Bring him here. These are not necessary anymore." He rattled his wrists. Marcus laid me on a chaise lounge in the corner, brushed my hair back from my face and then headed over to Claudius. There was a metallic ca-chunk sound as one cuff and chain dropped to the floor. It was followed by another thud.

"Get food and some blood packs, Marcus. Hades can get excited and tends to forget to take care of his partner." I closed my eyes against the physical pain I felt but the inner core of me...it hurt so much more. If this was what drove Father into recklessness, I could understand it. It was almost as if doing something suicidal made the pain lessen. What a stupid thought. I twitched as a hand lay on my forehead. I opened my eyes and looked up at Father's blue orbs.

"I don't even need any special ability to know that you've been raped repeatedly today. He didn't even try to give you pleasure, he just took what he thought was his. My Fallen...I'm sorry for driving you to do this." He leaned over and pressed his lips to my forehead.

I thought I had used Shade as my box of tissue, but I burst out crying again. I curled around him, savoring his embrace. He held me and let me get rid of my anger, frustration and helplessness.

"I'm sorry...I kicked...you...face." I blurted out between sobs.

He pressed his cheek along the side of my head. "So am I. It hurt, Fallen. But what I have endured is nothing compared to what you have faced today...because of me. I gave you pain. That is the last thing I wanted to do."

316

"You hate me…"

"No. No, my Fallen. I do not hate you. I am proud that you and Armor ganged up and kicked my ass. I could see Azrael and Armor working together but you…you surprised the hell out of me. If what I felt is one tenth of the agony I put you through when it is my turn to stop you from attacking Hades, I sincerely apologize. Seeing you on his lap, kissing him with your wings extended…I felt as if I was stabbed through the heart with a dagger of ice."

I winced as I sat up. Father waited until I was sitting, and he moved between my legs, kneeling there looking up at me. I leaned over, wrapping my arms around his neck. "It was petty of me to do that. While Hades was on me, I realized I did it to hurt you. You should hate me…I'm not worthy of your love."

Claudius moved so fast, I barely had time to flinch. He was on the chaise and I was sprawled flat on my back. His fingers dug into my shoulders as he pinned me to the leather. "Do not EVER question my love for you, Sex. You do not get to doubt me. You have seen the lengths to which I will go to keep you safe. If I cannot…."

His grip lessened. His voice dropped to almost a whisper, "If I cannot keep you safe, I will carry out your wishes. I will burn your body to ash. I will court your sister. If there are Blues, I will raise them to know that their Uncle was the greatest Lord Emperor who touched so many in so short a time. As long as I live, you will be in my heart and in my soul, my precious Fallen."

Father carefully laid his weight on my body. His eyes searching for any sign that I was about to freak or in severe pain. I knew I was safe now. With him, I knew I would always be safe. I wrapped my arms around his chest and buried my face in the crook of his neck. I could feel the warmth of his locket brush against my temple. The soft touch of his fingers against my cheek as he swept hair back from my face.

"I know you have to do this, Fallen. I know that if you do nothing…it will be a cowardly death for you and Azrael. I will tell you now, I do not like it, but…I will not stand in your way. Fight, my Fallen

Angel. Fight with every inch of your courage and talent. Fight to stay here."

Claudius shifted and ran the back of his finger down my cheek. "I am your sword. If you wish me to protect your family, that is what I will do. Armor is your shield, let him stand with you. That is where he belongs. If you fall tomorrow, you will not go alone. I will send my eldest with you."

I closed my eyes as he pressed his lips to my forehead. "I always thought of myself as a good father, but I have failed both of my sons miserably. My protection came too late, for both of you. Anything I do now is too little, too late."

I squirmed my arms between us then pushed at Claudius until he finally let go. I matched his sad gaze with a glare so heated I was surprised that I wasn't snapping into my crystal blue flame. "Don't you dare accept that I'm dying tomorrow."

I could feel my eyes flare with anger. "I'm not dying tomorrow. I've got too much to live for. I'm not going anywhere. Do you understand me, Claudius? I'm not going anywhere."

"Then why are you crying?"

"I'm tired…let me sleep in your arms, Gorgeous. Keep me safe here for a little while. Hades hurt me today, but I want you inside me. I want you to be there instead of him."

"Rest, my little Fallen Angel. You need not fear anything tonight. I will keep you safe, I will keep you warm. I will guard your heart as you guard mine."

My throat was tight with more unshed tears. "I didn't think I could love you more, but it feels like my heart is bursting over."

Claudius shifted, and I felt a kiss on the locket sitting at the hollow of my throat. "You know my core, Fallen. I throw nothing away. You are with me forever."

I patted his hand. "My precious little pack rat."

I laid back and relaxed. Claudius shifted me around until he was under me and I was pulled back and resting on his chest. His breath wafted across my cheek. He dropped a hand to my chest and held me gently.

"Sleep is the best thing for you now, Fallen. I'll wake you when food is here."

'He would have killed you this morning..." Inhaling his clove scent sent it straight to my head and heart. I could have lost him.

"I could not find a way..."

"He doesn't have his hemlock protection any more...I took it from him." Claudius stilled.

"Sleep, my Fallen. Let me ponder some more." I felt his lips brush my forehead.

I snuggled back into him and rested my cheek down on warm sand...damn it. My breath went oof as a heavy weight landed on my back. I was driven harder into the beach. "You...I don't know what to think about you. You are a wildcard that my Honey Bee thought he had securely in his deck." A giant hand ground my cheek into the sand, "But now we both know that isn't true."

I tried to thrash and was pinned harder down on into the sand as Liam laid his giantess on me. I cried out in frustration. He kissed my ear. "Claudius's little kinder -- fractured and fragmented yet out of all the enemies that I've seen over the centuries, you fragments are the ones to be wary of." Liam kissed his way from my ear down to the crook of my shoulder. His tongue snaked out and licked my skin.

"If you're going to fuck me, get it over with, I've had enough of your little wunderkind today."

Liam bit me. I groaned and tensed, making the fanging worse. Damn, I never learn.

"Sweet...your blood is so pure an essence. Cinnamon...an exotic flavor. You've freed my little Honey Bee. I was quite angry with you when you did that but then I was grateful to see that my Cillian hasn't changed all that much. He still is beautiful and gentle..."

Gentle? What the hell station was Liam tuned into? "What do you want?"

"Withdraw your challenge."

"Will you still try and take over X?"

"You let Cillian loose. I must now. I can't have him running all over the Nation. If you thought he was a menace before, he will be unstoppable now. I put that curse on him for a reason, little boy. I love him, but I know what he can do. Don't think of him as a victim. He climbed the Assassin's ladder all on his own. He's not even from the House of Du Bussey yet he's the Head. You and he are the only ones outside of lesser nobles that had made it into the House of Assassins. Both of you and he have climbed the pinnacle on your own merits. If I could, I would love to watch you both fight it out. Even though you are so young, little Emperor, you would give my Cillian a run for his money. You are unpredictable enough that you might win. That is why I can't allow it."

I relaxed under him. Tensing and fighting was getting me nothing but a face full of sand. "I blood my shield."

"Very good for a first try. You didn't wrap it around the bottom."

File that piece of information away for future reference. Was that a hand on my ass? "Get off me."

"You're lacking in manners. Your brothers had a bit more tact."

"I don't remember you sitting on Azrael."

Liam rolled off me. I rolled in the opposite direction picking up a handful of sand. I jumped to my feet and found myself in a short white kilt. The warm sea breeze blew my white hair across my face. I picked up a strand and looked at it. Both X and Az had returned to their normal red. "You are your brother's power source. You are the center post that everything hangs on; the lynch pin for all"

I turned and looked at the giant of a man. Crap he was bigger than Azrael let on. Liam's hair whipped around his head and he casually flicked his hand and the wind stopped. Holy crap. "Xavier thinks that he is brother number one. That is false, you are, Edward. He guilted you into stepping back years before Claudius' fragmented child came along. I was Mr. L with you, Edward – not Xavier that's why he really doesn't have any memories of his childhood friend. All those night horrors you experienced as a child were real. Those were the lesser Bloods coming to pay you fealty. Even they could sense your greatness running through your veins, but you 'saw' a little too clearly and far too early for a young human to understand and I had to drive them away because you couldn't handle it. That experience left you a little twitchy.

A little twitchy? I slept with a nightlight, okay all the lights on in my room for as long as I could remember. It wasn't until I moved off to college that...Wait...what was that? What did he say?

"You blamed yourself for that Lycan attack, as if a little boy can draw a female Lycan to him. After all the panic, fear and desperation your parents allowed you to witness...you reached your limit and willingly stepped back to let the brother number two take over."

"You're lying." I angrily wiped the sand off my face.

"Here, on this plane the truth comes out." Liam turned and stared down at me with all the force of his gray eyed gaze, "The gifts of the Emperor are coming to you first because you are the true Lord Emperor. You are the true owner of that body. You know it, yet you stay in the shadows."

I was shocked. Yet it rang true somewhere off in the distance of my heart. Liam stepped forward and brushed a thumb down the side of my cheek.

"Why do you think you can go through the hell you have and come out merely tired and sore? Others would have collapsed and been unable to recover. Xavier is strong because of you. Azrael is strong because of you. But if I kick out their support, what will your brothers do?" He hands turned into claws and caught my jaw. "What could they do without you?"

A good defense is a great offense. As Armor had pointed out on many occasions, I could be downright offensive. "So, you have no faith in your precious Cillian."

Liam's face broke out into a wide genuine smile. "I prefer to play with my own loaded dice. That is just the way it is little Emperor. I win. I will always win because I make sure there is no way to lose."

I tried to wrench my head free. It was like my chin stuck in a bench vice. "You don't have the brute force to break free, little Emperor, so just relax. I'll send you back when I'm ready and not before."

Nobody tells me what to do...not any more.

I willed out the Phoenix wings. Liam jumped back, evidently learning from the first time with Xavier. I forced them wide and danced backwards creating a small sandstorm as well as getting some distance between us. Thrusting my hand holding the sand into the fire of one wing I forced back a hiss as the sand began to sear my hand. I drew on the healing light and my wings flared brighter and bigger. I groaned as I shaped my molten sand into a glass point. If I was going down; I was going down hard and I wasn't going alone.

I felt a strong breeze as Liam called out his own huge white wings. He flapped hard at me as if trying to extinguish my flames. I brought my right wing up shielding my face. I was tired to begin with and I could feel the drain on me. So, what if I got trapped here...X and Az would be safe. So, would Armor and Marcus. The only one who would suffer would be Claudius. I didn't want that light to leave his eyes, but it might even if I fought for it.

Behind the shield of my wing, I called out more Phoenix flame flaring my wings higher as I fashioned a long bow out of the hand of light. My glass point set on a thin, long shaft of white flame. I pulled the thin string of fire back then dropped my wing. Liam saw my arrow and twisted but not fast enough. The glass point buried itself in his shoulder. He roared. The whole of the beach shook with his fury. I let the trailing edge of my wings run in the sand. It only took a mere thought to have newly formed glass chards rise out of the sand and fly to my hand. I formed a new shaft and notched my arrow again.

Liam ripped the arrow from his shoulder as I shot once more. This one he batted out of the air. I let the next one go. And the next. Liam was grazed in a couple of places, but my arrows didn't hit him full on again. I ducked behind my fire wing as some of my glass shards flew back at me as Liam flicked his wrist at them. They hit the fire shield and melted into flattened disks. I dropped my wing in time to see the foot

322

come up and kick me in the side of the head. I landed a couple of feet into the water on my back. The water hissed and steamed as my wings thrashed in it. I got to my feet and staggered sideways and fell again. My vision was out of whack. I blinked everything back into focus.

Where the hell was...? I flew about another ten feet out into the sea as a knee rammed into my back. I raised my hands to shelter my head and hit the water hard. I came up coughing and trying to get air back into my lungs. Liam flapped about twenty feet above me off to the right. He brought his hands together and out shot a ball of hand of light. I crudely fashioned a hand of light shield before it hit. I was driven back under the water. It felt like my wrists and elbows broke from the force of that hit.

I didn't have a quarter of his strength.

"If you drank enough of my blood, you would eventually match my strength. But it takes a lot of blood..." Hades words ran through my head. If I could get Liam's blood, would that show up in the real world? How much? He wouldn't give it to me. I gritted my teeth and shot up out of the water. I angled my Phoenix wings to hover above the water. Another hand of Light orb came at me. I dodged it, just barely. I zigzagged my way back to the beach and all my little glass missiles of death. I zagged when I should have zigged, and I got tagged hard by an orb in the right wing. My flame went out and I ended up playing skip rocks again this time flop bouncing up on shore. I landed hard, knocking the wind out of me. *Get up...get up. I couldn't move.*

I lay there panting, waiting for the death orb to come for me. Feet lightly touched down at my head. I stared at the giant toes inches from my face and dug my fingers into the sand underneath me. "If there was a way, I would love to have you as my right hand, Edward. I haven't had a battle like that in centuries. Nothing close to this since I first came to organize the Bloods. Impressive, little Lord Emperor. You tried not to use my gifts, to keep me off guard. You forget, I was in Sigmund. He had the Phoenix wings. I didn't have a long time to learn them, but they can be a powerful weapon. It is lucky for me, that you haven't had a chance to master them completely."

323

My fingers found a large icicle shaped piece of glass beneath me. One chance. I rammed that glass dagger through Liam's foot pinning him to the sand. I surged up and grabbed his thigh and dropped fang, extending them the furthest they would go. I ripped into his femoral artery and sucked as hard as I could. It took him off guard. He didn't know what to kick off first, the dagger or me. I swallowed and chugged as much blood as I could. He wailed on my shoulders and back, once.... twice I hung on and drank deep. The third hit knocked me right to the sand. Blood spurting out of his artery from my deep fang marks. He grabbed a hand over the wound and kicked me in the ribs. I landed back out in the sea. By the time I spluttered back to the surface he was in blue Healing light. I splashed my way back to the shore.

I saw Liam move but couldn't get out of his way. I brought my arm up and caught his wrist as he tried to stab me with the glass dagger he wrenched out of his foot. I caught his wrist and stopped him from driving it down.

"Impressive." He elbowed me in the temple from the other direction. I staggered off balance and he drove the dagger into my side. I cried out and rammed the heel of my hand against his jaw. His head snapped back and he lost his hold on the dagger. I danced backwards holding my wound. I called on my own healing light. When it finally spluttered to life and took care of the injury, I knew I was at the end of my endurance. My legs wobbled, and I dropped where I stood.

I want to go back to Claudius. I want to go back to Claudius. Go...go... I gasped as red hot agony ripped through my veins. I bolted upright out of Father's embrace. My mouth burnt with the taste of Cayenne pepper. I grabbed my stab wound. A red blotch was staining through my pajama top. I reconstructed my shield and made sure it was fully blood insulated.

"Sex..."

I fought my way off him. "Sex?"

"Burn...I need to burn...now." The power of Liam's blood was like a Hellcat's pure essence only five times stronger. Oh my...my flesh was sensitive. "Move...move..." I pushed Father out of the way and ran for the music room door. I wasn't going to make it to the burn room. Chesterton and the serving cart went flying. I hand of light orbed a large pane of glass out of the side of wall and dove out into the night just as the Eternal's power surge erupted.

I lit up the whole side of the building as I burst into Phoenix Wing. I caught my reflection in the windows of the building as I fell - the wings were larger, brighter, hotter. The whole flame shimmered with colors of the entire spectrum of light—red and purples to blues and whites and all the flickering colors of the rainbow. I snapped them wide and shot forward. I had to get away…burning too hot. Too many around to see. Too many….

I winced and sat up. What the fuck happened? Sex's memories were chaotic. I was floating face up in about three feet of water, naked as a jaybird, in another pool with the sides scorched all to hell. Wearily, I stood up and waded to the shallow end to climb out. Wait a minute...the sun was up, why wasn't I turning to a dried-out sponge? I held my hand up directly into a morning ray. It just felt like it used to when I was alive. I climbed out the pool and looked for anything to put on. There was a towel laying in a pile in the corner of the fence. More like a shop towel but it was better than nothing.

My stomach growled. Well that was normal, sort of. Disjointed memories flooded back to me. I remember, Liam was going to kill Sex on the beach. Somehow…we got stronger and we got back here. I held my head. I don't know what happened, but I needed to get home. I don't even know where the hell I am. Nothing looks familiar.

I held onto my towel and started walking looking for a phone booth. I'd have to beg for money when I did find one. A siren behind me made me jump. I turned and spied the friendly neighborhood squad car. They were better than a taxi.

325

I didn't have to touch them to get them to do what I wanted. Something big happened. I felt stronger in every which way. Sex wasn't talking to me. Was he even there? Even Azrael was silent. Maybe we just needed to rest. The cop car pulled up in front of my condo, let me out to the relief of the Loyal then drove off. I walked into the elevator in nothing but a smile and a towel.

The penthouse was still in an uproar when the elevator opened into the foyer. Shade sat in front of the elevator her massive red tail swishing the floor in agitation.

Can you hear me now? Her tone was pissed. As if I couldn't tell from her tail.

"I can hear you." I wanted a coffee. When was the last time I wanted coffee?

Where have you been?

"I don't know. I just woke up twenty minutes ago." Really. When was the last time I wanted coffee?

And you couldn't call?

I opened my towel and flashed her. "Don't exactly have any pockets for a cell phone or a quarter."

The tail stilled, and I got the Hellcat cat scan. *You're different, somehow X. You've got some color.*

"I didn't burn up in the sun. I think I got a slight tan."

Incoming.

Haley grabbed me around the waist, knocking the towel off me. "Alpha, you have everyone so worried." Why was he in a suit? What the hell happened last night? I have no clear memories at all. Sex? Nothing yet. I hope he's all right.

"Where is everybody?" I tousled his hair.

"Well most of the suits are out looking for you. Sensei Marcus and Claudius are in the Great Hall. Oooh, oooh, ooooh, you have to see it. It's done." Haley grabbed my hand and tried to drag me off to the Great Hall. The red tail slapped down on his hand and he yelped.

Xavier, get some clothes on, first. Haley moved to grab me again and Shade blocked me. *Hurry up, I can't do this all day.*

326

I grabbed my lost towel and wrapped it around myself. As soon as I did that, Haley realized that nakedness wasn't my normal mode of travel. "I'm going to change too!" He tore off in the opposite direction.

Shade followed me. I stank of chlorine. I hopped in the shower did a real quick scrub down then popped back into my bed chamber. Shade lay on the bed still flicking her tail, a sure sign of her continued aggravation.

Toweling my hair dry, I ended up draping it over my shoulders. *What?*

You have no clue what happened last night?

"I remember Sex falling asleep in Father's arms in the music room then I have some random images of sand in my face, of Liam and a beach then nothing clear until I woke up floating in a firebombed swimming pool. I have no clue where that is. I'm just going to have to rebuild all the pools in the city."

You blew out all the side windows of the mansion and jumped out the largest one. You burst into phoenix in front of the whole city, it was captured by a local TV station newscast, but it was dismissed as a hoax. You were gone for nine hours.

I pulled on some underwear then khakis that fit.

And, when the hell did you get that?

I looked down at my piercings. *Uh, Marcus gave it to Azrael.*

Was that yesterday? Jeez, that was only yesterday.

I can't leave you alone for a second can I. Have you got anything else pierced?

I didn't want to tell Shade, I don't know. I did a real quick shower, I could have depending on how wild Marcus and Azrael got. *Nowhere important guys. That's all I ask. Guys? Hey Sex!* I still got nothing but silence. What was going on? Should I start getting worried? I pulled a plain green tee out the drawer and yanked it over my head. Since my hair was still wet, I left it loose. I padded bare foot toward the Great Hall.

Haley bounded out of the kitchen, dressed, thank god or I would have been hearing from Hans within minutes, holding a tray with a silver cover on it. "Hans said this is for you. Cinnamon French toast, bacon and he's making an omelet. He said to wait but I thought you would be hungry, so I brought it anyways."

"Thanks, Haley."

I held the door open for both Shade and the Lycan then followed them in. Claudius was standing in the middle of the room with a one hand cupping his elbow and the other cupping his chin. "No, back the way you had it before."

He cocked his head in my direction and called out a greeting. "Xavier!"

"Hey, guys. What's up?" I followed Haley with the tray and picked up a piece of bacon. I turned around and got walloped straight across the right cheek. "What the hell was that for?"

Father pointed his finger at me. "Where were you? When did you get back? Where is Sex? What happened last night?"

"I woke up in a pool. I just got back five minutes ago. The Loyal have probably called their search off by now. I don't know where Sex is, he's not talking to me, neither is Azrael and it worries me, and I have no clue what the hell happened last night or for the last nine hours." I rubbed my face. "All I know is that I'm tried and I'm hungry and I want to go to bed with both of you." My face flamed red. "uh...I mean I want to sleep with both of you....er....just sleep, no sex...well maybe..." I turned to look at what was happening across the room. "Marcus! Nice painting."

Father caught me in a tight embrace and I thought my eyes were going to bulge out of my skull. The bacon fell out of my hand onto the floor.

"Haley don't eat off the floor." Claudius reached out and pulled it out of the Lycan's mouth.

Claudius clung to me. The marks from the cuffs at his wrists had begun to fade but they were still there. He had pulled the mooring posts out of the wall. Holy crap. Thank god, he only gave me a love tap just now. I really didn't need another concussion...with a fight to the death match less than eight hours away. Suddenly I lost my appetite.

328

Claudius did a classic Armor move. He sat in the chair and I ended up plastered on his thighs, then was hand fed. I was eating like a baby bird...again. I glanced at Marcus, he just shrugged and went back to straightening another of his masterpieces. I chewed and just stared at the painting. It was a work of art. If people didn't know how loony our pod was, they would expect to see three brothers just like the newest portrait envisioned.

"What are you calling it?" I called out to Marcus.

"Pod."

He was pulling my chain, right? "You are so not calling it that."

A slight chuckle came back from across the room. "No, it's just called Von Drachenfeld."

Claudius shoved a bite size piece of cinnamon toast in my mouth.

While I was gagged with food Claudius broached a delicate subject. "There is something I would like to request, My Lord Emperor."

"You're a Von Drachenfeld if you want to be, Father. I didn't know if you wanted to change Houses. It's kind of a given that I'm Head here."

"I would be honored to be accepted into your house." I got a kiss to the nape of my neck. Still no Sex. *Azrael? Come on guys this isn't funny anymore.* I yawned. Maybe both of them were resting. I yawned and leaned back against Claudius.

"Are you done?"

Was he talking to me?

Armor turned around, "He's done. Father?"

Apparently not.

Claudius stood up, Armor sat down, and I now ended up on his lap. "I do have other chairs you know." I groused lightly.

"You look better sitting here." Armor kissed my temple.

"Ha ha." I yawned. I pushed the fork away. "I'm really tired. Father, I know it's Sunday. I don't know where Sex is. I want to sleep. You can join us, if you want."

"Again, an honor, Lord Emperor." Claudius was a class act. Who else would be so damned refined when asked to join in a threesome. Even if it were only for sleep.

I elbowed Armor in the ribs and motioned with my head towards Haley. "Pup, you can come too. Sleeping only – with bottoms on!" Haley grinned and tore off through the doorway.

Shade? How the hell did I ask her that with a yawn in my silent speak. I must be more tired than I thought.

Too much testosterone for little old me. I've got some clerical stuff I must get done before this afternoon. I'll meet you at the arena, my Lord Emperor. Shade leapt at me in panther form. I squawked and raised my hands to snag a red fluff ball of a kitten out of mid-air. She purred, and I brought her to my face. Her little red head rubbed all over my chin then she bit me. Ow.

What was that for?

Making me worry about you all night. Get some sleep. You look like hell. I set the kitten back on the floor. She ran and within two strides morphed back into the full-sized panther I knew and feared and loved so much.

I hopped off Armor's lap and caught his hand. I offered Claudius mine. He took it without hesitation. By now the staff knew I was back, and they were off in skitter mode but they waited until they saw us pass by to scurry away. It must have been an amusing sight because every one of them seemed to have a smile on their face before they faded back into the woodwork. I plopped myself into the middle of the new bed. *Mmmm comfy. It was like sinking into marshmallows.* Claudius carefully undressed then lay beside me. I turned so I could get spooned. Armor was just getting ready to lie down then Haley slid onto the bed right where Armor was going to lay.

"I do not think so, Pup." Armor shoved him out of the way and lay in front of me. I pressed my head against his back and laid my hand on his waist. He moved slightly and dragged the wiggling Lycan to his chest. "Settle down. You are fine where you are."

"Are you all right, Xavier?" Father whispered into my skin.

I pressed my back against Claudius chest and shivered as his breathes tickled the back of my neck.

"Never better. I think pod life agrees with me." I let a smile cross my face and I sank into the softness and the warmth of a full life...and a full bed.

Chapter Twenty: Do what I must....

"Fucking die already!" I screamed out loud.

"I got you now."

"No...come on...shit." I dropped my controller on the floor as Haley killed me yet again.

Haley bounced up and down on the couch. "Again!"

"No, I'm tired of dying." I laid back and rubbed my eyes. I probably should have slept a little longer, but it seemed like I had gotten all the sleep that I was going to get when I was just lying there staring up at the ceiling.

"Alpha?"

My stomach gurgled right on cue. Twelve bells. I want lunch now. Haley popped up and patted my head. "I'll get Hans to get lunch ready."

I didn't have the heart to tell him that I would probably throw up if I ate. I yawned and debated about getting back into bed.

Brother. Sex's voice came in loud and clear.

I sat up grateful to hear him. *Where the hell have you been? Sex?*

Liam took me to his beachfront vacation home and stabbed me. He's royally pissed. Don't drop your guard for one second.

So why the silent treatment?

There was along long silence until Sex let out a deep sigh, grunt. *Liam said some things that messed with my head. I'll keep them to myself for now, until this fight is over with anyway. Have you noticed anything different?*

Haley's not dropping his pants and asking for dominance every time I turn around.

There was genuine laughter in Sex's voice. *No...in you.*

In me? Waking up in the pool and not getting seared like a shrimp-on-the-barbie was new. *The sun didn't burn me. Father smacked me one, but it didn't hurt as much as usual.*

I drank from Liam. A lot. I'm hoping that it gives us enough strength to carry on.

333

Is that why he stabbed us?

The bastard was going to stab us anyway.

So, you just helped him along.

There was that little bit of self-depreciating laugh again. *A little.... can I see Father?*

You going to screw around?

If he'll let me.

Where the hell is Azrael?

You don't want to know.

Why? I was a little bit alarmed. Did Liam do something to Az...er, Azrael as well?

Let's say the darkness has good acoustics and Azrael has been singing his own tune for a while now getting rid of excess energy.

What the hell did...*Ewwww.*

Trade with me, you can listen for yourself.

I blinked and then lay back and gave myself a good stretch. Hmm, noon. I pushed myself to my feet. Now, where was my black-haired master assassin? I trotted down the hall back toward my bedroom. The rings swung on my chest under my loose tee, just providing enough stimulation to remind me that they were there. I must have looked stupid jogging down the hall with both hands over my nipples. Nope, he wasn't there.

There was no reason to be back in the Great Hall. Music room it is. I slowed as I got outside the door, well where the door used to be. I ripped it right off its hinges last night. A piano and a violin were making beautiful music together. I stepped into the room and looked at 'our' lovers. For a kinky bastard, Marcus played with the heart of a muse. His face was innocence and light when he was lost in his music. He glowed with an inner beauty; it was as if music lit up his soul. I turned my attention to my love, my light, my black-haired beauty. He was dressed in Armor's pajama bottoms. His hair was carelessly braided into a single tail down his back. I could see the muscles in his back as he played. I sat on the floor and pulled my knees up, so I could rest my head there. It was their long-haired crap again, but I had to admit that it was beautiful.

334

The last noted faded and I looked up. Marcus looked at me for a moment, identified which of us it was then began to pack his violin away. Claudius looked over at him then glanced over his shoulder towards me. He said something to Marcus then got to his feet and walked over to me.

"Mne ni-kog-da v zshiz-ni ne-bee-lo tak ha-ra-sho. Tee vsyo, chto mne nuzsh-no. Ya bu-du zhit' diya te-bya, lubov moya."

It was fascinating that I could understand him even though he was speaking Russian to me. *Never in my life, have I felt so good. You are all that I need. I will live just for you, my love.*

He held out his hand to me to get me off the floor as Marcus began to play "*Mona Lisa*" by Nat King Cole. "Are you trying to make me cry?"

"That is your natural state, my Fallen." Claudius said with a smile.

I buried my face into his neck and he brought his arms around me. I have no idea what you call it but I call it snuggle dancing. Swaying is an option. I knew I had a sappy little smile on my face as we rocked. I closed my eyes and breathed in Father's clove scent. Some time must have passed as we swayed in each other's arms because when I opened my eyes, Marcus was gone.

I spoke to him in Russian, "Sasha, my love. Take me here and now. Don't make me wait any longer."

We stopped moving. "I offer myself freely to you, Fallen."

I pulled his head down for one of our regular intense lip lock. Our lips crushed together, and our tongues engaged in a familiar mating ritual.

"If you desire to mount me, my Fallen Angel, I will submit..." Claudius's words rolled off my heating skin like cool pearls or beads of jade.

I finally pulled my head back breaking the sensual spell we were weaving together, "I told you that you are not something to be rushed. When you show me how to please you to your deepest core, it's going to be all day. We can't even share today. I can't take my shield down

335

because Liam is hovering around out there trying to prevent this challenge."

I felt his hand slide down my back and cup my ass. A shiver caressed my spine in a damn fine way. "Have you healed from Hades touch?"

I look his hand and backed him toward the leather chaise then twisted around so I could try to lay myself artfully on it. I don't know about the art part but Claudius eagerly settled himself on me, hitting on the right places and cupping his.... aaaaahhhh.

"Liam's blood healed me."

Sasha.... I decided to call him that when we were together. It rolled off my tongue easier and sexier. Sasha and Sex. Sex and Sasha. He pulled back slightly to look me in the eye. "Why do I think that this Liam would never share his essence so straightforwardly?"

"I took it without asking. Hades put the idea in my head so when Liam tried to kill me last night I bit him where it hurt. He also said some other things that messed up my thinking, but we'll deal with that load of bull when we have to. When I came back, it was just like Hellcat essence only stronger. I had uncontrolled burns for about seven hours. I wrecked about nine pools last night -- some private ones but mostly public."

"That explains seven hours out of the nine you were missing."

"The last two were trying to get everything together and calm for today. I would have been back sooner, but there was a surprise burn. At that time, I was tired, and X took over. But I'm rested now...and I want you, Sasha. Run with me now...while we still can."

Sasha pulled my right leg up and hiked it over his forearm. He pushed his hips forward and rubbed his cloth bound member against my denim covered ass. Feeling his heat grinding against me was so good as he dry humped me. I arched up against him demanding more friction. Sasha stopped moving and he pressed his hips down hard against me. "We should not do this. You have to fight in less than two hours."

I bucked up to him. His whole body rocked in response. There was a look of shock as I lifted him again with just my groin. "I told you that Liam's blood made me stronger."

"How much stronger?"

"I don't know it was a spur of the moment thing." The scent of warm cloves surrounded me. "Never mind that now, I want you inside me, Sasha."

"Sex, we should find out…"

I reached up and pulled him down onto me. I lightly worried his ear with my teeth then ran my tongue along the reddened shell. I suck kissed my way down his neck and dropped fang just a bit to scrape his flesh. "I already found what I want."

"We have to…Fallen. There is not enough…mmmmm. Fallen, why is it that I cannot do the sensible thing when I am with you?" A ring of red flame encircled those arctic blues.

Arcing my jaw forward, I nipped the underside of his chin then laved it better with my tongue. My voice was low with desire. "Then be bad…be naughty, Sasha. I'll be naughty with you."

I laughed as I found myself lifted into his arms, on the way to the crimson piano. Oh yeah, it was fun the last time we played there. I wrapped my legs around his waist and carefully fanged his neck. He stumbled in his step and he gently tossed me up on the lid.

"Too naughty." He scolded me as his hand stroked the curve of my ass and down my outer thigh.

"There is no such thing." I licked my lips in anticipation.

Oh yes there was. Sasha showed me by ripping my pants off, literally. I squirmed on my back on the red piano lid as my love swallowed me whole. He pulled one knee over his shoulder, pressed the other to the side and sank his glorious lips down my shaft. His tongue slid along the underside of my cock pressing it up to the roof of his mouth. Two fingers traced my face. I sucked them into my mouth, licking them like they were his swollen member. I separated his fingers and flicked my tongue at the fleshy part between them. Then Sasha hit a

337

sensitive area with a little bit o' fang that sent me arching backwards, smacking the back of my head off the piano.

The newly wet digits entered me easily. I ripped off my shirt. Those blue eyes zeroed in on the new piercing but then settled on the warmth of the locket around my neck. I was reduced to panting as the corners of his lips curved up. I grinned back at him as he continued to suck me. I propped up on my elbows and watched his reddened lips work my sensitive flesh. He curled his fingers and searched for that sweet spot within me. My eyes open wide and I gave a sharp cry as he found it. He laughed while I was buried in his mouth. Oh my... nnnnuuuhhhh.

There was a loud wet pop as my cock slid free and slapped my stomach.

"Pull them." Sasha ordered.

My chest heaved in time with his finger thrusts. "Pull on your rings for me, Fallen. Put on a show for me."

He rose to his feet, his fingers still working inside my ass. I must have looked wanton. Pale, flushed pink, skin and snow-white hair contrasting with the blood red of the piano's finish. I arched my neck to the side and held my hand over the gold locket, his heart gift to me. I let one finger trace over its surface, swirling my pad on it as if I were caressing a hidden button. A groan ripped out of my throat. I trailed my finger down from the locket at my throat to my left nipple ring. My nipple was stiff standing at attention, wanting to be taken into Sasha's talented mouth. I brought my finger tip back to my mouth, wetting it with my spit.

Sasha groaned in a low lustful voice as I brought it back down to my nipple and let it slide over the hardened nub. "Pull it." He growled the order.

I took the ring and pulled it out from my body just as Sasha hit that spot again. I think I must have short circuited. I opened my eyes and felt his lips sucking at the base of my throat. His member was buried deep in me. I gasped as he moved slightly, bumping that bundle of nerves with unnatural accuracy. My right leg was over his forearm. He shafted me

338

again. I tossed my head back knocking it hard on the lid of the piano again. Ow....huuuunnn!

He twisted the other ring. I tightened up hard on his member. He swallowed my cry.

His tongue mimicked his cock as he pillaged my mouth. This vampire could make me cum from a kiss. I groaned around his possession. I felt alive. My fingers dug into his back as he pulled on the opposite ring. He arched hard up into me. I gave an exceptionally loud cry. He kissed his way to my ear and got down to the main event. His hips began to slam into me repeatedly.

His voice whispered, "*Lubov moya, lubov moya, lubov moya…*"

His words "my love" filled my ears.

I gritted my teeth and tried to stay with him as the pleasure intensified. He nuzzled my neck then bit me. Tears sprang from my eyes as he drank my essence. I was getting overwhelmed with sensation.

"Uh, uh, uh. Aaah…Sasha!"

"Be with me…stay with me…" Sasha gripped both rings and twisted them in opposite directions. I screamed. My cock erupted between us. My ass spasmed, milking my welcomed invader to completion.

Sasha rested his head on my heaving chest. I brought my arms up and hugged him hard. "You belong to me, Sasha, *moya mily. Vsyo idyot kak nado.*"

Everything is going to be all right. I whispered it to him again in Russian. *Everything is going to be all right.*

His flame was abated but flashes of crimson still flared in his beautiful arctic blues. "How can you be so sure?"

I stroked his back and pressed my chin to his sweaty shoulder. "I'm Lord Emperor. Hades is not. He has only been the Emperor's Consort. I'm not losing to him today."

I hugged Claudius tighter, "And if you come near me with that bottle of ether like you planned, I will chain you back to the piano. Keep the faith, Father."

"How did you…?"

"Mindfuckability. I don't have to touch you. You didn't want to do it anyway."

"I do not want this day at all." He stroked my hair. I sighed and closed my eyes. I listened to his steady heartbeat.

"I wanted to ask you to join the House, but I didn't feel I had the right. Maybe I don't. Damn, my thinking is still messed up." I lifted a hand to my forehead.

"Sex?"

I debated all for a heartbeat. I didn't want to keep anything from Sasha anyways. "Liam said some things. He said I was the original Sigmund Edward Xavier. He could be lying to confuse me, which is working. He could be telling the truth, which is still messing with my head."

Sasha pulled me up right and wiped the tears from my eyes. He pressed a gentle kiss to my lips then slapped me across the face. Sonofabitch! I stared at him and held a hand to my stinging cheek.

"Pardon my language, but Liam is fucking with your head. You will fight for your survival in less than two hours and you have allowed him to create doubt. Do your brothers know about this?"

"No."

"Keep it to yourself. Put it aside. Do what you must, to get what you want. What do you want, Sex?" Father's eyes had gotten cold. It wasn't Carnage, but it also wasn't my hot horny bad boy Sasha. "What do you want?"

That was easy. "I want to live. I want to be with you. I want the brothers to be happy."

"What do you have to do to get that?"

"Get my head straight."

That perfect jaw stiffened. "Let us try this again, what must you do to get what you want?"

I hated it when he did this, but I was missing something simple. What do I need to do today? "Kill Hades."

340

"That is the only thing you have to concentrate on. Center all your thoughts on achieving that goal. If you have any second thoughts just remember my little motto."

I'd heard that enough times. "Do what I must, to get what I want."

I grabbed Father by the back of his braid and jerked him forward until our foreheads touched. "Don't ever let me go back into the Dark."

"I have never stopped cherishing you, Sex. I never will." He caught my hand and pulled me off the piano. "It's time to get ready."

I showered alone. I worked at getting completely calm. Frosty. I had to be frosty and clear. Focused on the task at hand. I had asked X to trade but he said it was Sunday and it was my day. Big Brother made me smile. If Azrael finally stopped the deviant things he was doing in the Dark...I didn't even want to know.

Chesterton was standing beside the bed when I came out of the bathroom. On the bed was a leather outfit, sort of like Elvis' 68 special comeback tour gear, except it was a black and beaten silver in color. I can only guess that Claudius had picked this out. Maybe it would prevent some cuts. I glanced over at Chesterton who was holding a silver serving tray full of daggers, blades and sheaths. "Sir."

"Where's everybody?"

"They are getting ready as well, My Lord."

Do you wear underwear with leather battle gear? Since Chesterton had a pair of tighty whites laying there on top I guessed so. I got into them then slipped into the leather pants. They were skin tight. I pulled on a black undershirt then reached out for the tray. My hands hesitated over the forearm daggers. These weren't X's. A small discreet C and D were etched into the hilt of the tang. They were Claudius's. I buckled them on and tested each mechanism. They were well taken care of and were flawlessly smooth on the test draw. Of course, they would be; they were Father's.

I went to do something with my messy hair. "Master Claudius will see to your hair. Master Armor will see to your feet. These, My Lord will go into your boots."

I slipped into the leather shirt and found two long slits cut into the back. Wing slits? I pulled it on and snapped it together. I shrugged my shoulders and called on my feather wings. They slid out effortlessly through the slits in the leather shirt not binding or interfering at all. I spread my wings wide as I slid the small blade into the waistband of my pants. A few more experimental flaps and twitches then I dissolved the wings in a shower of light.

"Lord Emperor?" I shoved my hair out of my face, so I could see the butler's concerned face.

"Chesterton?"

"Kick his ass, Sir."

I really grinned back at him. I walked up and kissed his cheek. "Thank you for everything you've done up until today. Remember, we've got an engagement party tomorrow."

"Yes, Sir."

"Get everything ready the way the Baroness wants. I may have horny men in my life, but the women in it are absolutely terrifying. See you later."

I headed out of the bed chamber and sidestepped a Lycan lunge. Haley turned and looked at me. He was back in the suit he had on when X got home. "I'm dressed wrong."

Claudius approached from behind Haley. "You are dressed as your station dictates, little Pup, you look fine." Claudius was dressed totally in black. Beautiful lines on a custom-made suit made him seem taller. He had on a black dress shirt and matching tie. He even had a black scrap of material peeking out of his suit pocket. The absence color accented his pale skin and made the only color on him, his glacier blue eyes, pop.

Schwing.

Damn it. Claudius smiled and ran his eyes over me. "It looks good. Haley, go and get your Alpha's lunch. He will have to eat in the car." Haley turned and padded to the kitchen. "And get your shoes on."

Claudius turned back to me and arched an eyebrow. "That looks good on you."

"Ya, heavy leather in the middle of summer."

"Still looks good on you." Claudius stepped up, his eyes warm with love. I closed my eyes and lifted my face for a kiss. I gasped as I got a hand cupping my...I was jerked back to another broad chest.

"Father, please..." I glanced up and looked up to the underside of Armor's chin. "Give Sex some rest."

Armor was dressed for success as well. He was in a dark navy pinstripe three piece with a crisp white linen shirt. He had on a dark jade green tie and again a matching handkerchief. I couldn't help but compliment. "You clean up nice."

"Marcus has a better eye with color, so he picked this out. Are we ready?"

Armor handed me my mp3 player. "Good to go."

Haley bounded up carrying his shoes and a brown bag which I assumed it was my lunch.

Okay, I wasn't expecting it. All the staff was lined on one side of the hall leading to the elevator, the house security Loyal were lined up on the opposite side. Armor let me walk ahead after he whispered in my ear, "Let them see the Angel of Death, Sex. Give them assurance that you will be coming back."

I let my feather wings out. They were bigger than before, the ends trailed on the floor. I had to lift and open them slightly to keep Armor's big feet from stepping on them.

"Excelsior! Excelsior! Excelsior!"

What? Someone gave me a light shove in the back to get me moving. As one, all twenty-five staff and twelve Loyal dropped into reverent pose. Holy crap. Majorly impressive. I worked on keeping from making a fool of myself as I made my way to the elevator. I ducked slightly to get inside then moved to let my little motley crew in with me. Everything was all fine and dandy until I sneezed. My wings acted on reflex. They spread and flattened Father and Armor to the sides of the car. Haley had ducked down to tie his shoes and missed the feathered compactor.

"Put them away." Armor grunted at me.

"I'm sorry. Sorry."

They dissolved in the usual shimmer of light. I watched and bit back a laugh as Haley grabbed at the glittering orbs as it passed over him but opened his hand to emptiness. I glanced up and wiped the smile off my face. Neither Father nor Armor looked that all impressed with getting smacked around. Claudius pulled a feather out of Armor's hair then brushed some fluff off his lapel. "Urrr...sorry..."

"Come here."

I shuffled over up to Father expecting a reprimand.

My hair was still in disarray and tangled so it rather hurt as Sasha pushed it back off my forehead. "There is no doubt you are definitely stronger. Walk into the warehouse with your wings out. They are a part of you. Hades cannot complain. As you said, he has been a Lord Emperor's Consort for years; he knows that Wings are part of the Emperor. It will be a psychological advantage and every advantage helps."

"Just do not use them now." Armor rubbed his jaw where I hit him.

The bright afternoon sun didn't affect me. Comparing this feeling and the slight tingle Hades' blood left as I stood in the sun in the Ferris wheel made me think that maybe I got enough of Liam's blood to make it an even fight.

I grinned and bounded after Haley as he sniffed the car for bombs I guess. Clear! I jumped into the back and sprawled on the seat. Claudius came in and settled on the far side of the seat then pulled me back to rest against his side. Armor sat down, and I plopped my bare feet on his lap. I wiggled my bare toes at him. Haley slid in and sprawled on the opposite seat. The door shut behind us and the limo pulled away.

"What happened?" Father asked staring down at me.

"I just realized - I'm going to kick his ass." I twisted oddly to pull his head down for a gentle kiss. "I'm going to win."

I set my mp3 player on my chest popped in the ear buds and turned it on. Enya? I picked up the player and looked at it. This wasn't mine...this was Azrael's? Azrael and Enya, not a combination I would have thought. I left the music on and laid back on Father's lap. He brushed my hair…much better than the last time he did it with X. Armor did his feet massage thing…boneless chicklet mode indeed. I relaxed more than when X was in bed.

Something bumped my lips. I opened my eyes to see Haley on his knees holding a sandwich up to my face. What the hell? I went to take it from his hand but he pulled it back. "It's my turn now."

"What?"

"I get to you feed you, Alpha. You're my penguin now!"

Claudius burst out laughing. This wasn't a muffled laugh. He was loud and ruckus. All of us looked at him kind of unsure what to do. He ended up wiping his face with the back of his hand. "Of all the animals in the world, Sex, I would never have compared you to a penguin. Eat something. You need your strength."

I went to take the sandwich and Haley pulled it away. "I get to feed you now." He widened his eyes and attempted to stare me down. This was like a guard pup trying to be tough with a burglar the first day of training.

I held a hand to my forehead. That's all he has seen. My closest companions sitting me on their laps and hand feeding me breakfast, lunch and dinner. "Thanks guys, you've set a bad example."

"Just let Haley feed you, pengi." Armor returned with a slight smirk on his face. Which I would take from him. I still owed him an ass kicking on the books for getting stapled to Hades' wall. Armor put my socks and boots on me, then slid the blades into hidden sheaths in the shank of each boot. I shifted and sat on the floor in front of Father and he began to braid my hair.

Haley scooted around and held the sandwich up to my mouth again. Black Forest Ham, Swiss cheese and sweet honey mustard. Not bad. But I'm going to have Hans remove any trace of honey out of Von Drachenfeld now that Honey Bee was buzzing around all untainted now. The pup pulled out a bottle of cream soda. I watched him warily. He took a swig and moved in….no, no, no, no. I put my hand over his mouth.

"I'll eat a sandwich from your hands, but I draw the line at drinking from your mouth."

"You did it." He swallowed it and made a face.

"That was Xavier and it was beer."

"I only have this." Haley held up the pop bottle. I took it out of his hand. He looked like I just smacked him with a newspaper. I opened my mouth to assure him that I wasn't mad and got another mouthful of food. The pup was going to feed me that sandwich if I wanted it or not. Sometimes, it's easier to give in.

Claudius gave a couple of yanks on my hair. I brought my hand back and felt a sheathed stiletto braided and hidden up near my nape. Clever and devious or would that be considered well prepared?

"Kill him any way you can, Fallen." Claudius patted my shoulder and lifted me back up on the seat. I was locked and loaded for bear, or I guess it would be a Honey Bee.

"I think you should look at this." Armor gestured out the window. I slid over sideways and looked at about 200 limos parked around the warehouse. Haley popped his head up beside me and knocked me back onto Armor as he wiggled to get a better view. He knew better than to open the window, more than likely, the Loyal locked the windows so they couldn't be opened. Armor caught me around the waist and held me still. I muttered. "Well I guess it is not exactly a secret match anymore is it?"

Claudius straightened his cuffs. "What did you expect? You challenged Hades in Shadoe Inc. The news was probably spreading as you came down in the elevator. I think all the ranked assassins are here and our Loyal are still coming. It also looks like there are High Council members and their entourage."

"Sex." I turned my head back toward Father. "Do what you must to get what you want. What must you do?"

"Kill Hades."

"Kill him any way you can. If you have to burst into the Phoenix Emperor to do it, you do it."

"The training area isn't that big. You'll..."

346

"It does not matter if I get caught in your wake, Sex. I am not the only one who loves you or depends on you. Hades is Ancient. He did not get to be that old only relying on William to keep him safe. He will be reluctant to fight you at the beginning. Once he realizes that you are truly earnest in your attempts to kill him, you will have a vicious fight on your hands."

I nodded. The limo pulled around to a side door.

Olly, olly oxen free, X. Show time, big brother.

Sex breezed by me in a whisper of white, a shimmer of wings of fire, micro mini and ballet slippers.

Fuck'em up, X.

Sex had such a gutter mouth. I blinked as I settled into the familiar confines of this body aware I was in my favorite chair. Leaning back into my richly scented apple orchard, turned my head and nipped at his neck. I felt a chuckle in his chest as he presented it to me. I dropped fang and savored his nectar. I breathed deep inhaling his apple essence. "Have I told you how much I fucking love you?"

"Language, Little One. I fucking love you too." Armor hugged me gently. "Kill him quick. Marcus says be safe."

I had to laugh. "Azrael said to tell Marcus not to get used to driving."

Armor dropped a kiss to the nape of my neck.

Winter opened the back door and waited for me to move to the heavily guarded entrance. Haley popped out first glaring at everyone then took up position across from the Loyal. Claudius moved past us. "Remember what I said, Little Blue." He slapped me lightly on the cheek.

Armor kissed my booboo. "What do you want?"

"You."

"I will be waiting. Remember, you are the Lord Emperor. You have many skills and talents. Use them. I want you in my arms tonight, Little One." Armor slid out and joined Father making a line toward the entrance. The outer door opened, and Queen Nightshade sat there flicking her tail. She was flanked on both sides by six other hellcats. Holy mother of ….

Attitude will take you places, Xavier. Style will get you noticed. We will make them fear you.

Shade what are you doing?

Shut up. We are your vanguard. They are stupidly crowded in there. We will clear your path. Walk behind us, X. Make a statement. Many have heard of you, few have seen you. Make them know that the Lord Emperor walks among them.

Shade let out a hellcat roar. It was echoed six times over. I had to cover my ears and I still felt the reverberation rattle my chest. Holy crap. Everybody knew I was here now. I willed out my wings as I emerged from the dark recess of the limo. They vibrated, sending out the sound of glass chimes; I took a deep steadying breath as I stepped into the bright light of day. That was noted as well. I stood in full daylight without wilting like the fledgling everyone knew I was.

Suck on that, Hades.

Do what I must to get what I want. Right now, I wanted this day over.

Queen Nightshade bowed to me then turned and led her pack of six huge hellcats into the bowels of the warehouse. The Shade and the other Hellcats formed a wide empty swash behind her, forcing the crowds back against the side of the building then the corridor walls when we made it inside. Haley took point directly after Shade and I followed him aware that everyone was staring. I didn't look back, but I was comforted to know Father was on my right and Armor was on my left.

What must I do?

Kill Hades.

Chapter Twenty-One: ...to get what I want

Tide goes in, tide goes out. Tide goes in, tide goes out. Don't trip. Don't blush. Keep your wings up. Follow the red tail. Keep your eyes on the red tail.

Calm down, X. You're freaking me out. Shade snapped back at me as the tip of her tail flicked in annoyance.

I hope you know where the hell you're going. I have no clue. I felt a thousand eyes on me and the glass chimes of my wings shivered, however only the two vamps behind me knew I was shaking under the scrutiny, not because I was going to a possible death, but because this panic was a leftover from being the 'fat kid' who hated being the center of attention.

Well, duh. Shade's sarcasm didn't help.

Shade's feline humor wasn't appreciated at this time. *Be nice, this might be the last time you're talking to me.*

Shade let loose another Hellcat roar that ripped through the throng of vampire assassins. All conversation around us ceased. Every vampire with good sense backed up out of the way clearing a path that should take us to this arena. I would like to say that they parted like the Red Sea, but it was more along the line that they cringed before a tidal wave of red Hellcat fur.

Don't even joke about that, X. Her tail flicked right and left in agitation.

Who the hell is joking? Armor was correct. Every single ranked assassin was here. I really only dealt with the top fifteen. Anything lower than that got handed off to Billy Envoy and he texted the orders out, very impersonal but efficient. Still, efficient isn't always the best way. Hades was correct saying that the House was now fractured and seeing the Loyal men in black melt out of the crowd and physically clear a path for the Hellcat brigade only brought home that old adage -- a house divided cannot stand. There were going to have to be changes made when this was all said and done. I don't do impersonal. If someone is willing to put their undead life on the line for me, I want to know them. It might not be the most efficient way to do things, but that was just the way I roll.

We finally made our way into the training room. It was the same room where I had frightening memories of when I thought I killed Father, okay when Azrael and I killed him. Glancing up, I saw that the whole of the ceiling was now enclosed in glass just like an operating theatre. Unfamiliar vampiric faces ringed the whole arena. This was the *secret* House of Assassins? Too many people... er, vampires, were gathered here to keep this training facility as a viable resource. It was going to have to go when this match was said and done.

I walked forward a few more steps and saw Hades and his second standing on the far side of the room--Billy Envoy. Why the hell would Hades pick the man in white? He wasn't a fighter, he was a desk jockey. Well, wasn't that a kick in the teeth. My skills were considered so lowly that Hades didn't even rate me as a serious threat that he basically walked onto this killing floor alone.

I clenched my jaw. Fine, Hades was in for a big surprise.

Claudius dropped a hand on my shoulder and squeezed. I got a slight tap to my midsection with a red tail. Okay, concentrate. Tide goes in, tide goes out. I regulated my breathing. Hades glanced up and did a double take. He couldn't hide his surprise after doing that. He knew I was coming with Claudius. He should have assumed that Armor would be here. Maybe he even assumed that I would have the Lycan prince pup with me. His eyes widened at the amount of red fur standing in front of me then he canted his head back to take in my pure white wings.

Way to go Shade. I high fived the tip of her tail.

Hehehehehe. That was a little creepy to hear a kitty snicker in my head. *Come on boys, our work here is done for now.*

I was brushed on each side as one hellcat turned and rubbed on my right, another turned and rubbed on my left until only Her Majesty was left. She sauntered up and flicked her tail at the underside of my chin. *I'll be waiting for you outside, X. Don't disappoint me.*

350

Hades cleared his throat. "I knew you had a Hellcat, Xavier. I didn't know you had the Queen as your bond mate. I never thought that Hellcats would be slumming…and white? Really?" His eyes flicked up to my wings. "It's like the tavern whore wearing white for her wedding."

Claudius's grip crushed my shoulder. *Ow…what the fuck? Was Hades trash talking both me and Father?* "He is trying to rile you up. Do not play into his hands."

Hades continued with his king ass routine. "Honestly, Xavier, whatever were you thinking?"

Really? This was how we were going to face each other, like schoolyard bullies? "If you took the time to talk to me instead of screwing me up against a window or over furniture, you might have learned some things."

Hades's pale blue eyes narrowed and the expression on his face turned lascivious. "But the experience was exceptional."

I shut up. Mainly because I would have been playing into Hades hands, and the other was that I needed my clavicle in one piece. Father's tightening grip was bordering on freakishly strong. It was taking more effort than I wanted to admit keeping from groaning out loud. My silence was rewarded with Father removing his hand. The pressure was gone but the residual pulsing and pin and needle effects made me stretch my shoulder. Damn, that's a whole lot of foot pounds of pressure in those long elegant fingers. I gave Hades a thin smile. Off to Hades right, Billy Envoy stood at attention as always immaculate in white. Him and Claudius could be a salt and pepper set.

Damn, I missed whatever Hades was spouting. "What?"

"How the hell did you get to be First? You have the attention span of a gnat."

I returned in the same mild tone Hades had asked his question. I was anything but calm and mild. "Who the hell dragged me into the House to begin with?"

"Your natural talent drew you in and your penchant for defiance is why we are standing here today." Hades stalked toward the center of the

351

room crossing the distance to poke me in the same aching shoulder Father had bruised. My wings chimed with the force of his poke.

Haley jumped out in front of me causing Hades to take a step back. Armor caught Haley's shoulder and pulled him out of the room. "But, I have to protect my Alpha…"

"Do you not think I want to be by his side? This is the Lord Emperor's battle. This time, we can only watch."

The door shut closing off the gladiator's arena. Two men enter, one man leaves…well four vamps enter, two leave. You get the gist.

"There is still time, Xavier. Withdraw your challenge. You have witnesses that will vouch that you arrived on time. No one will question your resolve or your courage." Billy took Hades coat and headed back to his corner. Claudius walked off to our own corner. Hades was dressed in fighting leathers as well. His were a dark distressed brown. He had on a sleeveless side-laced leather shirt with bracers extending from his wrist to his forearm. "I am nine hundred years older than you. I am faster. I heal quicker and I have killed Vampires far more talented, over less significant things. You do not need to die today for simple rank."

I let everything get cold and calm, "We both know that running Assassins Incorporated has nothing to do with this."

"Who else is going to believe you, Xavier? A long dead and forgotten Emperor who's coming back century after century to guide the Vampire Nation to new heights is coming to possess your supermodel body? Tell anyone and they would say you take after your grandfather and call you cuckoo. If he still existed, my William would have come back to me centuries ago. I am drawn to his signature essence just like a bee to nectar. I've found his reincarnated body three times and fostered him back to the age we could be lovers once more. William has never possessed an adult Vampire and Sigmund's behavior was called into question long before this supposed merging."

If I thought Hades as a dink before, when he was trying he was even a bigger ass. I wanted to punch his fangs in.

However, I was Lord Emperor Ass. Leaning in, I whispered. "Now, I know more of the truth, I would gladly be compared to Sigmund. He lived a whipped life, but I know that was by choice. He died to stay free of that monster's taint and that was also by choice. I chose to keep my brothers. That's what I'm fighting for, Cillian. That choice."

"So be it."

Crap, the bugger moved fast. My cheek burned hot as he sliced my face open. I brought my forearm up, blocked the second slash and kicked Hades in the side of the knee. He went down but rolled. My own blade scraped on the concrete, covered by sand, just missing where he had stood. My wings dissolved in a glitter of light. I'd never fought with the feather form and I doubted that now would be the time to try. The light made him hesitate for a heartbeat and that was enough time to allow me to spin and slash out at the back of his calf as my other blade dropped to my hand so I could thrust it forward. My sweeping blade scored the back of his boot but didn't' cut through. My thrusting blade hit home. I caught his forearm in between the leather seam and rammed it straight through. He yanked his arm high as I pulled the blade back. Blood splattered everywhere. I spun on my knee out of his reach. My own hot liquid was pouring down my face and running under my leathers.

Hades hissed at me as he held onto his wound. "Not so pretty now, Xavier."

I focused on my forefinger as concentrated blue light danced on the tip. I ran it along my cut cheek. That was a bizarre sensation as the skin healed behind my touch. I let the blue light fade and ran the back of my fingers over my unscarred cheek.

"Pretty is as pretty does."

Hades eyes narrowed and he actually snarled at me.

I shook that finger at him, "Be careful, if I lose and Liam gets to me, you just might be sleeping with this face."

Hades zigzagged toward me then ran up the wall al la Gene Kelly. I twisted and rolled trying to keep him in front of me. He jumped over me. I ducked the flash of his blade. His kicking foot grazed the back of my neck. I didn't like being on the defensive. I charged forward arcing my dagger in a left to right swing. Hades ducked under it and I felt a

353

sharp stab in my side. I reversed movement by twisting my upper torso even though my left side screamed in protest. My blade buried itself in the back of his upper arm. He wrenched back. We both lost our blades. Mine in his arm; his in my ribs.

Fuck that hurt. It was a burning pain that pulsed with each heartbeat. Damn it.

He's better than me. Sex, have you got his moves down yet?

Azrael's voice came through loud and clear. *Heal up, brother. I'll cut him up a bit.*

Sex's voice came out of the Darkness. *He's holding back, Azrael. Make him come at you full force.*

I gasped and ripped the blade from my side. I pressed my elbow in tight stopping the blood from oozing down into my pants. *What? Are you saying that he's just fucking with us?*

Sex seemed to have the coolest, calmest voice of us all which just showed that while we might look all bad ass and bloody on the exterior, we were, well, I was freaking out. I could barely track Hades movements. *X, we all have talents. Yours is shooting. Let Azrael cause a little mayhem. I don't want to show myself too soon.*

I panted and forced myself into a Healing Light. I could feel my energy draining, but it was not like the weakness I was left with before Sex sucked on our progenitor. Liam's blood was some kick ass juice. Hades would have shared bloodlust with Liam. That's why he's so damn quick. But, he's hasn't had a jump from that battery in over 400 years. Good lord, what the hell would he be like if he was fully charged?

Ramp it up, Azrael.

Little brother's voice sounded real close when he replied. *Run at him, X. We move differently. I'll take over just before we engage. Remember he doesn`t know how quickly we can cycle.*

"You looked tired, Xavier." Hades taunted as blood seeped down his arm.

"I got three lovers to satisfy. I don't get much sleep."

"And that's why I couldn't be added?"

"No, you were just a punk ass kid who's used to grabbing anything shiny and new without bothering to find out if it belongs to someone else. That's why you couldn't be with me."

Hades healed fast, faster than a normal red blood vampire but not as fast as the Healing Light. He flexed his upper arm and shook it. He took a good look at the blade he pulled from his forearm. "I gave this to Claudius."

"I guess this is his way of returning it to sender."

Oh, that pressed some buttons.

Hades eyes glowed red. Right, left, leap forward. I back pedaled and caught his wrist as the dagger slipped past my ear. Azrael brushed against me so I fell back into Darkness.

X dropped all control into my hands in less than a heartbeat. I tightened my hold on Hades wrist and jerked him forward hard enough to send him off balance. Twisting my torso as he passed I punched Hades hard in the temple. He dropped like a load of bricks to the soft fine sand. I hit him again relishing the feel of my knuckles on his face. I kept a hold on his wrist, falling on his chest, digging my boney elbow into his side, forcing all my weight on his ribs. He grunted then shoved at me, gaining enough space to flip onto his back. I let go of his wrist and grabbed at his throat.

"Hey, Cilly… having fun, yet? I told you I'd be the one to kill you."

Hades eyes lit up in recognition. "Azrael."

I gritted my teeth as he hammered his elbow into my shoulder. If I hadn't reacted quickly, the bastard would have smashed my windpipe in. I grabbed onto his upper arm and forced my fingernails into his almost closed wound. I ripped it open again. The blood made it slippery to hang on. I tightened my hand on his neck. The bastard stabbed me in the thigh.

We both gimped away. I pulled the blade out but my hand shook with the effort. *Come on X. Heal me…*

I drag, crawled, myself back from Hades getting enough distance between us so I could use the wall to stand.

X!

I'm working on it.

I wiped my bloody hand on my leather and reached down into my boot. I pulled out a fresh blade. It glinted in the overhead light. Hades flexed his fingers. "Oh, yes, you can't heal can you, youngest brother."

X...needing some healing. Like NOW.

You're going to have to bite Father after this burn. We are getting too low. Make Hades bleed...slow him down.

Hades paused as my whole frame burst into blue light. I could see the light bulb go off in his eyes. "You're working together. As I've yet to see my lovely Edward, I'm going to take it he's just the fluffy plushie that looks best in bed. Good at games, but not really suited for real life. He's a good fuck. When you submit, I'll chain him to my bed. He looks best there anyway."

Was that supposed to throw me off guard? I knew Sex was a good fuck. I let a thin smile break my lips.

"You forget, Hades? This is to the death. Unless you're into necrophilia, if you win there won't be any sexy time." The Healing Light faded in a fizzling burst then I was hit with a wave of weakness. My knees buckled and I ended up on my hands and knees panting hard but I never allow my eyes to stray from my opponent. Good way to get yourself killed if you forgot that simple lesson.

"You can't even stand, Azrael. I can still forgive this." Hades raked his sweaty blonde curls back over his forehead leaving a streak of blood on his forehead.

"You've given a good accounting of yourself. No one would say that you did not try. Yield to me. Your penalty would be that you would give me Edward; pledge him to me. I will love him and keep him safe and we'll call this over."

I couldn't believe this guy. He was thinking with his cock at a time like this? My whole leg shook with effort as I tried to scramble back to my feet but I was so weak that I couldn't even shift sideways. Damn it. The one thing in my favor was that Hades wasn't interested in stepping over the short sandy distance and kicking me in the face. This also meant that he was out of stabbing range for me.

"You're just like Liam." I glanced up at Hades with one squinting eye. Sand was everywhere, grating against my skin under these leathers. He had to be feeling it too. "You're how damn old and you still don't get it? You want to own Sex. You want to keep him just like Liam kept you."

I felt his stare zero in on me. "That isn't love, Cillian. I'm the last to admit it, but what you're offering Sex isn't love. You almost sucked Claudius dry with your 'care and affection' and where did you learn that? At your beloved Liam's knee. He taught you slavery and dressed it up by calling it love."

"You don't know what you're talking about." Hades snarled.

"You master cursed you for four hundred years. He locked you in a chastity belt so you would have to wait for his return. That's not love. That's not even trust."

"Don't comment on something you know nothing about."

"Really? Why the fuck do you think this battle royale is happening, Cilly? We're the epicenter of all the shit that's been going on. You and me and your master makes three and even though some might call us crazy, we're not into ménage a trios."

There it was --a small flare of crimson in those pale cold eyes of his. Hades was stronger and he sure as hell was faster but if needling him gets him off his game, I was the brother to do it.

The most deadly assassin with the face of a golden youth snarled at me as if truly offended by my slight jibe. "This isn't about sex." Hades took a step forward, pointing his own bloody blade at my face. "It's a deeper connection."

"I'd say so. Liam is rather hung. Is that what made you into a size whore?"

Hades snarled something along the lines of bastard and lunged forward. I was waiting for this so was able to contort out of the way but the downward slam of my boot dagger was off the target slightly and I only managed to pin the front of the Hades toes into the sand. I had hoped that my strike would bury the blade into the floor but the sand prevented it. Hades back slash didn't miss. The hidden hair blade and sheath took the brunt of the cut but it was enough to slam up into the back of my head, ringing my bell, and still had enough to slice the side of my neck.

The scent of cinnamon exploded in the arena as blood spurted from my neck. Hanks of bloody white hair slipped off my shoulder and fell into my face as I slapped my hand across my wound.

X!

Get to Claudius now. You don't have enough strength...now! Move it.

I did a cardinal sin of the arena. I turned my back on my opponent as I walk-staggered over to Claudius. Father caught me before my knees slammed into the floor. Since I had gone to my Second, it was like it was the end of round one. Billy Envoy ran out and wrenched the dagger from Hades foot, helping him back to the opposite wall.

Claudius pressed his hand down hard over my cut. "What are you doing, Azrael? X is better at this."

"I need to fang you." Father flipped his hair back and held me up to his neck. Sinking my fangs deep into his neck I sucked hard as if I was blood starved. He hissed at the pain I gave him but his blood shot around my system like pure octane. X suddenly flared me into healing light, slowing the searing pulse that had been pumping my blood out over my shoulder and chest closed with a cool blanketing touch. As I took Claudius's vitality my legs strengthened; he took my weakness and his knees gave out. I lowered him gently to the floor and propped him against the wall.

"Thank you Father." The Healing Light had closed the fang wounds nicely.

Claudius leaned heavily against the wall, "He is wearing you down too fast. Get it over with."

"There is a plan. Keep the faith." I gripped Claudius's shoulder then rose up to my full height.

As I turned back toward the center of the room I saw that Hades was a bloody mess. I wasn't Mr. Clean and tidy any more either. The crowd of Vampires ringing up the upper walls had fallen silent the moment we crosses blades. There was still nothing coming from above. The silence was deafening. All I could hear was my panting and Hades low groan as he stood. He healed fast but blue blood trumps red.

"Azrael…this doesn't need to continue. This is my last offer."

Reaching down into my other boot I retrieved another dagger. "You know the reasons why I fight. They still haven't changed, Cillian. I will live free as I am, or I will die free as I am."

"You can't win."

I held up Father's bloodied blade. "That's acceptable."

The sound of Hades blades falling to the ground echoed in the chamber. "I have told you that I am a Royalist…I may be the most loyal Royalist you will ever encounter. I yield. You are my Lord Emperor. The day is yours." Hades lowered himself slowly, painfully down into reverent pose. Billy knelt beside him, propping him up.

Damn, I wasn't expecting that.

Sex knocked me out of the way.

"NO!" I shouted, my body was shaking with anger but I had never experienced it like this before. Not like this. "Pick them up. I SAID PICK THEM UP!"

Hades lowered his head, "I, Cillian Von Drachenfeld, Hades, former CEO of Shadoe Incorporated, former Head of the House of Assassin for the Vampire Nation, pledge personal allegiance to you, my Lord Emperor Xavier. Ask and it shall be done. Command and it shall be destroyed. Lead Angel of Death and I shall follow."

"You don't get to do this." I stormed up and grabbed Hades' short hair yanking his face up to mine, forcing him to stand and elbowing William out of the way. "You don't get to do all of that to me and then walk away just because you said some pretty words."

"Edward…" I shoved Hades as hard as I could away from me. He stumbled back and hit the wall. I took Father's dagger and stalked up to him, lifting the blade until I could drive it hard through his shoulder; ramming in a few more times with my entire body so he was stapled securely to the wall. His face was screwed up in agony. Oh yeah, I knew what that felt like.

I grabbed his head again and forced him to look into my eyes. "That's not my name."

Out of my peripheral vision I saw Billy come at me. My hand snapped out and I caught him by the face, fingers curling around the high curves of his cheekbones, squeezing hard. I maneuvered him back from Hades then I shoved him away from me hard. He flew off his feet and lay crumpled in the sand.

"My Lord Emper...." I turned back to the teenager's face. It was disfigured with pain and a mix of both of our blood. Cinnamon and Honey blended together with a sickly sweetness.

"You agreed to this Cillian...there is no forfeit." I spied another of Father's daggers on the floor. I held out my hand and wanted it. It flew to me easily.

"That is for stapling me to the wall. This one..." I held up Father's bloody blade in front of his face, grabbing his jaw to make sure that he looked at it. "This one is for raping my Sasha."

Hades hissed out through clenched teeth. "I apologized for that."

"No you didn't. You made a statement. Just like in the Ferris wheel, it fucking hurt but you didn't care. It was your good-bye.' I backed up about six feet, reversed my hold on the dagger until I was holding onto the blade tip. "This is mine."

I threw the dagger as hard as I could. Even back in the Manor when I was still wet behind the ears fledgling, I stuck Grandbitch to the concrete wall, well it was X but, I could do it better with blades. I watched it in slo-mo as it tumbled end over end streaking for Hades black, black heart. Billy Envoy threw himself over Hades still form as a fleshy shield. The dagger sank in to the hilt through his back, into his right lung and still came out far enough to pierce Hades' chest.

So be it.

They could die together.

I ran up and took hold of the hilt and rammed it further through Billy Envoy. The blond haired vampire groaned and coughed up blood on himself and on his master. I gestured for the other bloody blade lying in the sand.

"I knew you would be the death of my Honey Bee, Number One." Billy whispered as I stepped closer. The voice…that voice. That wasn't Billy. It was Liam. I hesitated. He, er, they caressed his hands down either side of Hades cheeks and stared at the smaller man.

"I came too late…"

"William?" Hades stood there his features a mix of pain and confusion.

The white haired man grunted and pushed himself off the wall, pulling the dagger point out of Hades chest. "Cillian…my gentle little shepherd boy…"

"How can you be here? How can…you're hurt! You don't get hurt…ever!"

Billy, no Liam, laid his head against Hades neck. "You've won, little Emperor. See to your lover, while I see to mine."

"I have to finish this." My knuckles cracked with the force of my grip on the hilt.

"It's done. You've won." Liam turned slowly keeping his body between me and Hades. "I merged with a willing host; I am here with this young one named William until his body dies."

He groaned and pushed at the dagger point sticking out of his chest. "See to your Father; you've drunk too deeply." I turned and found Claudius flat on his side. My heart leapt into my throat. I turned and ran. He was chalky white. Oh my … I dropped to my knees and grabbed him to me.

"Sasha!" His eye lids flickered and he looked up at me. I dropped fang and ripped my wrist open. I held it to his mouth and propped him up against me. "Don't leave me…it's not any better if you leave me alone in the light instead of the dark."

Blood trailed out of his mouth. "Drink…Father…" Slowly, he began to draw on my wrist drinking in his familiar way. I closed my eyes and buried my face into his hair.

He tried to stop drinking at three swallows. "More…take more. You need it."

"It's over?"

"Almost…I got to take care of you first, Sasha." I turned my head and stared over at the other spectacle across the room. Hades gave out a low scream as Billiam, a combination of Billy Envoy and Liam the Progenitor, yanked the dagger out of the wall and his shoulder in one vicious pull. Hades slid down the wall leaving a bloody smear on the wall behind him. Next Billiam knelt, blood staining his white suit, he groaned out an agonized moan as Hades wrenched the dagger out of his back. Billiam began coughing, spewing out brownish red blood from his lungs.

I was weak. I concentrated hard as I willed all the good stuff I could into the blood Father was still pooling in his mouth. A slight flush of pink crept under his skin. I was light headed but tried to keep my balance. When I could see straight I used the wall to stand. I had to finish this. We, my Vampiric and my human family would never be safe if Hades lived. The progenitor would come for him again and again. It was an established pattern. If I didn't end it, it never would.

I twisted and threw the dagger as hard as I could at Hades body as he sat against the wall. Billiam threw himself in front of the blonde vampire again. The blade dug into his upper chest.

"Stop it!" Hades dragged Billiam to him, wrapping his arm around his shoulders. "He can't heal…he's just a red. Stop hurting him."

I walked closer and gestured for the dagger Hades had pulled out of Billiam before. It rose from the ground and I closed my fist around it. "I don't want to hurt Billy. I just need to kill you. Everything wrong in our lives comes back to you, Cillian. Everything I could have been, what I was, the children I might have had but can't sire now, I can lie at your feet."

Billiam groaned but used his lean frame to place himself between me and Hades. "I won't let you kill him. If you want to lay the blame, I'll take it. I did it. I did it all."

I tightened my hand on the hilt. "Both of you then."

"FALLEN!" I stopped at Father's voice. "Mercy is a trait a good emperor must have."

Why the hell was I crying? Tears stung my eyes as I glared at them. I could feel the heat of the crystal blue clarity that came with my Flame burning behind my eyes. "Mercy…what mercy have I received from their hands?"

"Then show them, what you have not gotten. If you continue down this path, Fallen…I cannot follow you. Hades has sworn an oath to you. William has yielded. You are the victor. It is done."

The silence was oppressive. "Fallen, let it go." His whisper was a plea for my sanity.

"Maybe, I should have let you use the ether after all, Sasha. I have lived in fear since I was a child. A giant came to be my protector from the things that went bump in the night but he had an ulterior motive and has always been there lurking in the shadows. When Xavier finally came…I let him be number one because he took the fear away. I was only nine years old and I'd had enough. I remember now…" I looked down at Billiam's bloody form; Billy Envoy was losing a lot of blood really quickly. His face was ashen. I had given him a mortal wound. Grey eyes peered up at me through his pain.

"You would look at me from over the crib and let me play with your white hair. You walked with me to kindergarten and sat on the back shelves waiting for class to be over. You made promises to a frightened child…all in order to get me to agree to merge when I got old enough. None of that concern you showed was for me. None of it. It was all for your lost little shepherd boy. I haven't received mercy from you – I've learned betrayal."

I flicked my eyes up to Hades pain filled washed out blue orbs, "And you…both Father and I were merely substitutes. If Father hadn't given me back my sense of self worth, I would've happily played lap dog for you and you would have sucked my soul, just like you did to Father, until there was nothing left but a pretty shell of a doll."

Billiam pushed himself to his knees more with Hades assistance than on his own. "I, William, First Lord Emperor, pledge eternal allegiance to you and your House, Sigmund Edward Xavier Von Drachenfeld. I vow to protect your family blood line. I will only advise the Lord

Emperor, I will never take on that roll again. Allow me to be your protector as I once was. I offer this freely. Cillian is caught up in my wake as well as you. Accept my oath. If you still need to kill someone, I offer up this body for execution."

Emotional tides swirled around inside me - the pain of betrayal; the anger and righteousness of a blood feud; the fear of seeing Sasha laying there so still in the sand. I could end this all now...Liam's been sniffing around this body forever. The blade in my hand was growing heavier by the moment. They offered up oaths but were they trustworthy? What must I do? To get what I want I have to do what I must. What do I want? Not X. Not Azrael. What do *I* want? For a long time I didn't know. I had just wanted not be afraid. Not to be so alone in the Darkness with nothing but my thoughts, my doubts, my fears and loathing. What do I want? That black Russian with eyes as cool as the arctic glacier, the warm antiseptic scent of cloves and hands skilled with the deadliest of arts and yet able to make your soul weep with the beauty he wrought from piano keys. Sasha. To get what I want...

"Billy wanted more than one day with Hades, you ass."

"I want him to live more." There was Billy Envoy's voice all full of distain. He was in there with Liam.

"You do know that you've cut your life in half, Billy." I ran my hand over my hair...wtf? Half of my hair was missing.

"It's William, not Billy. I've always said that you weren't worthy to be his Consort."

I snorted. Yup, that was Billy Envoy. To get what I want, I do what I must. If Sasha said he couldn't follow me down the path of vengeance...I wouldn't walk there. I dropped the dagger down into the sand.

I felt Father's hand close around my shoulder and squeeze it gently. "The day is yours."

Xavier's voice cried out to me from behind the darkness of the veil that separated the physical. Sex...why didn't you tell me about our childhood?

Later. Finish this. Billiam is bleeding out and our tank is empty.

364

Sex brushed by so quickly that anger and pain hanging on him still made me stumble as I took over. He offered Hades and Liam mercy but at the cost of himself. He was a mass of conflicting emotions.

Azrael calmly spoke up. *I got him. Do what you gotta do, Elder Brother.*

I blinked. My body felt so heavy. I willed out my wings opening them wide to shield Hades and Billy from the countless vampire eyes above us. Father had moved back as soon as he felt Sex leave and was now in reverent pose. I heard the swishing of clothes and shifting bodies as more and more vampires offered allegiance. Not the time and not the place. Just a quick glance showed me that Hades and Billiam were a wreck. I gestured for them to stay where they were almost flat on their backs in the bloodied sand.

"Cillian, William. I accept your oath. I can't heal you. I've nothing left."

Can you say cue the hellcats? Armor opened the side door once it was obvious the main event was over. Seven regal hellcats stalked in and ringed the room. It was a rare sight to see one hellcat. Most Vampires never did. Again in impressive mode, the six came forward and circled me. Heads bowed.

Shade? I so did not like where this was going.

Shade came forward and bowed her regal head to me. For once her quick action tail wasn't at the ready to rap my noggin. *They are honored to have witnessed the birth of a Lord Emperor and to have this chance to be of service, Xavier.*

All of them...are for me? Even though I tried to temper my horror, I knew some of it leaked out as Shade stepped in and rubbed her head against my chest.

It will be spectacular, Lord Emperor. Heal those you can then let them run. You can burn this building down to the ground. It is known now anyway and will have to be destroyed.

Did you know about Sex?

Shade was quiet for moment. *I am bonded with you Xavier. That is what I know.*

I knelt and bowed to the six magnificent read creatures that surrounded me. "Her Majesty has informed me of your selfless offer. I am honored that you have chosen to come witness this day and yield your spirits to me." Wearily I climbed back to my feet. I glanced back at Hades and Billiam who huddled together lost in their private sphere. Nine hundred years, eh? Aside from High Councilor, Thomas, these were the two most powerful Vampires in the Nation—and they knelt at my feet. I called on the Hand of Light and made my own light sabre. It was smaller than usual and thinner but the blade was bright and seemed like more than able to do the task required of it.

Azrael counseled from the darkness. *One stroke. There is no need for them to suffer.*

I'll try and make it quick.

"Forgive me." I pivoted on my heel and swung the hand of light around me. There was positively no resistance. I finally truly understood the phrase 'like a warm knife through butter.' When I was done, I was covered in Hellcat blood. One by one little green specks of illumination emerged from the feline corpses. I held out my hand and drew all those hellcat souls to me.

This was going to hurt.

I closed my eyes and gritted my teeth as those six souls blended into my flesh.

The Healing Light I called forth was a bright as a lighthouse's beacon. I had to screw my eyes closed and it still felt as if it seared into my core. At first the Hellcat rush was warm and tingling; spreading out from me, widening to fill the room, passing through the inner, then the outer walls and pushing up for the roof. My feather wings spread wide and I screamed from the sheer power running through my body. It came out of my throat as a roar -- a hellcat roar.

Then the screams started high above me. The ranked assassins and the noble visitors were bolting from the upper viewing chamber as the light intensified. They didn't know what was going on, only that it wasn't good. Anything dealing with Lord Emperor's and eating Hellcat souls was never a good thing in the Blood Nation.

Squinting I saw Armor drag Father through the door. Hades carried Billiam past me. But I saw the slight bow of his head before they hurried out into the corridor. It was too much. Too much power. Too much pain. Too much truth. I couldn't handle the intensity. It was too much. The Phoenix wings were coming and I wasn't the brother who could control them.

"SEX!"

The Phoenix wings flared up the white feathers, burning them away in a searing agony that made me see a shade of white that made these flames appear smudged with blue. They were bigger than before. A simple flare had them touching the arena walls, sending the walls into a smoldering black sooty smear where I touched them.   Way too much. Hand of Light energy built in my stomach begging to be released. Raising my arms high my hands formed a blue ball of energy that grew and glowed brighter, moving from blues to pastel and then another flash of blinding white. I blasted a hole in the glass of the training room, up through roof of the warehouse and higher still. The world turned to fire around me. My clothes flash burned off my flesh. The remains of my Docs were oily smears in the mirror like sand.

The Phoenix wings pulsed and expanded again powered by multiple Hellcat souls. Debris began to land in the arena and one I beam landed a little too close for comfort. It was a chore to start moving but I was naked as the day I was born as I slowly walked from one end of the warehouse to the other, burning everything in sight. Walls began to collapse and still I carefully set one foot in front of the other. The Phoenix wings came up over me on their own accord and sheltered me as more ceiling debris began to fall.

X's voice broke through the overwhelming roar of the flames. *Sex, don't do this.*

Do what, brother?

Don't give up. Claudius never said he was leaving you. He just asked you to stop. You know he is waiting for you. It's still Sunday. It's your day.

Just a day...a single day...I don't even deserve that much.

Sex!

I've been Edward all along. You have no idea much I hate that fucking name.

X's voice changed to a heartfelt plea. *Don't leave us to die here, Sex. We all have someone to live for. Dying shouldn't be easy.*

What was I doing? *I don't want to die. I don't want to.*

I called a Hand of Light orb and threw it at the wall in front of me. It exploded outwards leaving a big enough hole that I could get through. I stepped over the debris field and walked out of the burning warehouse. The wall behind me collapsed inward with an earth shaking rumble. I flared the Phoenix wings letting the burn go harder than it ever had, allowing control to slip away as the flames forced the remaining Hellcat essence out of my system. I shivered as a cold presence padded across my soul, then they were gone. X didn't even get their names this time. The wings snuffed out. As soon as the wings were gone, I could feel the overwhelming heat of the warehouse fire behind me. Holy crap! The ground was burning the souls of my feet. I danced over the rubble, blinking as the smoke stung my eyes and chunks of concrete rubble embedded with sheered rebar cut at my bare feet.

The wind swirled the smoke around me like tornadoes from Hell stinging my eyes with fine debris, arid smoke and ash. I winced as I slipped and twisted my ankle, landing on a hot piece of blasted concrete. I scraped the heels of my hands and hurt my wrists from the harsh jolt. Scrambling off the heated rubble I wrenched my ankle again, losing my balance and fell face first into a pile of black ash.

I don't know how long I lay there. I heard a crunch, crunch, crunch noise and then warm arms set me up on my knees then encircled me.

"Alpha...don't cry."

The little Lycan telling me that only made it worse. I leaned into the pup and let go. It was over. All this...hell was over. All the choices made now were ours; Xavier, Azrael and mine. All the successes. All the failures. I didn't even move when Haley let loose a hunting howl even though I was sure it did something to my left eardrum. The aftermath of the hellcat burn was decreasing. I was exhausted, drained and as limp as a wet noodle.

It took more effort that it should have to raise my visibly trembling hand to my forehead. Hair blew into my eyes making the smoke sting even more irritating. Long strands of it were wafting in the heated breeze, even on the side that Hades had sliced off. The sound of someone running toward us broke the abnormal silence. I leaned heavier onto Haley's shoulder not able to give the effort to be alarmed at the sound. I was exhausted to my core.

"Alpha..." He stroked my hair and licked my ear. Okay...enough of that. I sat up under my own power and wiped the spit from the side of my face. Haley wiped the tears from my cheeks. "Your face is dirty, Alpha."

"A lot more is dirty than just my face, Pup." I looked up into Claudius' concerned eyes as he knelt beside me.

"Are you injured, Sex?"

You are our strength, Sex. Lean on us, we are here for you. That is what brothers do for each other. I could have ignored it if X said it, but this was Azrael—the blunt spoken younger brother who considered himself the loner, the outcast for not having wings.

I nodded and buried my face in my hands. Father caught me in a hard embrace. It felt like my back was going to crack. "Never let me go." I whispered to him.

Claudius picked me up like I was a china doll. "I promise that I will never let you go."

Haley lead the way out of the smoke and smoldering rubble to the limo that had fortunately been far enough away to be outside the Hellcat/Lord Emperor blast zone. Armor hurried up as we got closer to the car. "Is he...?"

"Sex is just very tired and a little worse for wear. He needs to rest." I wrapped an arm around Father's neck and rested my head against his shoulder. Once we were safely inside, Father set me gently on the seat, propping me against Armor. He started pulling out his wet thingies to clean my face. He hissed as he saw my hands. He took my left hand and

369

began licking my scraped, ash covered skin. Armor took my right and began healing it as well. I leaned my head back and stared at the roof of the car. Haley sat on the floor and leaned heavily against the side of my calf.

My thoughts were scattered. What had just happened? I was now CEO of Shadoe Inc, and Head of the House of Assassins and every member of that secretive house and the whole of the High Council had witnessed the fiery birth of the next Lord Emperor. And now, I had a very private and secretive army at my disposal.

Haley wrapped his arm around my leg and rubbed his face on my knee, reminding me of another fact.

I had the beginnings of a war with the Lycans on my doorstep.

I stand or fall on my own. There would be no one to blame but me...er, us now.

Claudius pulled me over to him and settled me on his lap. "Do not doubt that I love you, my Fallen Angel. If you killed Liam after he offered you his oath in front of all of the House...they would have turned against you. Sex?"

"I don't want to be number one brother. I failed at it before." I was bone tired and depressed.

"You will always be Number One with me, Sex. Know that your Sasha will always place you as Number One in my heart."

Gently, Armor turned my body towards him, leaning me back against Claudius. I started as Armor caught my ankle and eased my leg up over his thighs to him. He began wiping my foot clean with a wet thingie. It stung enough to bring tears to my eyes, then I stared as the brown haired vampire lifted my abused foot to his mouth and began licking it. It ached but it was strangely soothing.

"You are one sick man." My voice was raspy as my throat was dried out from the heat and smoke.

"My salvia has healing properties." Armor met my eye and gave me one long lick from toe to heel. "We are even, Sex. Our book is clean."

I looked at him for a second then nodded. I turned back to Sasha, "I don't understand. I couldn't kill Liam, but I could kill Hades?"

He ran his fingers experimentally over my neck checking for any signs of the slash that could have killed us. I shivered as my skin relished my lover's touch. "Hades accepted the challenge. His oath to you could have been seen as a bribe when the battle turned against him. Liam, surrendered to you before he offered his oath. You kept your head, Sex. I am proud of you. Relax, allow your family to take care of you now. Let us go home."

A light blanket was tossed over my nakedness and eager hands tucked it around me. "Thanks, Haley."

He leaned up over me and gave me a kiss to the forehead. "Sleep, Alpha, I'll guard you while we travel safely home."

So simple a statement that he meant to keep.

Go home. I already was home. I lay in my Sasha's arms. Armor set my bare feet on his lap. Slowly he began to massage them.

Sasha whispered into my ear, "Sleep, my Fallen. I will watch over you."

"Sasha..." I relaxed in his hold and it seemed like it was the first time in an eternity I felt completely safe, warm and cherished. I slept in the freedom we earned. The world was our oyster...for now.

Chapter Twenty-Two: Lessons in Love

Haley crunched on the gravel of the roof then crouched down in the shade beside me. "Claudius and Sensei are looking for you, Alpha."

I looked over my knees out across the city roof tops. "I know. I just need some air."

"I brought you this." I flicked my eyes over at the brown bottle. I moved to take it and he pulled it out of my reach. He took a big swig then leaned over me. I had to laugh. He was so damned determined to penguin beer into me. Fine. I shifted and angled his mouth across mine. I swallowed the cool liquid. Haley gave me a teasing, playful kiss then handed the long neck bottle to me.

"That's all you wanted?"

"Yes, Alpha." The pup dropped to his knees then flopped over onto his hip. He leaned heavily against me and sighed. "It is crazy downstairs."

I couldn't argue with that. "Why do you think I'm up here? It's not every day a Lord Emperor gets engaged."

Haley flopped backwards and looked up at me. "Alpha, you don't like girls. Why are you marrying one?"

I've been asking myself the same question. I couldn't produce children. I wasn't going to make Claudia happy even if I truly tried to. The pup nudged me with his head. How to put it in terms he understood. "The Nation wants me to have pups. I can't have them with Armor, or Marcus or Claudius."

"Or me."

I reached out and ruffled his hair.

"Or you."

"If the Baroness knows you don't like girls…why is she marrying you?"

I took a drink. "I guess she wants pups too."

"She could get pups anywhere."

I chuckled. That didn't come out right, but I knew what Haley meant. "She wants royal blue pups."

"And only you have that."

Genetics 101 ripped through my mind. Shayne could be the Empress. She could bear the Royal Blue bloodline. Yeah, right. Hell would freeze over first. She was a Hunter through and through. She was in line to be the next Regent Hunter…the next Queen if you will. There would be no way she would consider becoming a Vampire like her poor little brother and my nieces would end up with the same terrifying childhood that Sex had. I reached out and patted Haley on the head. And she hated Lycans with a passion that I could understand. I hated and feared them myself once upon a time.

Speaking of Lycans…

"Pup, you need to tell me what a *Zsigmond* truly is. Whenever it's mentioned to a high ranking Lycan, it's like I've just stabbed them through the heart."

Haley looked down and made a move to stand up. I held his wrist and pulled him right against me. "Don't make me mindfuck you, Haley. It's not fun. I know that through personal experience."

"It's what I said. I have pledged my life to keep you safe…"

"And…" The memory of how Bruce the northern Lycan reacted came to mind. It was more than that.

"And all those of my blood line. I have bonded my pack, my mate and pups to you and your House."

I brought my hand up to the bridge of my nose. Oh dear Lord, it's worse than I thought. No wonder Grandma Wolf wants him back so badly. He just bonded a branch of the royal Lycan bloodline to the Vampire Lord Emperor's House. "Haley, did you know what you were doing when you offered this?"

"I'm forty-five years old, Alpha. I've lost my milk teeth a while back."

"Britta won't let this die out."

"I won't go back to her house. She disowned me. She killed Derry. I won't go back." I reached out and gathered him into a hug. I handed

374

him the rest of my beer. He leaned into me and quietly watched the sunset with me.

Finally I broke the silence. "So you're going to have pups, eh?"

"I could mate now. I've had offers, but I want to wait until the time of change. The pups would be guaranteed to be Alphas then. You will need a strong pack to guard you, Alpha." I glanced over at the tawny head. His profile stared out across the darkening city. He took a drink from the bottle and swallowed it down. There were deep thoughts and a strong constitution in him regardless of his puppy like behavior.

"Why don't you ask me to dominate you anymore?" I was surprised that popped out of my mouth.

Haley lowered his head. "I don't want to make your life any more difficult. Too many want so much from you. I don't want to be one of them. Besides you told me that even being like this..." He snuggled against my side "is proof of your protection."

I had to laugh. He did listen. "I like spending time with you, pup. I get to relax. It's like I'm playing with a little brother."

"Like we're littermates?"

"Er...yeah."

Haley turned and gave me a dazzling smile. He took a big drink and descended on me again. I drank down the beer and laughed. Really laughed, the first time all day. I nipped Haley's ear and rolled him over. I jumped past his arm and ran smack dab into a broad chest. Ooof.

Armor grabbed my shoulders and I ended up in a deep dip parallel to the roof top staring up into his hot chocolate eyes. "I think you need glasses again, Little One. I am not exactly small."

"Ha ha, Sensei caught you."

"Hey." Since the moment I woke up today, every waking moment was planned. I've been photographed, medically investigated, fingerprinted, washed, fluffed and dried. At the end of it all here I was dressed like I escaped from a "My Chemical Romance" video or a college marching band. I have never worn so much braided cord in my life...or death.

Armor tangled his hand in my ridiculously massive amount of hair and sucked my fangs out. I wrapped my arm around the back of his neck and arched up into his body. This act was the first thing I wanted to do for myself all day.

"Hey." He smiled against my mouth.

A tawny head popped into my line of sight again. He pushed his forehead against Armor, butting like a pup at a teat. Oh, bad imagery. Armor drew back with a puzzled expression. I got another kiss drink of beer. This time Haley wrinkled his nose and disappeared. I flicked my head at Armor drawing him back down to my mouth. I passed a mouth full of beer to him. He swallowed then pulled me upright. He licked his lips. My eyes followed that trail of tongue. I wanted him, right here, right now.

"Welcome to the penguin club, Pretty." I felt my flame dance around my eyes.

Armor let out a deep sigh. "Your guests are arriving. Bank your flame, Little One. We cannot do what you want."

"How do you know what I want?" My eyebrow arched in a teasing manner.

A hand cupped my hardening cock. "I know your body, Little One."

"Don't call me Little One when you're holding that."

Armor pulled down my zipper and cradled my erection. I groaned as his thumb swirled my sensitive head. "How about one size fits most?"

I popped my eyes open. "What? Are you calling me....Armor!"

The next thing I knew he was on his knees, my pants were passed my hips then he swallowed me down to the root in one motion. My fingers snaked into his hair. My knees quivered at the sudden sensation. Armor countered that by wrapping his arms around my thighs, under my ass and pulling me hard against his chest. His head bobbed up and down my length.

"Uuuh...nnnnnhhh...aaaah."

I thought I was making enough noise as it was then he started to thrust the back of his wrist up against my asshole, awakening that orifice as well, while driving me deep into his so very talented mouth. "Armor…..Armmmmm….aaaahhh I'm ….."

I couldn't string a sentence together. I felt my balls draw up and my body exploded. I literally saw stars as Armor drank my essence down. I think my eyes must have rolled up into my head. I twitched with aftershocks as Armor licked me clean. He rose to his feet, keeping his arms locked around my upper thighs. My big man. I steadied myself on his shoulders then he slowly, languishingly, slid me down the front of his body. I shivered and my cock perked up for round two.

Armor buried his nose in my hair. "Do you really need to cut your hair?"

Huh? What was that? I had to blink some of the sensual pleasure away. "Are you going to wash and dry it every day."

"Yes. It would be a great honor." Fingers stroked through the long pale strands then began to pull them forward over my ears. . "I love to see your body encased in it, like gossamer threads binding you to my bed."

Those words sent a shiver down my spine. Wasn't expecting that. "Are you getting as kinky as Marcus? When the hell did you start using words like gossamer?" I arched an eyebrow at him.

"Language, Little One." I got a quick peck on the forehead. "I can do more than just grunt, I will have you know. Marcus has a firm grip on the English language so I thought I should take a couple of pages from his book. I am more physical but I know that everyone likes to hear the heart spoken aloud once in a while."

My own heart went ba-dunka-dunk.

"Allow me any liberty you feel comfortable with, Little One." I was quickly wiped clean with a handkerchief then securely tucked back inside my zipper. "I only ask to keep your hair long…and your feet sexy."

Isn't that like barefoot and pregnant? He flashed me a wide grin as I stood there gapping like a stunned fish, picked the half empty beer bottle and took a drink. He caught me by the back of the neck and angled my face up to his and I got penguined again. The taste was something different now, the beer was flavored with the lingering remains of my cinnamon discharge yet the fruit crispness of ripe green apples was there too. I wanted nothing more than to wrap myself around this big man like a wet newspaper on a windy day but he kept most of me at arm's length, our fingers entwined as we suck, drank, and kissed.

"This is not what I meant when I asked you to find Xavier, Armor. You two look like you are at a kissing booth." I turned and looked at Claudius. He had on the same drum major's outfit I had except his was scarlet and silver, while I was in black and silver. I blinked and glanced at Armor. He just had tailored Armani on. Just. Damn he cleaned up real good.

"Hey, where's your marching band suit?"

"It burnt up in a fire." Armor returned easily.

Oh, yeah. Crap. I still needed to fill out his wardrobe. Licking my lips to savor the last of this unique flavor I caught the hint of a crimson flame catch in Armor's eye. Damn. If Father was up here...why was Father up here? I shook my hands loose from Armor's touch.

"Xavier, Dr. Maxwell is looking for you. He says he has some urgent information regarding the tests you've taken. As to what they are, he would not tell me." Claudius turned his attention to his son. "Armor, Marcus will be needed soon. He will need time to prepare."

Armor nodded and straightened his clothes. I don't know why he bothered because I was grabbed again and claimed with Armor specials. Finally he let me go and laughed as I staggered sideways a little brain muddled from the kiss. Father caught me and held on until I was in control of my faculties again. By that time, Armor had disappeared down the stairwell. I pulled down on the hem of my overly ornate jacket and made a move to the stairs.

"How is Sex?"

I paused and leaned back against the railing. "Quiet. Very quiet. He's here, he's just subdued which really isn't like him but he won't share his burden."

"May I speak to him?"

378

Sex. Father has come all this way to see you. If you can't lean on us...

Brother even pulled the black veil back for me so I could pass. He really was a class act. I turned and pressed my forehead against Sasha's chest. I felt his arms come around me and I leaned heavily into him. We stood like that for a while.

"You told X, you wanted to speak to me?"

"I lied. I just wanted to hold you in my arms." He tightened his grip and I brought my arms up and around him. I sighed. It felt nice. Father murmured in my ear. "Tonight, I give you to my daughter. That is strange."

We stood holding onto each other for a little while longer, and then I confessed. "Technically that's not me. I told you I abdicated, didn't I?"

"Pardon?"

"I officially gave up my ranking as Brother Number One. X does a better job at it anyway. I hope you don't mind. It will be the same status quo as always." It didn't take a whole lot of soul searching, but I buggered off when I was a kid and left X in charge. I didn't have the balls to try and take it back...not even though the selling point was being with this black haired sensual demon in the sack it wasn't reason enough. I didn't have the patience to be the Lord Emperor. It was X's gig and he, for whatever reason, wanted it.

"If that is what you must do, Fallen. I am happy with it." Sasha tucked a finger under my chin and urged it up. I closed my eyes and waited for his kiss. I waited. I opened my eyes and he smiled down at me so warmly. "I want to see your green eyes darken with desire."

"I think they're already dark. X left me with a hard on." I grinned as Sasha dropped a pale hand and cupped me. "If you do that, I'm going to be sleeping through the whole party. Armor has a mouth on him."

"Well I will have to be content with this then." Sasha tore into my mouth with his regular gusto. I bit his lip and lapped at the blood welled there. I flicked my tongue along his plump flesh lips.

"I got a present for you." I whispered to him.

Both of his hands curved around my ass lifting me up against him. "A present?"

I leaned forward and offered up my lips. My Sasha took advantage of them eagerly. I had to push myself back. "Naughty Russian…"

"Only with you, *lubov moya*."

I stilled as I felt something new press against the mental shield we had learned to blood. Liam said a lot of shit and I wouldn't believe half of it so this blooded mirror ball mental casing was a precaution against ending up in Liam's wonderland again. I sent my thoughts out and they caressed that 'signature'. "Your present is finally here."

"It's a person?" I got dropped to my feet suddenly. Ow…

I caught his hand and pulled him after me. Once we were down in Von Drachenfeld proper, the frenzied energy that had forced X to the roof to escape washed over us again. I paused in front of a hallway mirror and looked over my reflection. Yeah, it looked like I was basking in sexual satisfaction. My green eyes were a darker jade and my cheeks were flushed. My lips were red and slightly swollen.

"Fallen?" I glanced at Sasha. His eyes were ringed with red flame. I flipped my knee length hair to the side and offered up my neck. I shivered as Sasha ran his finger nail down my neck, tracing my vein. He lowered his head, keeping his eyes centered on me in the mirror. That was one of the most erotic things ever to watch, gaze locked to gaze, as he dropped fang and buried them into my life's pulsing stream. I brought my arm up and tangled in his hair as he savored me. My own eyes suddenly were ringed with blue flame. My mouth dropped open and I moaned softly.

Click. Click. Click. Claudia stopped in the middle of the hall. "You might want to take that into a smaller venue, Daddy." She cocked her head sideways. "Sex?"

Claudius sucked and licked my neck clean and dry. "Busted, my Fallen."

"Baroness." I nodded in her direction

"I was asked to inform you that Hades and William are here."

Claudius stiffened slightly. "That is your present?"

380

"We have unfinished business with them. Both of us do."

Claudia crossed her arms over her ample chest. "You're going to be killing here? Tonight?"

This reaction was mild compared to the cyclone she turned into when the rest of the Nation heard about the hostile takeover of Shadoe Inc. before she did. The reports of the burnt out hull of an assassin training ground didn't go over well either. Our sudden meteoric rise to CEO-dom wasn't that appreciated either. Hell hath no fury as a woman…period. It didn't matter that she couldn't have come to the fight because she wasn't an assassin. Her only demand was that she be included in all future mayhem. She didn't say stop it. She just wants to know. Strange, strange girl.

"No. I won't be killing anyone." I reached up and patted Claudius face. "I accepted their oath of loyalty. You didn't. You don't have to kill them, but I do want Hades hurt."

Sasha shook his head. "I cannot raise a hand to Hades. He is above me."

"You forget, I'm your boss now. You're my First." I chucked him under the chin. "Hades is just an ex-offico. If he wants back into the House of Assassins, he's gotta start at the bottom and work his way back up."

Carnage grinned down at me, "How hurt?"

"Until you get an apology you believe."

"What about William?"

"He's still my PA. I got him covered. Let's get this done."

"Wait!" Claudia pulled a black lacquer hair clip from her hair. She crossed behind me and hiked my hair up. She did something artistic and quick that pulled it up and out of the way. "Try not to get any blood on your clothes. You won't have time to change."

"Thank you, little sister." I took her hand and kissed her knuckles.

She shivered. "This is still…eeeewwww. I'll have Marcus start playing. You've got ten minutes before introductions start."

381

I made sure we were further down the hall before I asked Claudius what was on my mind. "You got a nice daughter, there. Why the hell is she settling for X?"

"She can do more good for the Nation as Empress than she can as CEO of Whitcombe Inc. I have told her that I will not step from your side."

"Damn straight you're not stepping aside. What no comment?"

"I agree with you. What is there to comment about?"

I lead Carnage into the room I had picked out for this to happen. This was not going to end easy between us, the elder Von Drachenfeld and us young upstarts--until Hades gave us a real, sincere apology. Rape seems to run in the House. That was going to stop. Here and now.

Hades and Billiam were standing beside each other. They had the stance of new lovers about them – close and satisfied. That was all good for Billy Envoy. He had loved that little blond bastard for what, a hundred and forty years now? Hades saw us walk in and he turned with a smile on his face.

Carnage walked up and punched him square in the jaw. As the teenager staggered backwards, I flicked my wrist and caught the dagger as it emerged then brought my arm up over Billy's shoulder around his neck and yanked his head to the side. He tensed until I gave him a pinprick to the helix of the ear with the tip of the dagger. "On your knees."

I could feel Billy's inner struggle as Carnage put the boots to Hades' ribs. I whispered along the platinum white blonde head. "You've been watching for a while, Billy. You know I ice-picked my own grandmother. If I have to stick this blade into your ear, you know I will do it."

"You invited us here." It was Liam's voice that answered, tinged with anger. "Your hospitality is less than impressive."

He lowered himself to the ground so I didn't have to stand on my tippy toes. It wasn't safe for him if I didn't have good balance either.

"Well, X invited you. We need to clear the air if we are going to work together." Hades popped back up and pulled a dagger from the small of his back. "CILLIAN!"

He flicked his eyes to me, saw how compromised Billiam was then froze. "We want something from you.""

"Whatever you want, I'll give it to you. Don't hurt William."

"You should know what we want from you, Cillian." He shook his head. "Then you take a beating until Carnage feels you've had enough."

Hades tensed. I pressed the dagger up against the soft flesh just in front of Billiam's ear. A stream of red blood trailed down from his lobe down his jaw and neck. Hades paled. His eyes following that crimson ribbon. I leaned over and lapped at the blood. *Oh my god, gack. Cayenne and pineapple.* I wanted to spit it out and rub at my tongue. Ghastly. I glanced at Hades and I thought I saw what I wanted there in his pale watery blue eyes. "What are you feeling, Hades?"

"Feeling?"

I couldn't bring myself to taste Billiam anymore, so I finger painted his neck with my thumb and his blood. I stepped between his bent legs and forced his knees wider. I pressed my lower body up against his backside just like Hades had done to X in the glass cube. Billiam was taller than me, so I couldn't run my crotch on the back of his head, but I rubbed on his shoulders. He tensed. I shifted my grip on the dagger and pressed it back to the channel of his ear. He stopped moving. I glanced up at Hades, "Feeling...Helpless?"

"Yes."

"Afraid?"

"Yes."

"Feeling despair?"

"Please, Edward....I mean Sex. Don't hurt William."

"Which one, the owner or the parasite?"

"How dare you..." His tirade was cut short as Carnage popped him one right in the mouth. He staggered sideways, his palm up to cup his bleeding mouth and aching fangs.

"Do you understand yet?"

"I don't know what you want." His face showed total confusion. He had no clue. Absolutely no clue.

"What's it like to watch a loved one suffer and not be able to do anything about it?"

"It's horrible. Stop hurting him…if it's something I've done…take it out on me."

"You hurt my Claudius."

"You hurt my Sex." Carnage returned evenly, coldly. "If I had known what you were going to do to him up in that Ferris Wheel. I would have tried harder that morning to kill you. If I had succeeded, Sex would not have been in such a great deal pain. It cuts deeper than a blade. It hurts worse when you see your beloved in agony and know you can do nothing to ease it. All you can do is hold him in your arms as he cries."

"I never thought…."

"No, you never have thought of any one's pleasure but your own. Reap what you sow, Hades."

Hades turned his head away and then wiped at his eyes with the back of his hand. He actually shed tears. Slowly he lowered himself to his knees. His face was twisted in stark realization of what he had turned into habit. "I'm sorry, Claudius."

Claudius turned and walked to me. He offered his hand and I used it to pull myself up. I reloaded the dagger in my forearm sheath and leaned back into my Sasha's embrace. He kissed my temple through my hair. "Thank you for this gift, *lubov moya*."

Billiam grabbed at his ear and looked at the blood still clinging to him. "You like making me bleed, Little Lord Emperor."

"You tasted better on the beach – not so fruity."

"You play a dangerous game, Little Lord Emperor." Billiam pushed himself to his feet the crossed over to Hades who was still on the ground. His face was beginning to discolor from Carnage's blows.

"Can't work with someone I despise."

"You despise me?" Hades glanced over at us but turned his attention back to the small little pinprick I left on his lover's ear.

"Not now. You're not on my best friend list; but, I'm not actively hating you."

"I thought we were friends." I bit back the sharp snarl I was going to give him because it sounded like an honest remark from him.

Claudius hugged me as if he knew the enormous effort it took to keep everything calm and even. "Friends don't rape friends."

Billiam gathered his little shepherd boy close and I looked down at them. Considering how old both of them are, I'd never met anyone so self-centered—to themselves and to each other. Gees.

Girding my hypothetical loins, I broached the request X wanted offered. "Hades, can you work for me?"

Hades cradled the blond's head and began lapping at the wounded ear. Billiam reacted as if he suddenly was plugged into some sort of love machine. Now they were wrapped up in their own little four hundred year over do honeymoon ritual, again.

Ahem, I cleared my throat rather theatrically. "Cilly..."

He didn't even bother to look over at me. "As an assassin?"

I shook my head. "You're too high profile. I want you to work as my PA. Basically, you take over Billy's job."

"My name is William." Billy Enoy's voice came out loud and strong. Creepy.

Okay, I hate being called Edward. "Apologies, William's position is in within the House."

"I'm fired?"

"I want you for Von Drachenfeld. Think of it as a step up. You'll be working for the Lord Emperor now."

"It's more of a lateral move than a promotion." Liam's voice now sounded and that was just creepy. At least when the brothers switch out, we have the same voice. But then, it's just fragments of one psyche, it's not a totally separate entity. *Damn, what was that?*

"You really do have a short attention span, Lord Sex." Hades spoke up.

"Shut up."

"Manners, *lubov moya*." Claudius tapped me on the side of the head. Tapped? He slapped Claudia's clip right off the back of my skull and it went flying somewhere so now my hair was hanging everywhere.

"What could we do for you as your personal assistants, Little Lord Emperor?"

"Number one; stop calling me that. Number two; while you are here and from what I understand, you cannot use your powers in that Red body—you could teach me how to use mine."

"So I am moved from your rival to your mentor."

I furrowed my brow. "Rival?"

"For my Honey Bee's affections."

"How many times do I have to say I don't want your Honey Bee's affections? I never wanted your Honey Bee's affections. This body has enough lovers. I have Claudius. I don't need anyone else."

Liam rolled to his feet with an ease that didn't match how I've seen Billy Envoy's body move and then suddenly he had my chin in the palm of his hand. I blinked...something was different. Wait a minute. Billy Envoy had blue eyes...these were now gray. "I have knowledge I could teach you, Number One. You have powers you have not even attempted to call upon. The Blue Line is strong in your family. The Royal Line is strong within you."

Liam lowered himself on one knee, one hand down on the floor and head bowed. "I will teach all that I know. You will be the river; I will be your tributary. I will feed you all you can handle so you will wash all your enemies from your sight. I will pledge this to you on one condition."

"Condition?"

"You do not lay with my Cillian again."

What part of I don't want your Honey Bee doesn't he understand? Listen when someone is protesting about someone's undesirability! Crossing my arms over my chest I easily replied, "Done."

"All of you...and him." Liam stared over at my Sasha.

"I can tell you right now without conferring with the brothers, that we will never have sex with Cillian, aka Hades, aka Honey Bee ever again. Claudius?"

Sasha's delivery was rather deadpanned. "Gladly."

"Hey!" Hade actually had the gall to protest.

I gestured to Hades. "You get that oath from your shepherd boy and we're a done deal."

"Cillian?"

"I will not approach the Lord Emperor for sexual favors." It sounded forced and petulant to my ears. Apparently it sounded the same way to Liam.

"My Lords, if you will excuse us. My consort and I have some negotiations to get through before we can join you in the Great Hall."

Claudius and I left the room. I glanced back to see Hades backing away, one hand up to his bruised jaw, the other out trying to ward off his maker and his lover. I looked down at Claudius' fist. His knuckles were red and swollen. "Can you play the piano like that?"

He flexed his hand. "I may have over done it. Claudia should be able to fill in for me if the swelling doesn't go down right away.

"How to do you feel?"

There was a long pregnant pause then I got a rabbit kick to the heart as Sasha gave me a wide smile. "At peace."

"Really?"

"I know I am, because it is a feeling that I have not had for centuries. Thank you, Fallen."

"You looked like you enjoyed pounding the crap out of him."

"That was his punishment for what he did to you." Claudius turned and caught me by my cheek. "As long as there is blood flowing through my veins, Fallen, I will punish any who seek to harm you. Be it blade, bullet or by malicious word. I only existed before you. I live for you now, my beautiful Fallen Angel; my heart; my reason for being."

I burst into tears. "You ass! Everybody's going to know I've been crying."

Claudius tilted my head and kissed the tears away. "I told you once, the day you cannot cry, is the day I will be seriously worried about you. There…all better."

All better. Oh gees. I forgot. "Azrael has to talk to Marcus."

"He is in the Great Hall." Claudius offered his arm. I grinned and ducked under it to get as close to him as possible. It would be six days before we could be together again. At the doorway, Claudius untangled himself, gave me a smile that went to his eyes and headed into the room the announcement was to take place.

Dang, he even walked sexy. *Little Brother you ready?*

Switch up. Sex whizzed by with that spark of his that had been missing for the past couple of days. I'd never admit it but, thank God. A quiet Sex makes us brothers worry worse than when he's hyperactive.

Claudia popped up beside me. Are we supposed to see each other before the announcement or is that just a wedding superstition thing? She brushed aside my train of thought as easily as a flyswatter through a spider's web. "Are they still alive?"

"They were alive when we left them. Hades however needed an attitude adjustment from Billiam. How that little session goes is anyone's guess."

"Can we get started?"

"One more thing." I turned and looked at X's girl. That was so weird. Big Brother has a girl. "By all rights, I should hate your guts, Baroness. You're horning your way into a perfectly good ménage a six, but you have spunk. I admire that."

Claudia turned and stared at me. "Azrael?"

"Got it in one. While you don't do anything for me, I have to tell you, you looked really good in that Chinese leather dress. Makes the sadist in me appreciate the lines and cut."

Claudia took the comment in stride. She was her father's daughter. "And you're with?"

I gestured with my head over to Marcus as he was finishing up his solo. The sound of that violin sent shivers right to my groin…which didn't help matters much down there.

"Marcus? But everyone says he's an artist—sweetness and light. Well until a few months ago."

"Hey, everyone is entitled a couple of mistakes. Besides…he painted that for X." I nodded to the large portrait hanging on the wall. That blank spot that was there was now filled with Haley sitting all puffed out chest proud at being included in the pod. I'd have to search him out later and give him kudos for sitting still.

I was proud of my fangy Puppy. He had talent coming out the ying yang. I bit back my sigh of disappointment as he lowered his violin, his shoulders slouched again. I'm going to have to get him a back brace or something. Eventually, osteoporosis is going to kick in and he'll be staring at the floor for the rest of eternity. The people in the Great Hall applauded politely. There was an awkwardness there in the room and it was all about my Puppy's past stalking behavior. The House had taken its pound of flesh and as far as I was concerned that bill was paid in full. Nobody puts my Puppy in a corner. I put my fingers in my mouth and blew a loud whistle. I didn't care if everybody turned and looked at me; I was just looking at my man. His face broke out into a smile as he made his way over to me.

I caught his hand and pulled him out of the room. It was X and Claudia's party. I wasn't that much of an asshole to try and steal their thunder. I glanced around, saw we were alone and pushed Marcus into a corner. Nobody puts my Puppy in a corner but me. I climbed him just like a lumberjack on a redwood and French kissed his musical soul.

"Master…"

"Hey there, Puppy. Nice playing." I picked up his hand and kissed his palm. "You are a musician without equal."

I smiled as he flushed red. "You paint pretty good, too."

"Thank you…"

"You fuck me even better, little seme."

"I...I thought you didn't like it. I hurt you."

I bit his lower lip and lapped at the cider pooling there. The lingering taste of cloves mixed with Marcus' essence for something oddly different but nice. Hmmmm. "I didn't mind the first five times, but after that….it was a killer."

"I won't do that again."

"Of course you will. I want you to...just not as intense as last time. We'll work something out, like a safe word." I loosened my hold and slid down his body. He leaned into me and enfolded himself around me like a big warm Pendleton blanket. I let out a big sigh, leaning into him. "Puppy, I got something to ask of you. I need you to do it."

"Master?"

I took his hands into mine. "You make such beautiful things. You delight the eye. You stir the soul. I need you to…no, we, all the brothers, need you to become Second of Assassins. We need you as the left hand man; our fall back guy. I'm now Head. Claudius is First. I need you there as Second to support us. Use Armor if you have to in order to challenge your way up."

Marcus stilled. He flexed his hands then leaned his chin on my shoulder. "Give me twelve days; I'll be Second by then, Azrael."

"I will be your second at every challenge." I offered my unwavering support.

I received a gentle brush of lips on the side of my neck. "That won't be necessary, Master, but thank you. I can handle this."

"What are you going to do?"

"I'll mindfuck them into submission. I can only challenge once a day so it will take me that long to reach Second."

"Thank you, Marcus." I leaned my whole weight up against him and he responded by leaning back just enough to keep us balanced.

"If that is where you want be me to be. That is where I will be. I love you, Master."

I patted his artistic hands. "You can call me Azrael. Sex really isn't into the word "Master" right now."

"I will call you Master, because that is what you are to me. Keep me grounded. Keep me focused. Give me my crazy kind of love. You are the Master of my Heart and Soul."

Well, someone had been giving Armor language lessons. Tilting my head back I stared up into those warm chocolate brown eyes. "Give me some sugar, Puppy."

This was a lazy kind of kiss. It lingered. It meandered. Tongues touched and shyly twisted together. Marcus fingers traced down my shoulder, slipping under the small gapping space of the ornate band uniform top and circled my hardening nipple. I groaned into his mouth and pulled back. He blinked and his eyes were dark pools of wicked promise. I'd gladly walk back into that six hours of sexual torture again for this Vampire. My muse. My Puppy. My Marcus. I never said it, but I knew he knew. He owned my heart and soul as well.

Chesterton came around the corner and discreetly, "Ahem".

We broke apart. "Milord, Claudius is ready to announce the engagement."

X, it's done. "See you Saturday, Marcus. You've got nothing to be ashamed of so please stand up straight."

Marcus felt the shift and backed off me like I was drenched in acid. Azrael had him pinned in a corner and there was nowhere for him to go.

"Be right there, Chesterton." I called back over my shoulder.

I took a couple of steps back giving both of us some space. "Thank you for agreeing to move ranking Marcus."

"As the Lord Emperor commands." Marcus turned his face away, looking down at the floor.

"Look at me, Marcus." I waited until his brown eyes matched mine. "It's forgiven. It's forgotten for the sake of peace in this family. Don't ever hurt me like that again."

"I will only hurt your enemies, little brother."

"Good enough." I sighed and stepped back to let him pass. He paused in front of me then turned. Slowly, he moved closer allowing me time to get away if I so desired and his kissed my forehead.

"Be happy, Xavier." He touched foreheads with me briefly then turned and walked back into the Great Hall.

How the hell happy can I get? I'm a sterile gay man marrying a woman for the sake of having children to make a Vampire nation feel secure. This was just not going to be pretty. There was a loud claxon flourish as I stepped up to the doorway. *Where the hell did they get horns?* As one the room dropped down into reverent pose. Claudia stepped up to my side and I offered her my arm. I looked across the lowered heads and saw Claudius, Armor, Haley and Chesterton standing underneath the lifestyle portrait of 'The Pod." I had love in my life, tons of love. I escorted Claudia forward. I had friendship in my future. I could get as happy as I wanted. I let a genuine smile cross my lips and led my future wife up to meet the rest of the family of Von Drachenfeld.

Chapter Twenty-Three: The Collective

It's all fun and games until your engagement party gets crashed by a Blood so mysterious that none other than the Progenitor of our species has ever seen one.

Up until that moment, this was the party I envisioned as my Introduction to Vampire High Society. Crystal stemware full of crimson liquid, men and women fully dressed to the nines and chatting about events of the day or upcoming venues but most of the conversation was about the burnt out hull in the woods. It was so refined I was falling asleep. The only entertainment was Haley pestering Chesterton for more snacks that he would try and penguin me until Father lead interference, oh and the debauched late arrival of Hades and Billiam.

They were fully dressed but you knew damn well what the hell they were up to. Claudius's bruises that he left on Hades face were gone but there was a honking big hickey on Billiam's pale skin at the base of his throat and healing fang marks on Hades' neck. They came in, dropped down into reverent pose then headed over to the free flowing fountain of blood and proceeded to try to empty it. I guess 400 years of pent up sexual tension requires a lot of top ups. They drank it down like they had just walked out of Death Valley.

My wife-to-be was a schmoozer. Thank God for that. My schmoozing was less than stellar and I couldn't remember everybody I had been introduced to. To be honest, the only two I could remember was the Baron and Baroness Whitecombe and that was only because he was supposed to look like Claudius but the only thing that I could see that they had in common was the black hair, blue eyes and the height. The Baron was a desk jockey. Maybe once he had Father's lean frame, but now he had a few extra pounds that I kind of envied....ooh speaking of pounds.

I searched out good Dr. Maxwell. His face lit up as he saw me approach. "Lord Emperor Xavier. I have to offer my most sincere apologies. There was a mix up in the lab."

"I don't have post burn hypermetabolism?" I was really hoping for a yes. Armor had set up the home torture chamber known as a gym earlier during the day and I was so not looking forward to having to start that program. I want to be a couch potato playing video games till my thumbs fell off. It was rather embarrassing to be known as First of Assassins and to get my ass kicked on a multitude of game titles by a pup of a Lycan.

"No, there is no doubt that you have that condition. The good news is you're not sterile!" Conversation died off around us. I felt my face burn red. Even Dr. Maxwell had the grace to look embarrassed when everyone in hearing distance was now wrapped with unabashed interest.

"Thanks for announcing that to the Nation, Dr. Maxwell." My sarcasm was thinly disguised.

The doc dropped his voice and moved closer to me. "My apologies, Lord Emperor. We ran tests today mainly because of the concern we had regarding the incident on Sunday and we were unsure if the Hellcat power spike caused more damage than just the destruction of a building. The Healing energy that you can produce has apparently healed your reproductive...."

"Okay...the boys can swim." I cut him off. "Why can't I heal this post burn hypermetablism?"

"Every time you burn, it's a new instance. Your body heals from the burn, then you have to burn again, it forces your body back into healing mode again. It's a cycle. I wish I had better news regarding that aspect of your health, Lord Emperor."

"Thank you for delivering this news in person, Doc."

Chesterton slid up with the unobtrusive skill that had made him Head Butler, holding a tray full of blood goblets. I played the good host. "Help yourself to some refreshments. Food will be served shortly if you are so inclined."

"Congratulations on your engagement, Lord Xavier."

Claudia ghosted up beside me, and snuck an arm around my upper arm. "Thank you, Doctor. Please, enjoy the party." She smiled then I

394

got pinched in the fleshy part of my inner arm. Holy crap that hurt. She smiled sweetly up at me. "You were sterile?"

"Not when you got pushed on me."

"Pushed on you?" She was still smiling but her eyes got that icy resolve. She was her Father's daughter. "I thought this was a mutual agreement."

"I told you at the club then you took off in a huff."

"I thought you were lying to me to get out marriage."

"I'm gay. What the hell do I know about women and procreation? I mean…" *Ow, ow , ooowww.*

"Go sit down, before I hurt you." Her kung fu grip tightened. Holy smokers. Suddenly she let go as she waved at another couple. "Now!"

My eyes actually watered. *Oooh, that hurt.* I think I'm missing a filter that goes from my brain to my mouth when it comes to women. And it must be a genetic thing, or maybe a gender thing that women can threaten and terrify you through clenched teeth with a smile on their face. Haley met me at my leather wingback chair with a glass full of blood.

Immediately his whole body went on alert as he knelt by the chair. "Alpha? What's the matter."

I wouldn't say I threw myself in the chair but it wasn't an elegant recline. "I pissed my female Alpha off."

"That's never a good thing, Alpha." The Lycan physically relaxed.

I discreetly rubbed at my bruise. "I'm finding that out the hard way, Haley."

He grinned at me then his face froze. He snarled and jumped to his feet, placing his body between me and the door.

I glanced around Haley's body and felt myself grow cold and still.

Chesterton's voice called out from the Great Hall's door. "The Seer."

Everybody stopped what they were doing. Claudius and Marcus had been playing that long haired crap of theirs up near the front of the room but that came to a crashing halt. Haley shifted slightly so I could really see this Seer. All I could think was—yowzah! Orlando Bloom as an elf had nothing on this guy. He was tall, really tall. He was half a head

395

taller than my Armor. His pale blue hair was sweeping above the floor as he walked forward. So this type of Blood, a Seer, was able to see both sides of the mirror – future, present and past, I suppose. His skin was a dark surfer tan. He glided, more than walked into the room even though he was a monster of a being. He was in an unadorned navy blue suit but it was cut to perfection to accent his…well physical perfection. He halted in front of my chair and graciously lowered himself into reverent pose. All that blue hair pooled around him as if he were crouching under a gentle waterfall.

You could have dropped a truck load of pins and heard every single one drop.

I felt Claudius and Armor come up behind me. Claudia ghosted up in her silent walk and stood at my left. Haley still stood in front of me, quivering with tension and then the silence was broken by his low threatening rumble of a growl.

"Lord Emperor, Xavier Von Drachenfeld, the First." This Seer's voice matched his appearance. It didn't belong of this earth. He opened his eyes and looked past Haley at me. The iris was crimson. Something warm washed over my mental shield. His mouth turned up at the ends in a smirk as he hooded his red eyed gaze. He had just tried to send me something and it was just intuition but it involved mixing blue and white hair on a bed of orange roses. *WTF?*

"I beg your forgiveness, Lord Emperor for the lateness of our reply. Our Blood Collective received your summons; however, plans had to be finalized prior to an envoy being dispatched to you. My name is Lanseng. I have been given the honor of serving your office and I bring to you an object left in the Collective's safe keeping eons ago."

Another of Chesterton's staff walked up carrying a rolled scroll on a golden tray, Lanseng pushed himself from the floor, rising and rising until he towered over Haley who was not backing down from his role as protector. Lanseng swept his blue locks back off his forehead then reached out for the scroll. Haley snatched it off the tray.

"Ah, the Lycan." His cocked his head sideways examining Haley as specimen under glass. "You are still an untested pup. Interesting."

Claudius took the scroll from Haley gesturing him to move to the side and when the pup did shuffle slightly Armor tucked him to a position under his shoulder. Meanwhile Father carefully opened the scroll and checked it for...danger? He handed it to me.

This was like every fucking nightmare I ever had about public speaking. The upper crust of the Vampire pie was here in my home and I could feel every eye burning a hole in my actions. The Seer stared me in the eye and spoke in that soft ethereal voice. So melodic and sweet. I could feel the blood drain from my face as my heart began pumping to a frantic beat. I could feel it pound in my ears.

Shut up, shut up, shutupshutupshutup!

The Seer's voice echoed the ancient Vampiric glyphs, that I had learned how to read when Hades allowed me to his mind. My eyes skipped along the dark black markings as Lanseng spoke aloud the damning words.

> *In the end of days,*
> *He will come upon fiery wings,*
> *A creature no Blood can call its own.*
> *Through a storm of fire and silver he will walk*
> *Rendering asunder all we have known*
> *Or can remember.*
> *Remaking the world in his own image.*
> *Harbinger of destruction.*
> *Destroyer of darkness.*
> *He will walk in blood and light,*
> *Hasmallim, the Illuminated*
> *Let all the Blood tremble before him.*
> *Revere him, love him, fear him*
> *Hasmallim the Assassin;*
> *Lord of the new Blood Nation.*

The tall elegant man lowered himself back down into reverent pose. "The Collective, acknowledges and swears loyalty to Xavier the First.

We have foreseen what you will build; your seed will tend to your vision and grow it into a strong and healthy Nation, under one banner – Von Drachenfeld. I am Lanseng, the Collective's Envoy. I swear personal allegiance to Hashmallim, the Destroyer of Nations and will serve the resulting future Blood Emperor to the best of my abilities. All that I see, you shall know. All that I know, you shall see."

The rest of the room followed the Seer's example. They almost dropped in unison. "Von Drachenfeld. Von Drachenfeld! Von Drachenfeld!!"

Blood Emperor?

Father, Armor, Haley and Claudia lowered themselves around me. I sat in my leather wing back chair staring out across all the bowed heads. An invisible hand was squeezing my chest. I was getting ready to bolt when a hand landed on my shoulder and pushed me back into my chair. Another hand pinned down on the opposite shoulder. A hand curled around mine and a soft thumb rubbed my knuckles. Finally a warm body pressed up against the side of my leg as the chanting of "Von Drachenfeld" grew intermixed with "Blood, blood, blood."

Oh, holy crap.

Continued in Caramel: Book Five of the Blood Nation Novels

www.ingramcontent.com/pod-product-compliance
Lightning Source LLC
Chambersburg PA
CBHW020931020726
47495CB00002B/446